DEATH

THE FAITH TRILOGY
BOOK 3

NICK NIELSEN

Edited by
LESLIE WATTS

LUMINIS PRESS

PROLOGUE

Hello again.

Welcome back.

You're serious about this. Aren't you?

It's tough. I know. The holes are deep.

But sometimes, they just need to be.

Otherwise, how would we rise?

1

A DISTANT BANGING spears my consciousness.

My head spins, and I come to blinking, the darkness so thick before my eyes. My gaze immediately finds Natasha. She's stretched out at my side on our solitary mattress, the outline of her back barely visible in the gloom. Her torso moves faintly up and down under the sheet.

Finally sleeping.

Sitting up against the wall, I hold my breath and train my ears to the sounds outside. Growling engines, barking dogs, and distant shouts all permeate through the wooden board I've hauled across the bedroom window. The low clanging of some kind of bell echoes around my head. And of course, I hear the muffled sound of our neighbour's television coming through the holes in the brickwork.

The television prattles on, but I hear no obvious bangs, no explosions. It's the twenty-four-hour news channel with the end of some panicked report about the crazy August temperatures and more harvests failing. Drought. Pestilence. I start to hum to drown out the sound, but my eyes find Natasha's sleeping form again, and my cheek muscles relax.

Then another voice filters through the wall. It's Paul Hawcross, our new prime minister.

" … we are a people of faith and humanity – understanding, welcoming, inclusive. Yet wherever possible, people should remain in their own countries. We are all struggling, and the huge pressure on resources compromises everyone. I'm sure many like-minded nations would agree …"

My shoulders tense, and I turn away, my gaze drifting over the surrounding space.

My old bedroom in my childhood home. The domain of my earliest memories is now a shell of bare floorboards and stripped walls with a jumble of makeshift furniture. I spy Natasha's plate of food sitting on one of the crates we use for chairs. It's Mrs B's cooking, a mixture of spiced vegetables and rice. Yet only half eaten.

My heart sinks.

The sound comes again. Three quick raps on our bloody front door.

This time, I scramble to my feet, my whole body tight as I close the bedroom door quietly behind me and hurry out onto the landing, making sure not to wake Natasha.

At the top of the steps, I spy Mrs B with her back to me, hovering in the entrance hall outside her room with two of her children – Hassan, who's thirteen years old, and Amira, who's nine. Normally immaculate, her headscarf hangs loose down her back, and she's whispering intently to her daughter and younger son, her hands gripped around their arms. They both stare at her, pale-faced.

I hasten down the stairs, and Mrs B swivels toward me, opening her mouth. My finger goes to my lips.

The banging comes again, shaking the door. *Fuckers.* I jump the remaining steps and stride toward it, but Mrs B grabs my arm.

I pivot and whisper, "It'll be okay."

She clenches me tighter, her knuckles white.

"Don't you worry," I say, holding her gaze. "If it's the gang, we're not due yet. Rent day's not for another week." I try a smile. "I'll deal with them. You go back inside."

Finally, she nods and turns away, shooing the children into her room. I face the door and take a breath.

"We know you're in there!" a voice shouts from beyond, the tone sing-song.

My head tilts. It doesn't sound like a gang enforcer, but the image comes of Natasha upstairs, wrenched from sleep. I yank the door open to find two guys standing there, the nearer one almost right in my face.

The light from grimy streetlights illuminates a shaved head, beady eyes, and torn overalls. The guy behind him is taller, dressed in faded jeans and a T-shirt. But both are heavyset with muscled shoulders and callused hands, plainly able to handle themselves.

I glance from one to the other. Though neither smile.

"This place yours?" the nearer guy asks with a nod toward the house.

"What if it is?" I say.

He ignores me and gazes past my shoulder. "You on your own in there?" he asks, his voice gruff.

I simply fold my arms and stare at him.

Jeans Guy lifts his hands, palms up. "Look, friend, my name's Callum, and this is Dan. We're from round here. See?" He fakes a smile. "A group of us are checking the neighbourhood. Just want to make sure our families are safe."

I raise an eyebrow, heat climbing my chest. It's all too clear where this is going.

"From?" I ask.

Callum shrugs. "A lot of foreigners arriving in these parts, looking to stay," he says.

"Well, no one's here," I say.

Dan frowns, creases forming across the top of his block-like head. Then he leans forward and sniffs the air over my shoulder as if he's actually trying to smell someone out. I keep my eyes on him the entire way. His mouth thins in some kind of smile, and he whispers softly into my ear.

"We can help you get rid of 'em," he says before stepping back.

I suppress a shudder. "Get rid of who?"

Yet at that exact moment I hear a noise behind me. Scuffed footsteps in the hallway. I clear my throat to try to cover the sound. Dan's smile widens.

Then he tries to dart past me into the house, his movement a blur ...

My thoughts still immediately, flames sparking at my core. The veil peels back a fraction – weirdly easily – and time slows. In that instant, I can sense everything ... the guy shooting toward me, his elevated breathing, his stooping posture, his fingers grabbing for the inside of the door frame. Energy fires down my legs, and I throw myself to the side to block him off, power surging up my torso. The guy crashes into my chest, but I hardly budge while he staggers backward.

He gazes at me, his lips parted.

"It's just a cat ..." I say, the veil slipping back before my senses.

Dan's beady eyes narrow into slits.

I raise my hands. "I'm sorry. It's late. I was sleeping when you knocked. I've been working all day."

Dan remains standing there, staring at me, his fists balled. He makes no movement to leave.

No movement to leave at all.

With a clenched jaw, I force my lips into what becomes a pathetic smile and step toward the guy to pat him on the shoulder.

"Look, friend," I manage to get out. "No one's here. There was before, but they ... left. Know what I mean?" I even raise my eyebrows a couple of times.

Eventually, Dan's face breaks into a broader grin. He claps me on the shoulder in return. "Good to hear it," he says, his voice equally low. "We got to be careful. These heathens ...

Their home countries are sending 'em here. Thousands of 'em ..."

I nod along as he continues to spout his bullshit – something about bombs, curfews, and our nation being bled dry. Eventually, he turns and slopes toward Callum and the road.

I take a deep breath in, prepared to sigh with relief ... to shake it all out.

A few feet from the gate, he stops and glances back. "There's a local meet at Immanuel School," he says. "Thursday night. Eight p.m. Come along."

I stick a thumb in the air and force another nod.

"And put a white ribbon in your window," Dan adds. "We all got to take a stand. And it'll tell everyone you're part of the effort."

My thumb remains held aloft, and I add a wider smile.

Dan turns back toward the gate and has almost reached it when a shout comes from further down the street.

"I got him!" a shrill male voice calls out. "I got him!"

I follow the sound and spot a young, wiry guy with bad acne hurrying in our direction. He's frogmarching Hassan down the pavement in front of him, a hand on his collar. Mrs B's younger son is clasping a plastic bag to his chest, holding on to it for dear life.

"I found him out back!" Acne Boy says to Dan and Callum. "Just like you said. He was trying to sneak stuff out of the house."

I can only watch as Acne Boy thrusts Hassan forward by the neck. The kid stumbles, his body trembling and eyes like plates, though he doesn't let go of the plastic bag. He simply grips it tighter.

My insides plunge. That's what I heard behind me: Mrs B sent Hassan out with their prized possessions, expecting her rooms to be raided.

And somehow, these fuckers knew.

My gaze finds Dan, who lingers unmoving at the gate, an

eager smile on his lips as Hassan is shoved ever nearer. Callum's a bundle of energy – bobbing forward and back, his hands opening and closing. I shift my weight as Dan's gleaming eyes swivel toward me.

"Good thing we stayed," he says.

2

Acne guy propels Hassan to the gate, the kid still clutching his bag of possessions to his chest. Dan stands there immovable, the shadows somehow deeper around his shoulders and face.

"You see?" he says to me, his voice becoming a growl. "They steal stuff. Valuables. Government handouts." He grips Hassan's bag and tries to yank it out of his hands.

My heel bounces, my eyes on the guy, and Natasha's many pleas come back to me … *Just stay out of things. Then everything will be okay.* But of course, her obvious fear lies underneath it all, the terror she won't give voice to – that we're corrupt, and all we do and will ever do will be tainted.

Callum edges down the side of the concrete yard, his weight on the balls of his feet, poised to edge behind me if I move, desperate to get stuck in. I tense my legs and keep my focus on Hassan, my thoughts screaming at him to let the bag go. But he continues to clasp it tightly, his face almost white now and his arms frozen rigid.

Dan pulls harder, and then harder again. Finally, the bag rips, and papers tumble out along with a few candlesticks and some clothes. The bundle unravels in mid-air, letting slip two golden picture frames and a small wad of money. The notes flutter down to the cracked concrete.

My toes grip the insoles of my shoes while Callum and Acne Boy ogle the fallen cash. Dan peers down at the frames, however. They're beautiful. Maybe gold-plated. And each frame contains Arabic words written in gold on a black background.

Dan's nostrils flare, his entire face reddening. "Fucking heathens," he says and jabs a finger at the scattered notes. "Where'd you get this? Sold the handouts, right? *Right?"*

"No fucking way," I say under my breath.

But Dan's not paying attention to me. He's still eyeing the cash, leaning down to examine it. My gaze is on Hassan. With the bigots focused on the money, the kid's bending his knees, tensing his body, turning away from Dan ... While my gut twists, my fingers clenching and my calves stiffening.

Hassan leaps for the gate. Dan moves like lightning, even more quickly than before. His arm snaps out, and he grabs Hassan by the collar to haul him backward. And amid the smell of baked dust and refuse, a new acrid scent hits my nose. Cordite?

My heartbeat accelerates, and my eyes scour the darkened street.

Nothing. And then the whiff's gone.

"Where you going? You fucking savage," Dan says, dragging Hassan around by the collar.

The kid struggles to get his legs underneath him. However, each time he tries, Dan kicks them away again. Hassan gropes at his neck, straining to inch his collar away from his windpipe, but Dan yanks him off the ground with just one hand. Incredibly strong.

Almost unbelievably so.

The thoughts barely register, though, as the flames roar higher inside me, tightening the muscles in my legs, my shoulders, my arms. I find myself stepping forward when a scream sounds from behind. Mrs B pushes out of the doorway and scrambles toward her son, her fingers clawing the air. I barely get in her way to hold her back.

Callum plants himself between Hassan and Mrs B, her arm extended toward her son. Mrs B strains harder against me, but still I hold her firm. Callum starts to bait her, his voice sickly sweet, urging her to get the boy.

My eyes search the nearby houses, the many darkened windows and the few lit ones. But the yards remain empty, the doors still firmly shut. No one is coming to help.

And the kid's turning blue. Dan continues to hoist Hassan around effortlessly by the collar like he's some kind of rag doll. Then he shoves the kid's face toward the frames and money on the ground.

"Go on, take your pretty picture and your heathen shit," he says. "Your money, take it!"

Mrs B screams behind me, ripping at my arms with taloned fingers, and the chaos only drives the flames hotter in my chest. Yet I swallow them down and grip her more firmly by the shoulders. These guys know where we fucking live.

But again, my eyes find Hassan. His eyes are drooping, and he's no longer even scrabbling with his legs to push himself up. Dan keeps going, lifts Hassan high in the air while squeezing his throat more. And still the street's as empty as ever.

So I let go, let the fire rage inside me, and surge toward Callum.

A wild grin splits the guy's features. He swivels and reaches back with his fist. My thoughts still, the veil again so insubstantial before my senses. I peel it back and, for the first time in an age, get a proper taste of the shimmering world.

Surfaces glimmer. I feel myself connected to everything – the ground beneath my feet, the air around my skin. And every one of Callum's movements imprints itself on my awareness – his upper body spinning, his weight shifting forward, the bared teeth, the arc of his punch.

I dart just to the side of the strike and grab his wrist as it passes my ear, while shooting my other arm up behind his elbow. With the power seething through my limbs, one thrust is all it would take to shatter the fucker's arm.

Then the vision comes of me pouncing on him, grinding his smiling face into the ground. I glimpse it all in my mind's eye, almost able to feel the joyous fury and the darkness inside me banished. I can see the guy destroyed on the floor—

In the next instant, I find my breath and instead pull the thrust of my arm just in time.

Callum goes to backhand me, but I clasp his wrist and yank it downward. Then I slam my forearm into his shoulder to spin the guy around. I get him in a lock, his bent arm pinned to his back, and hold him there.

Hassan's eyes are closing, Dan's fat fingers still gripped around his collar, and Callum struggles to free himself. He's ready to hurl himself at my back if he's released. I jab the guy's pinned elbow upward. His shoulder pops, and he yells in pain. Then I kick him behind his knee, and the guy sprawls to the ground, opening a path to Dan.

I fling myself toward him. Our eyes lock, and he grabs Hassan with both hands and shoves him in my direction. The kid stumbles toward me across the hard concrete yard, his legs like jelly. Yet I keep going. Don't veer off at all.

Dan follows up behind him, his eyes burning, the muscles bulging in his neck. He draws back his fist, goes to punch me over Hassan's shoulder, and the image comes of his lightning movements from before.

I skid to a halt before Dan, let Hassan bounce off my chest but don't catch him. Instead, I hold my arms out and anchor myself on my rear foot. Then I start to spin, letting the kid's head slide down my chest, under the trajectory of Dan's punch.

The guy leans forward, teeth gritted, his fury like a wildfire. I feel it rampaging through my torso. His punch flies toward my head. I twist away. And he still catches my chin with a glancing blow. But the pain hardly registers. The guy's anger builds my own, drives the river of fire faster through my veins ... peels back the veil further.

I channel the growing power up my rear leg, into my hips, my shoulder, and down my arm as I swivel around Hassan's slumping body. My fist careens toward the guy's neck.

I imagine him darting out of the way, pulling back with his incredible speed. So I go in hard and fast.

Yet Dan barely moves at all. He simply remains there, his arm stretched out, as my extended knuckles smash into his throat.

I hear a crunching sound, and the guy's eyes balloon. He hangs in mid-air for a moment, desperately trying to breathe and clawing at his neck with straining fingers. Then he drops to his knees, his face growing first white ... and then as blue as Hassan's was.

I can barely move.

Eventually, a faint wheezing's audible – Dan sucking air in through a crushed trachea. My leg muscles slacken, and I take a faltering step back.

Hassan's sitting up on the ground, finally breathing steadily again. Acne Boy surveys the scene, his eyes blinking as his mouth opens and closes.

I swallow, trying to find my voice.

"Just get them out of here," I manage to say, all too aware of the void blooming inside, the growing darkness at my core.

Callum limps toward me, toward the gate, one arm clutched around the other. Dan's still on his knees, struggling to breathe.

Acne Boy jabs a shaking finger at me. "You!" he spits, his cheeks burning. "You're fucking worse than they are!"

The shout peppers me with spittle. His rage is so powerful that fire surges in my chest, yet it dies so quickly, the abyss claiming my insides instead. And I just remain there as Acne Boy and Callum lift Dan to his feet. The guy can barely stand.

Then they lug him down the pavement and away. As they pass, I glimpse a figure on the far side of the street, the faintest outline in the shadows. Black on black. And again, the same metallic scent permeates the air.

A shiver runs through me, and I peer closer.

They're both gone – the image and the smell. All that's visible on the pavement opposite are pools of darkness between the working streetlights.

Mrs B drops to the ground at my side and helps Hassan up, tears shining on her cheeks. She presses his head to her chest and rocks him back and forth, mumbling something in Arabic. Hassan stares at me the entire time.

I avert my gaze and lean down to help Amira gather up their valuables. We start with the golden frames, wrapping them up in the clothes, before collecting the spilled banknotes.

With Hassan safely indoors, Mrs B hurries back over to me. I open my mouth, words of apology on my lips.

She squeezes my arm and says, "Thank you … thank you." And she's crying again, her fingers held to her lips.

I grip her trembling hand and make a quiet shushing sound as my eyes search the surrounding street. It remains empty, including the pavement across from us where I glimpsed the strange outline.

And questions whirl …

The veil so thin before my senses. Dan's incredible speed and strength. How the bigots' rage registered in my body, just like it did with the emissary in the heavenly realm. And the fleeting scent of cordite.

Angels? Emissaries? Here? It makes no sense.

With the possessions cleared up, I usher Amira and Mrs B toward the house, but my thoughts flit to Dan. He'll return with more cronies. All because of what I did. And the image forms of Natasha, still so vulnerable upstairs. Plus Mrs B and her family.

I grip the door and squeeze it, ignoring the splinters digging into my palm.

Why the hell did they have to come here? I fume and thrust the door shut behind me.

It slams hard, the resulting crash vibrating my skull. The entire house quakes with it, and the abyss plunges away deeper inside me.

My lungs emit a groan, and I go to shuffle for the stairs when I see a flicker of movement in my peripheral vision. Something long and thin topples from behind the door and falls to the hallway floor with a thwack of wood on wood. A prickling sensation spreads across my back.

I peer forward, my mind not quite able to compute what I'm seeing.

Father Thomas's walking stick.

I rack my brain but can't recall bringing it back with our stuff from the church.

Leaning down, I pick up the stick, and the memories form of the old man cradling it in his kitchen. Shining eyes. Wide smile. His lectures about humanity liberated, humanity's potential realised, the spark of faith, about how this must all be intended.

I shake my head. Then there was Pergamon, only six weeks ago. His broken body lying at the bottom of a shallow grave. His lineage at an end. A vain sacrifice for a world with the devil released. And all my fault.

My eyes dip as I straighten, my gaze still on the stick, and more memories come. The priest's endless practices – all for nothing. Trying to bend laws, to slow time, to speak with his command voice, to defy gravity. All fucking pointless.

Again, the embers smoulder within, and I dump the walking stick back behind the door. Yet Father Thomas's final words return to me ... *Trust this.*

I spin away.

Hassan's shuffling toward me from the kitchen at the end of the hall. He's holding a cup of tea in his shaking hands, a nasty purple bruise forming around his neck.

"For you," he croaks.

I smile. "No, but thanks," I say, my thoughts already on Natasha upstairs.

This is what the priest told me before he died ... *Soon, you'll need to be there for her. But she'll be there for you before the end.* Whatever that means.

I leave Hassan and head up the stairs, taking two at a time. Then I pause at the top before pushing the door open gently.

Light from the open door falls on Natasha, the blanket pooled around her knees.

I tiptoe into darkness, and she rolls onto her back to face me.

"Is everything okay?" she asks, her voice faint.

I edge the door closed behind me, leaving only a faint sliver of light from the landing to illuminate the room. The sound of the television next door drones on through the walls.

"Everything's fine, Nat," I whisper, padding toward her.

She continues to stare at me, and in the reflected light, her eyes are as distant as ever. Maybe more so. I force a smile, though the void grows wider at my core.

"I promise," I say.

Eventually, she smiles weakly and rolls back over to face the wall. Her fingers hold her tiny crucifix, still tied by its chain around her neck. I gather up the blanket, lay it softly down over her, and then start to clear the remaining plates.

"You are not involved. Are you, Jake?" she asks, her voice barely audible.

"No way," I say. "Didn't need to be."

Though the image of the priest's walking stick flashes through my mind.

I busy myself with cleaning up and start folding our clothes to stow them away as quietly as I can.

Finally, Natasha rolls onto her front, her eyes closed, and pulls the blanket tighter around her. My shoulders relax a fraction. And the news channel prattles on, invading the silence. Its commentators complain about a deteriorating situation in the Middle East, accusing its governments of using immigration as a weapon against the West.

"Could you?" Natasha says.

"Sure," I say.

And with clothes in hand, I hum a tune to drown out the sound of the television. I continue as I clean, shifting from song to song. Gradually, Natasha's breathing deepens, though the commentators' voices continue to poke at me.

"We don't know what they're making in their basements, in their garages," one says and rails on about the increase in terrorist attacks and the need to reclaim our religion, our identity as a Puritan nation.

I pause in the blackness, the ragged cloth gripped in my hand.

It's time to go. I've got to organise passage out of the country.

And the other commentator adds, "Never fear. A reckoning is coming, Mike. And it won't be long."

3

I PASS the final roundabout and begin traipsing down a long residential road. It's after midnight, and most lights are off in the houses. The few glowing streetlights cast distant cones of light across the darkened pavement. The place is deserted, totally quiet aside from the echo of an engine starting up and some distant shouting at least a couple of roads away. I ignore it all and keep to the shadows, my mind revolving around recent conversations.

Two cargo ships to Poland – one leaving in ten days and the other in five. I shake my head. Probably too early for Natasha. It's been three days since the bigot visit, and she seems weaker, not stronger. I summon my remaining energy and quicken my stride.

As I approach the end of our road, a tiny figure comes into focus, sitting on a wall, legs dangling. I peer closer. It's a young boy. Maybe six or seven years of age. He spots my approach and jumps up, shouting something over his shoulder before turning back and chattering loudly at me.

My pulse throbs, and I thrust my palm forward to hush him. But he jabbers on and starts waving his hands in the air. I glance behind me, a shudder rolling across my back as memories flash of the shadowed outline from outside our house. Yet there's no obvious sign. The street's still empty.

I hurry on, and by the time I'm ten feet from the kid, he's bouncing up and down, babbling in Arabic at a hundred miles an hour. Only one word is intelligible – the name of Mrs B's son.

"Hassan?" I ask.

He nods vigorously and points behind him. Toward the road at his back. Toward our house.

A sense of cold grips my insides while the image of Acne Boy and the bigots lances my mind. I take off and sprint toward our street. The boy runs at my side, trying to keep up.

Reaching the last corner, our side of the street's swallowed in the darkness, the far end gleaming brighter. I train my gaze on our home, only a few houses down, and barrel toward it. The front door is shut, the yard empty. No lights on. No obvious movement.

I let out a deep breath, my feet slowing.

Several more kids scurry toward me down the pavement, Hassan at the front of the group. Like him, they're all of Middle Eastern origin, their ages ranging from around seven to twelve. And they're all focused on me. Hassan skids to a stop only a few feet away.

"What is it?" I demand, my throat tight.

He gives a wild grin, his eyes gleaming. "It's happening!"

"*What?*" I ask.

Hassan grabs my wrist and starts yanking me further down the road, toward our home. But his eyes are fixed on the end of the street.

Only then do I spot it, thirty buildings away. At first, it looks like the far end of the street's been floodlit. Then I realise it's a crowd poised in the middle of the road. Maybe two dozen people, all facing a particular house, some gesticulating angrily and others holding torches in their hands. Naked bloody flames.

My feet stumble to a halt outside our front yard, and Hassan grips my forearm tighter.

"I told them," he says, his gaze still focused on the scene up ahead. "Told them what you did."

The chill prickles my skin.

"Who?" I ask, though my brain's barely functioning.

"My friends," he says.

"*Kids?*" I say, the word tumbling out.

He nods, his eyes gleaming. "And they stopped people coming into their home," he says. "Just like you did."

Hassan gazes up at me while the rest of his group jabber in Arabic, most of them jumping up and down now. My eyes are still on the throng ahead, my mouth opening and closing.

Our front door flies open, and Mrs B stomps out onto the concrete yard. She starts yelling at Hassan in Arabic and then jabs her finger back at the house. She spots the mob, and both hands go to her mouth as she starts speaking to herself, her voice high-pitched and the sounds unintelligible behind her palms. And I find myself nodding, the weight building in my chest and my heart beating ever faster.

This could be a fucking bloodbath.

Two of the kids sprint down the road toward the mob.

"Come!" Hassan says to me and pulls at my arm again.

"Hassan, *la*!" Mrs B shouts.

But he's already turning, his knees bent. A couple more of his friends chase after the others.

"Hassan, wait!" I bark.

And this time he stops and spins. I grip his arm, yanking him behind me, and with the darkness filling my insides, I hurry down the street toward the mob.

Hassan and the remaining kids amass at my back as we go, like I'm some kind of saviour. And so, I pace down the middle of the pavement, positioned directly in front of them, trying to act as a screen.

Yet more Arab neighbours – young and old – join us from other houses across the street till there's around twenty people behind me. With teeth clenched, I find myself blundering on at the head of the maddest procession, now only fifty yards away from the riled crowd.

I scan faces, searching for the three bigots. But even with the torches, it's still dark, and a lot of people have gathered on the road – twenty-five to thirty of them all amassed around its middle.

I jerk up the hood of my shirt to hide my face in shadow and come to a stop a good ten yards away from the front of the mob. The group of kids and other neighbours halt behind me. We're still in the relative darkness of the broken streetlights, well outside the pools of light from the naked flames, and from here I take in the entire scene.

The mob's mostly young men. Several of them hold lit torches made from varying constructions of sticks with rags wound tightly around them, soaked in some foul-smelling fuel. And well over half of the crowd carries some kind of weapon, many of them half concealed. Bats are held up sleeves and chains wound around wrists. Some even hold bricks. Many of them wear white bands – simple bits of cloth tied around their upper arms. And yes, they're all facing one particular house with eight people lined up across the pavement in front of it.

Hassan's friends.

They're all boys of Arab descent, all between fourteen and seventeen years old. And they all sport taut expressions and tense postures. A few of them grip rudimentary weapons as well – a chair leg, a broom handle. And on the far side of them stands a line of older Arab neighbours, mostly parents and grandparents, between the mob and their younger family members yet out of the way. Simply looking on.

I remain still as someone shouts from the front of the mob – a much older man poised five or six feet from the line of young neighbours.

"Don't touch me!" he says. "You're filth!"

The guy's in his sixties or seventies, whip-thin and

stooped with long wisps of thinning grey hair. He clutches a bell in one hand and stabs a bony finger at the line of young people with the other, a real frenzy to his movements.

One of the older kids in the defensive line shouts back, "You leave our home!" His chest's out, and he's a few inches taller than the others, with a chair leg in one hand and a belt looped around the other.

"It's not your home, this ain't your country. You weren't born here, and you don't belong!" the older guy shouts, clanging his bell. "And we're coming in to search the house!"

The old man strides forward, as does the young neighbour, till they're only a foot or so apart. They face off with jawlines taut, and I can feel the anger all around me like flames burning in my own chest.

I take half a step forward and then stop, the skin tightening across the back of my neck. A dozen of the larger guys in the mob push forward at the old man's back, almost every one of them brandishing a weapon.

And although they're facing a much larger army, the young neighbours hold their ground, their own weapons gripped firmly in their hands.

I feel the gaze of the older neighbours on the far side. Several stare at me, their eyes shining with a mixture of anger and expectancy. I tug at my hood, making sure it's covering my face.

"You got no rights," the old man says and steps even closer to the young neighbour, staring him in the eye. "If you don't budge right now, we're ploughing right through you."

On cue, one thug advances to the old man's side and unravels a chain from his arm, letting it clang to the ground.

I glance from the old man to the neighbours. Still they hold their line. The taller kid glares straight back at the old man, his chin jutting out. And though new onlookers continue to approach the mob, they just hover at the back, staring on. No way they're going to stop this.

As the tension builds, the heat continues to rise inside me, my fingers squeezing together. Natasha's voice chimes strongly in my head. *You're not involved, are you?*

The old man rings his bell louder, and the thug lifts his chain behind him.

"Wait!" I say and throw out a hand.

Only a couple of people turn toward my half-hearted yell. Plus, I'm a good twenty feet from the confrontation, positioned in the shadows.

More thugs converge on the young neighbours. The guy with the chain raises it higher, and another guy grips a crowbar with two hands, bringing it forward. The collective rage continues to stoke the flames inside my chest, sizzling, burning. Plus, they're only fucking kids.

I channel the fire and power up my throat. "*Wait!*" I shout, using a bit of Father Thomas's command voice this time, though I make sure to keep my feet anchored to the spot and not step forward.

And this time, almost everyone swivels to face me, including the old man.

"We don't need to do this," I say, extending both arms out.

"And you are?" the old man barks.

The weight of everyone's stares presses in on me. My palms grow sweaty. And I just stand there, blinking.

Hassan and his group shuffle closer at my back, whispering encouragement, egging me on, like I can work fucking miracles. Yet the darkness congeals around my insides.

My arms drop.

The old man leans closer, trying to peer under my hood.

I tilt my head further down and retreat half a step. "Nobody," I say.

"Well, *nobody,*" the old man says, "we *do* need to do this. There's stolen goods in that house, and we're gonna find them."

He spins back to face his mob, one arm held aloft.

"These people are thieves!" he shouts. "Jewellery and other bits have gone missing from three homes, and locals saw these guys out after curfew. And we *know* they're hoarding the government support packages."

I shake my head. The same bullshit. And while the young neighbours mutter in disgust, several people in the crowd yell with approval. Others nod. More of the thugs from the midst of the crowd shove toward the front, weapons carried brazenly in their hands now. I open my mouth, but the old man blathers on.

"And even worse than that, there was an *attack* the other night," he says, his voice shaking with outrage. "People badly hurt. Our friends and neighbours."

The words die on my lips, and I shrink back, the weight growing ever heavier in my chest. I can't help scanning the mob, searching again for any sign of Acne Boy, of anyone staring in my direction. But there's no one obvious. Except ...

A man toward the back of the crowd, dressed in grey clothes, I think; they're not quite visible. And I can't make out his face, either. Like me, he's standing in the gloom, away from the torchlights. The only thing that's definite is that the guy's eyes are fixed on mine, his gaze unwavering, his head tilted.

The old man clangs his bell. "It weren't always like this," he calls out, pulling my attention back. "I've lived around this neighbourhood for over *thirty years*. It used to be a nice, God-fearing community, close-knit, where you knew your neighbours, where everyone *helped* each other."

The very air seems to quiver with his voice. His supporters clamour louder, and the veil's strangely insubstantial before my senses again. I sniff the air. Yes, there's a new acrid scent, unplaceable with the smell of the alcohol-soaked rags so powerful in my nose.

"But now it's a cesspit, reduced to ruin," the old man goes on, turning his scowl on the taller kid. "Every second house has got you people in it. You're a fucking stain." He jabs a finger at the guy's chest.

"You will leave!" the taller kid shouts back, his own voice shaking now.

His friends thrust their makeshift weapons out. And a half dozen of the thugs lumber out from behind the old man, teeth bared and eyes shining. A few of them grip bloody torches like they're looking to burn these people out.

Yet still the neighbours don't move or show any sign of backing down.

My shoulders bunch as Hassan's group murmur expectantly behind me. The veil's still so thin, the collective rage building the fire at my core. My arms tense, and I imagine peeling the veil back, feeling the power coursing through my limbs, smashing through—

However, my eyes find the figure in grey again. He's still staring at me, but it's more than that. Someone with a torch has drifted right next to him, yet the guy's as ensconced in darkness as he was before, the shadows somehow clinging to him like some kind of shroud.

Despite the heat, a shiver runs right down my spine, and my thoughts clamour ...

The angels, the emissaries. They've finally found us, have come for justice for us getting the final binding angel killed, for helping release the devil. Images flash of Satan, face pale as smoke, mismatched eyes gleaming as he proclaimed us Adam and Eve, Gabriel lying entirely broken behind him. Natasha and I the symbolic bearers of a new age. His fucking age.

My pulse hammers, and I rip my gaze away, squeezing my fingers together to try to find some calm and stop them shaking.

"I won't be leaving," the old man shouts at the taller kid and then jabs him in the forehead with his finger. "*You* will. This is *our* moment."

Somehow his words vibrate my chest, just like the priest's command voice, while the flames lick higher around my insides.

I tense my neck and push them down while making sure not to glance at the strange figure, to keep the veil firmly in place, to use no hint of its powers. Because the bastard may be trying to smoke me out.

The taller kid lifts his chin. "Fuck you!" he yells.

The old man grins. "*God* has spoken, you little savage," he says through gritted teeth. "Your lot will be cleansed!"

Then he takes a step back. Pauses. And spits at the taller kid, the spittle landing right in the middle of the guy's torso.

The rage burns on both sides of me, driving the river of fire higher in my chest. The taller kid's two friends spring forward on either side of him, one with his chair leg lifted high. The thugs behind the old man react immediately, stomp forward, and raise their own weapons.

And I find myself darting right into the midst of them.

4

"STOP!" I yell as loudly as I can, the flames burning up my throat, yet I make sure not to use my command voice.

Nevertheless, everyone turns on me – the mob and the neighbours alike. The young neighbours gaze on expectantly from in front of the house while the thugs eye me, hands tight around their weapons.

The fire ebbs in my chest, a clammy sensation taking its place, and again, I just stand there between them like an idiot with no fucking plan.

The old man's eyes narrow in suspicion.

"You think they've stolen goods," I say to him, my mind racing. I deepen my voice and keep my head down under my hood. "And you want to search the house. Right?"

The old man says nothing. He simply squares up to me, his eyes burning into mine. I grit my teeth and try to force my stuttering brain into action.

I scan the crowd again. The old man won't leave till he gets what he wants. He'd lose standing. And behind him, the thugs swarm about, their gleaming eyes fixed on the neighbour's house. Any search would surely be an excuse to wreck the place, but the young neighbours continue to stand firm. Shoulder to shoulder. And the mob keeps growing, more onlookers at the rear just standing there, staring on. More scrutiny, more damn pressure.

An idea hits me.

The old man opens his mouth, but I cut the fucker off.

"Well, let's get this over with, then," I say.

Exclamations of shock erupt from both the young and some of the older neighbours, which quickly morph into accusatory shouts. And then five of the bigger thugs with weapons push forward past the old man, heading for the gate and looking to barrel right through the young neighbours' defensive line.

I step right in front of them. "No, not you guys," I say, keeping my voice loud.

Before they can react, I shove past them and stalk right into the middle of the crowd.

Some hold torches, others weapons. And none of them look happy. A few stomp into my path, their anger driving the fire within me again, the veil still so thin before my senses. I make sure to weave around them to keep my thoughts running and the shimmering world far away as I force my legs on in a measured pace.

The torches scorch my vision, and I unfocus my eyes, training my gaze for sudden movements or attempts to surround me. It'd be so easy. My overall plan is a truly idiotic one.

Yet my lips stretch into a grim smile. If it *does* work, it'll calm the situation and get me out of here without attracting any more attention.

And with my thoughts rabbiting on, I get all the way to the back of the mob before realising I'm near the place where I spied the strange figure.

My head turns automatically, and my eyes focus to seek him out, my brain trying to conjure up his image. But it won't come. Medium build, angular features, and bright eyes … maybe?

Yet I avert my gaze and make sure not to search. Even

though every part of my learned behaviour screams to identify the threat.

I swivel to face the rear of the crowd. The spectators here don't hold torches or weapons; they simply stand and gawk from the safety of the back. And while the flames smoulder on inside me, I scan their number for my willing volunteers. A man and woman back away. Both middle-aged, and both well-enough dressed – the man in trousers and a jacket, his wife in a long patterned top.

"Hey, you and you," I say, pointing at them. "And you." I indicate a skinny guy in a leather coat with the collar up who's turning to hide among the surrounding people. "You three are coming with me."

The couple glance at each other, their faces pale. The skinny guy lifts his hands at me and shakes his head. None of them move.

"Look ..." the skinny guy says, keeping his voice low.

I spin toward the mob and yell, "Hey!"

The skinny guy cringes.

"We're here to find stolen goods. Right?" I shout and lift my hand in a fist.

No one from the mob replies. Several thugs have formed a wall in front of me, blocking my way back to the front. And most of the crowd look on confused.

"Right?" I say again, even louder, and thrust my fist higher in the air.

I hold the silence. And eventually, several muted grunts of agreement emanate from the front.

I swivel back to my three not-so-willing volunteers and extend an arm out toward the front of the mob. All sound dies. The entire crowd is staring at my volunteers now. The three of them stand there, wringing their hands and tapping their feet as I hold my ground.

Eventually the scrutiny's too much, and Skinny Guy dips his head in defeat. They all trundle toward the neighbours' house. Faced with the three volunteers, the line of thugs parts as they approach. I follow closely behind them, using them as a shield to drive my way through the crowd.

The thugs press in close, making hardly any room. Padding between them all – between their torches, weapons, and hard stares – is like passing through an oven, embers broiling on all sides, the heat continuing to pump through my veins. I keep stalking forward behind my volunteers, my head down and face obscured under my hood.

Finally, we reach the old man at the front, whose breathing is fast and shallow, his eyes protruding. The young neighbours look even more furious – teeth gritted and weapons held out before them.

The old man waves a finger at me. "Now, look here," he says, and again I can feel my sternum vibrating, the tug of his command voice.

"No, *you* look here," I say, tensing my chest, damming the fire. "You want the house searched?" I jab my finger toward the volunteers standing mutely at my side. "These people can do it just as well."

The old man stares back at me, his snake eyes blinking, and it's as if I can see the calculations going on in his head. He's at the top of the pile here, so he can't be seen being told what to do. Yet he can't claim that any of his flock aren't a worthy part of his effort.

"You said it yourself," I continue, my jaw clenching. "God has spoken. That's why you're here." And I nod at my three volunteers. "*All* of you."

The old man's mouth forms a thin line, but he doesn't stop me as I stride past him up to the line of young neighbours, ushering the three volunteers with me. The thugs and the older neighbours all mutter angrily among themselves.

The young neighbours maintain their line, however. They just stare me down, a mix of disappointment and fury in their expressions. I'm forced to stop a couple of paces before them.

We hover there, like a troupe of actors on stage. The thugs stand behind me as an audience with the neighbours' friends and older family members standing on both sides, watching on from the wings. No one speaks while the tension squeezes my throat, the fire burning ever wilder in my chest. I take a breath and lean in toward the younger neighbours.

"Two minutes," I whisper, gazing along the line of them. "That's all it'll take. And then we can all go home."

The taller kid's mouth curls, and he pokes the end of his chair leg into my chest. Then he starts to shove. The thugs edge closer behind me, their shuffling feet and rapid breaths growing ever louder in my ears.

I don't retreat. In fact, I push in closer toward the young neighbour, letting the fire inside me dull the pain from the stabbing wood. My gaze locks with his.

"Or they destroy you," I hiss again and tilt my head to both sides. "And your friends are so young."

And there I position myself, my feet anchored. The young neighbour's gaze flicks between me and the thugs at my back, the weapons held in their hands. Ten seconds pass. Twenty. The thug rattles his chain against the tarmac road.

Finally, the taller kid gives me a last shove with the chair leg and grunts before stepping out of the way. His friends moan bitterly at him, but eventually they part as well. None of them look at me, their expressions still tense with rage. And while the fire burns on inside me, it becomes engulfed by the void, the darkness.

This'll violate their only sanctuary.

I swallow and steel myself. "Go on," I bark at the three volunteers behind me, trying to keep my tone hard. I motion them past the defensive line and into the house.

"Look everywhere!" the older man calls from behind. "In cupboards, under mattresses. We've got people waiting round the back. They can't escape!"

I ignore the comment and plant myself between the groups again. The younger neighbours continue to mutter in Arabic among themselves, still refusing to glance in my direction, and some of their friends or family members opposite cast angry glances at me. On the other side, many of the thugs eye the neighbours, faint smiles on their lips, fingers twitching around their weapons.

I stand firm between them all, my face down, and force my breath into a steady rhythm, darkness and fire mingling within me.

At one point, the taller neighbour jabs a dismissive finger in my direction and yells at the crowd that fetched me. A few of the kids shout back.

"Speak English!" the old man hollers at the neighbours, his tone patronising. He clangs his bell repeatedly and several of the mob hoot and howl along with him.

Still I avoid their gaze.

The old man roves back through the crowd, inciting people as he goes. I find myself searching for the strange figure, the guy who was staring at me, but he's no longer at the back of the crowd. In fact, he's now standing much closer, only ten feet from the line of elderly neighbours. And he's watching the front door, his gaze fixed. Till he gives me a sideways glance, as if he knew I'd had my eyes on him the entire time.

I spin away as exclamations of excitement break out from the mob. The three volunteers are hastening back through the front door followed by an elderly Arab woman who's hot on their heels, yammering at their backs.

The patterned-top volunteer shakes her head, while Skinny Guy says, "We didn't find anything."

My gaze tracks to the old man, who stiffens. Then he lunges toward the house again, his hands grasping at the surrounding crowd.

"It's in there!" he shouts. "I *know* it's there. They're hiding it on their persons, in their clothes!"

He shoves his way through the midst of the mob, thugs tussling to line up at his back. The young neighbours re-form their defensive wall, weapons still in hand. And again, the flames build so quickly, the river of fire bubbling and frothing in my chest. I keep my head tilted down and step directly in between the neighbours and the approaching thugs before anchoring my feet.

The old man can't attack. He's founded his authority on the moral high ground. On casting the neighbours in the role of thieves, of sinners—

But my gut starts to twist – my internal alarm – and I sense my gaze drawn to the side.

Someone's flying forward through the crowd, inhumanly fast. The shock stills my thoughts, and with the veil so thin, it peels back a fraction from my senses. Time slows, and I get a glimpse of the figure. It's the one who's been staring at me, and he's speeding toward us.

I plant one foot behind me, channel the growing energy into my legs and hips, and raise my hands.

But he's not heading for me, nor the old man. He's darting behind the row of elder neighbours, the guys looking on from the wings. And the older man scrambles forward on their other side, weaving through his band of thugs.

My shoulders tighten and my heart pounds at my ribs, visions forming of what the strange figure's going to do and the inevitable carnage that will follow. I'm ten feet away from the old man with half a dozen thugs standing in between.

I still my thoughts and use the burning fire to plunge myself fully behind the veil. Sensation inundates me – the movements of the crowd, the old man scrabbling forward, people turning to let him through – every motion, every distance effortlessly weaved into my awareness. I throw myself forward, dart into gaps between the thugs before they even appear.

The strange figure speeds up and gets ahead of the old man. Then he pushes himself behind two of the older neighbours and thrusts a leg between them, making it look like they did it. He clips the old man's ankles as they pass each other, and the guy sprawls forward, arms flailing for any kind of purchase.

I concentrate on the flames at my core, channelling the power down my legs, and then leap forward and fling out an arm. The dive sends me crashing down on one knee, but I ignore the muted pain, focusing only on the old man's tumbling body. And with one hand, I barely catch him under the shoulder.

He teeters, his arms reaching, and starts to spill from my grip. I thrust both hands under him and push myself back to standing, my knee throbbing from the fall.

And finally, I'm able to shove him back to his feet.

For a moment, the old man stands there, blinking, his facial muscles twitching. Then he focuses on me and bares his teeth, his eyes ablaze. I step back and tug my hood back into place.

"Get away from me!" he yells and shoves himself backward off my chest.

I bow my head, the veil slipping back before my senses.

"This isn't over!" he says and stabs a finger in my face. "We'll be back, bigger and stronger. You'll see!" He spins to face the line of young neighbours. "You'll see what's coming. You can't stop it." He sweeps a shaking arm over the watching neighbours on both sides. "None of you can!"

I just stand there as he stumbles back through the crowd, many of them turning to follow. However, a few of the thugs linger behind, casting narrowed glances at the younger neighbours. Mutterings break out among the neighbours as well, and a few of them brandish their weapons at the retreating thugs. I avert my gaze, unable to face either group and powerless to ignore the growing void inside me.

This hasn't stopped the violence. It's only delayed it and probably increased its scale.

A hand touches my arm, and I swivel, my muscles tense. But then my shoulders relax. It's Mrs B, staring up at me, a wan smile on her face.

"Come home," she says and tries to tug me gently toward our house. Toward Natasha.

Members of the mob continue to hover on the streets behind me. Lots of onlookers, too, some glancing toward me.

"No," I say and shake my head, my voice barely audible. "You go."

Eventually, Mrs B nods and shuffles back down the street. Hassan's waiting for her twenty feet away on the pavement. He doesn't meet my eye.

I turn back to search the diminishing crowd for a glimpse of the strange figure.

But of course, there's no sign.

5

I TRUDGE through the front door, my limbs heavy. The street outside is finally empty of the mob, of neighbours quarrelling, of older people trying to pull younger relatives indoors, and of the bigots jeering at anyone different they could find. And my thoughts dart to our bedroom above, to Natasha.

I shut the door silently and then take two steps down the hallway before a noise grabs my attention. The sound of low talking. My head swivels while my legs lumber on toward the stairs.

The neighbours' door stands open a few inches, Mrs B's voice coming from behind it. And with my eyes on the thin wedge of black between the door and frame, my foot comes down heavily on the bottom step. And the fucking thing creaks.

Sounds cease inside the room, and I freeze as well.

Is she waiting up for me? Probably worried about what happened, what's coming. I don't move, only holding my breath in the darkness. I've got no answers.

Eventually, the talking resumes in the neighbours' room, and I start up the stairs, slower now, my gaze still fixed on their door as my feet pick out the quieter steps. I get halfway up the staircase before giving a massive start.

A figure sits on the top stair, right by the wall and almost entirely cloaked in darkness, completely still.

"Nat?" I ask, my voice hardly a whisper.

She doesn't move at all but just stares blankly over my shoulder. I climb the rest of the staircase and stand above her at the top. She tilts her head back to meet my gaze.

"Are you okay?" she asks, her voice so soft. "What happened?"

I stare back at her, the familiar distance so obvious in her eyes. The void's there again in my stomach, the darkness so oppressive inside me and out.

I try to ignore the sensation as I gently lift her to her feet. She leans on my arms as she rises, her body so weak again.

"Nothing," I say. "All's fine."

I nudge her back toward our room, toward her bed. But she won't move. Despite her frailty, she stands like a rock.

"What *happened,* Jake?" she demands. "I woke up to shouting … screaming, and the ringing of a bell. And you were gone."

Then she wrinkles her nose, leans forward, and sniffs my chest. "And you smell *awful,*" she says. "What is that, kerosene?" Her shaky voice is louder now.

My eyes find Mrs B's door, still ajar, in the hallway.

"It's nothing," I say in a hushed tone and try again to usher her away from the stairs. "Just a bit of a ruckus down the road."

Still she stands there, immobile, with one hand gripping the wall. "A ruckus?" she repeats, narrowing her eyes at me.

"Some people causing trouble for our neighbours," I say, keeping my tone light.

But the image comes of the strange figure and its shroud of darkness. Just like the outline I saw when the bigots came.

The thoughts must show in my expression, because

Natasha's face screws up an instant later. "*Who* did you see?" she sputters. "Was it only *people*?"

I try to smile but fail. Natasha pins my gaze and opens her mouth.

"I can't say for sure," I say quickly. "It might be nothing."

Her eyes widen. "Angels? Emissaries?" she asks, her tone higher, more strained.

I squeeze her shoulders. "I don't know." I try to keep my voice calm. "It may have nothing to do with us. Whoever it was, they targeted our neighbours, *not* me. And they may have been there to stir religious anger, to build devotion."

Yet the obvious thought strikes me. If it *was* an angel or emissary, it's inciting people, interfering in their lives, going against Michael's orders. Why?

Natasha's eyes haze for an instant, and her legs wobble. I grip her shoulders tighter and try to steer her back into our room again. This time, she lets me.

A triangle of light falls on her back as she scuffs across the floor, her movements faltering and slow. More doubts come: the near impossibility of getting her onto the ship to Poland. Plus, we'd be leaving Mrs B and her family and friends unprotected.

Natasha reaches the mattress and then turns to fix me with her gaze.

"This trouble, will it happen again?" she asks, her eyes scrutinising my face again.

I exhale slowly and try to relax every muscle in my face. But a knot forms in my stomach, and my cheek twitches as I hear again the old man's promise to return.

But when? And with angels in tow?

Natasha places her hand on my arm, and in that moment, the old man's words morph into Dan's, and I feel the bigot clapping me on the shoulder. *Meet up … come along … Thursday night … eight p.m.*

The words are out of my mouth before I can stop myself. "I could find out."

My fingers go to my lips, and Natasha's eyes narrow again, that single line creasing her brow. I drop my hand quickly.

"They're holding a meeting," I say. "In a local school. Tomorrow. I could go along to see who's there and what they're doing."

Natasha grips my forearm. "Jake ..." she starts, her tone strained.

I raise my hands. "I'd just go to observe. Nothing more."

Which is insane. I could so easily be recognised.

Natasha continues to frown at me.

I take her hand. "It's okay, Nat," I say, my voice quiet. "It'll be helpful. I'll learn more and be able to help out our neighbours with what to do." I squeeze her fingers. "Plus, I'll be there and back before you know it."

Natasha doesn't reply. But eventually, I manage to coax her down on the mattress and then drape the blanket over her.

She doesn't close her eyes but simply lies there, staring numbly across the floorboards. I sit beside her and begin stroking her arm.

After a while, she pulls the blanket further up under her chin and her eyes close. I continue to stroke her arm, tracing the curve of her shoulder up to her neck and back again. I breathe the night air in and out, simply watching her.

"Stay with me," she murmurs.

And I find myself smiling back. "Always."

Though the knot in my stomach doesn't ease.

6

I REACH the corner of another residential street and scour its length. The houses are in better repair than most, with glass in all the windows and front yards free of rubbish. The road's empty. Just a group of kids playing with a tattered ball. Everyone else is either locked up indoors at this time of the evening – a bit after eight – or they're also heading to the bigots' meeting.

Striding on, I chew my cheek, my thoughts flitting to Natasha back at home. She was even more distant than usual, a faint look of worry in her eyes. But again, I vowed not to engage. Only to listen. And finally, she gave me a weak smile. Then I left.

The kids are chucking the ball, so I skirt around the game. Yet all five stop playing to stare at me, their heads swivelling as I push on. I keep my eyes forward, right till the end of the street, before glancing over my shoulder.

They're playing again. And no one else is staring, no suspicious figures. Just the bloody white ribbons in so many of the windows. I shake my head. My feet take me around the corner and there it is, directly ahead …

The school. On the far side of a T-junction, seventy yards distant, it's a two-storey rectangular block with multiple lighted windows on the first floor that resemble probing spotlights.

A crowd mills before its entrance, a dozen people queueing in front of a couple of guards. And with the shadows faint around me, the sky still a dusky blue, I take a breath and flick back my hood to reveal my face to the world. I keep striding toward the crowd, right down the middle of the road, in full view of both guards.

Each one's casually dressed – shirts and jeans. The first scrutinises the crowd while the second checks people in. Slowly. Keeping at least a dozen in the queue. He's making the meet-up seem popular, like the place to be.

My lips form a half smile.

Then it falters. I'm thirty yards out now, and neither guard has glanced in my direction. I have no clue as to whether they recognise me or not. And the final junction to veer off lies only fifteen feet ahead. I continue forward, searching faces for the strange figure. I can't pick out any sign of him. No hint of cordite in the air. And the veil's not that thin before my senses.

Ten yards out. My heart beats faster. Still both guards stare the other way. I cough loudly. The first guard snaps his head around. Then the second. However, there's no tightening of postures, no whispering together. They simply fix me with hard stares.

I swallow, lift my chin, and force myself on, sweat itching at my lower back. They eyeball me right till I get to the queue, before turning away.

Standing there, my feet jiggle, and I press my toes into the pavement, the guards still pinned in the corner of my vision.

Gradually the queue creeps forward, and I shuffle with it, covertly taking in my surroundings. The building has a tiny playground on one side, butting up to the road. And at its back, a grassy space extends a hundred yards to rows of houses on all three sides, hopefully with escape routes beyond.

More people line up behind me, and I scan the thinning crowd. It's comprised of all ages – young and old, even kids – and while not all are white, we're by far the dominant group. A few people wear Puritan grey, but most are dressed in normal clothes. Also, a sense of anticipation lingers in the air – people speaking that bit louder, that bit faster – as we inch toward the gaping entrance, a large crucifix secured above it.

Eventually, the guard waves the young couple in front of me into the building, and I step up to him.

"You live round here?" the guard asks. He's bulky with very little body fat. Several savage-looking rings adorn his fingers.

I nod back and fix my attention on the muscles around his eyes and mouth.

"Which road?" he asks.

"Church Vale," I say. It's not our road, but it's close.

The guy's eyes narrow. But only a fraction. "Lived here long?" he questions.

"Was born round here. You?" I answer in a sharp tone.

He doesn't rise to my jibe at all but simply stares back at me. I fully expect to be given my marching orders.

But the guy gives a faint smirk and steps aside, prompting me to stand there, immobile, a building full of bloody bigots ahead. I face the glass doors. Dozens of them stand around the corridor beyond, and my eyes scan desperately for anyone I recognise.

Savage-ring guard folds his sizeable arms and starts tapping his feet. His colleague glances over. I grit my teeth, stride up to the doors, and then shove through them into the school's entrance hall.

It's fifty yards long with doors to classrooms and a couple of bisecting corridors. The walls are covered with kids' drawings and Bible quotes. And several of the people glance at me as I approach, a couple holding their stares.

Instinctively, I go to put my hood up and barely stop

myself in time, just avoiding hastening under the bright lights.

Most people are drifting toward the end of the corridor, and so I follow behind, glancing down each junction we pass.

The passages continue straight as well, with additional classrooms along their lengths. By the second junction, I'm only searching in one direction, these corridors ending in more glass doors. A push bar is the only thing between me and the playground and green fields.

Near the middle of the main hallway, several people linger around an open set of double doors, a sliver of what looks like a bigger room beyond. I make a beeline toward it, the noise of animated conversation building with every step and a growing buzz in the air.

An elderly woman in a threadbare dress stands by a table with a large urn. She offers me a tea and a leaflet from a dozen coloured stacks in front of her. I decline with a raised palm and a smile. I press on for the double doors but come to an abrupt halt on the threshold.

The room's not big but huge – a cavernous sports hall already filled with hundreds of people, an empty stage to my left. Just like outside, people are hanging around in groups, chatting animatedly – all under the watchful eye of another large white crucifix above the stage, with more biblical quotes scribed around the top of the walls.

Multiple attendants stand in lines to either side of the doors, holding leaflets and blocking any chance of slinking rearward along the wall to find a place to hide. More people push in through the doors at my back, shoving me further on, right into the middle of the room. My legs tighten, and I swivel in place, searching for the strange figure. There's no obvious sign, and there's still not a hint of cordite in the air.

My eyes find the back of the room – the folded tables and stacked chairs with plenty of secluded spots in between. Suddenly a voice pierces the loud chatter.

"Welcome!"

I sense the word directed at me and find myself turning.

A man's slipping through the crowd in my direction. He has a slight build dressed in black robes with a dog collar, and for several seconds, I simply stand there blinking, the image of Father Thomas strong in my mind – though this guy's much younger, with a narrow face and long dark hair tied back in a ponytail. He weaves steadily between people, never taking his eyes off mine, with a beaten-up Bible held in one hand.

I shake myself, starting to pivot to get out of there. But an instant later, the pastor steps right up to me.

"So *glad* you could make it," he says and offers his free hand to shake.

I glance down at it, my mind blank, and more nearby people turn in our direction. The pastor doesn't withdraw his hand, so eventually I take it. The guy's skin is cool to the touch, his grip surprisingly firm.

"The movement *needs* people like you," he says with a smile, the words subtly vibrating my chest. "You've come to the right place."

I simply nod but say nothing.

He remains standing before me, however, his gaze fixed on mine. And people continue to fill the surrounding space through the double doors. My skin prickles with discomfort. I swivel to the side, potential excuses filtering through my brain.

"So, you're local, but you must have been away," the pastor says suddenly.

My attention darts right back, and the word tumbles from my mouth. *"What?"*

The pastor simply smiles, his eyes inscrutable. I sniff the air for cordite.

"I only surmise," he says. "As we haven't seen you in church recently."

He smiles again, and more of the crowd in our vicinity are staring at us now.

I swallow and force a smile. "That's true."

"Well, we're very glad you're back," he says, clasping his Bible in front of him. "To have you aiding our efforts."

And with this, he winks at me, spins, and glides back through the crowd, away from the doors. I manage a half turn toward the back of the room when the man's voice rings out again, much louder this time.

"Ladies and gentlemen, I think we'll make a start," he says and heads fast for the stage, where he bounds up the steps.

And I achieve only a single step away before a hush grows around me, the silence deepening. My eyes flick from side to side. The crowd's packed tightly around me now, unmoving, with all attention on the stage. And I remain standing there, trapped, right in the centre of the hall.

"Thank you *all* for coming," the pastor says, his voice booming despite the lack of a microphone. "It's so good to see so many supporters here."

I avoid his eyes as they sweep over the room, people murmuring their acknowledgement as his beaming gaze passes over each section.

Then he steps forward and holds his Bible out in front of him. "You know that our numbers grow every day," he says. "People called to our mission not simply because they're asked but because they know it's *right.*" His eyes linger on me for a moment before moving on.

I barely suppress a shudder.

"We are here for a holy purpose!" he says and lifts a finger to the sky. "We built these homes, this neighbourhood, after the second great war. We came together to defeat sin then, and we *will* do so again."

I hear louder expressions of approval from parts of the crowd. And I lean away as a lady shouts "Yes!" by my ear.

"And make no mistake, this *is* war," he says and thumps a fist down on his Bible. "Countries are sending these immigrants to poison our way of life, to threaten our families, and to eventually take us over."

I just stare at the guy, wide-eyed.

"And that's why you're here," the guy goes on, his voice continuing to grow in volume and power. "You see the threat to our beloved country, to our beloved faith. You believe in something better."

I can only watch as he closes his eyes and holds splayed fingers out toward us. He tilts his head back in some kind of swoon.

"I want you to imagine fewer people, less pressure on resources, more to go around. A proper community spirit. Better security and worrying less about your elderly, your children." His eyes fly open. "That's what we're building."

And while his voice has been growing progressively louder, he's made it rise and fall, the experience hypnotic. I almost nod along to his words. But then clench my jaw. It's bloody crazy.

I sniff the air, a metallic taste at the back of my throat. I find my gaze drawn to the wall, to a figure standing behind the line of attendants by the door. Medium build. Familiar sharp features. And the same bright eyes I remember from the mob last night, crystal blue in colour. But I can't make out much more about him – his clothes or his posture – with so many people in the way.

And he's staring directly at me.

My pulse races, and I blink. No … no, he's not. He's gazing at the stage.

The speaker begins again, his voice booming louder. "And, yes, it's the heathens' fault," he says, jabbing his finger at the door. And then his voice quietens. "But it's ours also." He gazes solemnly at us all. "We have been negligent. Distracted. Consumed only by material things."

My shoulders tense. It's like listening to Gabriel.

"We need a resurgence, to purify ourselves," the speaker goes on, slowly building in volume again. "And it's happening. Communities have been taking back their neighbourhoods. The profane fleeing in droves, swept before God's mighty hand." He makes a fist.

I scan the surrounding faces for responses and see only shining eyes, gritted teeth, and clenched fingers. It's fucking insane. The void grows in the pit of my stomach.

"And make no mistake, God has ordained this!" the speaker says, and the shouts of support grow louder from the crowd.

My gaze finds the strange figure again. Is it his influence? But he's not doing anything obvious. Only standing there, staring at the speaker like everyone else.

"The Lord placed a Puritan at the heart of government, a man of faith!" the speaker continues, pressing his palm down on the Bible. "And miracles happen every day." He raises an arm toward the back of the audience. "Theodora Clarence, healed from stage four cancer." Several people toward the rear whoop. "Dan Jefferies, recovering from his injured throat in record time." More whooping.

I keep my eyes fixed dead ahead, making sure not to react.

"And little Samantha King, saved from her awful coma." Everyone in the crowd cheers this one.

"Yet we still have so much more work to do," the speaker says. "Making collections. Managing distributions. Deploying security. Please see our coordinators to volunteer."

He lifts an arm, and I follow his point toward the six or seven people by the door. Sure enough, one of the larger guys is wearing a white band around his bicep.

"And we must redouble our efforts," the speaker continues. "To send a signal to all migrants that they're not welcome here! To root out the unclean! And we'll be doing that and more in only a couple of days' time."

I keep my eyes on the white-banded coordinator, the heat rising at my core.

"But this is only possible with your help," he says. "We are so grateful to those who are new to our cause. Brothers and sisters! Those of you who've attended before, please put your hands together to welcome those new to the fold!"

The speaker extends both arms and steps back. Instantly, the surrounding people applaud. My hands twitch, caught between blending in and not.

The folks around me are already turning in my direction, applauding me specifically. The speaker's staring at me also, an open hand pointed in my direction. And my arms remain by my sides, nausea rising at just the thought of clapping for this shit.

The speaker grins at me for an agonising twenty seconds, the applause ringing in my ears. Then he lifts his head, and his smile vanishes. The clapping subsides.

"But we must be careful," he says. "For while we burn brighter every day … Every bright light attracts insects."

Insects? My insides squeeze. The language of the angels.

"And the worst of all infestations is one that comes from within our own fold."

I edge backward as his gaze sweeps the crowd.

"But it reminds us to be vigilant," he says. "Without vigilance, sin *will* creep in." He leans forward and narrows his eyes. "And traitors run the risk of corrupting everything we've worked so hard for."

The lights directly above me seem to brighten as he stands there, staring. And I control the impulse to glance up and check.

"So, I invite you to look among you, at our newcomers, at those not known to you, for any sign of Judases," he says.

People swivel toward me, more sets of eyes zeroing in. And I can only stare back as perspiration breaks out across my chest and sides.

7

I PERCEIVE movement in the corner of my vision and spin. Someone's slipping through the crowd toward the double doors, twenty feet away.

The strange figure.

I watch him as he heads through them and out into the school corridor, my mind racing ... Angel? Emissary? Adversary? Or just a normal fucking guy?

The speaker continues to hold the silence while more and more of the surrounding people stare in my direction. Sweat beads on my temples. My pulse beats faster, and a part of my brain screams at me to gaze around, to join the search, to hide myself.

Fuck it.

I lower my shoulder and plough my way toward the exit. People back out of my way, damn well everyone staring at me now. I keep shoving, and a few people jeer at my back.

Reaching the doors, someone steps out of the corridor in front of me – not a guard but a woman holding a stack of green leaflets. And she doesn't move aside.

I tense up, waiting for the tirade, the accusation. But she only smiles and extends a leaflet toward me while a hundred sets of eyes burn into my back. In full view of her. The jeering grows ever louder. Her smile slips, her brow furrowing. I grab the flyer and pocket it. She steps aside automatically, and I plunge out into the corridor.

I let out a slow breath. The hallway is mostly empty, just a few people standing around and chatting in low voices. No guards, and no one's focused on me. My gaze finds the front entrance at the end of the passageway, darkness and anonymity beyond.

And there in between, twenty yards down the corridor, I spy the strange figure. Dressed in normal-looking grey trousers and a black shirt, he's ambling past the group of people. Then he turns down a bisecting corridor and strolls out of sight.

I throw myself after him. The guy seems entirely ordinary. No flowing movements. No playing with the light. Plus, I detect no cordite in the air. But maybe I'm too far away to notice.

I drive my legs faster. The people in the corridor turn to stare, and I fly past them, reach the junction in only a few seconds, and careen around it, ready to pull up short.

Yet somehow he's already at the far end of the corridor, still twenty yards away, poised before a glass door.

My pace slows. The guy doesn't turn but simply pushes the door open. He heads out into the darkness of the playground and green fields.

Again, I run after him, my feet beating hard at the rubber floor. Reaching the glass door, I jab my hand against the push bar and lurch out into the muggy night air.

To one side, the steel surfaces of playground equipment glint in the reflected light from the school windows. And to the other side, the wide green field extends away from me, most of it lost to the darkness. Between the playground and field stands a hedge, over two metres tall, only the near side of it visible from where I'm standing.

And the strange figure's already nowhere to be seen.

I dart forward a step and then stop, a sliver-like concern biting at my mind …

The last two times I spied him, he was right at the point of disappearing. Perfect for leading me on.

I pad out into the night, going slower now. And in the open air, my breath comes a little easier now that I'm away from that damn crowd.

My feet take me across the concrete ground, my eyes searching the darkness. I still see no sign of the figure on the playground or the field. I step beyond the hedge and glimpse someone halfway along it, striding toward a row of houses blocked by a fence. Again, with an entirely regular gait and posture.

I don't stop. Don't wait. Just sprint after him. I get halfway along the hedge before the figure disappears through a gap in the fence at the end. I reach it several seconds later and shove myself through into a narrow passageway.

Wooden fences line both sides, each one well over head height, brambles stretching over the top. In one direction, the walkway dog-legs quickly to the left. And in the other, it continues straight until it meets a road with streetlights illuminating large swathes of tarmac, at least fifty yards clearly visible that way. But no sign of the strange figure. Or anyone else, for that matter.

Which is weird in itself.

I gamble and spin toward the dog-leg. The passageway winds right and then left before hitting a fork where a broader avenue opens onto another road. But I don't take that either. I still see no sign of anyone.

The passage now snakes between houses on both sides, and I rack my brains for memories of this place from childhood. But nothing comes. In fact, seeing only the outline of the high fences, the shadows masking almost everything else, it's like being in some kind of dream. There's no sound, no wind. Only the faintest humming in my ears, the air thick in my lungs. Padding through the darkness, I get that feeling that I'm the only person for hundreds of miles. The same sense of timelessness I remember from being with the janitor.

I glance around me but spy no sign of him.

Reaching another corner, I turn to find the passageway continuing straight on into a yawning blackness, the end invisible.

I sniff the air again, trying to sort the scent of cordite from the perennial smell of refuse and fires. I fail and then take a breath before pressing on more quietly, placing my feet down gently on the earthen ground.

After several feet, the faintest light pricks the darkness, right at the far end of the passageway.

I peer forward. Possibly it's another road, a streetlight. Maybe forty yards away. It's almost impossible to be sure, but there seems to be a large pool of shadow in between, the light filtering back through what look like overhanging branches from trees somewhere up ahead. And of course, I see no sign of the figure.

A gust of wind cools my cheek, and I sniff the air again.

Cordite. Indisputable.

I shudder, my heart pounds, and my mind conjures images of the fork a few corners ago, of the figure hiding there and then creeping up on me from behind. I resist the urge to stop and turn. Instead, I back right up to the fence and edge forward along it, putting more distance between me and the last corner.

After a couple of steps, the wooden fence becomes a brick wall at my back, seven feet in height. After a few more paces, the fence disappears opposite me also, the line of trees taking its place. Their branches overhang the path between me and the road, creating the deepest pool of darkness that's only ten feet further on.

A thicket of trees stands between buildings – the perfect fucking place for an ambush.

Again, my eyes find the broken glow from the streetlights

up ahead on the far side of the shadows, the lit streets not far away. Only seven or eight seconds at a sprint.

Easy.

Too easy.

I force myself to stop, my eyes searching for any sign of the figure in the trees to the side and up ahead. But the darkness between their trunks is unnaturally thick.

Cold fingers tap up my back, while my gut twists – my internal alarm.

A huge impulse to run seizes my legs, yet I dart only another few feet forward till I'm directly under the overhanging branches in the deepest point of the gloom. And there I halt, my heart racing, and fix my gaze on the trees again to wait for my eyes to adjust.

Still, there's nothing. Only chasms of pitch blackness between the tree trunks. However, the branches up above and to the sides glow that bit brighter, their outlines clearer in my augmenting night vision. I ignore them and focus on the darkest patches. And in the next heartbeat, I go rigid, suddenly able to see.

Not one but *six* black shapes stand poised in an arc around me. Each one resembles the dark outline outside our home as well as Gabriel when he bound the shadows around himself before the final gate of hell.

I tense my body and lower my centre of gravity, preparing to be rushed.

But the outlines of black don't move. They simply hold still between the trees. I blink and peer closer. Shapes play before my eyes, the pools of darkness expanding. A gust of wind brings another whiff of cordite, but when I sniff the air again, it's gone. All the while, my gut twists further.

I take a breath and blink again at the darkness. The wells of black are definitely approaching now, slowly but steadily, the shapes overlapping. I back right up against the brick wall, the cold filling my entire spine.

Another huge temptation grabs me to turn and run.

However, I grip my legs and hold myself still. I try again to peer into the dark pools, desperate to catch a glimpse, but they remain simply holes of absolute blackness, indiscernible though only fifteen feet from me now. And getting ever closer.

Still I hold firm and continue to stare while clenching my hands to stop them trembling. Somehow, the dark deepens further. The shapes block out the sky above, the faint light of the road to my side, and even the branches above my head. A faint hissing starts up in my ears, like faint whispers, and it's as if I can hear my coming death.

I bend my legs and build the flames at my core. Then I spin and leap, grasping for the branches above.

But as soon as my back's turned, the darkness rushes in at me like a wave. The black floods my vision, the hissing becomes a roaring, and my hands shake as they close on shadows. I barely manage to clasp them onto a larger branch.

I grit my teeth, summon whatever power remains in me, and yank hard with my arms, desperately pulling up my legs to scissor them over the wall.

But a numbness is spreading through my calves and thighs, wrenching me down like weights. And when I hoist my knees, I'm barely able to clear the wall with the first foot while the second drags along the top.

The numbness has reached my waist now, the hissing now a full screaming. Tensing my stomach and chest, I give one last pull with my arms to haul the rest of my body over, my throat howling with the effort.

I hear a splintering crack, and the branch gives way above me. I go into free fall, my pulse galloping. My legs slip off the top of the wall, and my body twists in the air, my head a good distance below my feet.

Thoughts still. Time slows. And my lungs seize. The black wells merge into absolute shadow all around me, like I'm plummeting into dark waters. The hissing sound rages in my ears. My arms flail, and it's as if I fall forever, the sensation of numbness seeping into my mouth and my eyes and taking over my whole body.

Then the ground comes, crashing into my side. Something pops in my chest, and I yell with pain. The hissing dies as the numbness disappears.

My eyes shoot open, and it's like a shroud's been lifted. I peer upward, now able to make out the trees and bushes before me. A faint glow filters through the branches above my head, as if someone's switched on a light in the houses behind.

I just lie there blinking, one side of my ribs throbbing with pain. I see no sign of anything or anyone. No smell of cordite.

Shivers rack my body.

I scramble to my feet, teeth gritted against the pain, and spin toward the distant glow of streetlights.

Then I start to run.

8

Twenty minutes later, I find myself stumbling toward a shop doorway. The glow from inside spills out onto the pavement, a splash of light in a street of darkness. A couple of drifters lean against the entrance, gabbing on at each other in loud tones, one of them occasionally swigging from a bottle.

Approaching the pool of brightness, my shoulders loosen a fraction – the rest of my body so damned tight – and I slow my steps. Then I swivel to glance behind for the hundredth time, and a pain grips the lower right side of my chest.

I bite my cheek and cradle my rib while scanning the empty pavements, the parked cars, the dark houses. But I still see no pools of black, still nothing obvious following me, as if I invented it all. Six bloody angels.

How am I still alive? I shake my head.

"Oi!"

My body jerks and pain flashes down my side.

It's one of the drunks. He's wobbling on his feet, motioning me over. "Hey, guv'nor …" he says, his words slurred and his pointing finger swaying as much as his legs. "Come … lend an ear."

I ignore him and hurry past the row of shops. The guy totters after me, one hand still flapping, the other gripped around the bottle. I start to jog, and by the time I'm at the next corner, he's well behind, though his garbled shouts still echo in my ears.

Striding on, I waggle my arms and legs, trying to ease more of the tension. Then I hasten down a residential street toward home, the school a couple of roads over. I listen hard. But I hear no clanging bells, no distant whooping from a crazed mob outside. Just a couple of revving engines, and the soft padding of my footsteps against the pavement.

I get a quarter of the way down the street when three guys stalk into view at the far end, heading my way. They pass under a working streetlight, and I spy one dressed in Puritan grey, and a white band on one of the others' arms.

I skid to a stop and stare. They're fifty yards away, probably came straight from the meeting, and will recognise me for damn sure.

The guy with the armband's motioning at houses to his side, prattling on at the others, both of them nodding along. Then Armband Guy swivels back in my direction. Heart racing, I dart to the side, leap over a knee-high wall into the nearest front yard, and crouch down, pain stabbing at my rib.

I clench my teeth and keep low as I edge behind one of the pillars that a fence would have been attached to. I put my back to the narrow stack of bricks, my body hidden by the thinnest bar of shadow imaginable.

My insides tighten, and I glance back down the road, picturing myself running.

Their footsteps approach across the cracked pavement, the sound of their voices growing clearer. I hunch there, my rib aching.

"Two families in 'ere," one says. "Both heathen filth."

The heat climbs my insides, and I press my back into the stone pillar, the ache diminishing.

The three guys skulk closer – only ten yards away – still muttering about raiding nearby houses and forcing families off to the new migrant camps. The heat ignites into sparking embers, my legs twitch with energy, and I clench my teeth, thrusting my hands into my pockets.

My fingers touch a crumpled bit of paper.

I glance down in the darkness and pull it out, the guys' footsteps drawing ever nearer. It's the leaflet the woman gave me outside the hall and contains a familiar narrative. It describes a new dawn for the country, new possibilities ... Blah, blah, blah. None of the nastiness of the speaker from the school, but it's not too hard to see how easily the words could be warped.

I scan the text down to the bottom, complete with its biblical verses, and the invitation to join local groups with national phone numbers to help coordination. And there, right at the base of the leaflet, a familiar logo and slogan.

Rise.

It's Paul Hawcross's organisation. Ben's organisation. My eyes go wide.

Has *this* been the angels' plan? Infiltrate his network and use it to incite country-wide devotion to shore up their power before the devil attacks?

I start to push myself upward right as the three guys stalk past me down the pavement.

I freeze, my back to them and the top of my head above the cover of the pillar. Puritan Guy glances around, his eyeline only just above my exposed dome. And White Armband Guy jabs his finger at a home ten feet further down the road.

"Fucking Judases in there," he snaps and spits into the front yard. "Been supporting the heathens."

I hold my breath, keeping entirely still as my heart beats loudly in my ear. Finally Puritan Guy turns back to face the house. He scrawls a quick note in a handbook. Then the three guys march away, their footsteps ebbing into silence. I rise slowly to my feet, my eyes on the leaflet again.

Ben.

Could I get to him? He and Paul Hawcross have dedicated

their entire lives to bringing down the pantheon, to empowering people. He can't be aware of what's happening.

My pulse beats faster, and I scan the road in both directions. The three guys have disappeared, and I see no sign of anyone else. But there's a lot of shadow around – lurking between cars, in front yards, under trees.

I jump over the wall and hurry on down the road, the pain in my ribs little more than a nuisance now. I feel a new lightness in my chest. Because if Ben's organisation is coordinating the local groups, could I get him to de-escalate things around here? Last time I turned up at his headquarters, he saw us, and he listened.

Plus, another question nags at the back of my mind, my steps quickening.

Is Ben okay? Have the angels removed him?

I reach the street corner at the end of our road and pause to scan the street. A couple of people lumber away down the pavement thirty yards further on, plus one guy's sorting through scrap in his front yard.

My eyes find the corner, my mind already plotting a route around the block to prevent pursuit. But my body teeters, my legs suddenly so heavy as the adrenaline finally bleeds from my system.

I stumble toward the front gate, and my eyes take in our house beyond – its boarded-up windows, its reinforced door. Our lockup for six weeks now. And the sense of lightness starts to fade from my core, more thoughts circling.

Ben. I never reached out to him, never confessed what happened in hell. He had concerns before we left, yet he helped us anyway, and look what we did.

With a growing weight, I lumber to the door and unlock it, the hope dissipating like mist as the customary darkness reclaims my core.

It'd mean leaving Natasha for longer. And I've got to be realistic: the chances of seeing Ben at the headquarters are tiny. My fingers squeeze the door handle. We're cooped up here while he undoubtedly travels the world, most likely busy night and day. It'd probably be one big fucking waste of time.

I shove the door open and freeze.

Father Thomas's walking stick is lying diagonally across the wooden floorboards in exactly the same place as last time, as if I never put it back.

The hairs prick up across the back of my neck, and I peer into the darkness of the entrance hall. My mind conjures up the image of the old man standing there, the customary smile on his lips.

But there's nobody. Only the shadows of an empty hallway. No Natasha sitting at the top of the stairs. No sound from the neighbours.

Alone again.

The abyss plunges even deeper as I close the door behind me. Then I hunch to pick up the stick. This time I cradle it, feeling the old man's presence along with the pain of his passing. His familiar sermons resound in my ear …

See the bigger weaving. Have faith. The darkness exists to help us find the light.

But what fucking light?

Standing there in the murk, the embers glow at my core, the heat building. We're totally stuck. Natasha's not strong enough to travel yet. The next boat's four days away. And the fucking mob will descend on us in only half that time.

I grip the stick tighter with both hands, the fire hissing inside me and the leaflet crumpling in my palm.

Could I go to see Ben?

But Natasha's unstated fear rings in my head that everything we do makes things worse – from foiling Gabriel's plot to going to Turkey … even to me fighting with the bigots. And what if I visit Ben and bring him harm?

And so, I just stand there with the priest's stick, blinking into the gloom.

9

I PICK my way through the park, keeping to the main paths, each one surrounded by parched earth and wilted trees. The last remnants of dawn are fading from the sky, and orange reflects off the neighbouring apartment blocks like the glowing elements of a grill.

Five a.m. and it's already crazy hot out, the base of my back itchy with sweat.

Images swirl of Natasha, lying alone in our box room, and my chest tightens. I didn't tell her. Didn't want to worry her further. And I've probably got three or four more hours before she wakes.

I keep my pace up, my rib a low ache, while several people bustle onto the path around me. Some are in work attire, others are laden with bags for the black markets, and most have hard faces, slight sneers in their expressions. I glance to the side. They're all skirting an old skateboard park, now transformed into shelters with strewn mattresses and sleeping bodies. The vast majority are immigrants, running from some global drought or famine, turfed out of neighbourhoods like ours.

My fingers grip Ben's leaflet in my pocket, and I pace out of the park onto a major street.

People are sleeping on corners here, too. Individuals and families. Some clutch crucifixes, mumbling prayers with eyes closed. Others beg. And a few huddle before hand-cranked radios, glued to news reports, something about the climate crisis. The sense of despair hangs so thick in the air.

I keep my head down and press on. The closer my destination gets, the more the crowd swells around me. First a handful and then many more, like we're part of a great tributary system.

I continue to glance over my shoulder, but there's still no sign of angels or any kind of tail. I wind my way into the midst of the flow nonetheless, making sure to keep myself hidden.

I round another corner and there it is – Paul Hawcross's campaign headquarters. Box-like, seventy yards wide, with tiled walls and a flat roof. An old community library. It stands on the corner of a block with a sprawling concrete space along its front, already rammed with people.

I slink over to the cover of a bus shelter and stare. Maybe a thousand supporters, half of them dressed in Puritan grey. Many sing and pray, the collective din loud in my ears, while others hold up framed photos, scarves, or baby clothes, like they're looking for fucking blessings.

Snatches of television reports come back to me … *Paul Hawcross saved my daughter, my son, my grandfather …*

My fingers curl.

And whether or not they're bearing sacred items, a large number strain to get closer to the building, jostling with those around them.

I stand there blinking, watching people giving their agency away, not reclaiming it – exactly the opposite of what Paul Hawcross claimed to be for. My breathing quickens.

Is Ben still in charge at all?

I scan the building's entrance, halfway down its long side. Two revolving doors are bordered by walls of tinted glass that line the ground floor. A horde of supporters press around them, some holding banners and many of them shouting, the words inaudible from here. The crowd's being kept back by half a dozen security guards, though they've established no kind of channel yet. There's just a mass of people in between me and the entrance, with time ticking past.

I crane my neck to study the doors and the guards. My spine tingles. *Their suits.* They're pale grey in colour. The same as those who protect Ben.

One might recognise me.

I dive into the crowd, head lowered, and thread my way toward the entrance. The throng swarms around me, most of it pressing forward as well. And every few paces, I scan my surroundings, searching for familiar faces or unusual movements. I still see no sign of the strange figure. Still no obvious scent of cordite.

I push past groups of Puritans, some huddled in prayer and others chanting together. The closer they are to the doors, the more of them carry signs – all a mixture of anti-immigrant messages – and the more of them shoot me dirty glances, striving to cut me off.

Hunching my shoulders, I try to weave between them unnoticed, but soon everyone's closing ranks before me. No gaps at all. Their intensity sparks the energy in my core, my rib throbs more with each contact, and the shouting's louder in my ears.

"Foreigners out!"

"Shut the borders!"

Twenty feet from the entrance, I shove my way toward a guy holding a banner. He's got his back to me, busy yelling at the doors. I extend an arm to squeeze past when someone bumps it against him. The guy spins and grabs my shoulder, his fingers digging in. His eyes burn, his lips drawn back over his teeth, and he shoves me backward, sending me stumbling into the crowd behind.

The fire blazes inside, and for an instant, I begin the count, stilling my thoughts. The shimmering world is already spreading out around me. So easy. I go to grab the guy's arm, to fling him aside, to rush forward through the gaps—

Then I stop, sniff the air, and pivot, searching for angels again.

The guy swivels back to face the doors and plants himself side by side with several others. Like a bloody wall in front of me. And they continue yelling their bullshit.

I grind my teeth and then dig my hand into my pocket and yank out the crumpled leaflet. I open it out and start to fold it into a tight square.

People push forward on either side of me as more hands grip at my shoulders and torso, trying to haul me backward. I anchor my feet and shut out the growing pain in my ribs. I focus only on the paper, on making the final creases. Then I hoist the square above my head and make one last check for any sign of the strange figure.

"Important message for Paul Hawcross!" I call out, my voice swamped in the surrounding clamour.

A couple of people in front of me swivel, frowning.

"Details of an imminent attack!" I yell louder and thrust my hand with the folded leaflet high.

More people turn, the fervour morphing into worry. One steps out of the way, creating a small gap, which I dart into.

"A terrorist cell!" I shout. "About to be activated!"

A few more people step out of the way. Others try to block me off, eyes narrowed. I plough forward, diving into the gaps that appear. The entrance lies only fifteen feet away now, and I fix my stare on the nearest guard.

"There's real danger!" I yell. "I need to speak to Ben Whittaker, his special adviser!"

The guard spins and locks his gaze on mine. Thus I redouble my efforts, using my momentum to shove past the final few people and sending a few of them stumbling. The crowd's bellowing even louder, now; some angry at me while others shout their concern, the zeal so high now it vibrates my skull.

I lurch to a halt before the guard. A simple rope cordon separates us, but he doesn't open it. Instead, he extends his hand for the bit of paper I'm holding.

My throat goes dry, my pulse speeding up. All the other guards are staring at me now. I scan their faces, desperately hoping …

But I don't recognise a single fucking one of them.

My ribs constrict, and the yells increase behind. Hands pull at me, and the guard motions again for the folded leaflet.

My mouth opens, but nothing comes out. Suddenly, it's as if I'm standing before Ben, the imagined words tumbling from my lips, the void like an ocean at my core … *We failed you. Got the final binding angel killed. Released the devil …*

"Hey!" the guard shouts at me.

I shake myself.

"Give it here," he says, his hand still raised.

I offer the leaflet to him. He goes to grab it, but I palm the piece of paper and clasp the guy's wrist instead. I yank myself toward him and out of the grip of the people at my back.

"I'm sorry, but I need to see Ben," I hiss.

The guard glares at me and then shifts his gaze down to the fingers I've got wrapped around his arm.

"Do you have an appointment?" he demands, his voice low.

I give a quick shake of the head. "But he'll want to see me," I say, trying to keep my voice steady.

The crowd clamours ever louder at my back, and the guard tries to slip his arm out of my grasp. I grip him tighter and lean in, the darkness growing inside.

"I was in Turkey," I say, forcing the words out fast. "Ben funded the trip … a mission for *you*."

The guard rotates his head away, and one of his colleagues stalks over.

I jerk the guy's arm. "You guys train with swords. I *know* that."

The first guard whirls back to face me.

"And I know *why*. I know who you're protecting yourselves from," I continue. "*That's* what the mission was about."

Both guards gawk at me. The first stops trying to pull away, and I let him go.

"I've got vital information," I say. "I *need* to tell Ben what happened. That's why I'm here."

The guards gaze at each other for a long moment. Then, without a word, the nearer guy opens the rope barrier and nods me in the direction of the revolving doors.

I exhale deeply. "Thank you," I say and pace quickly toward them.

I'm about to pass the second guard when a thought hits me. "You still guard Ben at all?" I ask him.

The guy shakes his head. "Not any more," he says, ushering me into the first revolving door. "There's no need." And while my chest cramps up again, he's got a thin smile on his face.

"Mr Whittaker works here permanently," he says. "Never leaves the building. We haven't seen him in an age."

The tension doubles in my torso, a chill forming at the base of my spine. I open my mouth as the guy pushes the door around, and it spits me into the building.

10

ON THE OTHER side of the revolving door, I come to an abrupt stop. It's like walking into a different world …

A huge lobby area takes up the entire width of the building and probably half of it in depth. The ceiling rises twenty feet above my head, and a series of pendant lights hang down in a spiral. Red velvet sofas stand in pairs and threes around the edge of the polished floor, and the air-conditioned air cools the sweat on my skin.

Even this early in the morning, the place is a hive of activity. People sweep across the floor in all directions, moving from the sofas to a set of double doors in one corner of the space, to a manned reception desk opposite me, and to a narrow corridor in the middle of the far wall with a bank of lifts behind. Most of them are young – early twenties maybe, even younger than Ben – and they're all immaculately dressed in skirts and trouser suits, armed with tablets and laptops.

That's what's completely incongruent.

My eyes find the glass wall again. While it was opaque from outside, it's translucent from here, the frothing masses clearly visible through the panes. And these workers inside are completely ignoring them, striding around and talking with chins held high.

I stand and stare, my gaze eventually falling on the wide reception desk. A receptionist is eyeing me fixedly, his finger pressed to a button on the ear of his headset. I blink. He's one of three on duty already. The second is speaking to an older man at the desk. The third is engaged in a phone call on his headset.

Still, the first guy stares at me. Then his other hand creeps toward something at the front of the desk.

I shake myself and start in his direction. Three security guards stand by the corridor to his side with the bank of lifts beyond, and they're all eyeing me. Each one's dressed in a black uniform with an equipment-laden utility belt at his waist, complete with a hefty baton.

The older man continues beseeching the female receptionist, fingers spread across the white surface of the desk.

"He said to come here," the man says. "That he'd see me." His suit looks so creased he could have slept in it. "*Please,*" the guy adds.

The female receptionist simply shakes her head. Maintains the fixed smile on her lips.

I stop before the male receptionist.

"Can I help you, sir?" the guy asks, his voice terse.

He's got a thin build, large blue eyes, and blond hair swept immaculately across his crown. He's wearing the same pristine white shirt as his colleagues, one finger still pressing the button over his ear.

I take a breath, trying to concentrate. "I'm here to see Ben Whittaker," I say, staring intently at his features.

The guy's eyebrows raise a fraction. He opens his mouth and speaks after a tiny pause. "Do you have an appointment?" he asks.

I listen hard to the tone, concentrating on the guy's expression. His mask of politeness remains firmly in place. He simply stares at me, the faintest of smiles on his lips.

I shake my head. "No, but—"

"I'm sorry, sir," he says. "But without an appointment, you cannot see anyone."

Then he removes his finger from the button and spins away to resume whatever call he was on.

My toes tap against the floor, the tension re-forming in my chest while I replay the guy's slight pause in my mind. As I stare at the receptionist, the guy continues to ignore me. The heat kindles at my core – a gust of wind over glowing embers.

"Five minutes, that's all I need," I say. "He'll want to see me."

The guy doesn't react. Simply continues the conversation, staring off to the side. My fingers curl, the fire flaring.

"Just say my name – Jake – that I've got information," I say, the void still there inside, a bitter taste at the back of my throat. "Information about our recent trip."

Finally, the receptionist ceases his conversation and swivels to face me again. "Do you know how busy he is?" he asks, the words slow, the tone lofty, like he's speaking to a child. "Special adviser to the prime minister?"

The wind blows ever stronger inside me, the coals burning brightly against the background of black. And before I know it, my hand slams down hard on the desk surface. The impact shoots vibrations across my shoulders and down my chest, amplifying my aching rib.

The receptionist skids back a couple of feet in his chair. His eyes dart to the side, and I glimpse movement in my peripheral vision.

"Sir, please step away from the desk," a gruff voice says.

The receptionist doesn't start another call. He simply stares at me, a smile inching up the edge of his mouth.

I open both hands and raise them up, fixing the receptionist with my gaze as I breathe.

"Please, just let him know I'm here," I say.

The receptionist doesn't reply.

"Sir, we don't want a scene," the security guard says at my shoulder.

I scan him out of the corner of my eye. Large build, erect posture, hands poised over the various weapons on his belt – cable ties, baton, pepper spray.

"One call," I say to the receptionist, my jaw clenched, the embers still burning. "Ten seconds."

The receptionist maintains his smirk and shakes his head.

"If you don't come quietly, sir, I *will* use force to remove you," the guard insists.

My gaze flicks to the corridor in front of the lifts, blocked by two more guards. Ben is somewhere beyond, if he's here at all.

Several people slacken their pace across the lobby, glancing in my direction. The entrance hall is now fuller than it was when I entered. More folk notice me every second, the great machine slowing down.

An idea forms.

The receptionist gives a nod, and the guard grabs at one of my outstretched hands. He tightens his fingers around my wrist, which drives the fire inside me.

I let the river of flame flow wild as I start the count in my head. The pain in my rib vanishes, my thoughts still, and the veil peels back effortlessly, the shimmering world opening before me.

I feel everything – the slick floor under my feet, the solidity of the air in my lungs, the guard side-on from me, his hold on my wrist.

The guy whips out a cable tie from his utility belt with his other hand, his fingers clenched around the prepared loop with the tip sticking out, ready to be tightened.

Still I don't move. I just focus on the internal count, on the slowing of time between the numbers. And when the loop gets only inches from my hand, I spring.

With the fire churning through my body, I swivel to face the guard and twist my trapped wrist, breaking his grip. And now with both my hands free, I use one to grab the elbow of the arm I just broke free from while the other clasps the tip of the cable tie, the loop of which he's still clutching in his other hand. The guard tries to react, to pull back, but I'm too fast.

In slowed time, I thrust the guy's elbow to the side, propelling his hand through his own cable tie before I yank the tip of the cable tie with my other hand. And because the fingers of his other hand are still gripping the prepared loop, this tightens it around both the wrist of one hand and the fingers of the other, trapping his hands together.

The guard struggles to free himself. And with the flames still burning, I yank the tie upward, wrenching both of the guy's arms in the air. Then I knee him hard in the stomach. He utters a deep grunt and goes down, shins to the ground.

I hold both of the guard's hands aloft, the embers smouldering in my chest, and I spin around to face the reception desk.

The male receptionist has his finger back on his ear button, his mouth gaping. More sets of eyes are now trained on me – the other receptionists, visitors – people stopped in their tracks, staring on in a mixture of shock and amazement. More cogs in the machine grind to a halt.

I smile and eye the receptionist. "Call Ben. Tell him I've got information," I snap. "If he still doesn't want to see me, he just needs to tell you the country he helped Jake and Natasha get to, and then I'll go."

Still the guy stares at me, his eyes huge and mouth hanging open.

"Now," I say and yank hard on the cable tie.

The guard groans in pain. Then I sense more movement in the corner of my vision as two more uniformed guards hurry over.

I keep my gaze trained on the receptionist. "Otherwise, I'll stay and cause a scene," I say and manage a wide grin.

The receptionist shakes himself into action, presses a button on the desk in front of him, and speaks into his headset. A quick conversation ensues. He keeps his eyes on me the entire time. The guard shifts his knees, trying to get comfortable on the hard floor. I lower the cable tie.

"Sorry," I whisper, the fire bleeding from my chest, my rib aching again.

The receptionist continues to chatter into his microphone, blinking a few times.

"Someone will be down for you," he says, eventually.

I nod and help the guard back to his feet. The guy shambles off toward his colleagues, hiding his cuffed hands under his jacket. The other guards fix me with hard stares, but I turn away.

After a few moments, the receptionist takes another call, the other receptionists go back to working, and the guards disperse, the onlookers too. No one glances at me. As if the confrontation never happened.

Standing there, I shift my weight as doubts gnaw at my mind. I just used my fucking powers, right where they could be noticed. My heart beats faster, and my eyes search the corners of the space. Are the shadows deepening?

A voice calls from the side.

"Hello, Jake."

11

I SPIN AROUND. A young woman is crossing the lobby in my direction. She's wearing a fitted business suit and has dark skin with bright, intelligent eyes.

"It's nice to meet you," she says and stops a few feet away.

Another visitor begins arguing with a receptionist behind, but the young woman keeps her eyes on me. "This way," she says and motions toward the lifts behind her.

I scan her features. Her expression's relaxed, her posture too. And after a second's hesitation, I let my feet take me in the direction of the narrow corridor to the lifts.

She leads me past the guards and into the passageway. The corridor extends all the way up the building, a rectangular skylight high above. Natural light filters down around a set of bulbs that hang almost to ground level.

I follow my guide into a lift, and three people enter after us. I take a shallow breath, the cubic space seemingly hotter. Our companions ignore it, engrossed in a conversation; something about population numbers. My guide merely smiles and stares up at the ceiling as the lift climbs.

We reach the third floor, and the doors slide open. Sweat's forming up my back now, my shirt beginning to stick. The others exit while my guide remains inside, and we continue our journey upward.

The lift stops on the top floor, and my breathing deepens, my body expecting the sensation of chilled air. However, having stepped out of the lift, the atmosphere feels even hotter, almost stifling to my lungs.

I swivel back toward my guide, my mouth opening, but she speaks too quickly.

"This is where I leave you," she says and smiles again, her fingers already on the lift buttons. "Someone will be along shortly."

The doors close before me, and I end up staring at a fuzzy reflection of myself in their chrome surface.

I glance around and find myself standing in a wide corridor that extends in both directions, the ceiling high, a full ten feet above my head. The decor's functional, with nylon carpet, bare white walls, and wooden doors at regular intervals. And it's empty.

A porthole door stands to the side of the lift, a bannister visible beyond – the stairwell back down to the ground floor. I sniff the air. The smell of fresh paint and cleaning fluid is strong … plus another scent, something sharper.

I'm staring down the corridor when a door opens fifty feet down. Two large men step through. No security guard outfits nor grey suits, but dark blue jackets and trousers instead, with matching ties and handkerchiefs. Their white shirts are almost painfully bright, each one buttoned up to the top, and they pad toward me without a bead of sweat on their foreheads.

"You must be Jake," the nearer guy says, his tone upbeat and a faint smile on his lips.

He extends his hand to shake as he strides, a perfectly groomed goatee adorning his lower lip and chin. And while his colleague's clean-shaven, they both sport the same fine features, the same close-cropped hair. I just stand there, watching them approach.

Goatee Man stops before me, hand still out, and I find myself shaking it. His touch is somehow cool, and he holds my gaze while his colleague heads around my other side as if to surround me. I glance toward the porthole door at my back.

"You're here to see Ben?" Goatee Man says.

Ben. Not Mr Whittaker.

I give the faintest nod.

"Please," the guy says and motions me down the corridor.

And there they wait, entirely silent, an eerie smile on Goatee Man's face. An image forms of Ben lying beaten and battered somewhere. I take a deep breath and force myself on.

Both guys fall in behind me as we pad toward a set of double doors at the end. We pass a side corridor, and I search its length. Empty. Just five doors along it, all shut, the air so still.

Again, the memory comes of the janitor and his incredible sense of timelessness. But again, I see no sign of him.

My steps slow. The guys walk side by side behind me, blocking any chance of retreat. And despite the intense warmth, a cold prickle forms at the base of my spine, my gut now starting to twist. Automatically, I scan the wooden doors to either side. Each one with a keyless lock under a heavy-duty chrome handle. Each one undoubtedly a dead end.

I swallow and breathe, the air so hot in my lungs. The double doors approach, the right one ajar, and I pause in front of them. The guards halt at my back and just wait there, making no effort to open the doors or knock.

My ears pick out a low murmuring, and I lean toward the wood. The voice resembles Ben's, but it morphs as I'm standing there and turns into a muffled keening like someone being restrained.

The cold dread creeps up my spine while perspiration runs down my back. I force a sigh and edge a fraction to the side, positioning myself before the right-hand door. The two guys remain still.

I grab the handle and start to yank it open when Goatee Man thrusts a massive hand by my neck and slams the door shut. He pushes past me and stands a foot or so in front of the right-hand door. Then he folds his arms and fixes me with a stare.

"It'll only be a moment," he says and gives me another grin.

I inch away from him, feeling the second guy on my other side, behind my shoulder and just a little further from the left-hand door. And though both are still closed, a second sound filters through the wood. Higher pitched. Almost inhuman. And then it's cut off.

My gut twists even further. This time I don't think, don't wait. Instead, I picture Ben being tortured beyond the doors and focus intently on the image. It fuels the fire in my chest, and power rages through my veins.

I fling my hand toward the left-hand door handle and lean toward it as if I'm trying to dart through while keeping most of my weight anchored on my right foot. The guy behind me slams his body against the left-hand door, and my other hand's already moving. I grab the first handle again, spin my hips, and yank it open with the power burning at my core. It smashes into the shoulder of Goatee Man, who's only just started to move. And I slip through the open right-hand door.

And stumble into some kind of conference room. It's fifty feet long, with the same high ceilings and a large oval wooden table in the middle. A single door in the far corner beyond it. The lights are low, darkened windows lining one wall, and the place is in disarray. Papers lie scattered across the table, food wrappers everywhere. The air's even hotter in here, choked with an acrid reek.

Two people face each other at the far end of the table – one sitting, one standing – both side-on from me. My gaze is drawn to the guy in the swivel chair. He's leaning back, his face turned up toward the ceiling with a hand on the table, and I recognise the crumpled suit and the messy hair. The high-pitched sound comes again, and it's emanating from him.

Laughter?

I lurch to a halt and open my mouth, but nothing comes out.

"Ben?" I say eventually, my voice wavering.

He turns to face me, and his eyes light up.

"Jake!" he says, rotating his chair with both hands flung up in the air.

I'm vaguely aware of the other man in the room, of his shiny blue suit as he takes a couple of steps back from the table. But I can't take my eyes from Ben, his carefree posture, his smiling expression.

"Come in. Come in!" he says and waves me toward one of the chairs. "Make yourself at home." He points at various drink dispensers sitting on flat surfaces at the edge of the room. "Would you like tea? Coffee?" He raises an eyebrow. "Or something a touch stronger, perhaps?"

Still my mind stutters. I can only shake my head. Ben leans back in his swivel chair and hoists both feet up on the table. The guy looks the same. But something about him is also unrecognisable.

Finally, my gaze takes in the guy standing at his side. Medium build. Sharp features. Crystal-blue eyes. All too familiar …

My own eyes go wide, my pulse like a train.

The guy's staring at me now, grinning widely. Ben ignores this and reaches to the side of a pile of papers. He squeezes several empty cigarette boxes before finding a full pack. He takes one out, lights it, and then chucks the lit match over his shoulder. He leans back further in his chair, and the acrid smell suddenly intensifies, becoming recognisable.

Sulphur.

12

It's like steel bands are squeezing my lungs, all the air sucked out of me.

"You?" I say to Ben, the word barely a whisper.

Ben blows out a puff of smoke. He pulls the cigarette from his lips, contemplates it, and then nods.

"Me," he says.

"From the beginning?" I ask.

Ben smiles again and taps the ash directly onto the table before placing the cigarette down on the wood. "Even before," he says.

Then he glances up at the other guy in the room, the strange figure from our neighbourhood.

"Leave us," Ben says and waves a hand dismissively.

The man bows to Ben before shooting a look at me. His tongue flicks out between bone-white teeth. Then he strides to the door at the far end of the room.

Ben stares a few yards to my side and his eyes narrow, his face darkening. "And you," he says, his voice a low growl.

I spin around. Ten feet along the wall from the closed double doors, right in the corner of the room, sits a man perched on a tiny chair. And he's as different-looking to Ben as possible. Balding, diminutive, and in a dirty black suit. The small man rises quickly, his whole body trembling, and he bows low. But Ben grabs up a hole punch from the table and hurls it in our direction.

I flinch, which sends racking pains through my rib. And the small man shrieks and ducks, his movement super quick. Still, the metal hole punch crashes into the wall just an inch above his head.

The small man scurries behind me, keeping as low as he can with his hands over his ears and blubbering. He tugs open the double doors and lurches through.

As the doors swing closed, the smell in the room grows somehow worse – beyond just the reek of sulphur, to something like charred flesh. Plus, the scent of cordite's unmistakable, and the veil's so thin before my senses. I rotate back around to face Ben, my sides slick with sweat now, the air like a furnace.

And jump backward.

It's not just Ben sitting there. As with angels in the normal world, my vision flits between two images superimposed on each other. Ben, the man, and something else entirely – something much larger and much older.

It still wears a suit, but exactly half of it – the left-hand side – has been shredded, cut to ribbons, with fiery glows and wisps of smoke emanating from each of the slashes. And his face … I have to work hard not to look away. One side of it shines with an angelic beauty, while countless slashes crisscross the other, each one smoking. And the eye on that side of his face blazes a dark red.

A lancing chill claims my entire spine. I sense my mind crawling to a halt, the veil peeling back and the two images resolving into Ben's larger, more awful form. I drive my thoughts on to shut out the shimmering world, to focus only on Ben's human appearance.

"You're a …" I start.

Ben gives a mock bow in his seat. "Demon, *yes* …" His

voice is almost a purr, and I see a glint in his human eye. "Mammon, at your service."

My throat tightens.

"Not to be confused with the black creatures, you understand," he goes on. "The pneumas. Beings found a long time ago in distant realms. Easy to control but limited in their scope." He peers down his nose at me. "We demons are akin to angels. Like them, we transformed from mortals." Then he gives me a knowing look, one eyebrow raised. "Those of us who showed *potential*."

With the emphasis he places on the final word, I taste bile at the back of my throat, the void cavernous inside.

"This was all your plan?" I ask, speaking quickly.

Mammon sighs. "Sadly, no," he says and gazes wistfully at the wall. "Satan's plan, not mine." As he speaks, he rotates, so he's sitting side-on, his demonic half facing me.

Still I have to work hard not to avert my gaze.

"Two thousand years ago, he told us to wait and what to look for," he explains, examining the nails of a hand that's as scarred as his face. "And for a very long time, that was all we did."

Then he gazes straight at me. "And of course, he was right. He's always right," Mammon says with a smile, but his expression's hollow. "When we spied the pneumas appearing, we knew Satan's release was near, and because of their attraction to you, that you'd play a part." His grin widens. "Then Gabriel began killing the binding angels until only one remained underground, beyond our reach." His eyes blaze now with a kind of manic intensity. "We knew we had to ferret him out somehow."

The void grows in my gut, and I squeeze my fingers together, trying to anchor my feet for what's coming.

Mammon stretches out a limp hand and flicks his gaze away in a sign of mock disgust. "I couldn't have done it myself, of course," he says. Then he leans across the table toward me with a conspiratorial whisper. "Since the devil was bound, we've needed to keep a low profile under angelic rule, you understand." He waggles his finger in the air. "*Mustn't be noticed, mustn't use our powers,*" he says, singing the words in the melody of some twisted nursery rhyme.

I cringe at the sound.

"You were the perfect means," he croons with a tilt of his head. "All I had to do was give you a little push, and you dug Cassiel up nicely, delivering him right to Gabriel. You see, I know *exactly* what happened in Turkey."

The abyss plunges inside me. My legs wobble, and my mind screams at me to focus, to get the fuck out of there. However, I just stand still, barely breathing, the void so massive that any thought simply forms and dies.

Mammon stares at me for a long moment from his chair, his eyes burning brightly. Then he throws up a hand. "Come on. Don't grow reticent on me. Isn't this what you wanted?" he demands, a manic smile on his face. "To challenge the angels, to tear down the tyranny that's milked humanity for thousands of years?"

I stare back at him, my brain stuttering.

"*Well?*" Mammon says.

I open my mouth. But again, nothing comes out.

"Wait," Mammon says and his gaze softens, his mocking demeanour vanishing for the first time. "Don't tell me you're shocked." He pauses. "Did you *really* believe there was some kind of divine plan? That the powerful would be laid low by the powerless? That the meek would inherit the earth?"

I see genuine surprise in his expression, and something else … pity, disappointment?

I blink.

The look's gone, replaced by rage. And his demonic form grows before me. The tears in his suit spread, the fires blazing brighter inside them and the smoke billowing more thickly.

"Such naivety!" he shouts and slams his palm down on the table with a massive crack.

I stagger back a step.

"There is no God." Mammon spits the word. "No higher order, no divine justice. All that ever exists is the strong and the weak." He squeezes his scarred hand into a fist. "And those with power create the narrative, the story society believes. Life is terrible ... unpredictable, uncontrollable, with the threat of pain and death at every turn."

Mammon's stare burns into me. "Much better to personify the darkness, the evil. *Much* easier," he says with a nod. "Humans don't want to face their own darkness, the fragility of their lives. The masses aren't capable of it."

He leans back with a sigh, and his body stills. His demonic image shrinks a fraction in size. "It's a mercy," he says more quietly.

My brain reels, and the question tumbles from my lips. "*A mercy?*" I say, unable to keep the incredulity out of my tone. "And this is the gift the devil provides?"

Mammon shrugs. "It's a gift that works," he says. "And it's generated belief in him, has been the foundation for his power since the beginning."

He picks up the burning cigarette and presses the glowing end into the table, charring the wooden surface. "And if there is no divine plan, who wins?" he asks without looking up at me. He continues to rotate the cigarette between his fingers to singe the table. In the silence, that look of disappointment flits across his features again, all the crazed gleam gone from his eyes.

When I don't reply, Mammon nods. "The smartest," he says softly. "The one who understands the rules of the game better than anyone else. And there's never been anyone to match him." By the time he finishes, his voice is barely a whisper.

My feet shift, the void still so vast inside me. Nevertheless, I take a step forward, trying to channel the little fire that remains into my throat.

"If you don't like it, why support it?" I ask.

Mammon gazes back up at me with a faint smile. "Because we all need to make a choice," he says.

"And this is yours?" I ask.

Mammon's eyes gleam wildly again, like a switch has been thrown. His lips spread in their crazed grin once more. "You think this is the end?" he says, his voice growing louder. "This is the beginning! The devil has returned after two thousand years of incarceration. Do you know what a mind like his can accomplish in that time?"

Mammon gives a dramatic shiver, real or not. "How hungry do you think he will be after that much time away?" he continues, his voice almost shrill. "How quickly will he stamp himself back on the hearts and minds of men?" The demon shakes his head. "The angels and their short memories. They won't be able to remain transcendent for long. They'll need to act." And he barks a laugh that's devoid of any real humour.

I search his eyes. Any authenticity there ever was is gone. The look of disappointment, the genuine smile, a memory. Mammon spins in his chair like a child and ends up staring out at the darkened windows. Images flash of Natasha out there … alone. I picture the double doors behind me, only a couple of feet away.

I clear my throat. "So, what *is* coming?" I ask, attempting a relaxed tone.

"You don't know your scripture!" Mammon says and slaps his thigh so loudly the sound echoes. "Which reminds me, I must get on." He rubs his hands together with the same wild glee. "So much to do, so little time. For brother Satan, it's all work, work, work!"

He swivels to face the table again and leafs madly through the papers while I inch backward toward the doors at my back, those two burly fuckers most likely still on the other side.

"Big plans!" Mammon continues. "And it's global. Of course it's global. The little conflicts you've witnessed are only the beginning! There's so much one can do with the levers of government."

I continue my rearward creep.

"So many believers, so many extremists," Mammon says, and then he looks up at me suddenly and winks.

I freeze and hold my breath, trying to keep my face impassive while my muscles feel like rock.

The demon turns back to his desk. "With modern technology, the potential is enormous," he says, organising the papers into random piles, his fingers a blur.

I continue the painstaking backward shuffle. After a moment, my heel strikes the door. I bring my hands up behind me and fumble for the handles.

Mammon's arms still, and he speaks without looking up. "Your lady friend ... Natasha, wasn't it?" he asks, all lightness gone from his voice.

I stop dead again. The demon lifts his eyes and smiles such a cruel smile. The light in the room dims further, the fires in his suit blazing red and orange.

"How is she?" he continues, his voice silky smooth. "We *must* pay her a visit."

Amid the fathomless dark, the embers spark inside me. My fingers tighten into fists. The river of fire boils and froths. Power flares in my chest and flashes down my arms and legs.

"She was always *so* keen to help," Mammon says.

The door handles are just behind me, yet all I can focus on is the demon's wide grin, his taunting eyes. It drives the flames higher, and my hands shake as visions form of me leaping onto the table, grasping him around the neck, and squeezing.

I take a couple of steps in his direction, and my gaze finds the other door over his shoulder. No one would expect it. A grin pulls at my own lips while the fire blazes inside – so fucking hot.

Mammon lifts his chin as if taunting me. Power rushes

down my legs, and I bend my knees, leaning forward. Then I launch myself at him—

Something smashes into the back of my head. I feel an explosion of pain, of light, and my body goes limp. I sprawl to the ground and then the darkness slips in around me.

13

My eyes open, and awareness rolls in on me like a tide of sludge. I find myself lying on my side, staring once again at grey filing cabinets, the underside of a white desk, and a set of stacked chairs, all pushed against the far wall of my box room cell.

I shut my eyes, and my head aches as if someone's playing a drum against my temples. Images wash against the back of my closed eyelids, memories from a recurring dream …

First darkness. Then Natasha yelling in fear from somewhere up ahead. Hordes of people in between, hands clawing at me. The sensation of raging fire. Me bulldozing my way through limbs and bodies – gang members from my childhood, Ben and his suited minions, the black four-limbed pneumas. Fingers around my forearm, a broken body at my side, someone I've already smashed to pieces … My mother? No. Natasha.

I wrench my eyes open again, shove myself up off the filthy blanket and breathe, my chest heaving, my bruised rib a dull ache. I end up staring at the same damn whitewashed walls, the same stacks of office furniture, the same super high ceilings. The smell of sweat's dank and awful in my nose, and the air's scalding hot.

My eyes flit to the single window. It's darkening outside, the faint glow of dusk. How many days has it been? Three … no, four. With the artificial lights always on, it's been so hard to sleep, to keep track of time.

A metal click sounds behind me – the keyless lock – and I swivel, my body tense.

The door opens, and a man stands on the threshold; he's in a different three-piece suit, but still immaculate. Plus, that same scent of sulphur, almost sweet, and the same hungry blue eyes.

He drops a dog bowl of water on the floor and, as always, most of it slops over the side. He then glances down at the empty one at its side.

"Little one," he jeers, raising a sharp eyebrow, his voice layered with its customary dull screech. "You're not keen to try again?"

I wince, my mind conjuring images of my last attempt at something … Throwing the bowl at his face. But he caught it and hurled it back, his reactions lightning fast. It cracked me on the side of the head, and I blacked out.

And now the drum plays louder against my temples.

My captor steps forward, his blue eyes glinting. He grabs up the empty bowl and raises it high. My muscles tense, ready for the end, for the guy to finally kill me.

But he shakes his head, smiles, and swivels for the door. Then he turns at the threshold.

"Come now," he purrs. "Have some fun. Is there not someone you wanted to get back to?"

My captor gives a last grin, and the darkness fills my lungs like tar, the embers searing my insides again. I have to clench my hands to stop them from shaking.

He swivels and stalks away down the hallway while – not for the first time – leaving the door ajar.

For a good minute, my eyes just stare at it. Then, finally, I shuffle over, my heart pounding. A sliver of the far corridor comes into view. Only ten yards down the hall from Ben's conference room.

Much more fun to have me close.

I stop a few feet from the door, that sweet scent of sulphur growing stronger in my nose. And – not for the first time – I imagine my captor hiding a few paces up the corridor, ready to recapture and beat me in some twisted sport.

My feet twitch, only a few paces from potential freedom. But the guy's words return to me, and again, the other likelihood slinks into my mind. Maybe they want me to escape, want to track me back to Natasha. If they've not got her already.

The void's immense inside me. My legs sway, and I tense my body, shaking my head to clear it, and force my gaze back to the open doorway.

The sound of conversation echoes from the far end of the corridor. I go still. More chatter about some imminent event. The level of excitement's been increasing every day, and now a procession of people appears beyond my door. Several demons in their perfect suits. And mortals too – people from the Middle East, from Africa – all dressed up in traditional finery, maybe political or community leaders. They all file past, completely oblivious to me. I watch them go, my thoughts whirling.

Do they have any idea who's really in charge? Could I shout it to them, unveil my captors that way? I run my hand across my face, feeling my bristly cheeks, grimy skin, and scraggly hair. Who would even listen to me?

I take a step forward when another figure paces into view – an Arab man of slender build in a pristine white tunic. And when he gets to the point of disappearing, he swivels, and his gaze burns into mine, his eyes haunting. I stumble backward. It feels like ages pass. My mouth opens, and then he's gone down the corridor, as if he never existed. And I'm left blinking at the far wall.

I inhale deeply, shake myself, and prepare to edge out into

the hallway to find him. But the image comes again of my captor, waiting around the corner for me, so fucking vivid.

Suddenly, the door slams in my face. It locks with a click, and a voice sounds outside, one I've heard in the corridor before … female and silky smooth.

A shiver runs through me.

And like last time, I detect the faintest scent of spices plus the urgent desire to scramble and hide under the discarded furniture.

I force myself right up to the door, put my ear to it, and hear the sound of her striding by outside. Several other voices jabber questions, and she answers every one, commanding absolute attention, though the words themselves remain inaudible through the wood.

More thoughts churn. Why let me know they're planning something, and *what is it*? She continues away down the hallway, the other sets of feet scrambling to keep up. And finally, silence, the scent of spices gone from my nose along with the sweet sulphur.

I pivot, lurch over to the filing cabinet, and grope around till my fingers locate a twelve-inch strip of laminate I've stashed there. It came from the edge of a drawer, one of only two objects I managed to salvage from the office furniture, the other being three feet of cord from the broken blind.

Just enough to hang myself.

I hurry to the window and slip the laminate into the minute gap between the frame and triple-glazed glass. I squeeze it along the bottom edge, feeling for any kind of indentation – a screw or bolt – while moving extremely slowly.

This my third circuit. I've found nothing so far. Plus, the street's fifty damn feet below. And despite all the priest's practices and entreaties about defying gravity – *the pinnacle of my lineage's achievements* – I'd never survive the fall.

Yet I keep going. Minutes tick by. As I start my fourth circuit, my eyes find the nightscape through the glass – the shadowed outlines of the surrounding buildings, the skyscrapers of the financial centre beyond – while the devil's promise sounds in my head … *The world will burn*.

And Natasha. I tense my arms and shove the laminate on faster. She's out there in the darkness with no idea where I am. Undoubtedly she thinks I abandoned her. The thoughts gnaw at me, the void grips my insides, and my stomach growls like monsters rumbling in the deep.

The lock clicks open. My heart thuds, my fingers jerk, and the bit of plastic snaps in two. The door swishes open behind me. And I spin around entirely, thrusting my hands behind my back, the pieces of my broken strip hidden in my palm.

My captor stands in the doorway again, the corridor empty behind him. He carries the other dog bowl, and the smell of charred meat fills my nose. Never anything but meat. The demon doesn't drop it. He lingers, one hand on the handle, his eyes darting between me and the window over my shoulder.

I don't move, shielding the bottom of the window frame from view, my hands still behind my back. His smile vanishes, his features tighten in suspicion, and his gaze rakes my body, foot to head, his eyes burning black.

The heat prickles my skin, and the air burns in my lungs. I hold my breath and anchor my feet, the broken laminate still gripped tightly in my hand.

After what feels an age, the demon grins again, much wider this time. His tongue flicks out between his teeth, and he drops the bowl before stepping back and slamming the door. I hear it lock from the outside with another click.

I let out a steady exhalation. Then I glance from the door to the window to the stacked furniture, a new idea forming in my mind.

14

WITH HANDS SHAKING, I grip the final set of drawers and lift it up. Then I carry it across my box-like cell toward the door, sweat running down my sides in the heat.

Arriving at the opposite wall, I lower the drawers silently onto the top of one of the filing cabinets. I climb carefully onto an office chair and hoist them to the summit of my pile of furniture.

It resembles some kind of modern art structure right in front of the closed door with one upside-down desk, three filing cabinets, and now two sets of drawers piled on top. The last one is almost as tall as the door, six feet up, but the ceiling is a good deal higher still. And I've balanced another desk on its end to the side of the improvised structure, its surface only a few inches away from the door.

I scramble back to the ground, though my eyes remain glued to the drawers at the top, buttressed only on one side and probably still too unstable. And this is my third bloody attempt at the construction. My gaze flits to the window and the deep darkness beyond.

The demon could arrive at any moment.

My heartbeat accelerates, and I hurry over to the door again, grab up the few feet of cord I've attached to the handle, and begin tying the end around my wrist in a simple knot. Then I clamber back up my tower of furniture – *bloody stupid plan* – from the chair to the lowest filing cabinet while doubting thoughts whirl …

The demon won't take the bait, the structure will collapse, and escaping my cell doesn't mean escaping the building.

I breathe and focus on the climb, on moving as quietly as possible while holding the same vision of Natasha in my head … Alone, vulnerable, convinced I abandoned her. And with a final creak, I step onto the top set of drawers, the cord still tied around my wrist.

The structure wobbles, and I shift my weight. Forward. Back. Eventually, I find the point of balance and hold. I stand six feet above the ground, the closed door just in front of me and the high ceiling still a few feet above my head.

Keeping my legs dead still, I undo the knot and cradle the cord loosely in one hand, my other fingers touching the wall for stability. I breathe and start the count in my head, concentrating on the numbers to calm my thoughts.

And I settle in to wait.

A DULL CLICK of the lock opening, and I shake myself into readiness. The door swings inward. Quickly hits the surface of the table that's balanced on its end. And the tower of furniture wobbles beneath my feet, pitching me forward and off balance.

Automatically, both of my hands reach out, my fingers grasping for the top of the open door that's at knee level, just ahead of me. I get inches from it when the smell of sweet sulphur bites at my nose. The demon stands right on its other side. I freeze, gripping the wall with one hand and the cord with the other, and manage to steady myself.

The demon thrusts the door open again. Harder this time. It slams into the desk that faces it, which hits into the pile of furniture beneath me and goes no further. I anchor my feet, trying to imagine what my captor's thinking …

A barricaded door. His view blocked. The memory of me shielding the window, hands behind my back.

The demon shoves harder against the door. The tower sways a little, and I cling to the wall as my balance tips again. The demon utters a low growl on the other side of the door. The heat intensifies, as does the smell of sulphur in the air, and I feel the fire build in my chest, the veil starting to peel back—

I bite my cheek and force my thoughts on as my captor rams the door into the desk with the sound of a gunshot, far harder than I'd imagined. The cabinets shift and the drawers sway back and forth.

I grip the cord more tightly, barely managing to hold on. He continues to throw himself at the door, over and over, and with each impact, the tower of furniture sways more violently. It gets closer to collapse till I can barely remain upright.

At last, the demon gives up on the ramming and starts to shove harder. And with his immense strength, the hundreds of kilos of furniture all piled onto the upside-down desk begin to slide back across the room with me on top of them.

And as the door opens inch by inch, the structure continues to shift, the cabinets and drawers all slipping and sliding. I'm forced to jerk my weight from side to side, the flames growing ever wilder at my core.

Still, I keep my thoughts running, and the veil in place. The door opens further, the drawers almost half off the filing cabinet now, tilting under my feet. My balance starts to go.

Finally, I quiet my mind, focus on the fire, and use it to plunge me beyond the veil.

The shimmering world spreads around me, inundating my senses … Textures of the braided cord against my palm. The coarse wall against my fingertips. Distances to the top of the opening door below me. The balance points of the shifting structures beneath my feet. And the feeling of the air connecting everything. It all arises simultaneously against the background of my awareness.

The demon roars behind the door and gives a massive shove, thrusting the door further open and the furniture backward. The drawers slide further off the cabinet as the pile continues to collapse beneath me.

I grip the cord even tighter and hold myself ready.

The top of my captor's head flashes into view as he darts into the room, his movements lightning quick. He barrels straight for the window.

I force my feet down hard on the drawers as they topple, and make a leap for the open door. I scramble over the top of it, my arm out beyond its edge to ensure the cord doesn't get caught as I go into free fall on the far side. My body plunges toward the opposite wall, my stomach in my throat. The open doorway sits a few inches to my right.

Beyond the veil, I fix my attention on the solidity of the air and focus on wrapping it around myself like a swaddle. Yet still my body plummets fast downward, time slipping by so slowly. I concentrate even harder, sensing for the viscosity against my skin. And finally, my fall starts to slow …

Still, the ground comes all too quickly, and both my feet slam down, sending me stumbling forward into the wall. I hit my head and crouch there, stunned, my bruised rib throbbing.

A fierce hissing stings my ears, and I hear the scrape of swivelling feet. My whole body starts, and I throw myself through the doorway and out into the corridor, going down hard on my hands and knees.

I shake my head, the smell of sulphur so strong in my nostrils now, and the memory comes of Ben's demon form. An impulse grabs me to turn around to spy my captor and his hideous image.

I tense my neck, keep my gaze on the corridor wall, and yank hard on the cord still in my hand, forcing myself to keep with the plan. The door begins to close, the cord still connected to its handle, and now I start to swivel.

My stomach leaps up my throat. I get a glimpse of the demon's hulking, skinless form, just bones and muscles on a contorted body, with blazing eyes on top. He's spun around and is now darting for the closing door, reaching out a bony arm …

I scramble backward and yank harder on the cord. Beyond the veil, with time running at half speed, the door still swings shut so painfully slowly, and my heart drums madly against my ribs.

The door gets within inches of the frame when the demon reaches the handle and grabs it, the hissing ever louder. I squeeze my fingers around the cord, prepare to pull even harder—

Then stop. And focus everything on stilling my thoughts.

The door begins to open, yanked by the demon, while I spring to my feet and leap forward, channelling the growing power down my legs. I kick out as hard as I can at its wooden surface, sending it flying inward at the demon on the other side.

I hear a crash and another grunt, and I tug sharply on the cord again. The demon loses his grip. The door swings toward me again and this time slams fully shut. I dart forward and lock the mechanism with a click.

Silence.

I stumble rearward, my thoughts firing once more. The veil reasserts itself, and for a moment, all I can do is stare at the closed door.

I hear a vast roar, and something massive strikes the door from behind. Then an awful tearing sound starts up, like chunks are being ripped from the inside. I whirl around and scramble away down the corridor.

15

As I bolt along the empty passageway, the sound of roaring and tearing wood echoes in my ears. I barrel past the lifts, heading for the door with the porthole beyond. And I crash through it to find myself at the top of a stairwell.

Several feet down the side wall, the upper half of the wall disappears. I jump the first set of steps and lean over the railing.

I'm staring four storeys down to the ground floor, at the narrow corridor that connects the lifts to the lobby. Light bulbs hang on cords of different lengths from the dark skylight above, some of them almost reaching the ground.

I try to picture myself swinging down. With the veil peeled back, the air thick around me, there'd be no faster way.

But an instant later, cold hard reality hits me like a slap. *What the fuck am I thinking?* I'm not the priest.

I fling myself down the spiralling stairwell, careening around the corners, and burst through another door with a porthole. I find myself in another lit corridor, empty as well.

Office doors extend in both directions, and I sprint toward the nearest one, imagining myself getting help from any office workers behind it. But I stop after only two strides. Even if they're there, they'd be the next to die.

I dart beyond the lifts, plunging through the porthole door and on down the steps – from the third floor to the second and right on down to the ground. It seems to take an age. I hear no sound at all from above. The smashing noise has stopped, leaving the stairwell eerily silent. I reach the final door, the narrow corridor beyond, and halt. I plant my feet and stare through the porthole.

A thin slice of the lobby is visible beyond the corridor, yet most of it remains out of sight. The space is faintly lit and empty, the revolving door at the far end a hundred feet away.

I take a shallow breath and push at the door, my pulse thumping loudly behind my ears. It swings open without a sound, and I force myself to pad slowly through it, down the corridor, and out into the lobby.

The space extends around me, seemingly even larger than it was in the day, the scattered sofas and side walls almost hidden in the gloom. The only working lights hang in a spiral shape above the middle of the lobby, casting faint ovals of light on the tiled ground.

I creep on toward the revolving door, while searching the shadowy corners. Still, I see no obvious figures, no movement; nobody hanging around outside the building, either. The concrete space is empty.

I get halfway across the space, right in the centre of the weak glow, when a new scent infiltrates my nose – the mixed tang of cordite and sulphur – and my gut constricts, my internal alarm ringing like a bell.

The revolving door's only ten yards away now. Straight ahead. Entirely clear. And while energy pulses down my legs to run, a deep knowing presses in at the back of my skull.

The door will be locked.

I come to a halt, shake my body to loosen it, and then spin around.

A shot of cold slithers down my spine, my gut twisting

further. I'm faced by outlines of darkness, human in shape but larger, just like the one that came to my door and the six that confronted me in the copse. But twelve or thirteen of them hover here, all spread out in a line between me and the corridor to the lifts.

My head whirls to the side, my eyes searching for the double doors I spied in the corner of the space. The black wells fan out to surround me, cutting off my path in either direction, but they hold back and don't attack.

The sport is about to begin.

The darkness opens up at my core, but the fire is there also. I breathe into it, building the flames inside.

The pools of night continue to spread out around me, the arc almost a semicircle, and larger gaps appear between each pair. Keeping my head still, I eye the gap at eleven o'clock, thirty feet away. Ten feet separates the black shapes, and then another seventy feet to the corner door.

I start to swivel toward it when the smell of sulphur suddenly burns my nose, more powerful and sweeter, too. Plus, a new heat scorches my forehead, and my gaze snaps back.

The central outline in the semicircle has stepped forward into the spiral of light. And there stands my captor, stripped of shadow. As with Ben, my vision flits between his human and demonic forms. The latter's at least a foot taller with thin, whip-like arms and legs and a distended ribcage. It resembles a warped skeleton with an elongated head, a cavernous mouth, and those burning eyes. A snake-like tongue darts out from between its teeth.

My breath flees my lungs, and though a part of me is desperate to glance away, my eyes search the other black wells for any sign of Mammon or the woman with the silky voice. A shudder rolls through my body. The other dark outlines remain as impenetrable as ever while a new sound forms – a faint buzzing in my ears, creeping in from outside the surrounding arc.

My heart beats faster, the fire inside me continues to build, and my eyes probe the darkness beyond.

"Welcome," my captor says, his voice shrill and distorted. He smiles wickedly, his lip muscles pulled back over blade-like teeth.

The distant buzzing mutates into a familiar jabbering. The smell of sulphur's even stronger in my nostrils, and there in the lobby corners, I spy the outline of scuttling legs like giant spiders. My vision morphs. And I find myself staring out at the hell realm – a tortured wasteland of rock and lava – the black four-limbed creatures forming an arc around me, gazing on in reverence.

I desperately shake my head. My vision clears. But the black creatures remain. Dozens of them – the pneumas – scuttling steadily toward me from the edges of the lobby. Bulbs explode in the spiral shape above them as they approach, pulling the shadows ever nearer. And their black eyes shine in the faint light.

My feet stumble backward, the abyss plummeting away inside. The creatures continue their advance. The closer they get, the wilder the flames burn at my core, and the more images swamp my mind – the visions from my repeated dream, Natasha pleading at my side and me lashing out oblivious, killing her over and over …

I tense my arms and anchor my feet. With the fire raging, my jaw clenches, and I imagine throwing myself at the demons, taking at least one of them with me while the power surges through every muscle.

"Yes, yes!" my captor shrieks, his bone-like fingers clenched.

His voice chills my spine. I take a breath, trying to stem the fire.

More of the demons press forward as well, their shrouds of night falling away to reveal a barrage of images my mind can't handle. Bird-like heads, sharpened teeth, taloned fingers, towering horns, hoofed legs …

My captor's grin splits his distorted skull. He points an extended finger at me. "Come on, little one," he hisses. "Let's—"

A crash like a thunderclap behind me causes the floor to quake, and I end up lurching toward the demons. Shattered glass falls all around me, and I barely manage to keep my feet. My captor stares over my shoulder, and I whirl around.

My thoughts stagger to a stop. The veil peels back. And I blink, my eyes wide and my mind trying to make sense of what stands before me. Of *who*.

The janitor – poised twenty feet inside the shattered glass wall, ten yards to the side of the revolving doors – and beyond the veil … almost unrecognisable.

His blue overalls have become a flowing skirt with beaded trim. The top of his body's bare, his chest enormous and his muscles like boulders. And raised tattooed markings cover every inch of his dark skin. Swirls of gold encircle his massive biceps, and he wears a headdress of feathers.

Beyond the veil, he stands feet taller than me. His radiance sends the shadows scampering away from us, and like the times before, I sense a strange stillness in his presence, a timelessness, as if we're all insulated from the world outside.

The janitor. An Orisha – a god of spiritual purity, of freedom – that's what Father Thomas said. A feeling of awe seizes me, along with the desire to prostrate myself before him. It's not only the god's sense of eminence, of presence … it's his *age*. Staring into his glowing white eyes, I feel as if I'm glimpsing the aeons of the world, the birth of time. I breathe, trembling, in and out.

The Orisha mumbles something as the vibrations in the ground fade away. He surveys the scene, one arm dangling by his side – injured in his fight with Gabriel – and his glow diminishes, the darkness fortifying around us.

I shift my gaze to the demons. They remain poised in a semicircle with me at its centre, shrouded in pools of night once more.

"Obatala," my captor says after a moment, his voice lacking some of its shrillness. "You are a long way from home."

My eyes find the Orisha again. And for a good while, he says nothing. The hanging bulbs swing above our heads, arcs of light tracing shapes up the far walls like swaying branches in a storm.

Obatala lifts his chin. "I go where I am needed," he says, his voice like the rumbling of the earth.

"Indeed you do," my captor says with a sneer.

Then without a word, the demons divide into two groups. The larger contingent creeps sideways across the lobby, between me and the lifts, to form an arc around Obatala, while four shapes of darkness head off at right angles to the first set toward the glass wall.

This takes them only a few feet from where I'm standing, and as they pass, the heat sears at the skin down my arm and neck. The smell of sulphur is so nauseating it prompts me to gag. I scramble a few steps to the side as the images of their demonic forms seize my mind.

A new voice emanates from a well of darkness near my captor – a female voice, though not the silky one I heard in my cell.

"You've walked such a long time on this earth," she says, her tone almost musing, while she and the other black outlines continue to arc silently around Obatala's front. "Did you really mean to venture here?"

All the while, the four demons slink behind me and along the glass wall, toward the hole the Orisha created. The pneumas scramble across the lobby as well, keeping themselves at the back of the larger group of demons, a distance beyond the pool of light.

I shift my weight, though the Orisha doesn't move at all.

"Far longer than any of you," he growls.

The demons all come to a halt. The eight pools of night

form an arc between the Orisha and the reception desk, the remaining four on the other side cutting off his retreat.

My captor steps forward from the first group, the shadows sliding away to reveal his skeletal form again and his massive grin.

"You should not have come, ancient one," he says, his tone sharp once more. His tongue flicks out ever further between his teeth.

And as the shadows advance in on the Orisha, I hold my breath. Still he stands there, burning brighter than ever, his aura like a fire.

And then I notice that the ancient god is staring directly at me.

"Go!" I hear his voice in my head, just as I did with Qetesh and Eleth.

I gaze back at him, my mouth open. Images form of me leaving him with these creatures, and I can't help shaking my head.

The demons press in closer, only ten feet from him now, the darkness deepening on every side. Obatala pivots to face my captor and raises his good arm slowly, his fingers extended. He begins to trace the most beautiful movements through the air – shoulders swaying, hips rotating – like some martial art, some ritualistic dance. He hoists his limp arm, stepping with one foot and then another to draw the lines of sweeps and kicks, never stopping. Each movement is the beginning of the next. All the while, he remains in the middle of the encroaching circle of darkness.

I stare on as a female demon leaps in from the side, almost too fast to see. The veil peels back automatically from my senses again. Time slows, and I'm able to glimpse her demonic form as Obatala hits her with a wide sweep of his good hand, sending her flying. It was part of the dance – nothing altered, nothing changed – as if every movement was devised ages ago.

Another demon jumps from the other side of the circle,

and the Orisha rotates out of the way at the last moment. Then he slams the demon with the elbow of his limp arm as part of a spinning leap. His foot sweeps the demon's legs as another couple of demons surge toward him.

My hands tighten into fists as I picture myself aiding the Orisha. Two against twelve. Plus the pneumas behind. Could we survive?

The Orisha manages to keep the new attackers at bay while I dive deep inside, immerse myself in the void again, and feel for the spark, the river of fire. It flares behind my ribs, and the power grows in my limbs.

My captors are all facing Obatala now with no one focused on me. I tense my shoulders, channelling the energy into my shoulders, my legs. And prepare to leap, my gaze fixed on the nearest demon—

Obatala pauses his movements. "Run!" he yells to me, out loud this time.

I feel the word as a wave of power. It slaps into my torso and stops me in my tracks.

"This is not your fight!" he shouts.

Three more demons jump at Obatala, and then a fourth, and the Orisha speeds up his dance, barely fending them off. Yet having found their feet, they throw themselves again into the fray, swamping him now. His light goes down among the growing swells.

I can't look away, the void flooding my chest.

"Go!" The Orisha's voice resounds in my head again. *"Do not let this all be in vain."*

I can't move, can't imagine leaving him here.

They all pile on the Orisha – five, six of the demons at a time – the four-limbed creatures jumping and rearing behind. He continues his movements amid it all, but his light starts to vanish amid the dark.

"Go!" he bellows.

And even as the word hits my body, it takes everything I

have to wrench my gaze away. To spin around and aim my feet for the splintered glass wall. To stumble onward.

The void, the ocean rises up my throat like bile, monsters cavorting in the deep. I lurch through the broken window, my legs like wooden stumps, some part of my brain directing them while the rest focuses on breathing and keeping down the pain. I'm vaguely aware of tears tracing their way down my cheeks as I throw myself out into the night.

16

Buildings sweep by on either side of me. Wobbling spots of light against the backdrop of night – streetlights. The sound of my running footsteps becomes a metronome in my ears, the breath like fire in my lungs.

I focus hard on the discomfort and make it the entire sphere of my existence. But again, I see the janitor fighting … dying … and black waters swamp my insides, my thoughts akin to bits of wreckage among the swells while deep underneath lurks the crushing abyss.

I drive my legs harder, the metronome faster, the pain in my lungs ever fiercer. My whole body aches. Even so, I can't keep the questions at bay.

I'm still alive. *Why?*

Again, I turn my head and take a sweeping glance for anything following behind. Nothing obvious. Just the blur of buildings and cars along with the glow of fires on a few of the junctions, homeless people huddled around them, while the acrid smell bites at my throat.

Warning voices urge me to slow, to check again. But the void plunges ever deeper, more visions coming

Natasha. Alone for four days. With no word from me, no message. I lengthen my stride, the dark waters a constant companion, and my feet pound harder at the pavement, my eyes glued to the junction in front of me.

———

Thirty minutes later, which feels like an age, I finally find myself poised at the end of our road. My chest's heaving in and out, every muscle trembling, and I fix my gaze on the familiar house before me.

All the lights are off, as they are in the homes next door with dark alleyways in between. I swivel, checking the surrounding streets for any sign of movement. Nothing. No outline of dark figures. No hint of sulphur or cordite in the air. Yet still I force myself to the side on shaky legs. I lurch down a neighbouring road that's at right angles to our own.

The houses here are crammed together, their black windows eyeing my passing. And I keep to the shadows, my eyes on the well of darkness halfway down – the passage that runs between the back gardens of our road and the one behind. Hassan's route with his bag of valuables. And after another check of the street, I dart into the alley.

Dirt ridges bite at my soles while brambles claw at my cheeks from the tops of fences. I press on slowly, stepping over piles of rubbish and broken boards. And after eight houses, I reach the rear of our own and peek through a gap in the fence. Each of the windows is still boarded over. The back door as well. Steel reinforced and impregnable. I peer at the edges of the boards but see no obvious visible light in any of the rooms.

It is the middle of the night, however; maybe one or two in the morning.

I take another breath and then grip the fence post, vault the lowest part of the fence, and land in a crouch in the garden with wild grasses and hard earth all around me. There, I grab a handful of tiny stones from the ground before slinking on toward the house, keeping my head way down.

Twenty feet from the back wall, I stop, pause, and then cast a stone up at Natasha's window. It clacks against the wooden board and falls back to earth. I pause. My breath held. Ten seconds. Twenty.

No response.

And though a voice urges me to wait, I hurl more stones, peppering the rear-facing windows, including the back door. Each one creates a small cracking sound.

Still no movement. No sound. Aside from the thumping of my heart.

I take a single hurried step toward the back door, my mouth open to call upward. Then I clench my jaw and steal toward the side of the garden, padding silently along the fence and down the narrow alleyway that separates our house from our neighbours'.

Reaching the front yard, I pause and search the visible slice of road. Still empty. And there's no sound except for the revving of an engine in the distance. No smell aside from the familiar bitter scent of refuse, strong in my nose.

I edge along the front of the house, still keeping low. My fingers reach for the loose brick under the gang tags, our key hidden behind it. But when my gaze finds the front door, the breath stops in my throat.

It's open, just an inch, only darkness visible through the gap. Staring at it, a chill grips me from out of the shadows, clutching at my insides.

I jump up and dart forward, the road forgotten, with all of my attention on the door. It swings open with the faintest push, and I stagger over the threshold, my pulse stampeding now.

Shadows lie everywhere: in the entrance hall, the kitchen at the end, and Mrs B's room to the side. I scramble past and up the stairs, my whole body shaking. And after tripping a few times, I end up at our bedroom door and peer inside.

Nothing.

No Natasha, no mattress, no furniture. Everything

stripped. I just blink, my fingers gripping the door frame. Then the damning thoughts start to come, the barrelling darkness, my chest constricting. I thrust it all aside and careen around the house to scour every room. But there's no sign of Natasha, of Mrs B and her family, of any kind of note or message, of anything or anyone. It's all bloody gone.

Finally, I lurch back down the entrance hall, images swirling … my captor's wide grin, the numerous doors in Ben's corridor. Natasha might have already been languishing behind one, for all I know. Or the bigots. Maybe they've forced out Mrs B and Natasha in their fucking purge, leaving her without a home or protection, her soul shattered.

The darkness in the hallway presses in, and I dip my head. Alone. My mother gone, the priest too – the father I never had. And now Natasha. The void floods my insides, and all the while, deep in the black, I hear the call of monsters … *You left her.*

The dark ocean doubles in weight and then triples. I reel and then force a lumbering step toward the door, my mind conjuring images of tracking down the bigots, making them tell—

I come up short and find myself staring at something to the side of the door frame. A thin sliver of grey forms a line that's a fraction lighter than the blackness of the entrance hall. Five feet high.

I frown and lean forward. The priest's walking stick? The only thing left in the entire house.

And just gazing at it, my hands twitch, the faintest idea bubbling up.

17

I HURRY down another pristine city-centre street, right in the heart of the monied dominion. Pressing on, it's as if the towering buildings are squeezing closer, their lofty summits frowning down at me, calling me out to their rich owners.

I shake out the tension in my shoulders and glance between the office buildings. I see a tiny lightening at the edges, but largely the night maintains its hold with sizeable black clefts stretching between the pallid streetlights. I reach a junction and check both ways.

Empty.

I scurry across it, my legs unsteady, exhaustion like weights in my bones. I blink continuously. I must have been awake for more than twenty-four hours. And the same images crowd my mind – several sightings of a figure following me. My many backtracks and changes of direction since leaving the house have failed to lose them.

The skin prickles up my back.

I pass between two corporate behemoths and stumble to a halt. One has limestone pillars across its front, while the other has periodic square recesses of glass that span its height, creating a kind of ribbed effect with darkness in between. I glance over my shoulder and peer along the line of mirrored buildings.

No sign of my tail, and it's been thirty minutes since the last sighting. My eyes find the end of the road a hundred yards ahead, Father Thomas's church ten minutes beyond. I could be leading the fucker right to Natasha. *If* she's even there, and not dead or captured somewhere.

The priest's walking stick flashes through my brain …

Just believe.

I dart into a recess in the building front. It's only three feet square and deeply shadowed, with glass on all sides, providing a view in both directions. I turn my head to stare down the road behind, but tiredness grips me, pulling at my eyelids. With a yawn, I lean on the wall.

The glass radiates heat into my back as if the crazy warmth has been baked into the building itself. The air's completely still. Again, I blink hard to keep awake, but my eyes start to close …

A SOUND SLAMS me back to awareness – talking, along with approaching footsteps. Shock seizes me, my eyes fly open, and I spin to the side, my pulse firing.

Three guys in black uniforms are visible through the glass recess on my side of the street and somehow only ten yards away – a security patrol.

My entire body tightens, internal voices raging at me, and I shoot a glance down the road in the other direction, picturing myself running. The street's as dark as it was before – not bad for cover. But my legs are wobbling like damn jelly, and my mind conjures images of them calling a motorised squad – their standard tool for catching, beating, and ejecting trespassers like me.

My heart thumps, and my mouth goes dry. They're getting

closer, each one geared up like a soldier with a helmet, bulletproof vest, and a belt strapped with batons, cuffs, mace … and a bloody gun. The guy nearest the road is talking. He's bulky with a moustache and a gut, his voice a low whine as he kicks at something on the pavement.

I push myself into the back of the recess, right into the darkness.

The guy on the inside is checking every cubbyhole along the street, peering into each shadowy place. I hold my breath. He's wiry, almost ferret-looking, and he scans the nearest alcove with his close-set eyes, only ten feet away now.

Staring at him, my vision swims with fatigue. My limbs shake, and I catch a glimpse of my arms and legs, my clothes filthy; my own stink's strong in my nose.

Ferret Guy checks the pillars on the far side of the road, and I let my knees go, crumpling down the box recess with my back sliding down the glass. And I end up lying on my side, facing the street, curled up in the square cubbyhole.

The footsteps cease a few feet away.

"What do we have here?" a voice says. Ferret Guy. He speaks with a clipped accent.

I remain still, my eyes closed.

"Just a drunk," a whining voice says. Moustache Man. "He'll sober up in a few minutes and then fuck off. Doesn't need us. No one will notice."

A pause is followed by a whiff of shaving lotion, someone leaning down over me. I keep my face impassive, and the guy sniffs the air above my head.

"He's not drunk," Ferret Guy says. "No alcohol smell."

My jaw tightens, and I squeeze my eyes tighter shut.

"Let's wake him up," Ferret Guy says, straightening up. "Get him on his feet."

Two sets of rough hands grab my collar and arms, yanking me upward. I still my thoughts, focus on the fire inside, and peel back the veil. And as sensations spread out around me, I feel the pavement below me, picture myself connected to it, and imagine my body as heavy as lead.

Both guys continue to heave, their hands shaking while they pant. They manage to haul me to waist height as I flop between them. And beyond the veil, I focus on my connection to the ground as fiercely as I can.

Finally, one of them grunts in frustration. Their grips loosen, and they let me fall. The pavement slams into my side, and I lie there, slack again, the pain spreading from chest to hip.

"Wow, passed out," the third guy says.

"Let's see. Shall we?" Moustache Man says, an edge to his tone.

Still behind the veil, I make out the sound of the guy holding his breath, of his foot swooshing toward me. I tense my body an instant before his boot slams into my stomach.

The strike drives the air from my lungs, an explosion of pain in my torso, and flashes of light before my eyes. Plus, my bruised rib starts screaming once more. Nevertheless, I fight to keep my body still. And as Moustache Man steps back, I find my breath again, sucking tiny pockets of air into my aching chest.

"Let's leave him," Moustache Man says. "He's out cold. Won't be going anywhere. Police will find him first thing."

"No," Ferret Guy says. "You call a wagon and stay with him. We'll finish the patrol."

"Oh, *come on*," Moustache Man whines. "There's no time. My shift's up soon."

"We'll see you back at base," Ferret Guy says.

And he and the third guard stalk away, their footsteps growing fainter down the pavement.

Moustache Man curses under his breath. I open my eyes a fraction and squint up at him. The guy clicks on his shoulder radio.

"Base, this is patrol five, over," he grunts. Then he orders one of their motorised vehicles.

The radio crackles, barely audible, and I listen hard. *"Wagon ten minutes out, over,"* it says.

Moustache Man sighs and continues to pace, mumbling obscenities. I close my eyes again, keeping my breathing slow and calm, and wait for him to piss off.

But he doesn't. The bastard simply patrols the pavement, never more than ten feet away. And lying sprawled, visions come of the figure following me, of my tail well on the way to the church, somehow aware of where I'm going. My heartbeat speeds up, sweat trickles down my sides, and I have to tense my arms not to move.

And still Moustache Man traipses up and down, giving no indication of fucking off.

Again, I begin the count, trying to calm my mind. And with my rib still aching, I relive the memory of the guy kicking me, magnify it, and replay it. As the fire ignites at my core, I peel back the veil. My senses sharpen, and time gradually slows.

Then I roll onto my front, my hands under my chest. I moan a couple of times, squinting up at the guy again.

"You little wastrel," Moustache Man says. He plants one leg, draws the other one behind him, and drives his foot at my unprotected side.

In slowed time, I channel the energy in my arms and wait ... wait ... His kicking leg hurtles forward, his weight shifting back to counterbalance the strike. With power exploding through my veins, I thrust hard with my hands, throwing my torso away from his foot. While my upper body shoots backward, I pivot on my hip and swing my legs toward him along the ground.

His foot flies forward, misses me, and kicks the air above my body instead. He ends up arms flailing and off balance, with only one foot on the pavement. And that's the ankle I sweep off the ground with my swinging leg.

He tumbles to the side, his body flipping. And still beyond the veil, I spring upward from my other hip, grab his vest with two hands, and smash his helmet into the ground, just hard enough to knock him out.

And the guy doesn't get back up again after that. He doesn't move at all.

18

I SIT BACK on my heels on the pavement, my lungs heaving, Moustache Man lying before me. I check his chest. It's rising and falling. The fire ebbs from my veins, the veil slipping back before my senses while exhaustion seizes my limbs again, even heavier than before.

Rib throbbing, I force myself over to the guy's unconscious body, reach down, and grab his radio. I bring it to my lips and practise the voice a few times. Waiting till the timbre is about right, I click the send button.

"Base, this is patrol five again, over," I say.

No reply.

I squat there, waiting, my fingers squeezing the plastic casing tighter while images circle of demons prowling the city ahead of me, closing in on the church. I'm about to drop the radio when there's a crunch of static.

"This is base, over," a voice says.

I swallow, force myself to calm, and pinch my nose. "Cancel that wagon," I say, trying to mimic Moustache Man's whine. "Our comatose is now conscious, over."

There's a pause.

"The wagon's on route, only two minutes away," the radio says. "They can take him—"

I press the button too quickly, end up jamming his transmission.

I bite my lip, scrunch my eyes shut, and hit the radio against my forehead.

"Ah, negative, base," I say, my thoughts scrabbling. "This guy needs to walk. We need to have a … conversation." I draw out the last word, trying to make it sound ominous.

After another pause, the radio crackles to life. "Understood, patrol five," it says. "Wagon called off, over."

"Thank you, base … er, over," I say and click off the radio. I throw it down and glance both ways.

The street's still empty. For now.

With quivering hands, I strip Moustache Man's gear off. Vest, jacket, trousers, helmet, belt, radio. The guy's so bulky that it easily fits over my own clothes. And he's so senseless that he doesn't stir at all. I fold him into the glass recess and cuff him with a few of his own cable ties before darting off down the street.

I barrel across a junction and then another. Still no one. Rounding the third, I spot a few pedestrians and slow my steps, forcing myself to take deeper breaths. And from there, I stride forward on trembling legs, winding my way through the narrow, maze-like streets toward the church. My feet take me past a dozen more early office workers, a few vans making delivery runs. I spy no extra patrols, and while my eyes search constantly for signs of my tail, I see none.

Finally, I emerge into the west corner of the semicircular courtyard, office buildings all around with handfuls of dawn commuters marching toward them. The church stands on its near side with its familiar dirty stone front. Memories swirl, causing my feet to slow. I see Father Thomas, the very first time Natasha and I stayed. The glow in the old man's eyes. The warmth in his smile. And beyond the church, Gabriel's building looms dark and large. A shudder travels up my back.

A couple of workers glance at me with eyebrows raised – a

lone security guard without his patrol. Plus, I'm undoubtedly being searched for right now.

I shake my body into action and begin walking fast toward the church door. The same office workers follow my approach as I bound up the steps and take in the lock. It's clearly been smashed, a few of the wrought-iron struts around the handle hanging free. The mechanism's barely connected.

I grab the radio on my shoulder and mime pressing the button.

"Patrol seven to base, over," I say, raising my voice for the workers behind me. "Have reached church. Checking the reports of vandalism."

Placing my body in front of the lock, I wrench one of the struts from the wood and use it to lever the bolt out of the strike plate. It unlocks in an instant. I glance in both directions. The nearby office workers have lost interest and are ambling on across the courtyard. I shove open the door and dart inside, closing it immediately afterward. Then I turn around, and a gasp escapes my lips.

The glow from streetlights reflects against the stone window arches, the glass cracked in every one. Most of the statues stand broken, and almost all the pews have been either upturned or splintered. I blink at it all. The place is in ruin.

My feet shuffle toward the altar, and I scour the wrecked space. I see no sign of Natasha or anyone else. No sound or movement, only destruction wherever I look. Huge diagonal tears in the pulpit look like someone's taken an axe to the wood. And many of the religious carvings have been smashed in some kind of frenzied attack. I sniff the air.

And freeze, my entire insides cold as I pick up the faintest acrid scent. Sulphur.

My heartbeat gallops, and at the front of the church, I spy a flicker of movement – shadows shifting across the far wall.

My adrenaline races, my legs tense, and my shoulders spin toward the door behind.

Yet I maintain my gaze on the same shadows by the altar, on the gloom to the sides of the rear pillars. While warnings shriek in my head, I keep my feet planted and don't turn away entirely.

There it is again, a faint quiver, the shadows moving once more. They're a fraction lighter halfway up the far stone wall.

I straighten and force myself down the central aisle, edging between broken pews. Still, no one jumps out on me, and the darkness lifts a sliver. I pass the pulpit, stalk past two archways, and swivel.

There. Set on a black metal rack on the far side of one of the rear columns – a tiny, solitary burning candle. The acrid smell stronger here.

I take a breath and blow. The flame flickers, and the shadows dance against the stonework once more. While a lightness grows inside me, doubting thoughts still crowd my head, my mind conjuring all the ways this could be a trick.

But before I know it, I'm pacing toward the side of the church, to the door we used so many times. My fingers reach for the iron handle, and I turn and pull. It's unlocked. The corridor beyond lies in darkness, and the lightness within me fades a little when the burning scent fills my nose again, stronger here.

I stumble down the passageway into the black. My eyes adjust slowly, and I start to pick out the lines of walls and doorways. In the kitchen, a faint triangle of grey cuts across the corridor opposite the door, the contours of a table barely visible in the murk. Aside from that, nothing.

Nevertheless, I step inside, my gaze pulled toward the near corner of the room, the one deepest in shadow. I see the rough outline of a cupboard, the worktop, and something else leaning against it. Almost entirely still.

19

I GAWK AT THE SHAPE – an oval of black against a black background. The variation in shade against the kitchen counter is hardly noticeable. I don't move. The outline doesn't shift either.

I wet my throat. "Nat?" I say, my voice coming out as a croak.

Nothing happens. The shape remains still, and the acrid smell is far stronger here.

I take a trembling step forward. "Nat, is that you?"

As I approach the far counter, the outline doesn't vanish, and more details appear out of the black. Familiar features. A heart-shaped face, high cheekbones, and large eyes … gazing up at me with a look of surprise.

Relief comes like a wave – so powerful it almost fells me, my legs barely holding me up. Her mouth opens, and I lurch forward, wrap my arms around her, and hug her tightly. I bury my face in her neck, and she hugs me back. I can feel the strength in her arms and can smell the familiar scent of her hair.

I just hold on to her, but she lets her hands drop. Then she wriggles one up over my stomach and pushes against my chest. I let go of her automatically. She shoves me harder, thrusting me back toward the open door behind.

"Where *were* you?" she says, her tone animal-like. "Four … fucking … days." She spits each word.

And while the void's so heavy, staring at her tense jaw and the fire in her eyes, some of the tension ebbs inside me. She's more alive than I've seen her in weeks.

I reach out, but she thrusts my arm away before hitting me with both hands, pounding her fists against my ribs. And while pain flares with each impact, I don't make any move to stop her.

"You left us all alone!" she says. "Where the fuck *were* you?"

My lips close. My body shakes. She continues to glare at me, jaw clenched, eyes burning.

I clear my throat. "I was captured," I say, barely managing to get the words out.

She goes completely still again, one fist pressed to my chest. "What?" she says.

I raise my own hands. "It's all fine now. I'll tell you, but can we sit?" I say and motion to the table. "I want to know what happened to you."

In the darkness, Natasha glances from me to the chairs and back. Then she huffs and edges around the table. A drawer squeaks open, and a match flares to life. I avert my eyes from the sudden brightness, the acrid smell intense in the air once more.

She lights several candles already fixed to saucers and places them on the worktops around the room. There's only the cupboards, the counters, a sink, four chairs, and a table. Nothing else – exactly how I remember it.

I slump down in the nearest chair, barely able to sit upright as my rib spikes with pain.

"God, you look awful," she says, staring at me with lips pursed and chin raised – her nurse's appraising eye. I can't help but smile.

She bustles to the sink, fills a glass, and grabs a pack of biscuits. She dumps them on the table in front of me, and I watch her as she does so, her movements definitely stronger than before.

"And what's with the uniform?" she asks and nods at my outfit.

I glance down at the dark grey jumpsuit, the various tools at my waist. Then I undo the belt and dump it on the floor.

"Occupational hazard," I say, half smiling.

She doesn't return it and doesn't sit down; simply leans on the counter and watches me with a frown, her arms folded across her chest. She gave me the same look the first time we sat together in this kitchen.

I down the water and crunch through the biscuits, hunger claiming my stomach.

"So?" she says.

I point to my full cheeks. "You first," I mumble.

She fixes me with a hard gaze. I continue to chew, trying to smile at the same time. And eventually, she shrugs.

"The locals came," she says, glancing to the side. She reaches out and adjusts a candle, sending darting shapes across the walls. "They started in the middle of the night, a few roads over. Hundreds of people carrying weapons and torches. They knew exactly which buildings housed newcomers. Had their approach all worked out."

I stop eating, my insides tightening.

"Mrs Badr did not want to wait," Natasha continues. "She and her family were in such a state, so I helped them gather their stuff and packed up as well. I ended up going with them." She finds my gaze, her features taut with pain. "I did not think you were coming back."

The weight doubles in my chest, and I blink through the ache. "But how'd you manage?" I breathe. "You'd been so weak."

She ignores me and keeps speaking. "I took them as far as one of the shelters and made sure they at least had a place to sleep. But the organisers would not let me stay." Her voice falters, and tears prick her eyes. "And then I came here."

I push the food aside and reach out a hand. "I'm so sorry, Nat," I say, my voice giving out as well.

She heaves a breath, wiping her eyes, but makes no move toward me from the counter. "So, what's your story?"

My mouth opens, but I falter. Her features harden again as I chew my cheek.

"I went to see Ben," I say.

"What?" she says, her arms squeezing her chest, her neck muscles tightening.

I raise my hands. "I know. I know," I say. "But I thought it would help. Warning him about the devil, the angels. Getting protection for our neighbours."

She opens her mouth, her eyes still burning, but says nothing. Eventually, her features soften, just a fraction. "And?" she asks.

My fingers drum against the table leg, and I take a breath. "We were played, Nat."

Her frown deepens.

"Played by Ben," I say. "He's not who we think he is."

"He's a politician," she says. "They're never—"

"He's a demon," I say.

This time her eyes go wide, her mouth gaping. The candles flicker and still as she holds her breath.

"It was all a ruse. Following us from my squat, that time. Our conversation in the diner," I say. "Because of the interest the *things* showed in me, he knew I'd be important. So, he put us on the trail of Cassiel, and we dug the angel up for his master."

She blinks. "He's …" Her voice wavers.

"A demon," I say. "Mammon's his name. His form's hideous. And he works for the devil. The entirety of his team is a mix of humans and demons. It's all one massive political operation. They have Paul Hawcross installed as the perfect puppet, with Ben and others pulling the strings. They captured me. Kept me in a cell on the top floor of his building."

Natasha pushes off the counter, her arms still around her middle. "And you got *out* of there?" she asks, the bite in her tone becoming amazement and then suspicion. "They let you *escape*?"

My ribs tighten at her implication, heat sparking. But then the image slinks in of the figure tailing me.

I thrust it aside and push myself on. "It took me four days," I say. "But I got free. And then I came straight to find you."

For a long while, she just stares at me, and I hold her gaze.

Finally, she sighs, stands for a moment, and then pulls out a chair, settling down across the table. I keep my hand extended toward her, and she reaches her own fingers out, one side of her lips curving upward. And while my heart leaps at the sight, I can also see the growing distance in her smile, the flames ebbing from her eyes. Plus, the image comes of the priest's walking stick, the symbol that drew me here. I set my jaw, Ben's words sounding in my head … *You don't know your scripture.*

Natasha shifts her hand away and scans my face, her forehead creased. "What is it?" she says.

I take a deep breath. "Something I heard in my cell."

She's already shaking her head, her features tense.

"But, Nat, this is key. Father Thomas was *right*," I say, my voice rising. "They're planning something big, something political, based on a story from the scriptures. Ben said so himself."

She scrunches her eyes shut, bites her lip, and turns away for a moment, like she's thinking. And then with a blink, she's back.

"What is it?" I ask.

Again, she shakes her head.

My other hand clenches, but I keep it down by my side

and tilt my head, trying to keep my expression calm. "Nat, *please.*"

This time, she just fixes her gaze on me, her smile gone. I stare back at her, not breathing, and the shadows creep inward from the corners of the room, the candles dimming.

"Revelation," she says, her voice barely audible.

"The book?" I clarify.

She nods and holds the silence. I don't break it.

"That's what this is all about," she says eventually. "What it's clearly always been about. The devil's plan for an Antichrist. That's what the book describes, a charismatic leader who will unite the faithful and wage a world war to command *every tribe and people and tongue and nation,* on earth."

"A world war?" I say.

She shrugs. "That's what it describes."

I lean back again, blinking.

"Paul Hawcross the Antichrist," I murmur. "They've been preparing this for decades."

"For much longer, I think," Natasha says.

I find myself nodding. "And the black creatures were the trigger," I say. "The sign the devil's release was coming."

She sets her jaw and folds her arms tighter across her chest. The embers flare at my core.

"We've got to do something," I say. "We're the only ones who know the plan."

Natasha jumps up from her seat and spins away. The darkness looms inside me, and I cling on tight to the fire. I push myself to my feet also, my fingers pressing down hard on the tabletop.

"Nat, look at me," I say.

She keeps her eyes averted.

"Look at me, *please,*" I say.

She lifts her head and meets my gaze.

"We've got to at least *try,*" I say. "Sitting in that dark room was *killing* you."

She remains entirely still. More tears form at the corners of her eyes.

"I think he predicted this, Nat, before he died. In the car, driving to Pergamon," I say.

Natasha's eyes widen, and her lips part.

"Father Thomas told me that you'd need to be there for me before the end, whenever that is ..." I say, my voice trailing off. Then I say more strongly, "But that I'd need to be here for you first. I think *this* is what he meant."

Still, she just stands there, a tear tracing its way down her cheek.

"We have to do *something*," I say again.

"But what, Jake?" she asks, her voice rising, the sense of distance gone from her expression. "What *can* we do?"

"Enlist the angels," I say.

She throws up her hands. "Jake, that's insane," she says, the flames burning once more in her eyes. "Michael will *never* listen to us, never engage. He was in hell. He knows we were involved in the devil's escape."

I lean toward her. "Not Michael," I say. "But Uriel and the other angels we saw in hell. They tried to stop the devil. They acted. We could tell them what we know, and they could persuade the wider pantheon."

Natasha opens her mouth, but nothing comes out.

I press on, my pulse continuing to speed up. "There's something else," I say. "Something I've not told you."

She just stares back at me.

"He was there," I say with a nod. "He was there, the janitor – Obatala – the Orishan god. He broke through the front of Ben's building, just as I was going to be captured again, maybe killed." I shake my head. "He saved me, Nat. He was magnificent. And he *saved* me."

The void balloons inside. And my mouth shuts, my feet stumbling back. But then I thrust out the words.

"He sacrificed himself to get me out of that building," I say.

Natasha's hand goes to her lips, the tears coming more freely now.

"Why would he do that?" I ask, the rawness still there in my heart. Yet I don't turn aside from the darkness. At that moment, I feel it as fully as I can. "Why would he do that?" My voice cracks. "Why would he sacrifice himself?"

The question hangs there in the silence between us. Natasha doesn't shrug, doesn't shake her head.

"Unless he knew something," I say, speaking quickly. "Unless there's a reason we have this information."

Natasha lets her arms drop. And the memory comes of the priest sitting there at the table, staring at me with shining eyes.

"Father Thomas's walking stick led me here," I say. "You worked out their goal. And now we've got to get this knowledge to someone who can help."

20

Finally, the Puritan stronghold comes into view – All Saints' Church in Stepney Green Park – with the concrete path that connects the road and its entrance, fifty yards away. And of course, the place is bloody packed. I start to wind through the crowd before coming to a halt on the pavement opposite. Though the grey tide swamps the path and most of the road behind, the area around the church doors seems much emptier.

"Some kind of obstruction," I say, craning my neck. My exposed skin's already cooking in the midday sun, while my washed clothes remain barely damp against my back and legs.

Natasha stops at my side and crosses her arms. "You think it's the angels?"

"Unlikely," I say, only able to make out the tops of heads in front of me.

"Jake, Nakir wanted us dead last time," Natasha says. "And at least seven angels know we helped the devil escape. You think they are going to welcome us in?"

A shiver runs through me, and I turn to the side. "I'll check it out."

She grabs my arm. "Whatever happens, we stick to the plan, right?" she says. "Just pass on information."

I glance back at her. The tension's obvious in her shoulders and jaw, but the slightest flame shines on in her eyes – the glimpse I spied last night. A tiny part of her faith rekindled.

I nod. "That's it. We get in and get out. Nothing more."

She just stares back at me, and the Puritans continue to swarm around us.

I grasp her hand and lean in. "I'm serious, Nat. We'll get far away. Even out of the country. But we'll make sure we've helped first. Contributed in *some* way."

I smile. And eventually, she lets out a slow breath before nodding back. "Okay," she says.

Over her shoulder, I spy a flash of black across the road, and my head turns before I can stop it. A dark figure slips between groups of people approaching the crowd and then disappears behind the growing throng. My spine goes cold, and my fingers squeeze together, the faint scents of sulphur and cordite itching at my nostrils.

Our fucking tail.

Natasha's staring at me, her features more pinched. "What is it?" she asks.

I swivel my gaze back toward the church entrance, grab a nearby lamp post, and hoist myself up between two Puritans. Then I jump down again and clear my throat.

"Some kind of checking system," I say and nod in the direction of the path. I spied a line of guardians twenty feet before the open doors, queues of people formed in front of each one. "Come on."

And I take her hand and plunge us into the crowd. We start pushing forward.

The further we move, the tighter the throng becomes. People shove forward at our sides, many of them praying audibly and a few shouting their elation at the church spire. The collective energy beats my heart and sparks the fire in my core, but I keep my thoughts running, the veil firmly in place while I dart my gaze behind to search for the figure. Ahead, I catch glimpses of the guardians.

Slowly. Painfully. We approach them. I get my first sighting when we're only ten feet away. They're all Puritans in long habits with identical wooden crucifixes around their necks. And they're interrogating everyone who reaches their line. Most get through with nods, but a few are ordered away, almost all without the standard grey uniform.

I pull at Natasha's hand. "We'll be rejected," I say. "You've got to get us in."

Natasha whirls to face me. *"How?"* she demands, that sting back in her voice. "They're checking for community members. We are not known here."

My insides squeeze. And while pleas chime in my head, I keep my mouth firmly shut. Natasha continues to edge forward at my side.

The line of guardians is only a few feet ahead now, the Puritans pressing even more tightly around us. Several of them scream in fits of ecstasy. One guy speaks in tongues. The level of frenzy's like a gusting wind over the coals in my chest.

I take a breath and anchor my feet when a further whiff of sulphur invades my nose. My head swivels, and I catch another glimpse of the dark figure – fifteen feet back – while a note of familiarity rings at the back of my mind.

"Come," someone barks from in front of us.

I spin. We're right at the front of the queue, and the guardian is motioning us forward. Natasha stalks toward him, and I shuffle directly behind, making sure to keep her back protected.

The guy towers above Natasha, a good half a foot taller than she is, though his build's as slim as hers. Two stern eyes look her up and down, his mouth a sneer.

"Your congregation?" he snaps.

"St Catherine's," Natasha retorts and glares right back at him.

"Generation?" he says.

"Second," she says.

The guardian's brow doesn't unknit, and the Puritans shuffle more impatiently behind us.

I shift my weight, glancing between Natasha and the guardian as his fellow sentinels let more grey-robed worshippers pass on both sides of us.

Our guardian looms even higher over Natasha. "Trust in the Lord with all your heart!" he says. "And lean *not* on your own understanding."

Still Natasha holds his gaze. "In all your ways submit to him, and he will make your paths straight," she says without a pause. "Proverbs 3:5–6."

The guardian just stares, his lips parted. His forehead smooths just a fraction, and I step out from behind Natasha. The guy shifts his stern eyes to me as the crowd continues to seethe around us, the shouts of prayer and exaltation rising and falling, the fire continuing to build in my chest. Plus, another waft of sulphur hits my nostrils, and there's a growing heat between my shoulder blades. I tense my neck to avoid pivoting around.

"He is with me," Natasha says, without even glancing in my direction.

The guardian shakes his head. "Not good enough," he says. "He'll need to pass like everyone else."

My hands fidget. Natasha glances at me as well, the sense of distance growing again in her eyes. She gives a shrug. I bite my lip, potential schemes flitting across my mind.

But nothing sticks.

A grey-robed man pushes past me from behind, making my rib throb. Then another Puritan follows him. The guardian lets both through. I end up being spun side-on, people squeezing by on both sides. And I can barely protect my chest from each bump.

Again, I sense movement behind me – a dark shape slipping through the crowd to my side, only ten feet away. And my shoulders tighten, the void deepening inside while the flames erupt in the darkness, the fire prickling every inch of my skin. The figure moves like lightning, always just ahead of my eyeline. And that strange sense of familiarity jabs at my mind.

Swivelling back, the guardian remains there, letting the grey stream spill past him with Natasha at his side. I press toward him, my head down, and use my elbows like knives. The Puritans mutter and complain as I barge right back to the front of the queue. The guardian glares down at me, his jaw clenched and hands on hips.

"What are …" he barks.

I tune out his voice, take a breath, and begin the internal count. I still my thoughts. And with the help of the swirling fire inside, the veil peels back easily from my senses.

The sulphur bites at my nose, and the heat stings my back. As the shimmering world spreads around me, I shut out the bombarding sensations – shuffling footsteps, a cacophony of voices. Instead, I focus on the dark figure behind, reaching out my senses to *feel* it at my back.

Getting ever closer.

The guardian raises an imperious finger and orders me away, spittle flying – the sight and sounds stretched out in slow motion. Then I bound forward half a step before shifting my weight to the balls of my feet as the guardian leers down at me. And I wait …

There. Another waft of cordite.

I shove off my front foot and spin. In slowed time, my senses absorb the foaming crowd behind me, its movements unfolding in the dance I recognise so well, every shift perfect in its place. The dark figure's there, just a shadow behind two of the queues, only four feet away but moving so damn fast, bolting away to the side.

With the surrounding frenzy, I let the fire explode in my

chest, energy thrumming through every muscle, every sinew. And I spring forward into the throng, darting into gaps the instant they appear. My body takes over, and I sense myself aiming for a spot a couple of feet in front of the scurrying form, right in its trajectory.

The figure speeds up, racing to get away. I channel all the energy into my limbs and dive into the next queue. I plunge my hand between two robed believers, and my fingers close on the lapel of a worn suit.

Squeezing tightly, I yank the figure to a halt.

It bucks and writhes, almost pulling itself free. I drive energy into my forearm and shoulders, barely keeping hold of the thing and grunting with the effort.

Squawks of shock erupt from the surrounding Puritans. They back away, faces pale, creating a circle of space. For an instant, the figure stops writhing. It turns, shoots both hands up, and shoves hard at my chest. I clench my teeth, pain flaring in my rib, and barely manage to keep hold.

Sure enough, it's the diminutive figure from Ben's conference room. Short, balding, and dressed in the cheap, frayed suit. He's almost half my size and thrashes like a wounded animal in my grip. The flames burn higher in my chest. I channel more energy into my hands and fingers as I jerk him toward the guardian.

The Puritans scramble away, parting like the Red Sea before us, and I thrust the figure at the towering Puritan. The guy's face blanches, and he takes a step back, raising his arms. Natasha gapes at me from behind him.

"We need to get him inside!" I hear myself say, the fire amplifying my voice and vibrating its tone.

Faced with the church doors, the figure thrashes even more wildly in my grip. I clench my jaw and squeeze his lapel even tighter.

"A demon's taken hold!" I yell. "He needs exorcism … needs help, this instant!"

A good portion of the crowd is staring on, Natasha

included, a hush growing around us. The guardian takes in all the staring eyes, perspiration coating his brow. Again, the demon tries to twist out of my grasp. But still I hold on, my grip like iron, all pain lost in the wildness of my fire.

The guardian nods. "Very well," he says and scrambles out of the way. "Go now!"

I grab the demon with both hands and thrust him in the direction of the doors as a chorus of nervous mutterings breaks out behind me.

21

Lugging the demon toward the church, I hold my fingers tightly around his collar. The Puritans stare and give us a wide berth. And the demon strains harder against me the closer we get to the entrance, dragging his feet along the ground.

I keep my thoughts still, keep the veil peeled back, and with the energy firing through my veins, I haul the demon with two hands across the threshold, Natasha hurrying behind. It's like plunging into a maelstrom of sensation. The place is packed, the pews rammed while more press together in the side and central aisles. Dozens of people moan, faces pointed to the ceiling, features twisted in rapture while many hundreds of worshippers pray loudly, swaying back and forth.

The tang of their sweat's strong in my nose, mingled with the caustic smell of burning oils from lamps set in stone alcoves all the way around the church. The stink makes my head swoon while the general chaos drives the fire wild inside me. I keep a tight grip on the demon.

In the tumult, snatched words filter back to me from the pulpit. " … day of judgement is coming!" A man in a plain robe stands there, red-faced, shouting at the top of his lungs. "Prepare, my people, for the promised land!"

I grit my teeth.

The demon makes a dash for the entrance, spinning me around. He barges into a group of people, almost toppling them over. The fire gnaws at my chest, and floundering after him, I squeeze my fingers even harder around his collar. Again, I barely keep hold of him.

Then I yank him to the side, shoving him roughly in the direction of the back corner of the church.

"Jake?" Natasha says from behind me, an edge to her voice.

I keep my focus on the demon. I continue to haul him toward the rear wall – out of the central aisle and away from the Puritans pouring in and out of the church.

Several alcoves span the back of the church. They're triangular, just over the width of a man, and several feet from the Puritans bustling along the rear aisle. The first recess is blocked by the door, the second by a table with collection boxes, leaflets, and Bibles. So I thrust the demon on toward the third, ten feet further along the rear wall.

He thrashes and strains against me, and a couple of Puritans glance over. They give us a long stare as they shuffle down the rear aisle. Jaw clenched, I channel the energy into my legs and arms, and turn toward the Puritans, holding the demon still behind me. I force my lips into a tight smile. The Puritans keep moving, their eyes looking us up and down. I stare right back at them. And they hurry off toward the far walkway.

I swivel and bundle the demon toward the narrow recess. He almost stumbles, his arms flailing, and his hand barely misses the burning lamp that's hanging near the top of the recess. I grab his arms to quiet him, and slam his body hard into the narrow stone triangle.

And as soon as the demon touches the church stone, his body writhes, his face twists in agony, and his mouth opens wide. No sound comes out, yet a shrill keening explodes in my head, like someone's drilling out the insides of my skull.

I barely manage not to cradle my ears, to keep hold of him. Then I glance over my shoulder.

No Puritans react. They continue to bustle along the rear and side aisles, the sounds of prayer and shouted ecstasy as loud as ever.

The demon scrambles away from the stonework and tries to dart to one side of me. I anchor my feet to block him off. He goes to squeeze under my arm, but I don't move aside.

And in that instant, he wilts, ceasing all his straining and crumpling to his knees. He ends up quivering in the stone triangle, a bubbling sound escaping his lips. He grasps at my legs and stares up at me. I fidget, all too aware that Natasha's standing at my side, gazing on, along with a couple of Puritans behind her, their brows wrinkled and lips pursed.

I crouch before the demon. "Quieten down," I hiss and squeeze him by the shoulders, hauling him upward.

He stands there, only a few inches from my chest, holding himself as far away from the walls as possible. His head is down, body shaking.

"You're going to answer some questions," I say with a growl, my fingers gripping his lapel. "Why are you following us?"

"What?" Natasha says at my shoulder, and her gaze sears my cheek.

I keep my eyes trained on the demon. "Ever since I went back to find you at our house, this one's been tracking me," I say to her, keeping my voice low. "Maybe even before."

"Why?" she says, her voice trailing off.

The darkness blooms inside me, and I shift my feet.

She draws a sharp intake of breath. "It's a …"

"Demon, yes," I say. "He was in the conference room. Ben was furious with him."

"And you didn't tell me?" Natasha says, her eyes aflame and voice rising. Puritans still linger all around.

The heat grows across my chest, and I breathe. The demon continues to shiver before me.

I turn to look directly into Natasha's eyes. "Would you have come if I had?" I retort.

She goes quiet, her lips parted and expression blank.

"Nat, I'm not prepared to sit around, day after day, and watch you slowly die inside," I say, the void tightening my throat as tears sting the backs of my eyes. "I'm not."

Natasha just stands there, the fire ebbing from her gaze again, though the familiar sense of distance doesn't replace it.

I spin back to the demon. "So," I say, channelling the flame and grasping his lapel tighter. "Why are you following us?"

He shakes his head vigorously, hands fidgeting in front of him.

"Why?" I demand, yanking him back and forth.

He just shakes his head faster. I grab the demon with both hands again and shove him further back into the alcove, bringing his shoulders within an inch of the stone.

"Please, please, *please!*" he says, his arms windmilling at my sides. "You escaped! You escaped!" His voice is so high it's barely audible and sets my teeth jangling.

I ease my grip a fraction.

"He will want to know where you are, what you are doing," the demon says, his words tumbling out.

"Mammon?" I say.

He looks at the floor, and his entire body trembles, his bottom lip squeezed between his teeth. I tense my arms and go to thrust him back toward the stone again. He gives the faintest nod.

My head turns to the side, my gaze trained toward the drainage pools. Natasha stands directly in between.

"You're not thinking ..." she says.

I sense a fluttering in my chest, the same lightness as I felt in the priest's church, like a fresh wind blowing.

"Why not?" I say. "You said yourself that the angels

would never listen to us. We're insects, after all. But what about a demon? They could get the truth out of him."

The demon's body trembles wildly. "No, no, no, no," he blubbers, his head shaking so violently it makes me dizzy.

"We bring a demon into heaven?" Natasha says. "Jake, that's crazy."

"Is it?" I demand. And while my own doubts are yelling at me, I focus on the sensation of lightness and thrust them aside. "What if this is why it's here? What if we couldn't pass on what we know any other way?"

Natasha opens her mouth, but again nothing comes out. She simply stares at me, her muscles slack and eyes wide.

"Plus, we can't let him go either," I say. "He'd run straight to Ben to tell him where we are."

"I wouldn't! I wouldn't!" the demon says, his tone beseeching. He grips both my hands and collapses to his knees again. "I would go away. Anywhere you wanted. And wait. Wait for days. Say nothing ..."

He continues to babble loudly. I try to lift him up, but he won't come this time. He just remains on his knees, pleading, his hands gripped around my calves. More people are looking over now, slowing their steps as they pass. Two men whisper to each other from further down the rear aisle.

I glance over their shoulders toward the drainage pools. So many damn Puritans in between. No way we can get to them without being seen, let alone jump into the fucking water.

The demon babbles on. The fevered praying rings in my ears, and I take a deep breath in to begin the count in my head. I still my thoughts, and with the fire burning in my chest, again I pull back the veil. Then I let my attention wander over my recent memory of every detail I've noticed in the church ...

The worshippers in their grey robes, the stained-glass windows, the flickering candles and lamps, the defaced paintings and statues, the wooden pews and tables, the Bibles and leaflets, the rows of collection boxes.

My eyes find the table a few feet to my side, right by the entrance. The piles of leaflets on the top are thicker than when we arrived. I crouch down and peer under the table. Sure enough, two boxes stand side by side – one sealed and one open. Thousands of leaflets are visible inside the open one, the box almost full.

An idea starts to form, though a part of my brain screams madness.

With the veil still peeled back, I grab the demon and haul him up and all the way out of the alcove. Hoisted in the air, the demon stops blubbering. I set him down on the near side of the wooden table, and again, he scrambles away from the stonework. I hold him with one arm and then spin to face the front of the church.

Most of the Puritans who were staring have moved off, though one elderly woman remains, on the far side of the table, near the entrance. She has her gaze fixed on me, her eyes unblinking while I shuffle a few steps to the side. I stretch my leg under the table and hook the open box with my foot to begin dragging it toward the alcove.

A stream of Puritans shuffle by in front of us, and I keep my eyes on the preacher the entire time, one hand still on the demon. With just my foot, I haul the box painstakingly across the floor and position it in the recess.

The elderly woman narrows her eyes at me and then calls to someone over her shoulder.

"Jake, what are you doing?" Natasha says at my side.

"You'll see," I respond, backing further into the alcove, the veil in place again.

I reach up with my free hand and grab the oil lamp from its bracket. The case is hot and heavy, and the thing's issuing a foul, caustic scent. I hold my breath and bring the lamp's fuel tank to my mouth. The smell's horrendous.

A Puritan arrives at the elderly woman's shoulder, and she grips his arm, pointing in our direction.

Heart thumping, I seize the bung with my teeth and rip it free, the cheap alcohol biting at my lips. Then, with the wick still burning, I tip the lamp till the fuel's streaming down on the leaflets in the open box.

The woman's attracted more attention now – a whole handful of people staring. One heads in our direction and skirts around the table. The demon attempts to scramble away from the approaching Puritan, but I hold him tight.

"Jake ..." Natasha says.

I tilt the lamp further, increasing the flow. Oil splatters up out of the box onto the stone floor and walls of the surrounding recess.

"Hey, you!" the Puritan yells, only ten feet away now.

I grasp the demon and haul him across me, toward Natasha, toward the drainage pools at the back corner of the church. "Move, now!" I yell.

"Stop that!" the Puritan shouts, his voice shrill.

I crash the top of the lamp into the edge of the stone alcove, smashing the glass. The wick burns brighter once exposed to the open air, and I drop it directly above the soaked box of leaflets while spinning away.

I see a great whoosh of flame in the corner of my vision as I plunge along the rear wall, shoving the demon and Natasha ahead of me. A barrage of heat hits my back, and a crackling sound fills the air, followed by shouts of alarm.

"Get them!" someone yells from behind us, the words barely audible among the tumult.

I drive us on, the smoke stinging my throat, all the way till we reach the back corner. It's twenty feet square, the drainage pools right in the middle, and it's packed with people, almost everyone already on their feet. Some just stand there, while others shuffle forward toward the main body of the church, their necks craning to stare over our shoulders and peer along the rear wall.

I throw my free hand in the air and channel the energy up my throat. "Fire!" I yell and point behind me. "Quick, get out!"

There's a moment's pause, and then the square recess erupts into movement. Puritans scramble around each other, forcing their way out of the corner.

I press up against the rear wall, my hands gripping the demon to prevent him from being swept away in the grey flood. The smoke billows toward the ceiling, spreading to fill the massive internal space.

I squeeze Natasha's shoulder and yell, "Keep going!"

She nods, and I scramble behind her, around the corner and into the recess, squeezing past the throngs heading in the opposite direction. The square space is half-empty now, since many of the Puritans have already fled. I spy the drainage pools through many sets of scrambling legs as the smoke continues to thicken all around us.

I slot in behind the fleeing crowd, Natasha at my side, and we hug the scurrying feet right to the pools. However, with every step we take, the demon thrashes more wildly in my grip. His crazed movements, the Puritans' frenzy – it all drives the flames higher in my chest. I channel the power into both arms but barely hold him still.

"You first," I rasp to Natasha and nod at the nearest circular pool, my lungs already toiling with the smoke.

Natasha glances at the water, and then back at me, her face pale. She doesn't move. The demon flails more wildly, straining to pull away. And the reflection of the stained-glass window above is almost completely invisible in the smoke, our normal method of finding the angelic realm gone.

"We've got to go," I say as the accusatory shouts ring out louder from the entrance.

"But—" Natasha starts.

"Remember Father Thomas," I say and find her gaze. "What did he say the first time we were here?"

She heaves a breath, and I see that tiny spark in her eyes again.

"Just jump," she says.

I nod. "Don't worry about the reflection," I say. "Just see it there and focus on the memory of their realm."

And with that, she takes another breath, standing straighter, shoulders back. She turns and leaps for the pool. Her body freezes, her feet in contact with the water. I blink, and in the next instant, she's gone.

The shouts grow louder, along with the sound of people shoving through the remains of the fleeing crowd. The demon grabs at my hands, his crazed fingers clawing at my wrists, and the flames leap higher inside me.

I peel back the veil and channel power through my entire body. I grip the demon so hard my fingers hurt, and jump for the water.

22

Again I have the strange experience of falling upward, of flying. The wind wraps around me, cradles my body, and flings me through space – faster and faster – through swirling colours. Every other sight is banished. The customary sense of peace fills my insides, and no matter how hard I grip the demon's coarse jacket, eventually my muscles relax entirely, and he's gone.

I cast around, the colourful swirl coalescing into the familiar greys and greens and blues, all still hazy as I'm spun through the air. However, there's so much more grey than before.

Then the ground comes. The top of my head touches against something soft, and the rest of my body falls upward till I'm sprawled on a bed of grass, the smell of cordite strong in my nose.

I lift my head immediately to find myself lying on the familiar sloping bank. It continues up toward the ridge as normal, but beyond it there are no undulating hills across our strip of land. Instead, there's nothing. Just the expansive blue sky beyond, the grassy bank ending at some kind of rocky edge, only ten feet away. And there he is, the demon, curled up in a ball on the ground between me and the sky. He's rocking back and forth, a low whimpering sound emanating from his lips.

I spring toward him, grab him by the arm, and haul him upward, my gaze drawn over his shoulder. I scan the sky beyond the rocky edge, searching for the customary fingers of land that head in every direction.

They're not there. I see nothing but the expansive blue as I step toward the rocky edge and peer over the brink. Grey rock plummets away before me, and my stomach jumps up my throat. The strip of land's not paper-thin as it's been before. Instead, a sheer cliff face descends for infinity. I spy the occasional platform of grass jutting out of the wall, but my sight's quickly broken by the puffs of white clouds many miles below.

My head spins, and I stumble backward from the edge, the demon still clasped in my hand.

"What have they done?" Natasha's voice. Her tone low, the words breathy. I swivel.

She's standing on the opposite side of the pool of water, the familiar reflection of the church visible on its surface. Only the pool's much smaller than during our previous visits, just thirty feet across. She's facing away from me and staring up at something that towers far above her head. More grey rock. I tilt my neck back, following her gaze higher, and my head spins ever faster.

I'm staring up some kind of mountainside, its surface almost vertical. Our pool is in the middle of a square plateau that sticks horizontally out of this sheer rock face, its grassy banks bordered on two sides by cliffs that descend into cloud, and on the other two by walls that climb upward.

One wall is the main rock face itself, straight ahead of me. It rises two hundred feet behind Natasha to some kind of edge, the mountainside continuing beyond into more banks of white clouds high above. To my side, the other wall juts vertically out of the rock face and reaches up thirty feet, the top fringed by blue sky.

I peer closer at the walls. They're a mesh of large stone blocks, cracked pillars, and severed arches, as if the old islands of stone have been broken up and wedged together to build them. Tree roots wind in and out of gaps between the stones, and as before, the tiny yellow butterflies perch on the roots, the blocks, and everything else.

I stand there blinking at the vast mountainside. "What *have* they done?" I mumble. The place is like one massive fortification, all aliens to be kept out.

Cold shivers run down the rear of my calves. I swivel and search the corners of the grassy plateau, the top of the lower adjoining wall. And my heart thuds.

A familiar figure stands there with gold helmet and sparkling breastplate. His bare arms and shoulders are as massive as they ever were. The hilt of a sword's visible over his shoulder, and he holds a gigantic spear in one hand, probably ten feet long.

Nakir.

The demon scrambles behind my back as I tense my shoulders and arms. I anchor my feet, readying myself for the impending attack.

But the emissary doesn't move. He simply stares down at me from atop the wall.

"*Come,*" he barks and motions us toward him with a massive arm.

I frown, and my gaze finds Natasha on the opposite bank. She's facing Nakir. And thirty feet behind her is the edge of the plateau, our only possible escape route. And it's an infinite bloody drop into nothingness. My insides clench as I still my thoughts, peel back the veil, and try to shift gravity …

But it doesn't work. The shimmering world spreads out around me as normal, yet a new weight's pushing down on my shoulders, a strange resistance to flipping orientation. Plus, the customary sense of calm is gone, replaced by a thrumming charge in the air.

"Hurry, we must move!" Nakir calls and glances over his shoulder.

The obvious tension in his posture drives my heartbeat faster, and I step toward him, the demon blubbering audibly behind me.

"We need to find Uriel," I shout up to him. "Or one of—"

"We will see about that," Nakir says, his voice taut. "But first come quickly."

He motions us forward again, his huge biceps and shoulder muscles rippling. Then he disappears out of sight behind the summit of the wall.

I glance back at Natasha. She's staring at me as well.

"What d'you think?" I mouth. "Do we go ... then try to give him the slip?"

She shrugs but says nothing.

I sigh through gritted teeth, grab the demon, and shove him toward Nakir's wall. He digs his heels into the grassy bank and leans back on me, refusing to move.

I put my mouth to his ear and whisper, "Either you go with me, or I call back that nice emissary."

The demon gives a low shriek and scrambles away toward the pool. I grab his arm and hold him tight. Then, with my other hand, I cup my mouth.

"Na—" I yell, and get halfway through the emissary's name before the demon starts shambling toward the wall with a whimper.

With shoulders drooping, he climbs falteringly over the stones at the base. I follow right behind him, and though the wall is vertical, it's possible to chart a course upward. We step on the broken blocks and arches that make it up, numerous footholds sticking out of the wall's surface.

Nakir doesn't reappear over the top of the wall, and I make sure to keep well ahead of Natasha as we climb to breach the summit first.

And the sight steals the breath from my lungs.

The mountainside's actually a vast column, or spire, its

sides curving out of sight, both left and right, many miles wide. Its peak lies many more miles above us, the white clouds hiding much of the top from view. The surface of the spire is spanned by countless walls and plateaus, all jutting out at different angles from the mountainside like it's a building covered by gigantic scaffolding. And many of the plateaus are linked by sets of stone steps, some massive, others horribly narrow, and all of them over impossibly long drops.

I scan the spire. The number of features is overwhelming, no obvious routes anywhere, and no bloody way we can find our own path here.

"Faster," Nakir calls.

My head turns. Our wall connects directly with the mountainside, and the emissary's already fifty feet along it, poised above one of several sets of steps that descend from its top. This one links the wall with a much smaller plateau below before climbing up to yet another wall top, twenty feet higher than this one and further away from the central spire.

Nakir sets off down his steps as Natasha reaches the summit at my side.

"I'll go first," I say and push myself to stand atop the wall.

It's just two feet across, a massive drop on one side. I take a breath and force myself along it, shoving the demon after the emissary. He goes reluctantly, moaning the entire while and refusing to get closer than a dozen yards to Nakir.

I scan the vast space for places to hide, but I see no niches at all. Everywhere is so fucking exposed.

The emissary leads, and the three of us follow his crazy path, occasionally descending but mostly climbing jumbled sets of steps. We keep close to the near-vertical spire, close to jutting walls and overhanging plateaus, and gradually I find my gaze flitting more and more to Nakir.

He's scanning our surroundings constantly now, his features tense. And his agitation builds the energy in my core, driving my pulse faster.

"Where are you taking us?" I call out.

The emissary ignores me, climbing even more quickly up a near-vertical incline of large blocks. Each one is far too big to just use our feet, and I scramble to keep pace, gripping the stone with my hands and knees. But when the demon touches the stone with his bare skin, his moaning morphs into a high shriek that vibrates my skull.

Nakir shoots us a glance from the top. I clamber up in front of the demon, grab his hand, and haul him up the large stone block. My rib screams, but I ignore the pain as we continue like that. I do a mixture of urging the demon on from behind and helping him climb when we need to, my right side throbbing.

"We're almost there," Nakir says, speaking quickly.

He leads us across a stone walkway to a steep set of stairs up, a crumbling wall on one side and the spire on the other. Nakir bounds to the top of the steps, an overhang of rock a good distance above his head. He halts there and gazes down at us.

I can't follow him. He's only twenty feet above us, and the demon wails louder, refusing to get any closer. Natasha reaches the steps at my side and starts to climb.

"Come on," I hiss at the demon and grab him with both hands, forcing him upward.

With a higher-pitched moan, the demon eventually moves, and my eyes fix on Nakir. The emissary keeps glancing behind him, his posture tense and his features expectant.

My heartbeat's pounding now. Natasha reaches the top. And as soon as she does, Nakir disappears over the edge with her. I drive the demon faster ahead of me, scrambling up in his wake, my lungs heaving. And then I stare over the summit of the steps.

Natasha's standing in the middle of another grassy plateau. This one's smaller and sheltered by crumbling walls on two of its sides with the high overhang above. Nakir's poised a few feet from the edge, his gaze fixed on the blue expanse, one foot behind the other, his muscles taut and fingers gripped tightly around his spear.

I thrust the demon onto the plateau and shove one knee up just as a flash of light explodes before my eyes. A figure drops to the ground five yards before me. My whole body tenses with Natasha right between us.

23

Fire pumps through my veins, and I clamber to my feet, throwing myself across the grassy plateau toward Natasha. The newcomer swivels to face me, the blue sky behind. A woman in full armour – a golden helmet, boots, a sword at her back, and the same breastplate as Nakir. And I notice a familiar brightness in her smile, a fresh scent in my nose.

My shoulders relax, and I give a long exhale.

Eleth's features quickly harden. "Get under cover," she says and waves a muscled arm at the mountainside.

The demon tries to scramble away from me, back toward the steps we scaled, but I grip his arm and drag him in the direction of the stone spire. Natasha comes with me. And Nakir paces back and forth along the edge of the plateau, spear still held in his hand, posture as tense as ever.

"What are you doing here?" Eleth asks.

"We have information," I say, still hauling the demon toward the female emissary. Though the closer it gets, the more it tugs at my arm till I'm forced to remain ten feet away. "On the devil's plans."

Eleth grimaces. "I fear it will come to nothing," she says. "Michael knows you're here. Is hunting you as we speak."

With a drumming heart, I open my mouth at the same time as Eleth shifts her gaze to the demon. My lungs squeeze.

"Who's this?" she demands.

I clear my throat. "Someone who can help," I respond, trying to keep my voice level.

The demon huddles more closely behind me, stooping even lower under Eleth's gaze. I search her expression, but she gives no sign of recognition. Mammon's words come back to me … *Mustn't be noticed. Mustn't use our powers.*

I force myself on. "We must find Uriel," I say. "Or whichever angels are ready to fight."

Eleth shakes her head. "That's impossible. Michael's threatening every angel who acts with exile."

I blink. "Michael said that?"

"Not directly," she says, and then scorn laces her tone. "But his minions have made it clear enough. They've constructed this place for siege and are planning to rest up here and endure."

"That's crazy," Natasha says, the flames visible again in her eyes.

"It *is*," I say, my words tumbling out. "They can't not engage. The devil won't allow it. He's been planning this since before he was bound—"

"I agree with you," Eleth says, her intense gaze fixed on me, that faint smile back on her lips.

I shift my weight.

"But the pantheon has been fuelled by millennia of inaction," she goes on. "And the situation remains so finely balanced. Though some would act, every angel fears exile. With the devil released, without the strength of the pantheon behind you, it would mean certain death."

She smiles grimly, and my fingers clench, my ribs squeezing with the darkness blooming inside.

Eleth takes a step toward me. "No angel is going to want to meet with you," she says. "It is simply too risky."

Nakir stops his pacing and swivels to face us from the

plateau edge. "Unless we don't seek out a single Malakh," he says. "We address them all."

Eleth spins, and I swallow, my mouth dry.

"All of them?" I find myself asking.

Eleth pauses and then turns back. "The fortress meeting ground," she says, her voice an urgent whisper. "If we were able to reach it before Michael, we could summon the entire pantheon and ensure your information gets out."

I stare back at her. "But that would mean your exile, surely?" I say.

She holds my gaze awhile and then nods. "Perhaps," she says, her grim smile widening. "But I am decided, and we will need to move fast to get you an audience."

Nakir stands straighter. "I will lead," he says, his gaze fixed on Eleth, a pained expression on his face. "You follow behind."

He paces to the corner of the small plateau and then scales the surface of the spire in huge strides. I track his progress, the path forming in my mind – a mixture of blocks and tree roots – all the way up to the overhang above our heads.

"Let us go," Eleth says, urging me forward.

I take a breath and force the demon up after Nakir, keeping right behind him. Now sandwiched between emissaries front and back, the demon moans less and moves along faster. And we climb.

Nakir's route takes us up to another plateau above the first, and then to the top of a wall that runs out from the spire. We end up first snaking away from the pool we came from and then back toward it, continuing to navigate the walls and steps across and up the near-vertical mountainside.

We reach the bottom of a flat stone incline that butts up to the mountainside and slopes up and away from us. It's thirty yards wide, reaches twenty high, and Nakir starts to climb it while Eleth appears at my shoulder. She turns and points up the sheer surface of the spire to somewhere almost directly above.

"There it is," Eleth says. "If we can get up there, we can summon your audience."

I follow her pointing finger. The spire ends at some kind of ridge, well over fifty feet above our heads, and Nakir's sloping surface leads up to a series of massive steps that zig and zag up to the ridge.

Natasha and I hurry up the slope, the demon scrabbling between us with Eleth behind. By the time we're a third of the way up, Nakir's almost at the top. He peers over the edge and then darts back out of sight, gripping the incline tightly with both hands, his face ashen white. My heart pounds as Nakir thrusts his spear toward us, pointing behind us and to the side.

Eleth is already moving. She bounds down the rest of the sloping surface and hurries along the top of a narrow path at the base, in the direction of his spear, directly toward the vertical mountainside.

I throw myself after her, my adrenaline firing, and slide down the sloped surface as if it were a pitched rooftop, merely a free-running practice with the priest at my side. Gripping the demon's arm, my feet hit the bottom a fraction before Natasha's, and I shove the demon in front of me. We scramble toward Eleth and the surface of the spire. The ridge is still well over fifty feet above us.

"We need to climb," Eleth says. And I follow her gaze up the cliff face.

There are no walls, no sets of steps. Just sheer fucking rock with the tiny corners of stone blocks, arches, and columns jutting out of it along with the web of tree roots. My stomach goes cold.

"And we have to go *now*," Nakir says, arriving breathless at Eleth's side.

The demon quivers wildly, his whole body vibrating. He shakes his head violently. Nakir dumps his spear and goes to grab him, but I dart between them.

"No!" I say and thrust my hand at the emissary's chest.

"No ... Your touch will make him scream all the way. We'll attract every angel in the vicinity."

Nakir just stares back at me, and I scan the rock face, the network of protruding roots and stone ledges between us and the ridge.

"Go on either side of him." I say, motioning to Eleth and Nakir. "It's the best we can do."

Eleth leads us this time, Nakir right behind, forcing the demon in between. And they climb. The demon whimpers with every contact against tree root and stone, but he keeps moving upward, his arms shaking. Nakir remains a couple of feet from his side.

I push Natasha ahead of me and begin climbing at the rear. Somehow Eleth finds a route up the mesh of stones. It criss-crosses back and forth along the mountainside, and steadily we creep toward the ridge.

But the higher we get, the vaster the expanse below my feet, and the stronger the gusts of wind, the more they pull at my body. My heart pounds, and I have to focus hard on the jutting blocks and roots just to keep climbing.

Halfway up the cliff face, my foot slips off a broken arch, and I can't help looking down. Again, the breath congeals in my chest. The tapering cliff face descends into nothingness, just an expansive blue and clouds below. The countless walls, steps, and plateaus look minuscule when compared to the spire itself; and down to the side, maybe two hundred feet below, is our tiny pool, surrounded by grass, stone, and then nothing but air.

"*Jake,*" Natasha calls from a couple of feet above me.

I blink, grip the roots tighter, and force my head up.

She's staring down at me.

"It's okay," she says, her voice soft. "I'm here. We'll make it."

Her own hands quiver, her face is pale, and still she smiles. I barely manage a smile back.

She climbs again, and I continue up just behind her,

concentrating again on the rocky handholds while keeping her in my peripheral vision.

Twenty-five feet to go to the ridge. My arms ache, lactic acid etching out my veins, and my breath comes in spurts now, my ribs throbbing with each inhalation. Natasha's slowing down, too. Hardly moving. I struggle on.

Fifteen feet. The demon whimpers louder at my side. I turn my head. He's frozen on the cliff face, his head cowering between his raised arms. Nakir and Eleth have stopped also, both staring upward. I don't bother following their gaze since the glow from the ridge is creeping into the top of my vision, the heat already stinging the crown of my head and my heart hammering in my chest.

"Hang on!" I yell and throw myself up the rock face. I climb fast above them, trying to make it look like they're chasing me.

Ten feet. The blasts of wind are like hands trying to swat me from the cliff face, and it feels as if my entire body's going to give out. Sweat pools on my temples, my rib feels like it's on fire, and my fingers are shaking so much that they can barely hold the blocks and tree roots. I grit my teeth, channel the energy in my core, and grip harder. I focus fiercely on the top, hauling myself further up through the viscous air.

Five feet to the ridge. The heat scorches my forehead, the light burns my retinas, and more of the fire dies in my chest, the fresh glow like a blanket on my emotions. I'm forced to shut my eyes and climb blindly. My arm flails upward, my fingers desperately searching.

There. The ridge above me. I tense every muscle in my body, bend my entire focus on the flames at my core, and with a strangled yell, heave myself over the edge.

I lie there panting, the light streaming through my closed eyelids. The glow suffuses my insides, the wind caressing my skin. My insides feel bathed in peace, the pain a memory. I force myself to roll over and clamber to my feet. With my legs shaking, I open my eyes.

I'm standing halfway along another plateau, but a massive one. Almost two hundred yards wide, half as deep, and made of the customary grey stone. Behind me, the curved ridge gives way to nothingness with boulders dotted around the edge like broken ramparts. The plateau's three other sides are made of sheer rock, a set of massive doors carved into the cliff face before me, many hundreds of feet high. And in between stands the major source of the light, fifty yards away.

The archangel Michael.

As before, he's like the sun. My eyes burning, I squint into the brilliance till it gradually dims a fraction, and his colossal form appears out of the brightness. Three feet higher than a normal man and significantly broader, his muscled body resembles a gigantic marble statue, its colours and hues shifting from mother-of-pearl to white every instant. His face changes features from young to old and back again, and behind him stretch the vast arcs of yellow wings made up of a million butterflies. A billion.

To his sides stand twelve more angels, six on each flank. Identically muscled forms. Identical glowing radiance. And they all hover there, immobile, many of them with swords already drawn, as if they've been waiting for an age.

I scan their faces, my insides tightening. I don't recognise a single bloody one of them.

The angels fan out to surround me, moving entirely silently, golden boots sliding across the smooth stone. Eleth and Nakir appear at the top of the ridge with the demon, who scurries a dozen feet further along the edge before cowering behind one of the boulders. The emissaries dart to either side of him, standing there as guardians behind the semicircle of surrounding angels.

I scramble several steps away in the opposite direction, putting some distance between us all, and end up near the middle of the massive space, ten feet from the edge. Natasha stumbles to my side, breathing hard.

Michael glows on from the centre of the semicircle, impervious while the other angels stare at me, their beautiful features as sharp as blades. The void deepens inside, and I scan their expressions for signs of hurt, of rage, trying desperately to discern if they know what happened in hell. But they just hold my gaze, their faces still, their eyes burning into mine.

I try to swallow, forcing saliva down my parched throat. Then, with heartbeat racing, I channel the remaining fire up my chest, tense my arms, and open my mouth.

"I know I'm not welcome here!" I yell.

The wind carries much of the sound away. No one speaks. No one moves.

I force myself on. "But I've got a message for you—"

"Child, can you even conceive of your hypocrisy?" Michael demands. And as before, the words echo from every direction, his lips unmoving, his features still hidden behind the marble countenance.

Every one of the other angels in the semicircle jabs their sword point toward me in perfect harmony, and the movement's like a punch to my sternum.

I take a quick breath. Flames build in my torso, and I still my thoughts to peel back the veil. Though the calm weighs heavily, I channel my energy, imagine the river of fire like a spinning vortex at my core, and drive the energy up my throat.

"I'm here to say that you must face the devil!" I yell in the priest's command voice. And this time, the words echo back off the stone walls, rebounding all around me. "You can't just sit this out and hide!" I go on. "It's what the devil wants. He'll just grow ever more powerful!"

Still the angels remain silent as my words ebb and die.

"He's got a plan for it," I say. "And I can tell you the devil's scheme!"

The angels simply stare at me. And there's no sign of the massive doors opening, of wings beating. No new sound or movement.

I squeeze my shoulders, ball my fists, tense my neck, and shout the words even louder. "And I can tell you what Satan's going to do!"

The sound of my voice rebounds around the plateau. Once. Twice ... And finally, there's a change. Several of the angels shift backward and begin to scan the blue expanse beyond the plateau. Others gaze upward, their heads tilted, while Michael keeps his eyes on me.

And that's when I hear it – the distant sound of flapping, of wing beats, getting ever louder. My head snaps up, and the haze of light grows above me.

24

Dozens of angels come. Male and female. Floating down, wings outstretched, armour gleaming, swords strapped to their backs, butterflies flitting all around them. They land on the stone plateau behind Michael and his cordon of allies. The resulting glow's so bright that I shrink back, the heat searing my skin. So many of them. Maybe a hundred in total.

Natasha stands poised by my side while the demon cowers even lower behind his boulder, twenty feet further along the lip of the plateau. Eleth and Nakir press closely on either side of him, behind the growing mass of angels. I glance from face to face, and their perfect features remain as hard as rock.

Natasha leans in. "At least some of these must know about us in hell," she breathes, her voice shaky.

I nod, my adrenaline racing again. The void is pooling deeper around my insides as I anchor my feet and prepare to be rushed.

But none of them approach. No one speaks. Michael remains there at the head of them all, statuesque in his marble form, a colossus in front of the soaring stone doors.

I blink, and then it strikes me.

"He can't tell them about the devil's release," I whisper

back with a nod at Michael. "It'd mean admitting that the last two thousand years of their rule, his rule, has all been as the devil intended."

Still the angels remain poised, and I step forward, searching their mass for Uriel. But there's no sign.

I fuel the fire in my chest. "You have to fight—" I start.

"And *this* is your hypocrisy," Michael says, his voice echoing around us. "You previously desired nothing more than to rip down the pantheon. And now you ask for our help?"

My eyes go wide, and my legs tremble. Father Thomas. I glimpse him at my side when we first faced Michael. And I hear his words again, his vision for humanity liberated.

"This is why we must remain the sun, the inspiration," Michael says, his voice raised to his audience all around. "Compassionate, transcendent. We cannot involve ourselves in the fears and desires of humankind without eventually becoming what we deplore." Then he shifts his gaze back to Natasha and me. "Hypocrisy becomes inevitable."

My insides squeeze, and I can't help shaking my head. He blazes brighter, the heat scorching. And this time, when my mouth opens, the words evaporate from my tongue.

"I'm not entirely sure about that," an unfamiliar voice says.

A hush of surprise arises from the pantheon as I search out the sound of the voice. A single angel steps from the mass to the side of Michael and pads through the cordon.

He's male with curls of blond hair, green eyes, and the same flawless symmetry in his features, the same perfectly muscled form. He wears silver armour over his chest and shoulders and, instead of a weapon, he carries a small bunch of something between his fingers. I do a double take.

Grapes?

He pops one into his mouth and ambles in our direction across the middle of the semicircular plateau. His gaze isn't on me; it's trained on Natasha, and his eyes sweep up and down her figure, one side of his lips forming a thin smile. With each step he takes toward us, his glow becomes more intense. The sweat breaks out across my forehead. His presence has every one of my nerves tingling, and my breath comes quicker. Natasha flushes at my side and moistens her lips. The demon whimpers from behind his boulder.

The angel stops a few paces in front of Natasha to stare at her, his head at an angle. "I don't know," he says, his words slow and easy. "There may be some humans worth saving."

Angels titter behind Michael's cordon, voices indistinct, their attention entirely on the new angel now. I stand rooted, forgotten.

The angel starts to circle us, his gaze still fixed on Natasha at my side. The heat intensifies as he spirals incrementally.

"Haniel."

Michael's voice. A faint tone of admonishment.

The angel – Haniel – shrugs. "I'm only saying that some things may be worth preserving," he says.

His eyes never leave Natasha, and the smile grows wider across his mouth. She remains still, her hands clenched at her sides, staring straight ahead. The fire rises at the core of me, and I turn on the angel.

"This is no joke," I snap.

Haniel ceases his circuit at my shoulder, Natasha on my other side. He swivels to face me for the first time.

"I'll have you know that I take this kind of thing very … seriously," he says in a mock-sombre tone, which prompts louder tittering from behind the cordon. Then he reaches out a finger toward me, touches my shoulder, and pushes.

It's the merest movement, yet the shove sends me spinning away from Natasha, my limbs flailing and head reeling. I dart my hands out and stumble to a halt five yards from her far side.

Haniel begins to circle Natasha now without me in the middle, shark-like, continuing to press ever closer. He stops behind her for a moment, his gaze raking her back. Then he glances across at me and raises his eyebrows.

Energy flashes down my arms, my fingers curling. And the angels continue to chuckle behind the cordon. I loosen my hands, take a breath, and drag my eyes from Haniel. I drive the energy up my throat again.

"You have to listen to me!" I yell and sweep my gaze across the group of angels.

Haniel continues circling Natasha.

"The devil's plans," I go on, focusing on Michael at the head of the cordon. "They're already in motion."

Still the angels keep their focus on Haniel, on his circling of Natasha, many of them laughing out loud now. The void pulls again at my insides, so heavy.

I tense my chest and force out the words. "Something is coming imminently! I know this because I was captured, and I escaped!"

Some of the tittering dies down, murmurs taking its place. Several of the angels turn to face me now.

"The devil is enacting the book of Revelation," I say quickly. "His demons have managed to elect a Puritan leader. They're setting up this man as the Antichrist. Their plan is to spark a global religious war to pit the entirety of humanity against each other. With this story, think of the belief he will generate, the power …"

My words trail off as I can't shut out Haniel's purring at my side. "While the world goes to hell, wouldn't you prefer a life in heaven, my dear?" he says to Natasha.

She turns to look at him for the first time, her arms wrapped tightly around her chest. And when the words come out, they're laced with fire.

"A war is coming that will embroil the whole world," she says, her eyes fully aflame now. "And at this time, *this* is what you want?"

Haniel shrugs. "Sometimes, time is the only luxury we have," he says, his layered tones like ringing bells.

My shoulders tense, and I push myself to continue. "The Antichrist will create such hatred with his war, and he'll claim to see the devil in everything and everyone that opposes him," I shout at the angels. "*That's* how they'll build belief in their master." I stab a finger in the air. "And then when the war rages, and when his demons walk the earth, humanity will see it as the apocalypse prophesied in Revelation. It'll make the devil even more powerful. And they're starting it right *now*."

Haniel ceases his circuit in front of Natasha to tower over her. My train of thought dies.

"Time ..." he says, his tone musing. "How would you like to spend yours, my dear?"

Natasha looks the angel up and down. "I will fight," she growls, her voice shaking. "I would rather burn."

My heart beats faster.

"Haniel, please," Michael says from behind him.

"Indeed, dear brother," Haniel says and bows low before Natasha.

Her eyes continue to blaze.

Then he glances at me. "Maybe I was mistaken," he says with a wink and pivots back to the angels with a wicked grin. "It seems such a shame."

The angels laugh louder than ever. And the fire burns higher inside me, the energy pulsing in my veins and up my throat.

"You have to do *something!*" I yell, my gaze scanning all the angels now, searching their faces. "Revelation ... you could use the power of the story against him still, cast the devil back into his fiery pit."

Some angels remain focused on me. But most shift their attention to Haniel as he slips back through the cordon. Several slap him on the back as he rejoins the masses. The flames continue to smoulder inside.

"The devil's plan ... You don't believe me?" I demand, my pulse racing and my fingers clenched so hard that the nails chew the skin on my palms.

I glance at Eleth on the far side of the cordon, still guarding the cowering demon. She's gazing back at me, her eyes shining. And while visions of their likely exile swirl through my mind, the fire burns on amid the blooming dark.

I swivel back to Michael, to the angels, and take a deep breath. "Ask *him*!" I yell and jab my finger at the tiny demon.

He blubbers, shrinking ever lower behind the rock, twenty feet behind me and to the side. Still the angels don't react.

"He knows the devil's plans. He was there when I was captured!" I continue.

Finally, the tittering quietens a fraction and more of the angels gaze back at me, their perfect brows furrowed.

I force the words out. "He knows because ..." I yell. "Because he's a *demon*!"

The laughing stops entirely. Almost all the angels are staring at me now. Then they shift their gazes toward the demon, toward the boulder he's cowering behind. A few shouts ring out.

In the broken silence, the demon's snivelling grows louder. Then higher ... harsher. It morphs into a strange cackling. I spin. He rises slowly from behind the boulder, his hands around his belly, guffawing with laughter. He pads toward me around the lip of the plateau, swaying as he walks, as if he's drunk.

More shouts ring out. Several of the angels press right up to the cordon, their eyes trained on the diminutive figure as the heat builds. All the while, the demon makes straight for me. I swivel back to face Michael. He remains standing entirely still in his marble form, his glow so bright. The angels' exclamations grow ever louder.

"Please!" I shout and point frantically at the demon, my pulse like a train behind my ear. "Ask him, he's here to—"

Michael darts forward a step, his form blazing red. "He's here because the devil willed it!" he hisses at me. And the wave of heat's like being struck by a wall. The breath flees my body, and I almost go down on my knees.

Michael's features shine through the marble veneer – gleaming armour, gargantuan muscles, his dark angular face. His outline blazes, and I have to avert my eyes from the brightness.

"The devil let you escape, knowing you would bring a minion straight here," he says. "To see the state of our defences, our numbers, and then he will go right back and inform his master!"

My gaze finds the demon, who makes a show of scanning his surroundings as he approaches – the plateau walls, the stone doors – leaning back, pot belly thrust forward.

"Your defences?" the demon says, his voice unrecognisable – playful, taunting. "You think *that's* why I'm here?"

An angel leaps toward the diminutive figure from the edge of the cordon. He covers ten yards in the blink of an eye, his blade thrust forward. I shepherd Natasha back a step while the demon spins away from the strike and then continues to twirl toward me, turning the movement into some kind of dance.

"Easy, tiger," he says, wagging his finger.

None of the other angels move. The one who attacked glances at Michael, unsure. The archangel remains stock-still, his rigid gaze fixed on me, and the attacking angel retreats to the cordon.

The demon takes his place at my side, hands on his hips and eyes shining. A chill climbs my neck.

"No, no, no. Your politics are *far* more interesting," he says, scanning the mass of angels behind the cordon. "To see the web of fantasy you're spinning yourselves. Satan will receive the tidings gladly."

Michael swivels to face the angels behind him, his wings stretching high into the air. "You see, brothers and sisters," he calls out, his head turning to scan every face. He pauses an instant on Eleth and Nakir by the edge of the plateau.

"*This* is what happens when one sullies oneself in the quagmire of anger, of desire … in the morass and hypocrisy of mortal plans," Michael says. "We cannot engage without losing our clarity. Anything we did would risk perpetuating that which we might wish to change."

I search the faces more desperately now, but still I see no sign of Uriel or the other angels we saw in hell, though the glare is so bright.

Michael swivels back around and turns his gaze on me again. "The devil achieved freedom undoubtedly *because* of those who meddled in base plots," he says, his melodic voice suddenly replaced by a low rumble.

And despite his heat, a shiver runs through me.

Michael raises his arms at his sides. "No, we must not fight," he says, standing there, alabaster-white again, statuesque. "We must remain removed, transcendent. *All* of us." His massive wings stretch up to either side of him, his glow intensifying once more, almost too painful to look at. "The devil will need us. He knows that the shadow cannot exist without the light."

The embers spark again inside me. And the demon is laughing wildly now, his arms holding his shaking belly. Several of the angels step toward him through the cordon with swords raised.

Michael shakes his head. "We will not be baited," he says. "We will return to ancient times. We endured then, and we can endure now."

The fire blazes higher inside me, and energy seizes my throat. "But it's not the same!" I find myself yelling.

The demon nods at my side and jabs his thumb toward me. "The kid is right," he says.

I lurch a half step away from him.

"You think you can survive sheltered here?" the demon says to Michael, the lightness in his voice gone. "The world is primed like dry tinder, people *clamouring* to believe. Fear of him will spread like flame through every country." The demon hunches over and sweeps his hand across the space in front of him. "And with a population fifty times larger than when the devil last walked this earth, his power will become greater than you can possibly imagine. He will reign forever. While he'll keep you as barely a memory."

My gaze finds Natasha, whose jaw clenches and body shakes as the demon speaks. And a new silence spreads through the angels. Faces grow paler, auras diminished.

Michael remains unmoving, poised at their head, his face marble-like, barely visible in his glow. "Our role is to remain the light, the sun," he says. "While the devil tempts men's hearts, *we* will be their inspiration."

Natasha marches forward a step, her fingers squeezed together. "But how can you be an inspiration and do *nothing*?" she shouts and rips the crucifix necklace from her neck before holding it out in a shaking hand.

This time, Michael turns on her and leans forward, his face shining. Natasha retreats again, her head bowed with fingers grabbing her temples, the archangel rooting around in her mind. I grip her arm and hold her steady.

"And this is *your* hypocrisy," Michael says. "You ask us to intervene, to risk our lives and legacies, yet what have *you* done since the devil's release?"

Natasha stands there, her lips trembling, and the angels remain still at Michael's back. The demon steps behind Natasha and me, placing a hand on our shoulders.

"You're wasting your time, friends," he says.

I turn and shove him off. My hand burns with the contact, so I yank it away, the scent of sulphur now so strong in my nose.

I stand there, blinking.

His form has morphed completely. He stands as high as me, though his posture's bent almost fully over, animal-like. The skin of his face is cleaved into innumerable shapes like dried mud, and his tattered suit barely exists, hanging off him in strips.

"Oooh, touchy," the demon says, his voice crackling and his mouth widening in a strange grin. Then he stoops down and presses his bare hand to the ground. I hear no whimpering as he touches the stone, no shrieking. He just gazes up at me with that same grin on his face and winks.

I stumble backward, the darkness plunging deeper inside me.

Angry shouts ring out from a few angels. Several stalk toward us from Michael's cordon, all steadily closing in on Natasha and me in the middle of the plateau, on the demon at our side. Again, the growing heat singes my forehead and neck.

The demon raises his cracked hands. "Woah, woah," he says, the lightness back in his sing-song tone. The butterflies coalesce behind him, forming smaller iridescent wings behind his shoulders, and he pads backward toward the plateau's edge. "I don't want to go *too* early. Don't want to be missing out on any of the fun."

I remain still as the angels continue their advance, pressing in as a semicircle around us. The demon continues to dance backward till he's only five feet from escape off the plateau edge. The angels cease their approach, still over twenty yards from him on all sides, and my gaze snaps back to the demon.

I'm much closer – only seven or eight feet from where he's standing.

The demon flicks his tongue at me and grins manically. The fire burns in my veins, the veil so thin before my senses.

I channel the energy down my legs and lean toward the demon, preparing to leap and grab him—

And then I stop, the darkness dwarfing the flames as Michael's words come back to me ... *Anything we did would risk perpetuating that which we might wish to change*. I'd leap, miss the demon, and incite his escape instead, proving Michael's point even more than I already have.

The demon's staring at me, not at the angels, and despite

the void, I wrench my gaze away. I force myself to face Michael again, to face the angels around him. I raise a hand and focus on the dwindling fire within.

"The old balance is gone, and the devil's not interested in maintaining it!" I bellow, my voice straining. "He wants you weak!"

Several of the angels glance in my direction.

"It's true! He's right!" the demon croons from behind me.

I tune out his voice. "The Antichrist will control the story, and the devil will have total dominion!" I say. "In the end, you'll be forced to intervene to avoid extinction. You have to strike now!"

Slowly, Michael shifts his gaze to me. "This is beyond you, child," he says. "You are nothing but the devil's puppet."

I turn from him to gaze at the angels at his sides instead. My shoulders tense again, but as I open my mouth, Michael speaks directly inside my head.

"And what do you think my brethren would do if they knew of your role in the devil's escape? You do not think they'd tear you apart?" his voice asks.

His gaze burns into mine, and I stutter, my throat raw.

Michael advances on us, on the demon, with a slow, unyielding pace. He pushes past the angels pressing in around us. The horde falls in behind him, and the heat continues to intensify. It feels like my skin's blistering. I anchor my feet, holding firm.

A hand grips my forearm. Natasha. I search her face, already picturing darkness, the void within.

It's not there.

Instead, her eyes are narrowed and burning, focused on the angels and shining with fury.

"Let's go," she spits.

Still, I don't move, my gaze back on the angels, final persuasions whirling through my mind while the darkness builds inside me, the monsters cavorting in the deep once more.

Natasha pulls on my arm again. "We're wasting time here," she says.

"Yes, come ... come!" the demon says from the plateau's edge. He's motioning us excitedly toward him.

Natasha continues to pull, and I let myself be drawn. She leads me ten feet further along the edge of the plateau from the demon, thirty feet from where we scaled the sheer surface. The angels continue to advance. I can feel the heat searing my back through my clothes.

I peer over the edge, and again my heart's in my mouth. The rock face plunges down for what again seems like forever, dwarfed in the expansive blue, speckled with islands of white. And *there* ... Almost directly below us, the tiny plateau we arrived on, the pool right in the middle. It juts out of the sheer wall. Two hundred fucking feet down.

"It's been a pleasure!" the demon yells.

He's standing right on the cliff edge, grinning at me. Then he leans forward, preparing to leap.

"Stop them!" an angel yells.

I grip Natasha's hand, my pulse racing, as wings from a dozen angels thump the air behind me. The heat blazes the back of my neck, and with the fire burning inside me, I peel the veil back in an instant ...

Time slows, and the shimmering world floods my senses – the gusts of wind pressing at my body, the thickness in the air, the plateau hard beneath my feet. And along with the void, I can feel the angels darting toward me from behind us – their driving limbs, their raging anger.

"Enjoy hell!" the demon yells, the words distorted in slowed time. And he flings himself forward into the open air.

Beyond him, my eyes find Eleth for an instant, standing further along the plateau's edge. Her jaw's set, her features tight.

The angels continue to close in, swords drawn and arms stretched toward us. I can almost feel their blades carving up my spine, and my heart batters my ribs.

I yank Natasha's hand and yell, "Jump!" as I haul us off the cliff. I focus on the sensation of the surrounding air, on its thickness and its fluidity, just as a shouted word detonates in my skull.

"Hold!"

Michael's voice.

Natasha leaps with me, and we tumble through the air, the heat diminishing against my back, the glow abating.

The demon soars downward with his wings. Natasha's plummeting to my other side. And the pool's still nearly two hundred feet below me but approaching fast.

I still my thoughts, focusing everything on the energy inside, on keeping the veil peeled back, on thickening the surrounding air. It pushes up against us. Cradles us. Slows our descent ... But only a fraction.

My teeth clench, and I try to imagine Father Thomas at my side, the old man curbing our fall, suspending gravity.

So fucking hard.

One hundred feet. The air pummels my legs and chest. My rib wails while the wind howls past my ears. All too fast still.

Again, I bend all my will to my focus, to imagining myself as the feather, to believing we can float. Yet the void's still there, memories coming of Michael's words to me, of the demon laughing, all of it pulling at my concentration, dampening the fire.

Fifty feet. I grip Natasha's hand so tightly my fingers ache as I concentrate fiercely on my care for her, on the need to protect her. The flames burn brighter again, the shimmering world intensifying – the sensation of the barrelling air, the gusting wind. And finally, our fall starts to slow.

Twenty feet. The water so close. I pull on Natasha's arm, yanking her upward, and in turn, I smash myself harder into the surface of the pool.

25

EVERYTHING HURTS, every nerve end screaming. Waves of agony course through me, and I grit my teeth against each one. I'm lying on my side, cold stone beneath my hip, and my brain crashes with each painful surge.

Slowly, recent memories trickle in.

My eyes fly open, and I force my head up. I'm back in the church, curled up on the ground by the drainage pools. Natasha's there, a few feet away. I swivel, my pulse thumping.

The corner's empty. No Puritans. Just walls and floor covered in soot, an acrid scent heavy in the air. Plus, a scraping noise – something being dragged across stone – along with the sound of approaching footsteps.

I try to rise, but a tremor runs through me like a million electric shocks. It leaves each one of my limbs shaking.

Natasha climbs to her hands and knees, her head down between her arms. Her shoulders quiver, and she screws up her features. She bites her lip and then meets my gaze.

"God, I bet we both look pretty awful now," she rasps.

I can only nod. And again, I try to get my hands underneath me. My arms tremble, and my body shakes violently. I collapse back to the ground, and the scraping sound draws ever nearer.

"Come on," Natasha says and grabs me by the shoulders before hauling us both to our feet.

I swoon and nearly fall. Natasha grips my arm and tugs me behind a corner wall, propping me up against the stonework. I take a long breath. The electric shocks diminish a fraction, and I force myself to peer around the edge and scan the church interior.

It's much emptier than before. Only fifty or so Puritans, spread throughout, sweeping up the ash with cloths and brooms. The thick plumes of smoke are gone, replaced by a haze of dust, and the scraping sound's coming from the nearest Puritan. The grey-robed man drives his broom down the side aisle toward us, twenty feet away.

I duck back out of sight, my eyes on the rays of sun shining through the windows on the far side of the church – the opposite side from where they shone before we left this place.

I blink. That must mean four or five hours have passed, even though we were in the heavenly realm for only a fraction of that time. My chest tightens, my rib smarting, and I scour the church's shadowy corners and alcoves.

No sign of angels or emissaries. No one following us for our crimes. Yet.

"You okay?" Natasha asks at my side.

The fire's still burning in her eyes, the familiar distance absent for now, the darkness not yet taken hold. I nod and then clench my jaw as another wave of shocks seizes me, though it's weaker. I lean down and grip my knees as it passes. Natasha starts off along the wall toward the exit.

"Nat, wait!" I blurt, straightening fast.

But she's already pacing out of the corner, into the rear aisle of the church, and directly in front of the guy with the broom. He stops and stares, his mouth open. She keeps going and heads for the doors.

I scramble to catch up, my legs shaking, the sound of my stumbling feet all too obvious against the flagstone floor. Nearby Puritans stop and gawk. Then more of them, further back. I keep my gaze averted, focusing only on the doors up ahead. A constant stream of Puritans is passing in and out, some with basins of water and others with cleaning rags.

Natasha continues to stride on unchecked, the entrance only ten feet away now. An urgent whispering erupts somewhere behind us, the sound echoing around the stone interior. Its intensity grows louder, and a wiry Puritan darts toward her from the opposite corner of the church.

I start to run, straining to get ahead of her, when another wave of shocks grips my abdomen and squeezes my aching rib. I double up and then scramble onward, concentrating on placing one foot before the other.

Natasha meets the wiry Puritan at the doors.

"What are you doing?" he barks.

Natasha leans toward him with her jaw tight, fixing him with a fiery glare. Wiry Guy stands there, stock-still, as I lumber to her side. Then she pushes past the guy and out of the door, weaving around a man with a basin who's on his way inside.

The wiry Puritan starts and then swivels toward me, scanning my face, just as another stream of shocks courses up my body. I grimace and dip my head, going to follow Natasha. Then I end up face to face with the man with the basin. He's standing in the middle of the doorway, blocking it, his tub full of soapy water and a cleaning rag floating among the suds.

Wiry Guy slams a hand on my shoulder from behind. "I recognise you," he growls, and I hear the sound of hurried footsteps at my back.

Resisting the urge to shake off Wiry Guy's fingers, I reach out and grab the sodden cloth from the basin, tipping it downward in the process. Half of its contents splatters over the ground, soaking our feet and the surrounding stone in soapy water.

The basin holder darts back a step, and Wiry Guy snaps, "Watch it!" His grip on my shoulder loosens a fraction.

"So sorry," I say and dart to the side of Basin Guy before dropping the cloth in the air a foot or so in front of him.

With both hands occupied, he scrambles forward to catch the cloth in his basin. At the same time, I shoot my foot out, bumping his ankles together as they cross.

Basin Guy sprawls forward, his feet slipping and sliding on the soapy floor. He lets go of the basin to grab Wiry Guy, dumping the water all over him, and both of them go down in a heap.

I rush through the doorway, shove past a guy holding a pile of wrung cloths, and dash out onto the path.

The concrete's full of bustling Puritans with Natasha standing twenty feet further along, her eyebrow raised. She spins and strides away, leaving me a good distance behind, and I plunge into the crowd after her.

The space outside the church is almost as packed as it was going in. Many hundreds of Puritans spread out over the path, the grass of the park, and even the road beyond. Most of them stand or kneel facing the preacher, who's now camped himself twenty yards from the church wall on a small grassy rise.

"Be vigilant! Be watchful!" he shouts, his finger raised toward the sky. "The devil prowls around like a roaring lion, seeking those to devour!"

Pressing onward, the demon's words come back to me … *The world is primed like dry tinder. People clamouring to believe.* And while the electric shocks continue to diminish, the darkness grips my insides.

I hunch my neck and hasten on through the throng, my ears trained on the church at my back. Ahead of me, Natasha strides with her head up and her shoulders back in full bloody view of the entrance. Her gaze seems to be already fixed beyond the crowd, taking in the houses nearby and the

Docklands skyscrapers in the distance, the late afternoon sun glinting off their summits.

I search the surrounding rooftops for any sign of angels or demons. Then I open my mouth to yell at Natasha when a cry emanates from the church, only thirty feet behind.

"Brothers ... sisters, help us!"

I speed up and begin darting between Puritan groups while lowering my head even more. Natasha walks as tall as ever, her gaze still fixed ahead.

"A man and woman! Both trespassers! Both heathen!" the wiry Puritan shouts. "Stop them!"

I push past several young Puritan guys. The furthest one stares at me and blinks.

"Here!" he cries and clutches for my arm.

I spin away and end up bumping into another group. A few of them yell in surprise. The shouts intensify behind me, more people scrambling out of the way, and I weave toward the edge of the path. I grab up a handful of pebbles from the ground and then blunder on behind Natasha's striding form.

She reaches the end of the path, with me only five feet further back. The road is full of Puritans as well, many of them straining to see the preacher on the mound. But more of them are eyeing the crowd around us now, searching for the source of the commotion.

Natasha veers off and presses through the side of the crowd, east toward Docklands, taking us away from the main throng. The angry shouts continue at our backs, ever closer, and the edge of the crowd is only twenty feet ahead – the end of our cover.

I grab a small pebble and lob it high into the air, the arc taking it over the bulk of the crowd on the road, thirty feet to our side. Then I press on, head down, listening.

Nothing happens.

The shouts grow louder behind us. I lob another stone, pitching it a little further away. A few seconds later, a sharp cry of pain rings out from the main throng, followed by a shouted, "Hey!"

The yells become more heated behind me. Arguments about our location.

I launch the next stone and then the next, lobbing each one that bit higher, that bit further over the masses to our side. The sound of exclamations grows louder but more distant, our pursuing crowd following closely behind the path of outrage.

We break out of the mob, and Natasha continues stalking down the street but doesn't let up the pace. I hurry to catch up.

Beyond the park, the pavements border low houses, their walls dirty yellow brick. She passes the first junction, and then the second, but doesn't turn as she keeps pressing on toward East London.

After another corner, I grab her by the arm and bring her to a halt. "It's this way," I say, motioning to the junction behind us.

"Where?" she says.

"Home," I say.

She turns on me. "There is no home, Jake, not any more." Her hands go to her hips. "They know where we live. They know the church."

Darkness blooms wider inside. I shift my weight. "What about—"

"And we are not going to Poland, either," Natasha says. "I know that's what you were hoping, but you heard the demon. Nowhere will be safe, no community the devil will not terrorise." Her features harden. "And Michael was right. I cannot ask others to act while doing nothing."

The void deepens, a cavernous ocean in my chest. I push into the pain and take a step toward her. "Nat, we just brought a demon into heaven," I say, my voice low.

"Yes," Natasha says, and her lips form a twisted smile. "Hopefully it shook the angels up a bit."

I blink. "They might never act again," I say.

"They were not going to do anything *anyway*, Jake," she says, rage in her tone. "They are the only ones with the power to stop *him*, and they built themselves that ivory fucking tower." Then she shakes herself, nods, and calms her voice. "Maybe at least now, some will think twice."

I hold the silence as Natasha stares back at me.

"Do you have a plan?" I ask.

"No," she replies and swivels to face east. "But who knows? An opportunity may present itself."

Her grim smile returns, and she goes quiet, gazing into the distance again at the Dockland skyscrapers – the stalwarts of the financial centre of the city, half a mile or so away now, rays of sun still reflecting off their peaks. She tilts her head and continues to stare, and I glance from her to the towering buildings.

She's focused on one of the central skyscrapers, a giant lightning bolt fashioned out of steel and glass. And near the top, a floor extends out on all sides to form a giant platform, seventy or eighty yards wide, supposedly a cloud from which the bolt thunders down to the ground. And a spot of reflected sunlight shines like a beacon three-quarters of the way along the platform, tiny yet dazzling. I run through my memories of glimpsing that skyscraper when leaving the church.

My stomach goes cold.

"That light. It's not the sun. Is it?" I ask, a prickle climbing my spine – the sense of being watched.

"I do not think so," she says. "I noticed it outside the church, and it has not shifted at all as we've moved, whereas the other reflections have."

"You realise it's probably one of … them. Right?" I say. "An angel … or emissary. Sent to kill us."

She shrugs. "So? Much better to die here and now than drag it out, cooped up in some dark room as the world burns around us."

The fire's in her eyes, a mixture of abandon and fury in her voice. She turns to me. "Are you ready?"

I can only stare back, the priest's words resounding in my head ... *She'll be there for you before the end.*

Is this what he meant?

I take a slow breath and start down the road in the direction of the beacon. She falls in beside me and then leans her head toward mine.

"Plus, I am not letting you go up there on your own," she says. "You'd probably bungle it all and get captured again. You'd need rescuing."

My mouth opens as a wry grin forms at the corners of her lips. And for an instant, I find myself smiling too, the darkness retreating a little inside. We walk on toward the tiny point of dazzling light.

26

Ten minutes later, we reach Billingsgate Park, that massive public space that borders the luxury rises of the Docklands area. Entire groups of security guards patrol the edge now, scrutinising those passing over into the dominion of the crazy rich.

Natasha strides past the cordon, her posture erect and her chin up. Dressed in our casual clothes, we pace through the endless sections of lawns, trees, and stones with ornate paths and bridges in between. Escalators connect the ground-level paradise with a network of glittering shops and restaurants below. And security guards stand by metal detectors at each one.

A couple of nearby guards watch us intently as we pass, but they don't move. I glance over my shoulder, searching for … *there*. Three more guards, trailing us from the edge of the park but keeping their distance, maybe fifty yards behind.

We continue on, our pace steady, weaving our way past manicured flower gardens. My eyes find the skyscraper ahead with the beacon of light, still shining in the exact same location on its cloud-like platform. Clearly not a reflection. The building is only a hundred yards away now.

I scan the entrance. A sculpted glass fountain stands on a

grass island before it, encircled by a private road that butts up to the public space. And beyond the roundabout, a throng mills before the doors in shimmering cocktail dresses, ball gowns with ridiculous trains, and pristine evening suits. Seventy or so people crowd onto a bright red carpet. Some kind of members' club, opening for the early evening.

Security guards stand all around, five in a line along the border of the green space – between us and the club. More line the pavement ringing the roundabout, plus a few to either side of the queue. Their fitted jackets bulge with barely concealed guns.

"What now?" I whisper to Natasha.

"I don't know," she says with a shrug. "You're the master of this kind of thing. I have complete trust."

She continues to stride on, that wry smile back on her lips and the fire still burning in her eyes. More of the guards turn and stare as we approach. My gaze takes in the five standing along the park border, spaced ten yards apart. I head between the nearest two, the ones between us and the fountain.

We're only forty feet away when one of them moves to block us off.

Natasha waves at him. "Hi," she says, her tone light. "It's good to see you." She beams a wide grin.

The guard slows to a halt and stares quizzically. I wave too, lifting and opening both hands to show my lack of weapons. We get twenty feet from the roundabout before he reacts again and starts hurrying toward us.

I break out into a full run, sprinting for the gap between him and the nearest guard. Two more converge on me from either side of the roundabout, cutting us off in both directions. I plough straight on across the road, directly onto the central reservation. Then I vault the row of hedges and scramble around the glass fountain, heading toward the rear of the glittering crowd.

The queue's shaped like a wedge in front of the club's entrance, narrow at the front and forty feet wide at the back with ample space in between each person. Many of the guests parade between groups like peacocks.

Natasha runs behind. "You want … to join … the … *queue*?" she blurts between snatched breaths.

I jump the kerb on the far side of the central reservation just as the guards at the front of the queue start toward us. They skirt around the left and right edges of the tittering crowd, going to pincer us at the rear. Yet none of the guards hurry, none run, all well trained in avoiding panic.

Ten yards from the back of the queue, I slow to a jog. "It's only polite," I say to Natasha and scan the throng before me.

Several guests have turned in our direction.

"Just keep moving," I say over my shoulder before raising a hand. "Hello!" I yell to the crowd. "How you all doing?"

More of them turn and stare, dainty hands pressed to their chests, aghast. And the flanking guards scamper toward us along either side of the crowd while I plunge straight into the middle. The guests back away, expressions of shock and horror carved into immaculately made-up faces.

"It is so nice to finally be here!" I yell, striding on.

The guests continue to retreat, melting away to either side of us. They form a ten-foot blockade between us and the pincering guards on either flank.

"There's something you must see!" I say, glancing behind and waving those at the rear of the queue toward us.

None move, those at the back keeping their distance and leaving our path gaping wide for the pincering guards to follow.

"The lady and I have a treat for you," I say, raising my voice and motioning to Natasha as we press forward. "Something sponsored by the powers that be, something you wouldn't *believe*."

Natasha does a little spin. And finally, the guests form up behind us, curious looks on their faces, blocking off the path from the pincering guards.

"Watch closely!" I say, and we continue forward in our

bubble, guests following us on all sides, the entrance only twenty feet away now.

And it's extraordinary-looking. Sculpted entirely out of glass, it resembles the opening of a crystal cave, with channels of water that flow to either side of an overhang above our heads. In the middle stand two security devices, side by side: an X-ray scanner for bags and a metal detector for people, both coated with flowing glass, water trickling along rivulets down the sides of each one.

And they're the only way into the building.

A doorman in an evening suit and top hat supervises them, and he's currently assisting two ladies in matching orange dresses and four-inch heels. One's elderly with cheeks stretched to a plastic sheen, while a teenage version hovers at her shoulder. They're all three frozen in mid-movement – the young girl placing a clam-shaped bag onto the scanner conveyor belt while the older woman is being helped toward the metal detector – and all three staring at me.

I squeeze toward them through the crowd, my rib throbbing again, while yet another guard steps forward on the far side of the detector and positions himself directly in the way of the metal arch. Then he draws a huge taser gun, the type that packs enough juice to stop the heart.

I take a breath and hang back till Natasha reaches my shoulder. "Be ready to head straight through," I whisper, nodding toward the detector. "And whatever you do, keep moving."

The guard blocking it loads a cartridge into his taser and grips it down by his side. I stumble right up to the two women, who both stare at me, their eyes wide in horror.

"Such a pleasure to see you both here!" I say, reaching for the younger one's hand.

She whips her arm away with a high-pitched squeal, and the doorman lunges for me. He pushes himself between the women and reaches out to grasp my wrist.

I bare my teeth at the elderly woman and shout, "Boo!"

The lady shrieks. Her eyes roll back into her head, and her legs give way. The doorman retracts his grasping hand and dives behind her, catching her under the arms. However, the guard with the taser stands firm behind the detector.

I dart toward the girl. She's flapping her hands like she's trying to take off, and the taser guard's almost within touching distance of my side.

"It's okay," I say to her, raising both hands this time.

Then I start the count in my head, still my thoughts, and begin to peel back the veil, my focus fixed on my peripheral vision.

In slowed time, I catch a glimpse of the guard's coiling movement – leaning forward, knees bending, arm coming up. He dashes through the metal arch toward me, his taser raised. I spin away from him, and the detector gives an ear-splitting whine.

I scamper around the young girl and leap for the X-ray machine, shoving the clam handbag aside before clambering up onto the conveyor belt. The rubber strip disappears into a square tunnel at my feet, a yard across.

The guard flies after me and barges past the flailing girl. I grab the top of the machine and thrust myself feet first through the aperture, sliding along the conveyor as far as I can on my back.

My heart stops. My body goes rigid. The channel's much narrower than I thought, much longer, much darker, almost coffin-like. It's as if the sides are squeezing in on me, the top pressing down, memories coming of being trapped in the chest as a child, locked in for hours. The end of the tunnel's barely at my calves, the belt so fucking slow.

I wriggle forward desperately, wrenching my shoulders from side to side. The end of the belt's still several feet away. And beyond the veil, I can sense the guard leaning down toward the aperture. His breathing is fast, and I can smell his cologne.

As I struggle harder, my pulse thumps violently and my

rib throbs while my brain screams lunacy. I can feel the guard resting his arm on the belt, lining up the taser shot. And though the compulsion seizes me to scramble for the exit, I force myself to relax. To hold still in the darkness. To slow time and reach out with my senses …

I hear a faint squeak as the guy presses his finger to the trigger – a quick inhalation and then quiet as he holds his breath. I grit my teeth and throw myself to the side of the tunnel, just as a loud popping noise erupts behind me. Then I feel a sting of pain as something barb-like spears my hip.

But I hear no crackling sound and feel no rush of electricity. I rip out the single probe and hold myself pressed to the wall, making sure to avoid the second one. Finally, the darkness recedes, and the curved ceiling of the lobby comes into view. I scramble off the end of the conveyor belt.

Behind me, the doorman's still struggling to right the elderly woman while the guard with the taser is darting back toward the far side of the metal detector twenty feet away. Natasha's already through the arch, hurrying in my direction.

I barrel straight across the lobby. It's thirty yards square with a reception desk cut into the side wall, and a bank of five chrome lifts ahead, a bellboy before each one. The space is full of shocked guests, most of them staring at us and their expressions varying from curious to alarmed.

I hear the click of a door opening to my side, along with the sound of hurrying footsteps.

"Four more guards," Natasha shouts from my shoulder. "Coming from the right."

I keep my eyes on the lifts. Three are closed. Two open, each one with guests already inside.

"Twenty feet away," Natasha says, speaking quickly. "Fifteen."

The nearest lift's full of sparkling dresses, half a dozen pairs of nervous eyes staring back at us. Its doors start to close, and at least ten guests stand in between.

"That one!" I say and jab my finger at the lift.

I spring toward it, channelling whatever energy remains into my legs. The doors continue to shut, and I bounce into a lady in a green bodice dress, grabbing the handbag off her shoulder.

"I'll return it!" I say and hurl it through the crowd toward the closing doors.

It barely squeezes between them but breaks the beam. The chrome panels open instantly.

"Ten feet!" Natasha shouts from behind.

I scramble onward, the guests before me stumbling out of my way. The lift doors are starting to close again, and I lunge inside, a guest already screaming.

I spin around. Natasha clatters in after me as three guards bear down on us through the crowd.

Natasha jabs her finger on the close button while I reach down and toss the handbag back out of the lift.

"Please thank her for it!" I yell at the guards, just as the doors slide shut in their faces.

27

The lift shoots upward while tinkling jazz plays from surround speakers. The scent of flowers fills my nose, so strong it makes my stomach turn. In front of me, the doors shine like mirrors, reflecting six guests cowering by an identical set of doors at the rear. All of them are glancing between Natasha and me, their mouths clamped shut and expressions terrified.

"We will be gone in just a moment," Natasha says, a wan smile pulling at her lips. "Do not worry."

I shift my weight, and she turns to me, rocking playfully from toe to heel.

"Did you know?" she asks.

"What I was going to do?" I say. "No."

She snorts a laugh. "And now?"

"Not a clue," I say.

She shakes her head. "Amazing …"

I scrunch my eyes shut and then swivel on the spot, trying to recall the location of the unmoving beacon of light. Three-quarters of the way across the platform. And forward … maybe?

I face the front doors as the lift slows down; our journey

was only thirty seconds but that's easily enough time to get a warning up here.

The lift comes to a sudden halt, and the music warps for just an instant, like someone's playing off-key. I set myself, one foot behind the other. The doors slide open, front and back. My muscles tense.

I see no sign of security and no sign of the beacon, either. Still, my eyes widen and my lips part.

It's as if I've stepped into a fever dream.

The landscape's one of rolling grassland, dotted by trees I've never seen before. Some look like inverted umbrellas, while others have trunks like grey balloons. Bubbling brooks wind between the gentle rises, connecting waterfalls with crystal pools. And I spot four herds of different types of deer. *Four*. It's like we've been transplanted into a savannah of Africa. Spread out across the platform, guests stand in small groups, served by an entire army of barmen and women. And an atrium-like bubble extends high above us.

Muted exclamations ring out from the side, along with the sound of many clomping boots, all in a hurry.

"Jake?" Natasha implores, her gaze burning my cheek.

I don't move. I still see no sign of a dazzling light up ahead, and have no sense of being watched. There are just shallow rises and dips, all the way up to a row of trees and then the atrium dome wall, only a hundred feet away.

The security boots draw nearer. I spin and scan the savannah landscape through the other doors.

No sign of the fucking beacon that way either.

"Which way?" Natasha says, her voice tight.

My pulse thrums, and I leap forward out of the lift, Natasha just behind me. Half a dozen guards scamper toward us from the side of the platform, thirty feet away, black weapons on their belts – real guns, not tasers.

I plant my palm in the middle of Natasha's back and shove her in the direction of the nearest group of guests. "Keep close to them!" I yell.

Natasha starts to run while I sprint toward another group, only fifteen feet to her side. "Don't present a target!" I shout.

The sparkling guests gawk at us, rooted where they stand, and I dart from group to group. I continue to scan the platform ahead, searching for some sign of that damned beacon, so fucking bright from below.

But I see absolutely nothing, only crystal pools with snaking paths in between and the single row of trees ahead, the glass wall just beyond, only fifty feet away now.

Again, I try to fix on the memory of where the light was, but it slips from my mind, like the beacon was never there at all.

"Stop, *now!*" someone shouts from behind, followed by the sound of guns being drawn and chambered.

A realisation hits me, and I almost stumble to a halt. The beacon … a trap. The cleanest way for the angels to get us killed.

I lurch onward with my stomach in my mouth, careening between groups of guests. Natasha remains several paces to my side. The wall's only thirty feet away now, just the blue sky and the skyscrapers of Docklands beyond.

"Stop or we *will* shoot!" the voice shouts louder.

And suddenly, Natasha's out in the open – no more people between her and the wall. Only grass and trees and glass. I ignore the final group off to my side and barrel straight out into the open as well, my arms out to present a bigger target.

Still, I rack my mind for the memory. The beacon was three-quarters of the way along the platform, maybe forty yards from the centre, which would put it beyond the fucking glass of the atrium.

The adrenaline's like acid in my veins as I run, my lungs fit to burst, and my back muscles seize from the imagined stings of hot pain. Nevertheless, I sprint onward toward the wall.

The trees in front blur as light infiltrates my vision. My

ears ring, and my balance tips, a new numbness creeping up my calves as if I've already been shot.

"Jake!" Natasha's voice explodes in my head. The sound seems to come from everywhere.

I stumble. My mind screams at me to dive to the ground, to get out of the line of fire, yet I clamp down my thoughts, start the internal count again, and focus even harder on the memory – the beacon somehow beyond the wall, hanging in mid-air, above a two-hundred-foot plummet to the fucking ground.

I close my eyes, channel the energy into my legs, and throw myself forward between a pair of trees. Directly into the solid glass wall.

28

I SMASH INTO SOMETHING. It hits me full in the chest, knocking the breath out of me, and sends me spinning. A haze of blue and green flashes past my eyes while someone utters a cry of shock. Then the ground comes and smashes into my side, causing my rib to flare with pain. I tumble to a halt.

My eyes shoot open. A guy in a suit lies sprawled on the floor a few feet from me, groaning. Several people stand on his far side, all bathed in a warm glow. Natasha's there too, gazing straight ahead, her hand over her mouth and the familiar worry line etched across her forehead. Plus I feel a growing heat against my skin and smell the scent of cordite.

My heart gallops, and I twist around, my rib pounding. The word tumbles from my lips.

"Fuck."

The angel smirks, each side of his perfect mouth rising in a grin. "I don't think that's quite called for," he says, his voice like a tinkling bell. He raises an arched eyebrow at me. "At least, not yet."

Instead of shining armour, Haniel's clad in a suit that's so white, its lines fade as I stare at them. And with the veil in place, his image flits between a being of human height and one that towers a couple of feet taller. He holds a wide-necked glass instead of grapes, and he glows.

The angel glances between Natasha and me, the smile still parked on his lips, and his gaze burns with the same intensity. All my nerves are tingling in unison.

My heart beating faster, I scramble to my feet. And behind Haniel, the actual end of the platform is finally visible, the curved glass wall a further twenty feet away.

Haniel gazes off to the side. "Leave us," he says, giving a dismissive wave with one hand.

And that's when I properly notice them. Five guests – three women and two men – standing there with features blank and wide smiles. They're all young, and each one's extraordinarily beautiful, clad in extravagant clothes – long trains on the women and perfectly tailored suits on the men.

With Haniel's command, they all pivot away from us and begin padding along a wall of fog. Some kind of glimmering haze, it stretches across the row of trees I plunged between.

Through the haze, I can barely make out six guards. They're scanning the space around us, puzzled expressions on their faces, with their guns down by their sides. One guard looks directly at me, or through me, with no recognition in his eyes.

The guy I collided with gets up from the ground and tramps after his five fellow guests. The wall of haze spans the entire platform, blocking off this final section of the garden for Haniel and his entourage, which includes three more people on my other side.

Two servers dressed in black – male and female – are standing there with faces just as blank and beautiful as the guests'. A third person, a woman, is older than the others; maybe mid-thirties. Her strong features are both stunning and severe, with long dark hair tied up above her head. She wears a simple slit burgundy dress with calf-length trousers and very little make-up. While her expression's unreadable, her brown eyes stare intently at me. Not blank at all.

The six guests pad to where the mist meets the glass wall before passing through it.

My gaze darts back to Haniel. He's staring at Natasha again, his finger tapping his lip. I scramble to her side and anchor myself at her elbow.

"Fear not," he says and smiles a dazzling smile. "My intentions are almost entirely honourable. I assure you."

Then he angles his head toward the woman in the burgundy dress. "Harmony, would you be a dear?" he asks.

She doesn't bow but simply gives him a fleeting smile before turning to the servers at her side. She whispers something to them both, and they disappear back behind the wall of mist as well.

And though most of the guards have disappeared from the far side, one remains, still gazing at us. He's got his head at an angle, his gun still down by his side. I nudge Natasha backward toward him, toward the glittering wall.

"I wouldn't if I were you," a voice says.

I swivel. It's the woman in burgundy – Harmony. The servers having departed, she's staring at me again, and she doesn't glow at all. No special flow to her movements.

"So, why are we here?" I ask her.

"To enjoy yourselves," Haniel says and raises his arms. "I find myself often delighting in these gauche surroundings."

The female server returns with a tray laden with cocktail glasses in all kinds of iridescent colours and all kinds of sculpted shapes. Some burn with blue fire; others sparkle with precious stones. I just stare at the tray.

"Please," Haniel says and lifts his own glass toward us. "Think of it as camouflage. We need to make sure you blend in."

Still I remain rooted, and Natasha makes no move to take a drink either.

The male server returns, holding two identical black clothes bags over his arm.

"Harmony, my darling, what *have* you picked out?" Haniel asks, a child-like glee in his tone.

Harmony hands one bag to me and the other to Natasha.

"She's so very marvellous at catering to my extravagances," Haniel adds.

I hold up the bag. "You want us to *change?"*

"Of course! To blend in!" Haniel says. And while his grin doesn't falter, his features tighten, and he lowers his voice. "I simply want to talk, and you've already attracted quite enough attention. Don't you think?"

My eyes find the guard through the mist, but Haniel's shaking his head slowly. And I find my gaze drawn over his shoulder to the pristine blue sky beyond.

He smiles, some of the tension disappearing from his face. "Don't worry," he says and turns his gaze on Natasha. "I won't peek."

Harmony dismisses the servers, and the woman leaves her tray on the ground. I glance at Natasha. She's gazing back at me, the worry line gone from her forehead and the fire burning again in her eyes. I shrug, and we both head over to a clump of trees thirty feet away. Haniel doesn't move as we retreat beyond the branches.

Inside my bag, I find a charcoal suit and white shirt with seams so tiny they're almost invisible. I slip both on, and the material moulds around my body, perfectly sized. When I step out from behind the trees, Natasha is waiting for me.

My breath hitches. She wears a lustrous purple dress with open shoulders and material that hugs her figure down to the ankles. The slit up the side reaches her lower thigh.

"Now, that's better," Haniel says, his gaze on Natasha also, his eyes shining.

We pad back toward him.

"You were *born* for such attire," he says and tilts his head toward Harmony. "Didn't I say so?"

The same fleeting smile passes her lips. "You did, indeed," she says.

Haniel sighs and gazes back at Natasha as we approach. His fingers tap his lips again. "Though I'd have made a slightly scantier choice," he says.

Natasha doesn't look away. Doesn't shrink. She simply stops in front of him, her posture erect. Then she leans over, grabs up a red drink from the tray on the ground, and downs the entire thing. She coughs a couple of times, and Haniel's eyes widen along with his smile.

She sets the glass down and fixes him with a stare. "Why *are* we here, Haniel?"

"Because I admire you," he says to her, drawing the last words out as a purr.

The embers spark inside me, the flames building. My fists clench, my shoulders tighten, and I find myself stepping toward him.

Haniel turns on me and towers higher, his glow intensifying in an instant. His blinding white suit morphs into silver armour, and I can make out the outline of wings carved into the blue sky behind. His eyes burn, and he sweeps his hand across my face, leaving his arm hovering in mid-air.

I hear words shouted in my skull … *Can't breathe.* And like a seed, they grow in my mind. My lungs compress, and the same panicked thoughts spiral faster. *Can't breathe … Truly can't breathe …* My chest squeezes even more. My throat constricts, my heartbeat racing. My senses cloud …

"Jake?"

Natasha's startled voice seems remote, and I can barely feel her touch on my arm.

"Haniel, stop this!" she says.

"No need," Haniel says.

I can scarcely hear his words, my lungs rigid, all sounds growing distant as my vision blurs as well.

Finally, I close my eyes, stop trying to draw in breath, and start the count in my head, concentrating hard on the numbers. My chest feels like it's going to explode, but I ignore the sensation and bite down harder on my panicked thoughts, focusing everything on stilling my mind.

Gradually, the tension in my lungs eases, and I'm able to suck in tiny mouthfuls of air.

Haniel drops his hand, and the pressure vanishes completely. I take a massive breath, the aching intense in my rib again.

"Jake, are you okay?" Natasha asks, gazing up at me.

I can only swallow, my throat raw.

Haniel grins at me. "You see! I admire you *both,*" he says, his angelic glow fading to leave his pristine white suit back in place. "It's as I said the first time we met. I was perhaps mistaken." He turns to Harmony. "And it is rare that I admit that. Isn't it, my dear?"

She nods. "Indeed it is," she says in the same wry tone.

Natasha's hands go to her hips. "Mistaken about what?" she snaps.

"About you," he replies, glancing from me to Natasha. "I was too quick to judge."

My mouth gapes. "Wait … d'you mean this has all been a *test?"* I stammer.

"Of sorts," he says with a nod.

"Goading us in heaven … finding you here … messing with my breathing … *that's* what you've been doing?"

His smile returns, and he steps forward, leaning toward us. And while he diminishes his glow, I can still feel his heat prickling my forehead and neck.

"You see, the old man is wrong," he says, his voice soft.

"Michael?" I say.

His face flares red, the heat intensifies, and it's like my skin's aflame. I stumble back a step.

"We do not want to say his name," Haniel says, barely whispering the words. "Do you know what would happen to me if he knew we were meeting?"

I swallow and shake my head. He straightens back up and his bright glow returns. He forces a smile.

"But yes, sadly, he is wrong," he says. "The world *is* changed, no matter how my brothers and sisters may wish it otherwise. We have atrophied, withdrawn. Our power is not as it once was. We are far more remote in the minds of men. The olden days will not return."

Natasha frowns. "So what do you want?" she asks, her eyes still burning.

The angel grins again, but it doesn't linger. "For you to continue," he says.

"Continue?" Natasha says.

"Yes," Haniel says. "With your efforts."

"Against the devil? What can *we* do?" I ask, the words tumbling out and the darkness burgeoning inside. "We're insects … Plus we just united the pantheon against us—"

"Yes, that is what's so *impressive*," Haniel says, a genuine smile spreading across his features. "It is true that you perhaps aided our magisterial leader in his crusade. But I don't think you comprehend the larger context. You managed to summon a good number of the pantheon to hear you speak." He shakes his head, still smiling. "No mortal has done anything *close* to that for thousands of years."

Natasha glances at me while I keep my eyes fixed on Haniel. He returns my gaze, taps his foot, and purses his lips for a moment. Then he tilts his head.

"Harmony, dear, do you want to let Jacob here know what his name means?" Haniel prompts, his eyes never leaving mine.

I start at that version of my name. The only people ever to use it were my mother … and Father Thomas.

"His name? Why, certainly," Harmony says. "Jacob means … the usurper."

A chill passes down my spine. Natasha's eyes widen.

Haniel leans closer to me and points a finger at my chest. "And this is where *you* are wrong, my child," he says. "Yes, the devil is a supernatural being. And, yes, he is immensely deliberate, ruthless, and clever." He pauses. "Yet, like all the angels, the emissaries, and the higher demons, the devil used to be human once. He needs the belief of the masses, like all divine beings do. You *know* this."

Haniel gazes between us. "And what my esteemed leader does not realise is that the battleground will not be fought in the realms of heaven or hell," he says, his glow transforming from white to yellow fire. "It will be in the world of men. *Your* world."

His grin spreads till there's a hint of madness in his expression. I blink.

"You know the power of story," Haniel goes on. "And we know what he's doing – enacting Revelation. You bringing the demon to the pantheon helped confirm this. The devil will use every opportunity to spread his message, every weapon in the real world that he has. And you can stop him."

A flash of worry clouds Natasha's features, her brow furrowing and cheeks pale.

Haniel smiles directly at me and implants the same words in my head. "*Every weapon in the real world that he has.*"

And the kernel of an idea starts to grow in my mind.

Haniel glances between us; Natasha's expression has hardened again, the fire blazing once more in her eyes.

Haniel raises his glass. "I have great faith," he says.

My gaze finds Natasha, who stares back at me and then lifts her glass as well.

29

Natasha and I hike on toward the back of the massive structure. It's the kind of stage you'd find at the largest of rock concerts, with a curving roof that reaches high into the air. Dark clouds brood above the black-skinned top while the muffled din of a barking voice and cheering crowd emanate from the other side.

Natasha presses close among the hundreds of fellow event-goers, all hurrying to either side of the rear of the stage.

"Can you sense him?" she asks.

I head out of the flow and toward the cover of two Hyde Park trees. Natasha and I halt under the lower canopy, fifty yards away from the structure. And there, I close my eyes.

The air brims with energy, and I feel a prickle in my gut. But I can't detect the scent of sulphur or cordite. The smell of soil, sweat, and litter remains strong in my nose.

"Maybe," I say.

"Paul Hawcross is here, so the devil will be here," she says, total confidence in her tone. "The man is his main asset, and these speeches are key for them."

"But we still don't know what we're going to do here."

I utter the words, yet I can't ignore the seed Haniel planted deep in my mind …

Paul Hawcross – the devil's chief weapon and a mortal – groomed over decades for this moment. Meaning I could end his plot in one foul act.

Natasha's staring at me, and I glance away to settle myself.

She swivels toward the structure. "We just get backstage and find out their plan," she says. "If what Haniel says is true, an opportunity *will* present itself. It has to, right?" She slips a hand into her pocket and starts playing with her crucifix necklace. And while the fire's still there in her eyes, a darkness lingers there too, just beneath the surface.

My ribs squeeze, and I shift my gaze to the rear of the stage and the wide tent that extends the full width of the structure. "Right," I say.

She nods. "Is there a way in?" she asks.

I go up on my toes and scan the doors to the tented space, followed by the archways to the wings on each side of the stage. "I'm not sure," I say.

Everything's sealed off, every visible entryway closed. And worse than that, they've erected a perimeter of at least twenty feet around the entire structure, a kind of no man's land. The channel is patrolled by numerous security guards, far more than you'd think necessary.

Unless they're expecting a breach.

The skin tightens across my back. Then a new scent piques my nose, so faint. Something acrid. I scour the cordon straight ahead.

Between the guards in their fluorescent jackets, an additional figure stands poised at the edge of the perimeter dressed in a pristine blue suit and shirt. He's leaning over the railing, searching the moving crowd around us and scanning every face.

I dip my head and grab Natasha's hand. "Come on," I say.

She resists my pull. "What is it?" she asks, the hint of darkness growing in her eyes.

"Nothing," I respond, keeping my voice low. "There's no way in here, but we may find one around the front."

After a moment, she lets me tug her back into the flow of people. We skirt the rear of the stage in one direction and then continue on behind a line of platforms that they've erected on both of its sides, giving the whole structure a crescent moon shape. The platforms themselves rise fifteen feet in the air with rows of chairs on them. VIP seats.

Keeping us at the rear of the stream of event-goers, I glance periodically at the cordon. The damn thing borders the entire back of the structure, the twenty-foot channel constantly patrolled by guards, but there's no more sign of demons. All the while, the din grows louder in our ears.

We press on beyond the final platform and around one tip of the crescent moon. And there it is. The front of the stage, and the swelling crowd before it.

"Wow," Natasha breathes.

Maybe a hundred thousand people strong, the crowd stretches eighty or ninety yards at the back and tapers toward the broad stage complete with wings and an overhanging roof. Beyond the wings, the neighbouring platforms curve around the outskirts of the throng on both sides, making up the curved tips of the crescent moon shape.

I find myself nudged on all sides, event-goers milling about us. Some are dressed in Puritan robes, but not all. Many carry banners, others placards with Paul Hawcross's beatific face. An amplified voice resounds from the stage, each call drawing bouts of wild cheering from the masses. But it's not only cheers. My head turns.

Beyond the rear of the main crowd, a group of fifty protesters yell angrily at the stage, various accusations aimed at the prime minister. They're faced by a larger throng of Paul Hawcross's supporters shouting back. The collective noise is enormous. The frenzy drives the heat in my chest, and the clouds continue to darken above us, the brimming charge intensifying in the air.

"What do you reckon?" Natasha says.

I follow her gaze, her eyes shifting between the wings on either edge of the stage. They're walled off on the front and side, with a clear route to the backstage area and that tented structure at the rear.

"Looks pretty impossible," I say, the words tumbling out. They've created a twenty-foot perimeter directly in front of the stage also, with more guards in the gap.

Natasha keeps scanning.

"No, wait … look!" she says and lifts a finger. "You were right!"

She's pointing toward the far edge of the crowd. The throng extends all the way to the platforms on that side of the structure as well. And near the edge, a line of people hold items above their heads like framed photos and bits of clothing. I trace the line all the way to the front, where they queue before a set of steps that climb directly onto the fringe of the stage.

"That's our way in," she says.

Those at the front of the queue are getting shepherded into the wings one at a time.

My lips purse. "Could be," I say.

Natasha nods and pulls at my arm. She begins weaving her way diagonally through the crowd toward the platforms on the far side and the line of worshippers before them. I keep close behind.

We make good progress. The crowd's more sparsely packed at the back, only a few guards strolling around in their fluorescent jackets. My eyes find the stage. A preacher in black robes stands there, yelling into a wireless microphone. A massive screen on each wing projects his image while large racks of speakers amplify his baying voice. He grips a lectern marked with a giant crucifix.

"May the Lord *guide* our prime minister in his holy work!" he says, his voice booming, the cadence rising and falling.

"There is no more important task! We must unite *all* God-fearing people!"

I turn away and focus on the people seeking blessings, the end of the queue only fifty yards ahead of us now. Mothers hold babies. Relatives escort the elderly and the infirm, and ordinary folk with yellow sashes are helping them clamber backstage for a personal audience with Paul Hawcross – a once-in-a-lifetime opportunity.

Padding onward, my feet slow, Haniel's suggestion still revolving around my mind – *one foul act* – while the void swells at my core.

Natasha glances back at me and shortens her stride as well. "What's wrong?" she asks.

My gaze finds the steps running up onto the stage, to the wings and backstage beyond. I come to a halt. Natasha keeps her eyes on me while the crowd presses in around us, some shouting and others waving their arms at the stage. The energy pulses my ribs, and I notice a subtle twisting in my gut – my internal alarm.

"I don't like it," I say.

She blinks. "But this has *got* to be our way in," she says, her voice raised to make herself heard above the din. She motions toward the cordon. "There's nowhere else!"

I nod, my eyes on the single set of steps across the security channel, protected not even by guards but by volunteers. "That's the problem," I say.

Her mouth opens, but nothing comes out, more of the fire ebbing from her eyes. "So, what else can we *do?*" she splutters, her fingers stretching.

I dart my gaze over the stage. The preacher stands there hurling his words over the crowd as he describes Paul Hawcross and outlines his rise from a simple background. The people roar back louder in response, the shouts vibrating my bones. And after searching the wings, the throng, still I find absolutely nothing.

Natasha grips my arm. "Jake, we must go *now*," she says. "Our window's closing!"

My pulse thrums, and I try to focus, to shut out the sounds of the crowd, the preacher. He's moved on to listing Paul Hawcross's many achievements, progressing steadily to the present moment as his arms wave ever more excitedly in the air. Believers squeeze forward on all sides of us, and the charge builds further in my chest.

I force my gaze away, and my eyes alight on the two platforms on this side of the structure. As with the other side, they've been erected on a wedge of scaffolding that's flat on top, rises ten feet in the air, and curves diagonally away from the stage for seventy yards, forming one tip of the crescent moon shape.

Forty feet lie between the platforms, and both command excellent views. Twenty or so people mill around the one nearer the stage, but the farther one draws my gaze. It's smaller and already packed with twenty-five people jostling for position. Many of them carry television cameras and boom microphones.

"This way," I say and push Natasha toward the second platform. It's fifteen feet off the ground, the scaffolding full of easy handholds.

"Where are we going?" she asks, moving cautiously. "There is no route backstage—"

"They'll be briefing the reporters," I say. "Providing details about future events."

Her eyes find the media crews.

"Television's been a key weapon for them since the beginning," I say. "We *know* that."

After a moment, she nods, and we hasten toward the platforms, winding our way through the crowd. My internal alarm rings on, and I find my gaze drawn to the stage. Several figures stand there, right on the threshold of the wings, their dark outlines barely visible in the shadows. I hunch my shoulders, put my head down, and keep pressing forward.

"Wait," Natasha says and seizes my arm. "*Look.*"

She points over the crowd toward the media platform. I peer between people, and sure enough, they've created a perimeter here, too. A metal barrier runs along the entire raised wedge of scaffolding, ten feet in front of it with guards patrolling the channel in between.

My insides tighten, and my gaze follows the security channel all the way back toward the rear of the crowd, where a makeshift car park sits at its end. Twenty sleek black cars stand parked alongside media vans, two of them having just arrived. A couple of crews pile out of the back doors, armed with cameras and microphones.

The sound of a distant engine grows in my ears, a deep rumbling barely audible over the yelling crowd.

"Come on!" I say and grip Natasha's hand. I yank her rearward through the crowd, and we scramble between people, moving more quickly now and going against the flow.

We're still twenty feet away from the car park when the new media van bursts into sight between the trees, a satellite dish wobbling on its roof. The driver guns its engine down the pathway toward us, sending dust billowing behind.

I break out into a sprint. The van reaches the car park an instant before I do. It does a U-turn to slot haphazardly between two more trucks, the logo of a popular news channel plastered on the side.

A couple of guards stand at the end of the security channel, and I hurry past them, my gaze averted. My path takes me around more vans and several of the black cars. They're stretch limos with small flags on poles rising above the headlights – foreign diplomat vehicles.

The van's passenger door is already open fifty feet away, and a woman jumps out, a wireless microphone in her hand. Her face is flushed red, her jaw clenched, and she aims a shout into the cab of the van before slamming her door. She dashes between the two vans toward me, a security pass swinging from her neck. And I slow my pace.

She's a similar build to Natasha but with blonde hair instead of brown. Not a great match.

I bite my cheek and then position myself almost directly in between her and the security channel behind, one of the larger cars blocking the guards' view of me.

She continues to hurry in my direction, a few yards away, her eyes not on me but on the stage at my back. I set my feet. Lower my centre of gravity. And prepare to lurch into her path ...

But then I remain entirely still as she barrels past me. I don't move a muscle as she sprints on toward the two guards and the security channel beyond.

Natasha jogs to my side. "What's the plan?" she asks breathlessly.

I spin back to face the van, cursing myself. The reporter's colleague hovers by the driver's door, a large camera in one hand while he fumbles a set of keys with the other.

I scan the vans to either side of his.

"There!" I hiss to Natasha and motion at the nearer one. It's parked in the opposite direction, its nose pointed at us, and I jab my finger toward the far side of the bonnet.

Natasha frowns up at me. Then she glances from the cameraman to the bonnet, and the frown vanishes. She leaps toward the neighbouring van, skirts the bonnet, and crouches down.

The cameraman finally locks the door with the fob and then glances down to slip the keys into his jacket's inside pocket.

I bolt behind the rear doors of his van and out of sight. Then I fix my gaze on Natasha on the opposite side of the gap between the vans. She smiles back at me, the fire burning again in her eyes.

I hear hurried footsteps to our side. Natasha pauses a beat and then straightens and shoots out a hand toward the sound.

"Sir?" she says in her best plaintive tone.

I track the cameraman's swift approach from Natasha's eyes and then dart toward her across the gap between the vans, my knees braced and hand raised.

The guy's shoulder bumps into my chest, and I keep my legs angled away to avoid the swinging camera. The cameraman utters a cry of surprise, his gaze swivelling from Natasha to me. I clasp the guy's shoulder to steady him as Natasha darts across and places her fingers on his forearm.

"Oh god, I am so sorry," she says, giving his arm a squeeze.

Still stumbling between us, his eyes track back to her hand. I reach for the inner pocket of his jacket with my other hand, my fingers delving inside. I feel tissues and business cards but no keys. And the cameraman keeps moving, drawing out of my reach.

I take a couple of hurried steps, still searching, and my fingertips barely grasp the metal ring as he careens away, his eyes still on Natasha. His momentum draws the keys out of his own pocket.

"You okay?" I call after him, covering the clinking sound of the keys with my voice.

The guy doesn't turn but simply lurches on toward the guarded channel. I swivel, the keys clasped in my palm.

"Has he noticed?" I ask.

Natasha eyes the channel and shakes her head.

"And the guards?" I ask.

Natasha shakes her head again. "Ignoring us. Speaking to the man about something."

I nod and press the button on the fob. The van unlocks with a clunk. "Shield me," I say.

Natasha positions herself in the gap between the vans. I hurry toward the passenger door, jump inside the cab, and then squeeze my head and chest over the top of the headrest, my rib throbbing with every movement. Finally, I get my legs over too and tumble down the other side of the seat.

The rear of the van resembles some kind of rocket launch control centre with screens on both sides and a mine of equipment held tightly to the walls with stretchy cords.

I grab a spare camera, a hand-held microphone, a grey suit jacket and a couple of security passes. I dump them all over the headrest before scrambling back over and into the passenger seat.

Natasha yanks open the door. "Give it here," she says, motioning for the equipment. "They're about to close the channel."

I shove the jacket into her hand. "All yours," I say.

She smiles, and I leap down from the cab, spare camera in hand. Then I drop the keys by the van's front wheel.

Grey jacket on, Natasha spins for the media platform, a wailing crowd on one side and the clouds growing ever darker above. I scramble behind, heading toward the start of the security channel, right as the guards start to haul a barrier across it.

30

Natasha sprints through the car park, her arm raised. "Stop, wait!" she yells at the guards, her voice barely rising above the din of the crowd.

One of them ceases heaving the barrier and glances up at her, leaving the barricade three-quarters of the way across the media channel.

With hair billowing, she runs right up to him. I follow at her back, the camera swinging back and forth in my hand.

"Thank you … sir," she says, panting hard, her chest rising and falling mere inches from his.

The guard clears his throat and tries to focus on her face. "I'm sorry, ma'am," he says. "The media area's full."

I glance over the guy's shoulder and find the back of the platform bursting with crews, many of the reporters talking to their camera operators with no visible briefing in progress.

"It can't be. Can it?" Natasha says, flashing her stolen pass for an instant while beaming her widest smile.

The guard stares back at her, and Natasha inches through the narrow gap, keeping her smile fixed on him. The guy doesn't move at all.

"Appreciated!" she says and swivels away.

I follow right behind as we hurry down the security

channel toward the steps, the enormous crowd rolling and heaving beyond the metal barriers to our side.

It's still growing, more people joining at the back. Those in the middle shove further forward, squeezing into the space at the front. Not a patch of ground lies uncovered. Those queueing for blessings continue to press toward this side of the stage. A new preacher stands up there, hollering sermons in a rumbling voice, one hand raised in the air and his fingers clenched like pincers. Many thousands roar in response. The frenzy in the crowd continues to intensify, and the gusts of wind grow stronger, pulling at hair and clothes.

Natasha reaches the staircase and flashes her pass at a guard positioned at the bottom. She points at me over her shoulder, and I raise my free hand in a wave. The guard lets us pass, and we both leap up the stairs to the rear of the media platform.

It's thirty feet square with metal barriers running along its back and sides, leaving the front edge open, the one facing the stage.

I anchor my feet at the top of the steps and scan again for an official-looking person, for some kind of briefing. Nothing's obvious. Just three guards hovering at the back. Plus a dozen crews, most of whom have already set up their cameras while a few jostle to get the best remaining positions, some of them perched precariously close to the edges.

The nearest guard glances in my direction. I hoist the camera onto my shoulder to hide my face. Then I squeeze my way toward the front of the platform, pushing past grumbling crews while listening for any kind of information. Natasha pads just behind.

Right at the edge, I stop and then crouch down in the foot or so of empty space, directing my camera straight ahead.

Beyond our platform, the wedge of scaffolding arcs on toward the stage. It's thirty feet wide, flat, with the same board covering as the platforms, though it's a few feet lower. Forty feet further along it, with an even better view, stands the next raised platform, at the same level as ours but twice as big.

And fuller than it was. Ten guards hover around a group of three or so dozen people – men and women from all different nations. Each wears the formal attire of a diplomat or ambassador, and most of them have drinks in their hands.

Natasha hunches down behind me. "Is that odd?" she whispers. "To bring diplomats all the way here for just another of his speeches, for a glass of champagne? They could as easily watch it on TV."

I blink and find my attention shifting to the lectern right in the middle of the stage. Only fifty yards away now, with a lower wedge of scaffolding, the diplomat platform, and then the remaining wedge in between. All flat, wide, and easy to cross – maybe fifteen seconds at a run. Probably more than it'd take for the demons to notice, though.

I hear Haniel's words in my mind ... *You can stop him. I have faith.*

Staring on, another voice permeates my awareness, barely audible against the background of the cheering crowd and coming from the ambassadors' platform. My head starts to turn. The tone's familiar, a mixture of smooth charm and complete power, total assurance. My gut twists more with each passing moment.

And then the memory hits me. I freeze and spin back, the blood chilling in my veins.

Natasha leans into my shoulder. "What is it?" she whispers.

I swallow. The voice continues on from my side, too far away to make out the words. I try to rotate the camera to catch a glimpse, but my body won't obey, my internal alarm ringing as loudly as ever.

I stoop further down, trying to steady my voice. "Someone on the other platform," I say.

Natasha swivels while I keep my gaze fixed on the stage, the camera shielding my face from the diplomats. Technicians bustle about the lectern, placing bottles of water at its base along with an extensive collection of candles across the edge of the stage.

Natasha tightens at my side. "A woman," she says, her tone unsteady, "standing with the diplomats."

"I remember her from my capture," I say and then take a breath, tense my shoulders, and – against every impulse – thrust my head around. And I finally catch a glimpse.

My jaw goes rigid. My thoughts stop. The power emanating from her is so damn obvious. She's six feet in height and athletically built, wearing a figure-hugging grey skirt suit, with burning auburn hair that stands piled up on the top of her head like a bloodstained crown. Her hair, nails, and lips are so red they glow.

And she's delivering the briefing we've been searching for. Every diplomat listens to her in rapt attention – ambassadors from all over the world.

Staring at her, I feel the veil so thin before my senses. It starts to peel back. Her demonic form appears before my eyes as the grey suit morphs into shimmering silver, and large red eyes peer out of deep sockets. My heart thumps in my chest.

"Jake?" Natasha asks and places a hand on my shoulder.

I try to rip my gaze to the side, but panicky thoughts fill my brain, and I find myself stuck staring at her, muscles rigid and all too bloody noticeable. My body trembles, and I start the count, focusing fiercely on stilling my mind. The veil withdraws further and her demonic form continues to emerge. The shimmering silver resolves into shining plates embedded in her chest and stomach, and massive spikes jut straight out of her shoulders and arms.

The urge to banish the image – to abandon the veil – grabs me, but I keep the veil peeled back and channel the building energy up my neck. Eventually I manage to force my head around, back to the stage. And behind the veil, my senses pick up on the familiar scent – just a whiff. The many lit candles along the edge are unable to mask it.

Sulphur.

My heart pounds harder, and my thoughts babble, the veil slipping back into place. I search the shadowed wing of the stage, his image searing itself onto my brain …

Chalk-white skin. Mismatched eyes – green and blue. His suit as black as night while smoke issues from around his bare hands and feet. And there's the horned mask that covers half his face.

A sudden roar erupts from the crowd. Natasha clasps my arm, and I jump. The media crews scramble to attention behind me. Cameras click on as reporters start simultaneous commentaries. I shake myself.

A man strides toward the raised lectern in the centre of the stage, one hand held aloft and his fist clenched.

Paul Hawcross.

A normal-looking guy. Simple white shirt, grey trousers, thinning hair combed over. He's humble-looking in his gait and posture. The enormous screens project his smiling image to the onlooking thousands and to billions beyond through the cameras behind me.

The female demon continues her briefing to the diplomats, and I angle my head, trying to listen.

"Can you hear?" Natasha asks.

"Not from this distance," I respond. "Not without the veil."

Natasha shakes her head. "They could notice you."

"If they haven't already," I say, and my fingers tighten around the camera handle.

Paul Hawcross raises both arms to the crowd while my head turns, my eyes finding the security channel behind. My mind conjures images of us sprinting back down the steps, simply getting the hell out of there.

I scrunch my eyes shut. The female demon's voice purrs on in my ears, the words indistinct. Ideas swirl in my brain, and my pulse fires. And then, like a complete idiot, instead of hurrying to the rear of the media platform, I leap off the front.

31

THE BOARDS atop the wedge of scaffolding are only a few feet down, and I take the impact with my knees, the camera pinned to my shoulder. I scurry off toward the diplomat platform, toward the stage, in full view of everyone – Paul Hawcross, the media demon, the guards behind, and the entire fucking crowd.

I run in a crouch while my mind hollers at me. When my feet reach the open space between the two platforms, I hunker down all on my own with no cover and try to stop myself from shaking.

Her sultry tones are louder now, only twenty feet away, and a familiar scent infiltrates my nose, that mixture of spices. It's almost as if I can feel her heat.

My hands tremble and I fix the camera, the shield between us, to my ear. I try to breathe, the lens trained on the stage.

Paul Hawcross steps right up to the microphone. "Brothers and sisters!" he booms.

His voice pulls at my attention like a hook around my sternum, and I have to anchor my feet to prevent myself from stumbling in his direction.

All the while, the female demon continues her briefing to my side. I focus hard on the words.

" … flown in and out directly, first class," she says in her silky voice.

"From where, Madam Lucia?" one of the diplomats asks.

"City Airport," the female demon – Lucia – says. "It is only a fifteen-minute drive. You'll be provided an army convoy."

And still Paul Hawcross's voice seeps into my awareness, shoving everything else out. He's attacking corruption, the loss of Christian values, the risk from other religions from foreign invaders. I fidget and try to focus while the crowd roars louder with his every word, the fervour fanning the sparks at my core.

I notice movement in my peripheral vision. A guard jumps down off the media platform and strides across the lower space toward me. Only fifteen feet away.

The blood thrums in my veins, Paul Hawcross's words still tugging at my focus. I remain in a crouch, the camera pressed to my ear, and start the count. I risk peeling back the veil a fraction and concentrate even harder on Lucia's voice.

"It will be the first step in our global project," she continues, her words elongating as time slows. "We must do this together."

I can almost see her smile – the flash of white teeth between red lips.

"We need all of your leaders to be present," she goes on.

The guard continues to stalk toward me, only seven or eight feet away now. And Paul Hawcross grips his lectern tighter, his eyes shining brighter and his voice growing louder. Behind the veil, I sense the air throbbing with his power. Screams of ecstasy break out from parts of the crowd.

And the path to him cements itself in my head: platform, boards, stage. Only twelve seconds at a sprint. Then use the veil for the guards and maybe demons too. And again, I hear Haniel's words … *I have faith.*

My pulse fires even faster, a sense of lightness growing in my chest. I feel myself leaning forward, my knees straightening and muscles tightening with more thoughts coming … Yes, it'd mean death but also an end to the void inside me, the darkness.

Finally.

And then my legs go rigid, Natasha's words from what feels like a lifetime ago sounding in my mind … *Evil begets evil.*

The guard halts inches away and towers over me. "Get up!" he snaps.

The diplomat speaks again. "When will it be, Madam Lucia?"

I remain still and focus intently on the conversation to the side, on keeping the veil pulled back.

The guard growls, anger coming off him in waves. It drives the fire in my torso. He reaches down, and in slowed time I glimpse his fingers extending, the shift of weight. He grasps for my shoulder at the same time as I lurch an arm's breadth to the side, keeping low.

His hand closes on empty air.

"Four days from now," Lucia says. "But it will remain secret until just before. We've planned a grand announcement."

The guard hisses above me, "You little shit."

He draws back his hand and swings it at my head. Beyond the veil, I sense the movement and channel the fire into my shoulder. Then I jerk my free hand up to grab his wrist from out of the air, a few inches from my cheek.

He tries to pull backward, and I tighten my grip. I yank hard on his arm and, despite the flaring pain in my rib, use the power in my core to haul myself to standing.

The guy lumbers forward half a step and stares at me, eyes wide. I avert my gaze, my thoughts coming thick and fast, and the veil slips back before my senses.

"Apologies," I mumble and shuffle away from him. "Excuse me."

Keeping my camera trained on the stage, I retreat sideways toward the media platform. The other crews mutter angrily at me as I step back onto the raised scaffold. Natasha grabs my arm and tugs me toward the rear of the square space. Together, we squeeze between the crews, slinking past their hard stares, and my rib throbs more with each contact.

A female reporter plants herself in front of me – the one from whose van we stole the equipment – and opens her mouth. I nod and then slope around her, shielding my security pass with my arm. I feel her gaze on my back as we reach the rear of the platform.

Natasha presses in at my side. "What did you find?" she says.

With the camera still on my shoulder, I swivel it to block out the media crews, the diplomats, and the stage, and end up staring out over the heaving crowds.

The cheering's even wilder than before. Numerous people hold up phones and cameras, the flashes crackling like sparks of electricity. The wind's gusting harder as well, bringing swirls of dust, the clouds brooding and black above us, pressing ever closer. The platform vibrates with Paul Hawcross's booming words.

I lean my head toward Natasha's. "I know when it's happening, their declaration of war," I say. "They're inviting all Christian leaders to a summit in London, fifteen minutes from City Airport, only four days from now."

Natasha's staring at my cheek, and her voice tightens further.

"But why bring them all here just to tell them that?" she asks. "Is it group pressure ..."

Her words phase out from my mind, my attention drawn by movement in the crowd.

Just beyond the queue of those seeking personal blessings, amid the throng almost parallel to the media platform fifty feet away stands a man. He has Arab features and is dressed in a simple white tunic that extends down to his ankles with a hulking overcoat on top, despite the heat.

My gut starts to twist again. His face … familiar. Yet I can't quite place it.

Natasha touches my hand. "Jake, we should go."

I stare on, my thoughts stilling, the pain in my rib a memory …

Then the connection comes, and the shock's like a punch to the jaw. My cell. The door open. He walked past it and stared in. I can see still his haunting eyes.

And now he's edging his way forward through the crowd, mumbling something over and over, with the outline of a square and bulky object beneath his coat.

My heart stops. I grab the metal barrier at the edge of the platform and hoist a leg over.

"Jake, stop!" Natasha says, pulling at my arm. "What are you doing?"

"That guy," I say, pointing. "He was there when I was captured. He's part of the plan. He's got a …"

I trail off, Natasha following my gaze. She goes still, her face pale. The guy squeezes on through the crowd while the sound of the cheering grows louder in my ears.

Behind me, someone snaps, "It's him."

I spin.

"That camera." It's the female reporter, speaking to a guard and pointing in my direction five yards away.

I swivel back to face Natasha. Her gaze remains glued to mine, her fingers gripping my arm.

"Don't, please!" she says, worry lines etching her forehead.

"I have to, Nat," I say, hoisting the other leg over the barrier while my eyes find the steps up to the stage.

They've started to lead a dozen worshippers toward Paul Hawcross. His human shield.

"Hey!" the guard shouts behind me.

Natasha squeezes my arm tighter. "You don't have to do this!" she says.

"A great many people are going to die, Nat," I say,

meeting her gaze. "A great many religious martyrs. And that's what the diplomats are here to witness. It'll supercharge their war."

Tears form in her eyes as I squeeze her hand, gently prising her fingers from my arm. "Get out of here," I say. *"Please."*

"No!" she shouts.

The weight doubles inside me. Tears prick the backs of my eyes, and the wave of feeling's so powerful that my thoughts still and the veil peels away in an instant.

The shimmering world stretches out to every side, the air coalescing around my body, and I force my gaze from Natasha. I let go of the railing and thrust myself out into space.

32

As I leap off the platform, the ground plummets away beneath me, fifteen feet down – a far bigger drop than it looked. My arms stretch above my head, and I imagine the air like water, the wind buoyant against every inch of my body. With the veil peeled back, time slows as the bare floor of the security channel rushes up to meet me, the crowd a roiling mass before my eyes.

I manage to slow my fall a fraction, though the turf still slams into my feet. Pain stabs at my ankles, and I go straight into a forward roll before pushing myself upright, my rib aching, and stumbling on.

A guard yells from further along the channel, but I keep my head straight, my eyes searching for any sign of the bomber. My feet take me across the rest of the pathway, and I grab the top of the metal barrier, scissor my legs over it, and land amid the worshippers on the far side.

They're densely packed, all part of the seething throng. I keep the veil peeled back and unfocus my gaze, turning the crowd's movement into a choreographed dance. The connection forms with each person around me, like we're all linked by invisible threads, and I flow into gaps as soon as they appear, shifting between people. I hear yells and grumbles but continue on, leaving the angry outbursts in my wake.

I crane my neck, trying to peer over the crowd. However, my view's blocked by the many items held in the air – framed photographs, scarves, and other items of clothing – all being thrust toward Paul Hawcross while others train their phones on the stage.

I keep pressing forward, focused on my memory of the guy's trajectory. And a few moments later, I catch my first glimpse. Thirty feet from me and a hundred from the stage, flashes of his white tunic become visible through the teeming masses.

And with the images, my thoughts start up – doubting voices clamouring about what the fuck I'm going to do. The veil begins slipping back before my senses, and the shimmering world retreats. Time speeds up, the gaps disappear, and I begin bumping into people, drawing more rageful shouts.

A nearby guard in a fluorescent jacket swivels in my direction. I start the count in my head, trying to still my thoughts to peel back the veil. But my mind's a scrambling mess, images coming of the tunic man recognising me and then immediately triggering his bomb. The veil falls back entirely into place, the crowd now nothing but an unruly mass of bodies before me.

I claw at shoulders, yank at arms, and barge my way past people. Their yells resound in my ears, my heartbeat a constant barrage in my chest as my gut twists ever tighter. Nevertheless, I keep going, my gaze fixed ahead, peering for glimpses of the guy through the churning crowd.

And there he is, only twenty feet away now, still mumbling something – a prayer, a mantra. He's undoing the buttons on his overcoat, pulling it wide, exposing …

My throat clenches. He has an explosive belt, a set of cylindrical containers, eight inches high, all strapped together around his slender waist, connected to each other by many wires.

A few people notice and then a few more. A new silence takes hold of the crowd that surrounds him as people stumble away, creating a growing circle. I feel the pressure between my ears, squeezing my chest, questions forming about why he'd reveal himself—

My head turns, and I spot the camera crews. None of them have noticed him yet, but they will. And then they'll beam the devastation around the world.

I throw myself onward – and find myself pushed backward even harder with people retreating from the bomber. I end up wrestling through the crowd, shoving people left and right as my gut twists wildly, my heart hammering against my aching rib. I'm only a few feet from the brink of the growing circle.

The bomber puts a hand in his pocket and brings something out. A phone – the detonator. He fumbles with the buttons, his head down, while the crowd around him gaze on with wide eyes, many with their own phones gripped in their hands.

I reach the circle's edge and bump into a woman scrabbling backward. She swivels, her arm raised. I grab the phone out of her hand and then shove past her into the open space.

The guy glances up, ten feet away.

"Brother, wait!" I yell, the sound of my voice so loud in my ears.

The silence continues to grow around me, Paul Hawcross's words and the noise of the crowd somehow muted. The guy's gaze flicks to mine across the open space. His eyes are narrowed, while sweat trickles down his temples.

I come to a stop a couple of feet into the circle, the phone held down by my side and my pulse thumping in my neck.

"You remember me. Right?" I ask. "From the top floor?"

Still the guy doesn't react; he simply stares back at me and tilts his head. He's got one hand in his pocket, the other clenched around his phone, his thumb an inch from the buttons. His fingers tremble.

"Don't press!" I almost shout, raising the stolen phone before me. "You've got to use *this* unit instead."

The guy glances at his phone and then at mine. I edge toward him across the space, seven feet away.

"Yours has been hacked," I continue.

The guy meets my eyes again, his forehead furrowing beneath the beads of sweat. He takes a quick breath in and tenses his neck in preparation.

My adrenaline surges, and I lob the stolen phone at him, keeping it in his eyeline. It sails through the air toward his head, and he glances up.

I still my thoughts, the veil peeling back once more. Time slows, and it's as if the whole crowd's holding its breath. I quicken my steps – five feet away now – my entire awareness trained on his posture, imprinting every inch of him in my mind.

The guy raises his free hand to shield his face. He swivels his head away, just a fraction, which means his whole body turns. And the hand holding his phone – the detonator – lifts toward me, hanging there at waist height.

I leap forward and throw one hand at his face, my fingers spread to block his vision, while flattening my other hand like a blade and chopping it upward from my side toward the phone, out of his line of sight.

The guy blocks the stolen phone with his forearm while recoiling from my groping fingers. Then he clenches his jaw and starts to press down on the buttons of his phone. I tighten every muscle in my arm and yank my hand up faster, wedging it in between his phone and thumb just as he tries to jab the buttons. He presses down on my knuckles instead.

I squeeze the phone's casing and arch my fingers, maintaining a distance between his thumb and the buttons. The guy presses viciously down on my hand, using his entire body weight.

My arm shakes with the effort of maintaining the arch, which brings us chest to chest and our noses only inches apart. He grabs my shoulder with his free hand and goes to headbutt me while I spin to the side, dart my head backward, and use the rotation to drive my free hand up hard into the soft part of his armpit.

He grunts in pain. His grip around the phone weakens, and I manage to worm my hand between his fingers and the case. The detonator tumbles to the ground, but the guy makes no move to catch or retrieve it. I stamp down hard, smashing the phone beneath my heel.

Yet my gut doesn't uncoil, doesn't untwist.

A yell explodes in my ears, and I can't help spinning. Paul Hawcross's voice from the stage behind me, a great intensity to his tone, but the words indistinct with the veil still pulled back.

At the same time, the bomber takes a step away from me and plunges a hand into his pocket.

The breath stops in my throat. The man brings an oval object into the light – green and ribbed, a grenade. He shoots his other hand across, and with an extended finger whips the pin out, all in one practised motion.

The bomber keeps his gaze on me the entire time. My mouth opens, but nothing comes out. Still, he gapes at me, that same intense stare, the look from my prison cell. Then he raises the grenade above his head.

This time, the crowd erupts into screams all around me. Several people throw themselves to the ground, and I plunge even deeper behind the veil, trying to shut everything out.

Time crawls by as if through molasses. I lift one leg and lunge forward, stamping my heel down hard onto the bridge of the guy's foot. He roars with pain and reflexively jerks both arms down.

In slowed time, I bring both of my hands forward to intercept the grenade. With one hand, I grasp the guy's wrist while with the other, I tear the grenade from his fingers.

And there it is, hot and sweaty in my palm. I can almost hear it ticking, the seconds winding down. My heartbeat's like a train inside my chest now. Sound inundates me from all sides – screams of fear, shouts of alarm. I hold my breath, yank the grenade down, and then whip it upward, hurling it into the air with everything I have.

Another yell booms from the stage, elongated in slowed time. My eyes close, and then the explosion comes, a deafening noise ploughing through my skull like a wrecking ball. My body goes limp, and I wait for the shrapnel to rip me to pieces.

Nothing happens.

Distant sounds infiltrate the constant ringing in my head. A couple of gasps and shouts …

I open my eyes and flinch, but there's no death or devastation. The crowd remains in a circle around me, everyone staring raptly at the stage. Another shocked silence descends, even deeper than before. I follow their gaze.

Paul Hawcross. Standing there, looking directly down at us from behind his lectern, his arms raised in a V above his head. And my eyes find the massive screens at his back. They both show a picture of an immense V of smoke against the background of a cloudy sky. The muted shock erupts into yells of amazement, of awe.

I look up and step back. The same massive V of smoke hangs above us, white against the dark clouds, the wind no longer gusting.

My mouth falls open. The whole blast of the grenade diverted upward.

My gaze finds the media platform. Every camera's either trained on Paul Hawcross or on the space above my head. The veil slips back into place before my senses, my mind railing at the genius of it all …

A miracle with the entire world watching – the only thing

more powerful than martyrs. The void takes hold of me, the shock like steel bands around my chest and throat. My legs shake.

Members of the crowd scramble across the space toward the bomber, teeth bared and arms reaching. They get to within a few feet when several guards appear from nowhere and then wrestle the guy out of the angry throng and in the direction of the barriers behind.

Paul Hawcross shouts again from his stage. "This is why we can't be beaten!" he yells, the booming sound even louder. "We are the chosen people … and we will bring our enemies low!"

The crowd screams back in unison and begins chanting fiercely. The dark ocean rises further up my body, filling every pore, every cell.

I turn from the stage, and there she is – Natasha, standing amid the crowd, twenty feet away, staring at me. Her body trembles, her face drained of colour, the fire gone completely from her eyes.

She starts in my direction but is cut off immediately, bumped on either side by the surging crowd. She sways, about to collapse, and I stumble toward her. I thrust myself between people and just manage to get to her side to get my hand around her back.

People press in on all sides of us, the chanting morphing into yells of support, of adulation for Paul Hawcross. I shove people backward and hoist Natasha up by the shoulder while just waiting for a yell from a guard, for the fingers around my wrist. But of course, no one grabs me. And again, Michael's words sound in my head … *You are nothing but the devil's puppet.*

I stumble away through the crowd, the darkness taking me over entirely as Paul Hawcross's rousing voice echoes in my ears.

33

We trudge through the city in a daze, Natasha leaning on my arm, and my ears still ringing from the explosion. People swarm the surrounding streets, chattering excitedly, televisions on in every office and bar. The same images play of Paul Hawcross on stage, arms raised, the V of smoke in the air above the crowd. Some chant his name while others get down on their knees and pray.

We pass landmark after landmark in the dying light – the shops of Soho, the Centre Point skyscraper, the old city wall near Bank – the clouds nearly black above us and the occasional rumble of thunder audible in the distance.

And with every road, Natasha gets weaker. Her steps slow, her shoulders hunch, and I need to take more of her weight. All the while, memories spin through my mind …

Bringing the demon into heaven. The janitor swamped by demons. Those bigots searching our neighbours' home. The devil escaping hell. Having to bury the priest. My mother dead. Qetesh having her throat cut. All my fault.

The void's so wide inside me while monsters cavort down in the deep.

"Take me back," Natasha says, her voice a whisper.

I slow our steps. "Our house?"

She shakes her head, and her hand finds her pocket as she walks. She brings out her crucifix necklace and grips it tightly.

"The church?" I ask.

She gives the faintest nod.

"You know they've followed me there before," I remind her.

Natasha says nothing. She doesn't even shrug but simply continues to lumber on at my side through the city centre.

Because why does it matter?

The journey takes an age, but finally we reach the semicircular courtyard. The towering office buildings stand all around, our destination still dwarfed by Gabriel's skyscraper behind. And the space is almost empty, with only a few office workers hurrying this way and that.

The sky rumbles above us again, the thunder distant yet steadily approaching. The air thrums with static charge, the wind muggy against my cheeks. I don't pause. Don't scan. Just plod straight for the entrance to the church. The lock's still busted, and I heave the door open. Natasha slips through before me.

And there I come to rest at the start of the central aisle, the doors closed at my back. The destruction's as clear as before – the pews broken and scattered, the statues defaced, the pulpit splintered. And straight ahead, the altar with Jesus on the cross.

The memory comes of Father Thomas standing before it that very first time we met, bowing slightly before he hobbled off toward his rooms behind.

And I followed him.

I shake my head, and amid the cavernous dark, fire sparks at my core. *Trust this.* The priest's words. *Always fucking … trust this.* Would the others be alive if I hadn't? Would the devil still be trapped in hell?

I remain still as Natasha pads down the central aisle toward the rooms at the rear.

She turns. "Jake?"

"You get some rest," I say, my voice trembling, the void swamping every kindling ember.

"What are you going to do?" she asks.

"Walk ..." I say, trailing off.

Tears form at the sides of my eyes. I blink them away, but she holds my gaze.

I swallow. "To get some food," I manage to say. "We've hardly got anything left back there."

Still she doesn't move but only stares back at me. The abyss plunges away inside, almost bringing me to my knees. My body shakes, and my mouth opens, the sentence forming on my lips.

I'll be back soon.

Yet the words don't come. They're not true.

Natasha purses her lips in the shadowed light. There's no distant smile now, no vacant look in her eyes. Pain and exhaustion lie etched across every feature.

"You go rest," I say again, my voice barely a whisper.

And with a tremendous effort of will, I force myself to turn away. The tears leak down my cheeks, and my legs stumble fast toward the doors. My fingers grope for the handle, and I lurch back out into the growing night.

Across the courtyard, down pristine streets, the void's greater than ever, as if it's consumed my entire being, while my ears ring on from the grenade. I take the major roads, ready to be picked up by any passing patrol, to be beaten and ejected from the city centre. But none appear. My feet carry me south over London Bridge, streetlights reflecting in the dark waters. And I continue down into the urban neighbourhoods beyond.

It's clear where I'm heading, yet I don't slow. Nor do I veer off course, and in what seems like an instant, I'm there. Standing opposite the old community library – Paul Hawcross's headquarters – on the opposite edge of the wide concrete forecourt. I find my gaze fixed on the glass front, eighty yards away. It's intact now, the janitor's incursion swiftly repaired. A gaggle of media crews hover to the side of the doors.

I take a breath to settle myself. The abyss is still there, like a fathomless rent in my heart, but the fire's rising too, the flames tickling the inside of my ribs. I scan the building's windows. And while there's no cordite, no sulphur on the wind, it's as if I can sense the demons watching me.

I tense my arms and squeeze my fingers. Time to do what I should have done before – take one or two of the fuckers with me.

The image of Natasha infiltrates my mind: lying on the old beaten sofa in Father Thomas's rooms – shattered, alone. And for an instant, the void swamps the flames. But only for an instant. My neck tenses, and the energy builds in my veins again, the fire kindling and then raging inside me. I was wrong. There's no hope. I can't save her. The only chance she has is being away from me.

A light clicks on at the back of the lobby, and the media crews cluster excitedly. Cameras shove against each other to get a better view.

I grit my teeth. The priest was deluded. There's no divine plan, and if this *is* all intended, I'm truly damned. Everything I do aids the devil, Paul Hawcross now stronger than ever.

I stride toward the building, the same thought spiralling around my head ... *Stronger than ever.*

My pace slows, a new notion starting to form. And as it does, the entire world recedes around me. The sound of traffic quiets at my back. The rumbling thunder grows more distant, and the image of the old community library blurs, its many lighted windows becoming twinkling stars against the black background of my mind.

I come to a halt in the middle of the concrete forecourt, hardly breathing.

All intended.

My eyes widen, and it's as if hands clench my heart.

Energy floods my body while gooseflesh breaks out all across my back.

"Oh, god," I find myself whispering, my fingers on my lips.

Then I spin on the spot and dash back down the empty street.

THUNDER ROARS ABOVE ME. Lightning arcs across the sky. I run through the city streets, the rain falling in sheets, so intense I have to wipe it out of my eyes. My jeans cling to my legs, the water streaming down my cheeks and chest.

Finally, the church looms above me. I scramble up the steps and dart through the doors before dragging them closed behind.

I step into darkness as water trickles down my arms and drips from my fingertips. A shiver rolls through my body, my clothes cold against my skin, while doubting thoughts invade my mind.

I force myself to move again – on past the pews and altar toward the priest's back rooms, through the door, down the corridor, and into the tiny living room.

Natasha's already up on her knees on the sofa, her hands clenched on a blanket and her outline barely visible in the shadowy light.

"What is it?" she says, her eyes wide ovals.

"You were right," I burst out, the words snatched between heaved breaths.

"Right?" she says.

I crouch down beside her kneeling form. "To come *here*," I say and slap the wooden floorboards. "This time, and the time before. *You were right.*"

The ringing's still there in my ears, and my voice sounds oddly different. Higher pitched. Frenzied.

Natasha just stares back at me.

I take a breath. "The darkness exists to help us find the light," I say. "That's what Father Thomas told us."

She simply nods.

"Well, what if it's true?" I say, my fingers gripping the edge of the battered leather cushion. "What if everything that's happened was intended to?"

Natasha closes her eyes and turns away.

"All of it, Nat," I say and stand again, my voice rising. "*All of it*. What if we were supposed to release the devil? What if he was supposed to defeat Gabriel and bring the pantheon to its knees? What if we were supposed to help the devil at every step to help him lay the foundations for his global war?"

She shakes her head and shuts her eyes tighter. "I can't believe that, Jake," she says, her voice cracking. "I just can't."

I lean down and scoop one of her hands from her lap. Then I lift it toward my chest. She turns to face me as I squeeze her fingers gently and smile.

"What if the church didn't draw you back here?" I ask. "What if it was something else?"

And then I turn from her, and my eyes find the adjoining wall. The boundary between the priest's back rooms and the massive skyscraper beyond.

34

THE THUNDER CONTINUES TO ROAR, and the rain falls harder than ever, bouncing off my shoulders and streaming down my chest. Natasha simply stands there, staring up at the building in front of us, water dripping from her chin and her hair slick down her back.

"Jake, of all your ideas," she says, "this has got to be the craziest."

"I know," I say.

The building itself is unrecognisable. The fifty storeys still soar up into the dark sky with the same corporate majesty, but not a spur of light reflects off its granite-like surface. And the lobby before us is as black as a cave. No Puritans stand guard behind the wide reception desk. No incident lighting illuminates the slick stone floors. And the veil I sensed so thin last time is now almost completely absent.

My fingers squeeze the chunk of stone I commandeered from a shattered statue in the church.

"And he might not even be there," Natasha says. "He could be dead, for all we know."

"No," I say and shake my head. "Don't you remember? The devil said he'd leave Gabriel broken but alive. He wanted him to endure the ages, to witness his glorious victory."

Natasha purses her lips and then shivers in the pouring rain. "So, how do we know this isn't another one of the devil's tricks, that he hasn't suggested it somehow?" she asks, her voice soft.

Once again, the doubts clamour inside me. I take a long breath.

"We don't," I say. "That's the point. And we have to go on anyway."

I step up to the building's entrance and push at the revolving door, followed by the single glass door to the side of it. Both locked.

I glance over my shoulder. It's midnight now, and the courtyard remains empty in the squalling rain. A few lights shine from the offices opposite.

I lift the brick-sized stone, pausing for a thunder strike. Then I crash the chunk down on the chrome handle, splintering the lock.

No alarm sounds, and after I've broken additional bolts at the top and bottom, the door opens easily. I step inside, Natasha at my heels, and we quickly shove it closed behind.

The lobby's even darker than it was from the outside, the reflected light from the streetlights only able to reach ten feet across the floor. The darkness is like tar pooling on every surface. There's also a musty scent, the smell of rotting things, as if we're standing in a crypt.

I step over to the desk and rifle through the drawers on the far side for a flashlight. Yet I find only yellowing papers and old Bibles, already crinkled with time as if they've been left here for centuries, not weeks.

I glance toward the rear of the lobby, but I see no sign of the limestone flooring, the marble statues, or the winding staircase we encountered last time. Only darkness. It hovers before me like a physical thing.

My eyes find Natasha on the far side of the desk. "Ready?"

She simply nods and together we pad forward into the

black. It wraps around us so quickly. After twenty steps, the reception area vanishes behind me. Natasha too. The darkness is so deep it's like I'm drowning in it. I stretch out for Natasha, my heart pounding, and finally find her fingers.

"You okay?" I ask, my voice so loud in the silence.

She squeezes my hand, and I push forward.

There seems no end to the blackness, my bearings constantly shifting around me, the sense of where the exit is … gone. Still, I keep going, concentrating everything on placing my feet straight, on holding on tightly to Natasha. Finally, my foot strikes something hard.

In that instant, the outline of twenty steps appears before us. They're illuminated by the familiar flecks of glowing ash that float in invisible currents of air. It's not the majestic carpeted staircase I remember from before, no golden brocade or plush decoration, but it's still eight feet wide with bannisters on either side, made of bare wood, cracked and worn.

I test the first step, and the resulting creak sounds like a tree limb breaking in the silence. I freeze, my pulse galloping, and the faintest rumble resounds in my ears. My gut starts to twist – my internal alarm.

"Jake, what is it?" Natasha asks, her voice barely audible.

I shut my eyes and listen hard. There it is again – a distant rumbling out there in the darkness. The same tremor I've heard inside me – monsters roiling in the deep.

"Not sure," I say and begin to climb, placing my feet as quietly as possible, trying to ignore the loud creaks.

I keep to one edge of the staircase, holding on to bannisters where they exist. Natasha climbs at my side, my hand still tight around hers.

The stairwell spirals upward in the familiar square shape. But there are no walls, no tapestries, no candlesticks with flames blazing, just darkness encasing us on all sides. Plus, the floating flecks of ash and the twenty steps that remain visible above and below, like someone's directing a spotlight upon us as we climb. The notion sends a shudder across my shoulders.

We reach the first landing – a set of bare wooden floorboards that hang in space. Still no doors off it and still no visible walls. Several paces further on, the steps continue, the staircase in even worse repair. More missing bannisters and more gaping holes, like a gigantic mouth has gnawed chunks out of it.

We climb on upward, skirting the gaps, while I'm all too aware of the ongoing rumbling in my ears. The monsters either out there, or inside me … or both. My gut continues to twist.

Next landing. Two staircases this time. Both head up in opposite directions. We choose the one which looks in better shape, and all too quickly, our set of steps branches again. And then again.

Our journey continues like this. Multiple landings. Multiple staircases. Some end in nothingness and we're forced to retrace our steps till we come to the next set of steps heading up.

The further we climb, the more rickety the staircases become, and the more my mind spins as I try to remember our route. Have we been climbing for minutes or days? Plus, a new feeling of isolation presses in on me. The sense of being entirely lost, of being unimaginable distances from anywhere.

"Do you think we will find him?" Natasha whispers suddenly.

The noise brings me to a halt halfway across a narrow landing. I blink back at her.

"We'll find him," I say eventually.

A low growl emanates out of the rumbling sound. My eyes find the next staircase. It has fewer holes.

"This one looks better," I say and take the first step.

The wood vaporises as soon as my foot presses down on it, my leg plunging into darkness.

Heartbeat galloping, I throw out my arms to break my fall,

and my hip slams hard on the landing. While my body's seized by the desire to scramble out of the hole, I force myself to be still, to slowly take hold of the floorboard to my side.

Natasha grips my other hand and gradually helps me up to stand again. I place my foot gently down on the step above.

It holds fine. I exhale all the air from my lungs, my pulse still thumping hard.

"Let me go first," I whisper.

"No way," Natasha says and shakes her head. "You are clearly too heavy." And a thin smile forms on her lips.

I try to match it but fail, that sense of isolation, of aloneness gripping me ever tighter. She pushes past and climbs again.

We continue to weave between the gaps, using the bannisters wherever they exist. And after a while, there are no more landings, no more diverging staircases. Instead, the steps widen, the bannisters becoming more elaborate in design, though it's all still bare wood, cracked and rotten. And as we climb, the veil becomes that bit thinner before my senses while the rumbling sound grows ever louder in my ears.

Fifty feet further on, we reach our first branching staircase for a while. My head swims. One set of steps heads away from us on its side, with gravity flipped by a quarter turn. My stomach heaves just gazing at it, and I grip the bannister to steady myself. Natasha climbs past. Yet after another thirty stairs, she stops and stares upward.

"Shit," she says.

The staircase above ends in a solid wall, eight feet high. And at its top, the stairs continue directly above our heads, heading in the opposite direction. They'd require gravity to be flipped by a hundred and eighty degrees, so we'd be walking upside bloody down.

"We can't—" Natasha says.

"Wait," I say and climb up to the wall.

It's as broad as the staircase, with holes all over it. And a foot or so above my head, the stairs continue on into darkness behind us.

"Let's go back," Natasha says. "Find another way."

"It's alright," I say and place my hands flat on the wall at head height.

I start the count in my head and still my mind. The veil's there before my senses and, focusing on the energy in my chest, I peel it back.

The shimmering world stretches out around me. I can feel the steps above and behind me, the wall in front … and something else as well. Something much fainter, much larger – huge shapes shifting beneath us, circling closer, as if they're attracted by me using the veil. My pulse speeds up, and the shimmering world retreats.

I take a breath and tune out the thoughts, tune out the sensation of the approaching forms. I focus on my hands still flat on the wall and then concentrate intently on peeling back the veil again, on the feeling of gravity shifting. But more doubts slink in, my head swims faster, and the queasiness grows in my stomach.

"Jake?" Natasha asks.

I place my foot halfway up the wall and then bring back the memory of being with the priest in hell, of him flipping gravity, of the ground suddenly becoming a cliff face before me. I bend all my attention on it.

Eventually, the world lurches, the wall shifts to being underneath me, and I have to tense my arms to avoid falling face-first into it.

I breathe deeply. And gently push myself up to standing on the new ground.

"Wow," Natasha says.

I swivel. And the image of us at right angles to each other means my concentration slips. The world spins. The nausea grips me. And I have to focus hard on the ground again.

"Close your eyes and jump," I say, the words elongated in slowed time.

She clasps my fingers and leaps. I catch her in my arms, bringing her to me, chest to chest.

"Now open them," I say softly.

She does, and blinks. Then she looks around and fixes her gaze on the new set of steps above us.

"That was incredible," she says.

"Don't look back," I say and usher her forward up the stairs, driving my thoughts again till the veil slips back into place. Gradually, the nausea ebbs.

The staircase snakes up into the darkness. And soon, we're forced to shift gravity again, but it happens much more easily. Turning a flat section of flooring into a wall, the stairs continuing behind it. And with each set of steps, the veil continues to grow thinner before my senses.

We continue upward. More slowly now. The staircase becomes grander around us, almost twenty feet wide now with huge bannisters. Yet the decay's even worse – longer sections of railing missing, and gaping holes in the steps. I peer through them as I climb, and the outlines of monsters form in the darkness, colossal shapes below us, swimming ever nearer.

Natasha circumvents a large gap in the stairs a few steps ahead.

"We have to be close," she says, peering around.

There's still no sign of walls, of rooms. No sign of Gabriel at all. And I can't ignore the sudden twisting in my gut, the clamouring of my internal alarm.

My body stops mid-climb with one foot poised over the next step while Natasha continues upward, her eyes fixed on the top of the staircase. My mouth opens.

And in the next instant, an ear-splitting crack rings out, and the entire set of steps gives way beneath her feet.

My whole body tightens, and my thoughts still in an instant. The veil rips back from my senses, and time slows to a crawl.

Natasha's lips part and her eyes widen as the stairs fall

away. She starts to plunge downward, her hands rising above her head and a yell issuing from her open mouth. Every instant's like a freeze-frame.

I bend my knees, channel the energy in my legs, and dive head first after her while throwing out a hand to the side.

Her arms and legs flail, her waist plummeting through the hole followed by her chest. I concentrate fixedly on the shimmering world, on the sensation of the staircase passing beneath me, and on my connection to bannisters by my side. I don't look, just close my fingers on where I sense the nearest bannister is.

Natasha's head disappears through the hole, as my palm slams into the wood. I grab the bannister hard while throwing my other hand toward her vanishing form. My fingers tighten around her wrist as my legs fall into nothingness.

The wrench of her body weight almost pulls my arm from my socket. A shout escapes my lips. And I barely hold on, one hand on the bannister and one on her wrist, gripping them as tightly as I can.

And so, we hang suspended, feet swinging. And behind the veil, the rumbling sound continues to amplify in my ears, black outlines growing in the darkness below.

Natasha gazes up at me, dangling from my arm. Her jaw's tight against the pain, but she still smiles.

"Idiot," she says.

I almost laugh. Almost lose my hold on her. My energy's draining, my grip loosening as pinpricks of light appear before my eyes. I force my gaze above me.

The faintest image of a stairwell appears far above my head, continuing upside down, gravity flipped by a hundred and eighty degrees. Then it's gone. My vision swims with the growing pain.

I extend my neck and try to peer upward to catch another glimpse, but I only see darkness above me. My power's bleeding away, my arm shaking and my fingers straightening. Plus, the sound of rumbling morphs into gravelly laughter, and I can't help imagining demons out there behind the black.

"Let go, Jake," Natasha says.

I shake my head, grit my teeth, and focus intently on peeling back the veil, on shifting gravity, on the sensation of Natasha pushing down on me instead of pulling.

Nothing happens. My doubts yell at me as the pain builds in my arms, and I concentrate fiercely on it, morphing it into fire. Flames spark at my core, and I channel them up my body into my arms and bring back the priest's words ... *Remember, these realms are more pliable than you know.*

Still nothing happens. My arm just shakes more, and my doubts shriek louder.

Natasha touches my forearm and finds my gaze. "You don't need me," she says. "Go find Gabriel yourself."

I shake my head more violently, the weight in my chest like lead. I shove all thoughts away, thrust the veil further back, and focus everything on my memory of the thin outline of steps I spied. I use my mind to conjure the image out of the darkness ... above my head, yet upside down.

Pain screams ever louder in my shoulder and my injured rib. My fingers tremble, about to lose their grip.

"You're going to have to let me go, Jake," Natasha says.

My heart wails, the weight doubling inside, and I plunge deeply into the feeling, channelling it into fire, into energy. I fix all my attention on the sensation of us falling together into the darkness above and make it the entire sphere of my concentration ...

And after what feels like an age, gravity gradually lessens its downward tug on my body.

I focus even harder.

The world lurches. And we both tumble back through the hole and down into the blackness. Still, I keep my neck tilted back, my eyes fixed above me. And the outline of the steps solidifies as we plunge toward them ... a broad sweeping staircase forming out of the dark.

Then all of a sudden we're falling too quickly, wind rushing past my ears and the wooden staircase barrelling up to meet us. For an instant, my eyes just blink at it. Then I tense every muscle and concentrate again on the veil, on the solidity of the surrounding air. I focus intently on feeling the gusts pressing us back upward.

Gradually, the air grows thicker. The staircase careens nearer. I rotate my body and concentrate harder. Our fall continues to slow.

The staircase crashes into my side, Natasha still above my head. Pain explodes across my back and hip. Several steps splinter, and I bounce off the remaining ones, still focusing on the air like a shield around us.

Natasha collides with my chest. I barely catch her, and we tumble together down the rest of the staircase before ending up sprawled in the middle of a wide landing.

35

"Are you still alive?" Natasha asks, scrambling above me.

I roll over and end up staring past her shoulder into absolute blackness, cold stone beneath my back. My entire body aches, and my rib screams with each inhalation.

The veil's firmly back before my senses again, and gradually I test each muscle, each limb.

"I think so," I say eventually. And then, with several grunts, I sit up.

The landing's huge, both ends disappearing into darkness. Many broken staircases extend up and down in either direction. And the flecks of ash are more numerous here, hanging in the air and casting light on everything – fragments of wall on both sides, scraps of friezes torn down, the remnants of statues on plinths, most of them hacked to bits. Innumerable cracks cover the marble floor beneath me.

"This has to be it," Natasha says, her voice low.

She's crouched down at my side, her gaze fixed on the remnants of two immense doors that stand framed by fragments of a solid wall, each one at least a hundred feet high. The nearer one's been split in two, the farther one hanging from what must be a massive top hinge.

A chill forms at the base of my back, and I heave myself to

standing. I shove the throbbing pain to the rear of my mind as Natasha straightens, taking a long breath at my side. I squeeze her arm and then begin hobbling off across the landing.

The journey takes an age, each door gradually looming higher above us. And eventually, we find ourselves standing before them. I keep my focus on the dark gap in between. And before my mind can stop me, I push my way through.

Into a gargantuan room beyond, far longer and wider than a football field. It's covered by immense cabinets, statues, display cases, and arches, nearly everything destroyed. The place is like some kind of wrecker's yard, half the floor covered in bits of broken wood and stone, and endless artefacts lie strewn among the rubble.

I gaze around, seeing darkness shine through many gashes in the walls and ceiling. The flecks of ash float here too, gliding gently up and down and giving everything a ghostly hue. The air's colder, my breath misting in front of me.

I scan the far end of the room, and it takes me a moment to realise what I'm seeing.

Behind several cracked columns, deep in the shadows, stands a throne of hewn black rock with numerous fissures running through it, one third of it broken off. And sitting atop it, as dark and still as the stone around, almost impossible to make out … is a figure.

My heart thuds. My body tenses. I force myself to move, to slink toward a large block to my side, and Natasha quickly follows. We hide ourselves behind the chipped stone, and I listen hard.

There's absolute silence. Even the flecks of ash barely shift around us. I peer beyond the edge. Gabriel remains exactly as he was, sprawled on his hewn throne, his torso tilted to one side, a leg propped up on the remaining armrest while the other leg stretches out. He's entirely still, most of his body in shadow.

I step out from behind the stone block and begin padding toward him. My feet take me between countless bits of broken furniture, of smashed statues. And I never take my eyes off the archangel.

The closer we get, the more becomes visible – the outline of his leg bracers, his plate armour. But it's all bashed and dented, the flecks of ash bathing his entire body in a ghostly grey while his face remains cast in shadow.

His chest's not moving at all. It doesn't rise or fall.

My throat constricts, my gait lengthens, and I get fifty yards away before a low snarl freezes me in place.

"You need approach no closer," he says, the multiple layers of his voice horribly disjointed.

Electric shocks course through my body.

"If you've come to die … to be put out of your misery … I can accomplish that from here," he rasps.

His lungs make an awful wheezing sound. His face remains hidden, and the flecks of ash retreat away from us, the darkness creeping in from behind.

I set my feet and squeeze air into my chest. "We're here so you can rise again," I say, the words barely audible in my own ears.

He gives no reply and remains completely still.

I clench my fingers and force energy up my throat. "To challenge the devil," I say, my voice louder.

Gabriel barks a laugh that's like a thunderclap. It echoes around the massive hall. Then he descends into a series of hacking coughs interspersed with the horrible wheezing. I just stare on.

After a moment, he gets back control of his breathing. Then he leans forward, and his head gradually emerges from the darkness. "Have you not noticed?" he says, his layered voice growing harder. "I am not quite my former self."

His face moves entirely into the low light. Natasha cries out before grabbing her mouth. The archangel's perfect features have been cut to ribbons. A massive scar runs down his temple, across his nose and down the far side, while many more criss-cross the opposite cheek.

His lips part to reveal clenched teeth, a few of them broken, and his eyes burn, the grey flecks swirling wildly. My heart thumps harder, and I can feel Gabriel's rage, the embers sparking within.

Then it dissipates. He sighs and leans back into his throne, his face hidden once more. The flames ebb inside me as well, and the flakes of ash still around us.

"It is too late," he says, his tone hollow. "The devil has already triumphed. My brethren are fools." His voice falters. "Satan has played the game better than all of us."

The darkness continues to slink toward us from the corners while the air cools significantly, chilling my skin and lungs. My teeth start to chatter.

"For it is a game, make no mistake," he goes on.

Natasha grabs herself around the middle, and I clench my fingers to force the words out.

"But what if there were another way?" I begin. "What if the devil's release ... what if it was supposed to happen? What if it enables something that no one's achieved since the dawn of civilisation?"

The air becomes even colder. My whole body shakes, and every breath is painful, like the chill's permeating my chest from the inside, creeping toward my heart.

Again, I try to muster the energy in my core. "What if we could use the devil to free humankind?" I sputter, my throat raw. "To give people back their divine spark. To rob the devil of his power forever, to bring down his reign."

While the darkness continues to deepen, Gabriel's eyes shine like spotlights out of the shadows. And when he speaks, it's as if the voice echoes from every direction.

"I know what you ask," he says, his tone entirely flat. "You wish me to reveal myself in front of humanity."

I wet my lips and try to swallow. "In four days' time, they're organising a global summit," I say, scrabbling to get the words out. "Christian leaders are coming from all over the world. It's the perfect opportunity. The entirety of the world's media will attend, and the devil too. And there he'll spark his global war, to reign ongoing while the angels keep themselves holed up in heaven."

Gabriel says nothing but remains there shrouded by darkness. Two bright lights, fifty feet or fifty million miles away.

"Michael and the angels won't act. You know they won't," I say, trying to keep the pleading out of my voice. "Too much is at stake for them, but if you confront the devil and tell the entirety of humanity the truth, reveal their potential, show the true power of faith …" I pause. Set myself. "You'd end his reign forever."

The silence stretches.

"And that of every angel on the earth," Gabriel says eventually. And then his voice descends to a low hiss as the floor vibrates beneath me. "Why would I consider your … invitation?"

He spits the final word, his eyes burning, and I can feel his attention raking mine while the fire builds again in my chest. Then before I can stop it, the next thought flashes through my head, the revelation that came to me facing Paul Hawcross's headquarters.

I tense my jaw and keep my mouth firmly shut.

Gabriel leans his head toward me, and his lips curl. "I can discern your reasoning, little man, I can read … your … mind," he drawls, stretching each word out. "You think I am the only one who would ever do this." He gestures to the surrounding destruction. "Because I … alone … have nothing left to lose." Then the curl on his lips spreads into an awful smile. "Am I correct?"

Hearing my own thoughts articulated, my chest goes rigid, and my brain scrambles. And though my mouth opens, nothing comes out.

Gabriel's arms bunch, and the flecks of ash coalesce into

wings behind him, illuminating his cracked throne and the familiar black sword at his side. He grabs the hilt.

"And you wish for me to give this all up for *them?*" He hefts the six-foot blade and sweeps it to the side, motioning at the world beyond. *"For you?"* He stabs it toward us.

The muscles in his shoulders and neck stiffen into ropes as he draws back his wings and raises his sword. The floor shakes more violently beneath us, and the flames build at my core. I anchor my feet and throw an arm across Natasha.

She pushes right past me. "This is your role!" she shouts at Gabriel, the sound echoing around the space. "No one can do it *but* you."

Her voice ebbs into silence. Gabriel remains where he is, poised at the edge of his throne, sword raised, ready to leap.

I don't move a muscle.

Natasha stands tall and lifts her chin. "You have always been humanity's shepherd, have constantly strived to connect humankind with the sacred," she says.

Still Gabriel says nothing.

"And yes, we disappoint you," she says, "increasingly coming up short."

Gabriel's wings spread out at his sides again, and he brings his sword in front of him. I feel his rage prickling my skin.

"But that is because humankind has come as far as it can," she goes on. "You created the gospels, inspired the current age. And now with the devil's release, and the state of the pantheon, we are on the cusp of the next." She takes a breath, and her voice rings out. "You have *always* been the chosen one, have always done what others lack the courage to do. And you and your brethren have led us this far on our journey." She makes the sign of the cross over her chest. "Now, please, help us take the next step."

Gabriel lowers his sword slowly, and the embers cool in my chest. Natasha takes a deep breath and pads a couple more steps toward him. I need to bite my lip to avoid jumping in front of her.

"Archangel," she says, her voice tremulous. "What if there *were* a God? What if this *is* his plan? What if this is what you were ultimately *born* to do?"

And in that instant, Gabriel's glow disappears. The wings vanish, and darkness covers every inch of him again.

Silence reigns. The flecks of ash float up and down in the air. There's no wind. No wheezing breath from Gabriel. It's as if aeons pass.

I slip forward to stand at Natasha's side, making sure to keep my mind empty.

Finally, Gabriel's voice rings out but with less of the discordant quality. More like the layered music I remember from the angelic realms. "How would it work?" he says.

I open my mouth, my heartbeat accelerating. A million thoughts batter my crashed brain with the countless narratives I prepared, while sweat chills the back of my arms.

"What story do you envision weaving?" Gabriel asks.

"The summit," I stammer. "Paul Hawcross will be there, the Antichrist, and so we know the devil will be there as well. Too much is at stake for him to be absent."

Gabriel remains ensconced in darkness and says nothing.

"The media will be there too," I go on. "It's how the devil's controlling the world. You simply need to arrive and tell your story, describe how you were mortal once like us, and how you've used the power of faith as we all can. The media will beam it everywhere. We'll democratise power across the world in one moment. They'll be playing the footage forever ..."

My words falter, my mind stumbling again. Natasha squeezes my hand.

"You would live for eternity," she says to Gabriel. "Would be immortalised in the canons of history as humanity's saviour, as the one who connected every man and woman with their own sacred nature."

Gabriel's eyes burn in the darkness, and I feel them drilling into me. A new pressure builds in my chest, in my head, and the air hums. My throat's as dry as sandpaper, and I start the count, trying to still my mind. However, visions keep coming of Gabriel and every angel, every demon, losing their power because of this plan, losing their immortality – the true end of their reign.

Eventually, Gabriel sighs, and the gust of wind sends the flecks of ash swirling in eddies across the room. He retreats into darkness again.

"It is well conceived," he says.

I peer into the black. And in the next moment, a new light erupts from his throne, filling the room. It's suddenly blinding, and I stagger backward, hands over my eyes.

"An elegant scheme."

It's Gabriel's voice, but stronger again, more harmonious.

With half-shut eyes, I squint through my fingers into brightness. I can just make out his form standing in front of the throne, towering above us, his wings stretching twenty feet to either side. In the glow, the scars on his face lose some of their shape, and much of the rattling disappears from his breathing.

"Elegant, yes," he says, "but are you aware of who you're up against?"

You. Not we. My stomach drops.

Gabriel's tone becomes a hiss again. "This is the being who stood against the entire pantheon with a tenth of the demons," he says. "The being that presided over the angelic demise while bound in an impregnable realm. There is no length to which he will not go. No possibility he would not consider. Can we truly conceive what a genius can do with eternity?"

Gabriel stares down at us, a wide grin splitting his features.

I take a breath and set my feet. "It makes no difference," I say. "We have faith."

Gabriel snorts a laugh, and the sound echoes into nothingness around us. I shift my weight.

After a moment, he nods and raises a hand in front of his face as if to inspect his nails. "A summit, you say? You must realise how difficult it will be," he says. "I cannot simply … walk in. If the devil *is* present, then as soon as I use my powers, his demons will sense me, search me out, and make sure I never get near their master."

"We'll get you in uncontested," I find myself saying. "We'll make sure you can face him alone."

Silence spreads out around us once more.

Gabriel leans toward us, the grin growing lopsided on his face. "You're truly serious about this?" he says.

I swallow and ask, "Will you come?"

36

Billingsgate Park, three o'clock in the morning, an hour after getting out of Gabriel's headquarters. Clouds pepper the night sky, and the space is deserted, the underground shops and restaurants all closed. Yet several sets of patrolling guards still roam the edge.

Natasha and I pace down the main pathways, dressed in our posh clothes once more: Natasha in her evening dress, the tiny crucifix around her neck again, while I'm in the strait-jacket-like suit, the bloody material clinging to every part of my body.

The guards follow our progress, their eyes lingering on Natasha's bare shoulders and the flash of leg through the knee-high slit as she walks. Natasha lifts her chin and stares straight back at them. They make no move to stop us, and I keep my gaze fixed on Haniel's club on the far side of the public space.

Only a handful of lights shine across the skyscraper's thirty storeys. The platform's dark above, and the entrance seems empty.

"Damn," I say.

"Closed?" Natasha asks.

"Looks that way," I respond. "But it was a long shot. We'll

need to change" – I pull at my shirt cuffs – "and try the other option instead." My jaw tenses, my feet slowing. "That damn Puritan church."

"No way," Natasha says, keeping up her steady stride. "The heavenly realm's a fortress, and Michael will know the *instant* we enter." She shakes her head. "Haniel's our only chance. And we must have got these clothes for a reason."

She pats my arm while my skin itches under the tight shirt. I tug the collar from my neck.

She smiles. "Anyway, there might be an after-party," she says and nods at the building. "You never know."

I grunt, and we stride on, keeping away from the main cones of light. We get seventy yards from the club before I spot the two guards stationed in the shadows of the sculpted entrance. We come to a halt behind a cluster of high reeds, just wide enough to shield us from them both, and I peer through the stalks.

The metal detector and X-ray machine stand unattended, and a glass door's been pulled in front of them, the foyer empty beyond. All quiet. Though from this distance, a faint glow's visible against the domed roof of the platform, fifteen storeys up.

A prickling sensation climbs my back, and my gaze darts to the side. A third guard's pacing around the edge of the club building, staring directly at us.

I stiffen.

Natasha grabs my neck. "Kiss me," she whispers.

I just stand there, my pulse racing.

Natasha presses herself into me, stands on tiptoes, and angles her face up toward mine. The guard's stopped in his tracks. Still eyeing us.

"Hold me properly!" she hisses.

I fumble my arms around her waist and lean my head down. Our lips almost touch. My brain turns to mush. The sound of my heart's so loud in my ears.

"Is he still looking?" Natasha whispers.

I blink and glance back up toward the guard, my hands dropping down her back.

"Don't let go!" she says and shoves my hands back in place.

I swallow. "He's moved on," I say, my voice wavering.

The guard's striding toward his colleagues in front of the entrance.

"Come on then," Natasha says and pulls me in the direction of the club.

I anchor my feet and whisper, "We've been spotted."

She tugs at my arm. "Well, we cannot stay here," she says. "It will look suspicious. In all kinds of ways."

I let her lead me toward the fountain. She links her arm with mine, and we skirt the edge of the roundabout, heading to one side of the building. I can't help glancing at the guards, looking for any sign of recognition. All three of them are staring in our direction, the one who spied us whispering to his colleagues.

I avert my gaze but still glimpse the third guard turning away to start another circuit of the building. We pass out of sight of the entrance, heading around the opposite side, right into the guard's eventual path. I yank Natasha faster down the street, my eyes scouring its length.

Skyscrapers line both sides, their ground floors fronted with solid glass and steel struts. The entrances open out onto wide concrete spaces, all empty. Everything is shut up, with no obvious places to hide.

"Now what?" I ask.

Natasha's scanning the side of the club.

"Maybe an after-hours entrance?" she says, pointing.

And sure enough, a set of double doors are barely visible in the band of shadow that borders the building's flank, halfway down. There are no obvious push bars or handles, the surfaces entirely sheer.

"And?" I press, and my gaze flicks to the far edge of the building. "The guard will be on us in seconds."

"We knock?" Natasha asks. "Claim to be guests of Harmony? She must be known here."

My mouth opens, but nothing comes out.

"It's not a bad plan," a voice says.

I spin, the breath congealed in my lungs.

A figure's padding leisurely toward us across the road, the neighbouring building at her back. She's dressed in a black trouser suit, a white shirt, and a high-collared jacket.

"Christ," I say, my stomach still in my throat. "Where'd you come from?"

Harmony tilts her head. "Does it matter?" she asks. "I've been waiting for you. After your … performance at our dear prime minister's event yesterday, I figured you might be returning."

Her voice sounds playful, and she ambles to stand in front of us, a few feet from the club wall. My heartbeat doesn't let up.

"We've got to get out of sight. A guard's coming," I say and point over her shoulder.

"Well, that would be inconvenient," she says, tone easy.

And there he is. The guard rounds the corner of the club, only fifty feet from Harmony's back.

And in the same instant, she melts into the shadow bordering the club building, her white shirt vanishing behind a closed black collar.

"Hey, you two!" the guard calls, speeding up his approach.

I can only gaze on. Harmony's barely visible now, just a faint outline of black against black. As I stare at her, a silence grows in my mind, tingling energy climbs my legs, and I feel the veil that bit thinner before my senses.

The guard stalks straight past where she's standing.

"What are you doing back here?" he barks. "We're closed."

He halts right before us, various tools hanging from his

belt – stun baton, billy club, handcuffs, gun. He squints up at my face.

My lips part to speak when Harmony steps out of the shadows, only a foot or so from his back, her movements entirely silent.

"I recognise you!" the guard says to me, his features hardening.

I try to concentrate on him while Harmony mouths a word over the guy's shoulder.

"*Inconvenient*."

"I'm calling this in," the guard says, his fingers shooting toward his radio headset.

"Excuse me, sir," I say.

The guy's hand stops in mid-air.

I raise my own arm and point. "Behind you?"

He turns his head.

Harmony waves. "Hi," she says, her voice light and high.

The guy goes rigid and leaps backward into me. I still my thoughts and peel back the veil a fraction. With the familiar connections forming to everything around me, I dart one hand out, pop the catch on his billy club, and grab up the stick with my other hand. Then I knock it into the guy's temple.

He crumples to the ground without a sound.

"Finally," Harmony says and smiles.

I let out a shallow breath. "Is Haniel here?" I ask, the veil slipping back before my senses.

"No," she replies.

For a moment, I can only splutter. Harmony's smile remains.

"But we need him!" I manage to spit out. "Paul Hawcross is hosting a global summit. The only place we know the devil will be. We can challenge him there. We just need Haniel to recruit angels to help—"

"He won't recruit them," she says, her voice still light.

"But we've got Gabriel," I say.

Harmony frowns and pauses a beat. "Gabriel?"

"Yes, the archangel," I say.

"I know who—" she snaps.

"He'll face the devil at the summit, alone," I say, speaking quickly. "All the angels need to do is turn up, to shield him from demons. We can tell them where to be—"

"The good angel Haniel will … not … come," Harmony says. "And he won't recruit anyone."

I pause.

"Why?" Natasha asks.

Harmony turns her gaze on her. "Because Michael let it be known that you were involved in the devil's release," she says, her tone soft again.

My chest tightens, and perspiration breaks out across my lower back.

"And so, for Haniel to relay information from you to the angels would be to court exile, to become the easiest of targets for the devil and his servants," Harmony says, shifting her gaze to me again. "It would be suicide for any angel."

And with this, she beams a wide smile and turns away, padding back up the side road toward the front of the building.

"Wait!" I yell and reach out my arm.

She swivels and raises an eyebrow.

And I just stare back at her, my mouth dry. Natasha fingers the material of her dress as she shifts her weight at my side. Harmony turns to go again.

"*We'll* recruit them," I blurt out.

Natasha spins to face me, and Harmony's eyes narrow.

"We'll do it ourselves," I say. "We'll just need an audience of the most open to speak with. Haniel wouldn't even need to say what they were invited to."

Harmony stares back at me for a long moment, and I hold her gaze. A gust of wind cools the growing sweat on my neck, and I shudder.

"Very well," she says.

Then she continues along the side of the building toward the front. And as she reaches the corner, the obvious strikes me.

"Stop!" I say and throw out a hand. "The guards!"

Harmony disappears around the building, and no sound follows.

I turn. Natasha's still gazing at me, a strange look in her eyes – a mixture of curiosity and excitement. And that's when I notice the unconscious guard at our feet, lying there in plain view. A distant shout rings out from further down the street.

"Quick, grab his legs," I say.

And together we haul the guy into the band of shadow by the building's edge and then hurry after Harmony.

I reach the corner, pause, and peer around it. The front of the club is entirely deserted, with no sign of anyone beneath the overhang or on the roundabout beyond.

Padding across the entrance, I see the lobby light's been extinguished, the shadows deep in every corner. I keep going, my eyes trained on the glass doors.

There's now a gap in the centre, just a couple of feet wide. The skin prickles across my shoulders, and I slip inside with Natasha right behind me. The air's dryer and warmer with the slightest acrid scent, and I find my gaze drawn to the far side of the lobby.

A tiny display shines above the furthest lift. An illuminated G for Ground; all the others blank. Plus, a faint light spills through the doors, blackness to both sides. I pad toward them.

The call button's dark, though there's a slot beneath it, a key inside. And the same silence grows in my mind as before. I search the shadows to the side of the slot as Harmony emerges from them, her black collar still done up right to her throat.

"Is Haniel here?" I ask for the second time.

She simply turns the key, and the lift doors slide silently

open. Golden light blinds my eyes, and I shrink back, the heat so intense that my forehead burns.

Gradually, the glow dims, and I can make out the outline of a figure. His size morphs from colossus to normal man, and his form is clothed in the bright white suit. The heat remains, and sweat builds across my arms and shoulders.

Haniel's expression is flint-like from the rear of the lift, and his glowing reflection looks vast in its mirrored sides as he fixes me with piercing eyes.

"So … you come for my help," he says, his lips playing with each word. "And you have the mighty Gabriel on your side."

Doubts spring immediately, worries about whether the archangel will actually turn up. Haniel's eyes narrow, and I can sense him searching my mind, like fingers probing my brain. I start the count and focus hard on stilling my thoughts.

"And he's agreed to confront the devil at this summit?" Haniel goes on.

The fingers probe deeper, the pressure building in my skull. And an additional thought slinks in uninvited … *With the aim of robbing the devil and every angel of their power.* My heart speeds up, and I grit my teeth, focusing everything on the escalating numbers in my head and on shoving all else out.

After an age, Haniel smiles and the pressure releases. I almost stumble forward.

"Well, well, well," Haniel says.

After a moment, he gives a nod. Harmony pulls the key from under the call button and slips into the lift. She stands with her back to the side wall and doesn't meet my eye. I remain rooted as Haniel raises an eyebrow at us.

My insides tighten. "Now?" I ask.

"No time like the present," Haniel says with his familiar aristocratic ease. "Michael has eyes everywhere. The more time that passes, the more likely he will find out about your … plan."

Nausea bites at my stomach. Still Harmony doesn't meet my gaze. I shuffle into the lift and then back up just inside the doors. The heat's more intense than before, sweat rolling down my front. Natasha steps in at my side.

Harmony uses the same key on a lock inside the lift and presses a series of buttons on a keypad above. The lift doors close, and we lurch downward. My nausea grows.

"Where are we going?" I ask.

"Only one place exists that will suffice," Haniel says. "You see, any angels consenting to listen will demand complete anonymity. Won't they, my dear?"

He angles his head toward Harmony, though he keeps his gaze fixed on me.

"Total invisibility," she says after a moment.

The lift clunks to a halt. My arms tense. Harmony turns the key again, and the doors open behind Haniel to reveal a dark service passageway with concrete walls and the outline of wires in brackets. Neither Haniel nor Harmony move.

I swallow, my pulse thumping like drumbeats behind my ear.

"You must walk in the same direction as you arrive," Haniel says, and a grin pulls at his mouth. "All the way to the very heart of the ancient city."

At that moment, I feel icy breath against the back of my neck, and the cordite smell's far stronger in my nose. I spin. Then I stagger backward half a step.

The mirrored doors are gone. Instead, I see a film like a pane of glass, and beyond it stands a stone corridor, arched in shape, with pale bricks in the floor, the walls, and the ceiling. A patch of grey sky hovers at the end.

My gut starts to twist.

"You will find a large structure there," Haniel goes on from behind me, his voice starting to echo. "Stray not, tarry not. With it being an ancient battlefield, remnants of bygone weapons remain."

"What d'you mean?" I ask, swivelling.

The lift's empty. Haniel, Harmony, and the fierce heat, all gone. The far lift doors are already closed, the key vanished from the slot. I share a look with Natasha, and she grips my hand as we spin back around.

The image of the stone corridor's still there, stretching out before us, and I notice a faint pulsing at the rear of my skull.

I take a deep breath and stride straight toward the mirrored pane.

37

I PLUNGE through the back of the lift, through the film of glass, and the image of the stone corridor barrels toward me at breakneck speed. I shut my eyes and feel a tremendous tug on my sternum, the sensation of travelling countless distances. Hard ground slams into my feet, and I lurch forward several steps, the customary smell of cordite in my nose.

My eyes fly open. The grey corridor's ahead of me once more, but when I whirl around, only a wall of darkness lies behind. No sign of Natasha, of the lift, or of anything at all. I dart to the side just as Natasha stumbles out of the blackness. I grab her by the waist and bring her to a halt.

We both stare down the arched passageway, at the patch of grey sky at the end. The veil's clearly perceptible before my senses, and the pulsing sensation's still there, a faint vibration in my bones that sets me on edge. Haniel's words sound in my mind … *Do not tarry*.

"Come on," I say, squeezing Natasha's hand.

The cordite smell wanes as we stride down the stone corridor, a new smell taking its place – one of age, of dryness and decay. The passageway gives out into what once must have been a large courtyard, fifty yards square, and I stumble to a halt.

The courtyard's surrounded by enormous and ancient-looking buildings, the walls made of huge grey stone blocks with arched windows, battlements, and ornate columns and spires everywhere you look.

But everything's been destroyed, leaving gaping holes in every surface, the stone cleaved and shattered. Yet the remnants of roofs and walls remain hanging in mid-air with giant gaps around and between them, supported by absolutely nothing. It's like gazing out at a three-dimensional puzzle, only two-thirds of which has been completed, with many of the pieces hovering in space.

Above the buildings hangs a grey sky, its hue a fraction darker than the stone. There are no clouds, just the faintest marks of grey on grey. I peer closer but can barely make out the customary glowing flecks. They float fifty feet above the ground, far more distant than in any of the previous realms, their light barely illuminating the ruins beneath.

"We continue in the same direction. Right?" Natasha says, glancing up at me.

I nod, half of my attention on the dull vibration in my chest. It's a fraction stronger.

"Okay then," she says and strides across the hard ground, her footsteps resounding in the silence.

I scurry behind, and we pass the remnants of a fountain in the centre of the courtyard, now just a pile of stones with metal sculptures strewn about them – a set of horrendous sea creatures, fantastical in shape. And at the far edge of the courtyard, we find more metal objects: huge swords, shields, and spear points. Any wood or leather has rotted away, and a thin coating of dust covers every surface.

I lean down and run my fingertip along the top of a bronze shield. The dust comes off easily, and rubbing it between my fingers, I note it's very fine, far lighter than the pale stone around us. Almost bone-white.

A shiver runs through me, and I straighten quickly.

"What—" Natasha starts.

I hold up my hand because with each word, the vibration in my chest increases yet further. And it's now joined by a low drumming sound, barely audible.

"Can you hear that?" I whisper.

Natasha tilts her head, her brow furrowing.

"Not sure," she says.

I experiment with turning my head this way and that. The sound doesn't change, but the vibrations in my body do. I feel faint tugs from different directions, yet the twisting in my gut remains.

"We've got to get going," I say, trying to keep my voice level.

I lead Natasha down a wider avenue that heads off the corner of the courtyard. We reach a junction and turn, and then turn again, high walls and spires towering above us on every side, blocking our view in every direction.

The city's laid out like a maze. We pass huge cathedrals and castles, massive halls, and dome structures. All broken. All destroyed. Bits of stone archways hang in mid-air. Fragments of staircases hover over nothing. Thin towers stand with only a few lines of stone bricks holding them up.

And all the while, I keep us snaking forward, my head anchored in the direction we arrived in. The only sound's the echo of our footsteps while my bones vibrate more, the drumming noise growing in speed and volume, increasingly audible in the distance. I quicken my steps.

We approach a wall that runs a long way in both directions, blocking us off. My eyes find the yawning holes in the brickwork, many tonnes of masonry hovering unsupported above them, ready to crash down at any moment. I hold my breath and scamper through.

Nothing shifts. The fragments of the wall remain suspended above. I let out a slow exhalation. Natasha joins me, and we pace through the massive hall beyond under remnants of a vaulted ceiling high above and past broken statues and large silver plates lying scattered in the corners.

The same white dust covers everything. And having darted through another hole in the far wall, we emerge into another avenue.

Still no sign of the middle of the city, of any kind of central structure. Just another ruined castle lies straight ahead with shattered turrets and ramparts as well as a few staircases running halfway up the outer wall. And the drumming sound keeps building.

I shut my eyes, focus hard, and pick out the faint tugs from different directions. Four or five. Each one getting incrementally stronger. My gut continues to constrict.

"This way," I say and scurry up one of the staircases, the steps beneath me hanging in mid bloody air. I make sure not to look down but keep my gaze fixed ahead, craning my neck to peer above the lower structures for any sign of a large building beyond.

At the top of the steps, there's nothing. My view is blocked by more damn castle walls with only shattered buildings all around. The staircase passes through a gap in the broken wall and down the other side, while the remnants of a couple of turrets loom above us. Natasha pushes past me and begins descending.

"Wait," I say and clutch her arm. "I'm heading further up."

She turns as I grab a block at waist height and leap it. I start to scale the broken wall. My heart's in my mouth. The shattered stones are only a few inches wide and getting thinner, with nothing but fifty feet of space beneath them.

I keep pressing higher, foothold after foothold, my fingers scrabbling for purchase and legs burning with every gigantic step up. The turret's just a few feet above, a looming gap in the stonework below it. I jump for the rim, and my shoes thud against one of the remaining stone blocks. The drumming grows louder again, the single beats coming so fast now.

With my rib aching, I scramble up the rest of the wall and

push myself to standing on one of the few remaining bits of floor, the fractured rampart all around me.

Breathing hard, I stare out.

And there it is, far in the distance. The broken city gives way to an enormous circular plain at its centre, and at its middle, some kind of structure. A mere pinprick from here, it appears to be a fucking continent away.

My heart sinks, but while doubting thoughts clamour, I push them away and focus on the buildings before me.

More castles. A sprawling cathedral also, just off to the side with the ruins of four bell towers surrounding it, a couple of massive iron bells visible amid the collapsed stone. Directly in front of us stands a vast hall with a domed roof, plus a few smaller churches and a fort, its top a circular parapet. Broken ramparts litter the skyline, with staircases ending in open space and shattered walls like a million cracked teeth.

I start the count, still my mind, and focus on peeling back the veil. The shimmering world spreads out around me, and in that instant, the drumming sound erupts into a wild roar, the vibrations so powerful that my teeth rattle. And I feel my gaze dragged to the side, to the space between a couple of buildings a few hundred yards away.

A black shape appears there, a swirling hole in my vision, and it's as if its edges are reaching for me, dragging me in. The tugging sensation in my chest becomes so strong that I feel myself being yanked over the edge of the tower.

My adrenaline fires, and I reach out, barely able to grab the stone rampart. I hold on tightly and rip my gaze away. However, I can still sense the creature and another four of them, all tugging in different directions and all getting steadily closer.

My heart's pounding, and while every part of me wants to banish the shimmering world, to scramble back down the wall, I root my feet and keep the veil pulled back. I focus hard on the layout of walls and pathways ahead of us, trying to fix it all in my mind.

The roaring grows ever louder. I take one final look and then grip the rim of the turret to leap over the edge. My feet thump onto two of the floating blocks, and I scamper down the remainder of the wall, not pausing to balance. With one last jump, I land hard on the upper steps, the impact jarring my rib and my soles stinging with pain.

"What is it?" Natasha asks, her voice tight.

"Something's coming," I say and thrust a hand against her lower back.

She tenses under my fingers as I shove her on down the staircase and scramble immediately behind. We reach the avenue at the bottom and break out into a run, Natasha's face pale at my side.

"Don't worry. We'll make it," I say. "I saw the structure."

And again, the drumming noise grows. The barrage is so intense now that even without the veil, every part of my body is vibrating, the sound of our pounding footsteps almost drowned out.

I squeeze my fingers, trying to keep my focus on the map in my head. A straight avenue just ahead.

We barrel across a junction, and the tugging sensation increases, the creatures closer still. Less than a hundred yards away now, they're zeroing in from all around us.

I drive my legs faster, random ideas firing, different routes forming in my mind. But each one dissipates the instant it forms, every trail leading to a dead end or open air.

Starting the count again, I go back behind the veil. The awful roaring explodes in my ears, and I concentrate hard on tuning it out, on scanning through everything I've observed …

The pathways ahead, the towers, the halls, the cathedral, the castles, the items on the ground … stones, swords, shields. All bloody useless.

I scramble through a hole in the wall and sprint toward the side of the fort with the circular top, Natasha at my back. And still I hold firm behind the veil, trying to clear my mind for *something* to arise. A single memory keeps returning, over and over …

Natasha in the park, our lips almost touching, the warmth in my cheeks, the electricity up my back. *Fucking pointless.* And despite the doubt, despite the wild clamour in my head, I hold fast to the shimmering world as I run and let the memory unfurl.

Natasha and I hurrying around the corner of the club building. Harmony appearing out of nowhere. Then melting into the darkness—

I grab Natasha's wrist and skid to a halt. The veil slips back into place.

"Hide behind there!" I hiss, pointing at a wall. "Don't move and don't make a sound!"

Her lips open, and I lean in and kiss her on the mouth. She goes still, her eyes wide.

"*Promise,*" I whisper.

She nods, and I dart away from her, my heart aching as I barrel down an avenue to the side.

My mind brings up the memory of the buildings in this direction: a domed structure, a high wall, and the ruined cathedral just beyond. I sprint toward it and careen around the corner of a church into a narrower road.

The creatures continue to close in – three from behind and one from the front. The closest one from the side, only fifty yards away.

My feet pound against the hard earth, and I lean down and grab up a sizeable chunk of stone from the ground. I smash it against a bit of broken wall as I pass.

The resulting crack echoes off the stone, and the drumming intensifies even further in my head. The adrenaline's like lava in my veins now, my heart like a train. And while my warning thoughts scream ever louder, I force the veil back again and build the energy at my core.

I race toward the end of the road, toward a ruined building standing there, just twenty feet from the broken cathedral wall. I focus on the winding staircase at its centre, easily visible through the gaps in the brickwork.

Movement in my peripheral vision grabs my attention: spirals of dust approaching down an adjoining road. They whip through the air and tug at my mind, at my limbs. The resulting pull yanks me sideways, and I stumble, my balance starting to go. Still, I keep my gaze averted, channel the energy down my legs, and fling myself at a neighbouring wall. I bounce off it and barely right myself.

The creatures draw ever nearer, the closest one only ten yards away now with the ruined building approaching. I thrust my way through the outer wall and up the spiralling steps, my fingers clenched around the stone in my palm.

The barrage in my head has become a cacophony, all five creatures almost upon me, the pull intensifying from behind. I scramble up the last steps, the breath like flames in my lungs.

The staircase ends in nothingness, a fall of thirty feet to the ground just before me. My legs wobble and I focus forward.

The cathedral, its splintered outer wall and the top of its broken towers visible just beyond.

Behind the veil, I channel my energy from feet to shoulders, feeling it coursing up my body, and then I draw back my arm and heave it forward. I launch the stone toward the ruined cathedral with everything I have, toward the base of one of the towers.

38

THE STONE SAILS over the broken brickwork of the cathedral wall. I close my eyes in the next instant and focus all my attention on stilling my thoughts and giving over into nothingness. Instead of pulling the energy into my body, I send it outward into the stairs beneath my feet, into the walls of the ruined buildings to my sides. I concentrate on melting into the world around me, just as Harmony did.

The roaring in my brain doesn't let up. It augments till my skull feels like it's going to split apart. The compulsion to put my hands to my head is huge, to grip my ears. Yet I fix my arms to my sides and anchor my feet.

The wind slams into me from all directions, ripping at my skin, wrenching at my limbs, and pounding at my injured rib. The churning dust is like taloned fingers, and it feels like I'm being torn apart.

I scrunch my eyes even tighter shut, trying to block it all out and focus on becoming translucent. My body is as empty as my mind, the pain like dull echoes, all sound and sensation a memory.

And then the clang echoes around me, the stone having hit home, smashed against the fallen bell in one of the neighbouring towers.

The tendrils of wind howl again and then diminish. The tugging feeling dissipates in the clang's direction, and the roaring in my head ebbs away.

Still I stand there. Rigid. Till the sound's nothing more than a low thrumming, the vibration in my chest a faint buzz.

Finally, I open my eyes. The ruined cathedral reappears ahead of me with the broken walls to either side and the spiral staircase at my back. I take a breath and my body shakes, the adrenaline bleeding from my system.

Slowly, I reach down and inch my shoes off, one at a time, hardly breathing. Then I pad down the staircase and across the road entirely silently, making my way back toward Natasha.

It takes a good ten minutes to retrace my steps. And when I turn the last corner, her body tightens. Then she goes up on her tiptoes, her eyes alight.

My finger darts immediately to my lips. She freezes and settles back down.

I pad up to her, bend over, and trace a word in the dust.

Silence.

She nods and motions to my dusty hair and clothes with a smile. "You're back looking awful," she mouths.

I nod and smile back. She removes her own shoes, and together we steal through the labyrinth of shattered walls, always heading in that same direction while keeping our tread slow and quiet. And in the stillness, the pull doesn't grow again in my chest. The sound remains at a low thrum.

Our journey takes an age. Nothing but the ruined bloody buildings, one after another. My feet grow sore, embers sparking inside. But still I keep our pace steady, our progress silent.

Eventually, the buildings thin around us at the same time as the sky darkens above, fewer of the flecks visible. After a while, we're padding across an empty plain, the broken walls at our backs, the light having diminished to a round patch that encircles us. Nothing but darkness lies in every direction.

I peer forward, barely able to pick out some kind of feature on the horizon ahead, the tiniest outline of grey against black. The structure seems to disappear every time I look at it directly.

We plod on. Time loses all meaning. The passage of seconds, hours, days. There's only walking. Only blackness all around. The fatigue's like lead inside my bones.

Natasha grabs my arm. I shake myself and then stop dead.

A faint whooshing sound's coming from behind us. I remain still, my gut twisting again. The noise grows, approaching fast, its source travelling high above our heads. No sign of it in the black. Still, I don't budge. Don't breathe. My pulse far too loud behind my ears.

Finally, the whooshing noise diminishes toward the structure before us, leaving Natasha and me with silence and darkness on all sides. I let out a sigh. She squeezes my arm.

"Angel?" she mouths.

"Got to be," I mouth back.

The skin itches at my neck, the patch of light around us like a damn beacon.

"Come on," I whisper and pull Natasha on.

We trudge on across the plain, and the whooshing sound repeats itself several times. Each time, we stop, remain still, hardly breathing. And each time, it diminishes again.

And finally, the structure ahead seems to be getting larger on the horizon, a likely growing horde of angels within. My pulse thumps harder, the doubts swirling faster.

I turn to Natasha, open my mouth, and barely breathe, "What am I going to say?"

We pad silently on, and she frowns and blinks at me for a moment. Then she whispers back, "The minimum. That they only need to help Gabriel face the devil at the summit. No visibility. No risk. What have they got to lose?"

"*Everything*, Nat," I say, desperately trying to keep my voice quiet. "All their power, all their long life … gone." A weight's growing at my core. "And they can read bloody minds. How am I going to keep this secret?"

I swivel back and lurch to a stop, my body tight.

From nowhere, the structure's right before us, veering to the sides and above, absolutely gigantic and unfathomably high. Gazing toward the top, I nearly stumble. The jet-black walls sweep away in gradual arcs to both sides, the curves so big they're almost imperceptible. A row of huge pillars spans the entire front with massive gaps in between. I stare between them and prepare to be rushed.

Nothing attacks. There's no movement at all.

My muscles remain taut, and I sniff the air, a new scent emerging against the background of age and cordite – just a hint of a familiar freshness. I feel my gaze drawn to the nearest pillar.

The shadow becomes a fraction thicker on one side, and despite my quickening heartbeat, I find myself hurrying toward it. When I'm only ten yards away, a figure steps out of the gloom, their body swathed in darkness. The outline of their face slowly becomes visible in the dull light.

"Eleth!" I breathe.

"This way," she whispers, the word barely audible. "We don't have much time."

She heads off toward the immense pool of black between the columns. It splits down the middle, forming the contours of two massive doors.

I follow behind. The doors swing open entirely silently, revealing more darkness beyond, a slice of the ground illuminated by the grey glow seeping in from outside.

"Some have come," Eleth whispers, stopping at the threshold. "I do not know how many or for what purpose." She turns back to face us. "But they are here, inside, and have been waiting a while."

I stare beyond her through the open doors.

"It's an auditorium, immense on any scale," Eleth goes on.

"You won't see the audience, and do not attempt to. It will only anger them."

"Anger?" I ask. The same weight's building at my core, Natasha's words revolving around my mind … *What have they got to lose?* Everything. Eleth too.

I turn to her. "You should know—"

Eleth places a single finger to her lips. *"Say no more,"* she says, the words this time spoken directly into my head. *"Just go and speak your heart."*

And with that, she bows and backs away from the doors, padding along the side wall, her eyes on me the entire time.

"And try to stay alive," she whispers with a smile before disappearing between two of the columns.

My chest aches as I take a breath and shut my eyes for an instant. Then I focus again on the doors. The gap is wider than before, the immense darkness pulling at me. My gut's twisting ever more.

"I can't do this," I find myself whispering.

"You can," Natasha says, her eyes on me. "And I'll be with you."

"But my last speech didn't end so well, if you remember," I say. "And now they know we helped release the devil."

Natasha grips my hand. "Just trust," she says. "You were the one who told me this is all intended. It *has* to work."

I stare back at her, and she holds my gaze.

After a moment, I force a nod.

"Has to work," I repeat.

Then I squeeze Natasha's fingers, steel myself, and pad on into the blackness.

39

The doors rise bewilderingly high to either side of us. I keep my eyes trained on the darkness in between, scanning for any movement. Natasha steals forward at my shoulder.

We enter a wide corridor. The grey light filtering through the doors forms a path we walk upon. And eventually, the passageway expands out into an oval arena with high walls barely visible at the edge of the space. I start to scour the darkness above, peering out for seated rows, for the outline of angels.

"Jake, *no*," Natasha says.

I quickly avert my gaze, keeping it focused on the near-circular space, faintly illuminated by the pale glow shining through the open doors. And all the while a tingling sensation forms at the base of my back, the sense of being watched.

I pad on toward the middle of the oval space, my mind scrabbling to prepare my words. But my focus keeps slipping. The ground has turned from stone to sand, and I notice a growing smell of decay. It's clear I'm stumbling into a fucking coliseum, a place for sport and death. My gut twists further.

A faint hissing breaks the silence. The tingling sensation climbs my spine, and my heart thumps, while the air throbs with anticipation. I keep scanning the space, and then the outline forms before my eyes – a figure in the darkness, standing right by the curved wall, barely visible.

I lean toward Natasha and whisper, "Stay close—"

There's an explosion of noise like a thunderclap – the doors slamming shut – and the arena's plunged into absolute blackness. I spin.

A roaring sound shakes my skull, and a colossal form careens past me, right where Natasha's standing. A wall of wind slams into my chest, sending me reeling. Natasha's cry of shock rings out for an instant. Then it's cut off.

"Nat!" I scream and stagger to a stop. *"Nat!"*

I leap back to the place I'd been standing and cast my arms about in the pitch black. I probe desperately with my hands and fingers.

There's nothing. Just darkness and space along with the fading of the roar into the background hiss. It morphs into a voice in my head.

"How dare *you!"* it rasps.

Panicked thoughts fill my brain, and I keep scouring the gloom. Still there's no sign of her, or of the dark figure. Nothing but absolute blackness.

I clasp my fingers together and focus on calming my breathing, on slowing my spiralling pulse. Then I tilt my head up toward the rows above, trying to channel energy up my chest.

"Please!" I yell out, voice shaking. "We're here because we need your help! The devil. He's hosting—"

The roar of wind comes an instant before the impact – a glancing blow to the shoulder. I'm thrown backward, lose my footing, and end up sprawled on the ground with my shoulder and side aching.

I push myself back to my feet. The hiss is still there, and the words snarl again in my brain. *"We know what you are,"* the voice says. *"That you were welcomed in* hell!"

I try to shut it out. To concentrate again on the power in

my throat. "A global summit, two days from now!" I shout at the invisible rafters. "The devil will be there. We can—"

The figure smashes into my chest, and I'm thrown through the air, my ribs exploding in pain. I land hard on my back, much of my breath scattered.

"Gabriel," I try to yell but barely manage a croak. I thrust myself up to a sitting position. "Gabriel!" I shout again. "We have Gabriel."

There's a growing silence now, the hiss diminished. I stumble back to my feet, my legs shaking, my body throbbing with pain.

"He'll challenge the devil," I manage to get out while building the fire at my core. "One on one, but we need you to—"

The roar comes. I whirl toward it, tensing my torso and my upper body. But the impact takes me in the legs and sweeps them out from under me, sending me pinwheeling through the air.

I still my thoughts and peel back the veil, trying to slow my fall … And only an instant later, the ground smashes into my side. Pain shoots up my spine.

"Fuck!" I say, the yell escaping my mouth.

And the hiss starts up again. *"Devil's puppet,"* the voice says in my head. *"Why should we let you live?"*

This time I don't speak. Instead, I force my mind to quiet again and go back behind the veil. The pain amplifies with the increased sensation, and I grit my teeth against it. The shimmering world spreads out around me – the connection with the ground and the walls, plus the faintest echo of breathing reaching my ears.

I turn toward the sound. And behind the veil, shapes emerge from the blackness – the curved shape of the wall, and my attacker waiting before it. I get to my feet again, all my attention on the outline.

I open my mouth, my thoughts starting up again in my

head – my prepared lines. The shimmering world vanishes. The figure too. Blackness swamps my senses again.

I tense my throat as I try to spit the words. "We need demons kept at bay," I gabble, my eyes scouring the same patch of dark. "There's no risk, no need to reveal …"

The darkness stirs ahead of me with the merest shift. And in that instant, I stop my thoughts, peel back the veil, and catch a glimpse of the figure barrelling toward me. I channel the energy into my legs and spring out of the way. I get half a step before the shape bashes into my arm. Pain blazes across my shoulders, and I barely keep my feet.

I banish the shimmering world and yell again, "You'll remain hidden—"

This time, the figure hits me from behind, right between the shoulder blades. I crash forward onto the ground with my chest and then my forehead.

My mind swims, and I end up blinking into the darkness, my head aching and rib on fire. I have to focus hard to avoid passing out.

Slowly, I struggle upward, blinking away tears. Every movement is agony, the hissing ever louder in my ears.

I set my feet, take a breath, and try to still my thoughts. Again, my eyes scour the darkness, the veil gradually peeling back, the pain in my chest augmenting further.

And there … the dark figure poised by the edge of the space. Plus, the voice sounds once more in my head. "*Demon's friend*," it says. "*What torture do you merit?*"

A chill grips my spine, my thoughts firing up again, my mind careening between the impossibility of both evading the angel and getting the words out. The veil retreats, the figure disappears, and the blackness closes in on me.

The hissing augments in my ears, morphing into a low cackling. "*Guest of hell*," the voice says. "*Shall we make this long or short?*"

The flames course through my veins, my jaw clenches, and I thrust back the veil once more. And this time when my mouth opens, I don't search for my script. My mind remains blank and I just let the words come.

"Yes, I've been there!" I find myself yelling, my own words slurring in slowed time.

Visible behind the veil, the figure remains still, and the hissing diminishes a fraction.

More words come, my thoughts still banished. "I've navigated all six gates of hell!" I shout. "Iron and salt and ice and stone and fire and glass. I've faced the devil. Helped summon Michael. Yet we *still* failed to prevent the devil's escape. But I survived. Why?" I let the word echo around the oval space. "Not because I'm a puppet. But because I'm here to tell you what no one else will!"

I pause to draw a breath. The thrumming in the air reaches a higher pitch, the sensation pulsating my skull behind the veil.

"That Michael is lying to you," I say.

The hissing sound dies in an instant. The dark figure takes a step forward, arms out and knees bent. My mind starts to kick in. But I push all thoughts away.

"The devil's escape was no accident," I say, the words tumbling out.

The figure throws itself toward me, barrelling across the arena space. The fire rages at my core, and I plunge ever deeper into the shimmering world. Time slows, and I'm able to make out the shape of wing tips, a massive hand flying at my neck.

At the last instant, I channel the energy into my legs and spring diagonally forward, spinning under the outstretched wing. It misses me by an inch, the blast of wind buffeting my body.

I hear a gasp of surprise around the arena. I regain my feet and, anchored behind the veil, the words keep flowing.

"The devil chose to be bound," I say between breaths. "Just like he chose to return when you were weaker."

In the shimmering world, the feeling comes of the figure

rocketing toward me from behind. I throw myself at the ground, hands first, going into a forward roll. My chest throbs fiercely as the figure shoots over my head, the wind blasting in my ears.

The gasps intensify.

"With this war, he'll become unstoppable," I find myself saying while blinking away the thumping pain. I turn to face the dark outline. "You all *know* this."

The figure's back at the edge of the arena. It draws a sword from its shoulders, a huge spike against the background of black. I don't turn away. Don't alter my stance.

"Help Gabriel face the devil at the summit. Help him end this!" I yell, the words still coming. "I will get you into the building unseen. You don't even need to show yourselves!"

My arms end up raised to the sky, and I keep my gaze fixed on the figure, watching for the familiar forward step, for the sword to come cleaving at my head.

It doesn't move. And I find my eyes drawn along the wall to the side.

I blink. Another figure stands there … and another, twelve or thirteen in total, evenly spaced around the entire circumference of the arena.

My heart pummels the inside of my chest, and my body tenses. Amid trying to pick out the glint of swords, the darkness floods my senses completely. Even behind the veil, all sight and sound dies, as if every part of me has been smothered.

I spin about, my pulse firing, barely able to breathe. "We can do this together!" I say, though it comes out as a strangled yell.

And then the darkness vanishes, and the arena reappears. Much brighter than before, illuminated by the large square of grey light pouring through the open doors. I'm forced to shield my eyes. The twelve figures – plus my attacker – they're all gone.

I focus back on the doors, on someone running toward

me. Natasha throws her arms around my shoulders and squeezes tightly. The pain flares in my rib, and I bite my cheek as I hold her with one hand.

She steps back, the ghost of a smile on her lips, that strange look on her face again – curiosity or anticipation in her eyes.

A larger figure pads behind Natasha and stops in front of me, arms folded.

"Did it work?" I ask, my rib aching with each word.

Eleth grins. "You're still alive, no?" she replies.

40

Natasha and I turn the corner into another feeder road, and the summit building emerges into view once more, the space surrounding it fucking bedlam. Like nothing I've ever seen before. Hurrying down the street, we quickly come up short, much of the tarmac choked with people … again. The conference centre is still a hundred yards away.

On the river, half a mile from the Docklands area, the building is gigantic. It's rectangular and at least three hundred feet high with an open space around it the size of numerous football fields. And the surrounding crowd's so large – many hundreds of thousands strong – that it's spilling backward into these neighbouring roads and blocking us from getting anywhere bloody near.

Plus, people aren't just pressing toward the front. For some reason, they're surging across the outside space in all directions like some kind of angry sea, the collective din incredible.

"Can you spot it?" Natasha asks.

I go up on my toes to peer over the teeming crowd, scanning for the media enclosure – our planned ticket into the summit.

"Not yet," I say. The platform is still out of sight behind a building on the far corner.

I press on toward the side of the street and shuffle forward, keeping my back to an office front and trying to avoid getting pulled away in the currents of people. Their excited screams put me on edge, the air thrumming with energy and my heart already thumping.

Ten feet further on, Natasha grabs my arm, her fingers digging in. I follow her gaze and freeze.

A couple of guards are heading through the crowd in our direction. I duck down, trying to place their faces from the rally.

Natasha crouches at my side. "Another road?"

"Got to try," I say, though this is our tenth so far, and time's ticking down fast. "Further around, maybe?"

She nods, and with heads low, we push our way back down the feeder road. Then we turn at the next junction and run. Natasha goes to hurry down the next street, but I keep us going past two more roads till we're at one that's at a diagonal to a corner of the summit building.

This one's emptier, most of the street clear. However, the current's much stronger at the far end of the road, the throng surging across it. I scan the crowd. No sign of guards or of demons, either.

Natasha plants her feet. Hands on hips. "No way we can make it through that," she says.

"Not without the veil," I mutter.

Then I fix my gaze on the people streaming past, the flow moving parallel to the summit building. I tilt my head. "But maybe we don't need to." I hurry right to the edge of the seething throng.

Here the slightest scent of cordite pricks my nose, barely detectable under the smell of sweat and fumes. Then it's gone, though my gut starts to twist.

"Jake, what—" Natasha says.

A section of the crowd in front of us surges forward, and I grab Natasha's hand, yank her into their midst.

"What are we doing?" she asks, stumbling to keep upright.

"It's okay," I say, keeping my head down, shoulder to shoulder with the people swarming around us. "Just let it take you."

The current thrusts us first sideways, then toward the summit building, and then away again. And I make sure we simply go with the movement of the crowd each time, one hand shielding my rib and the other clamped around Natasha's fingers.

Pretty soon, the media enclosure comes into view on the far side of the single access road, a car park full of media vans behind it with a raised platform at the enclosure front. And this is crammed with camera operators and reporters, each crew recording last-minute broadcasts of the clamouring crowd. I spy a couple that have already finished hastening down the access road toward the conference centre.

The current continues to weave us around. And nearer the building, I spot several more platforms, each one with a preacher on top bellowing vitriol into a microphone. The people passing by them respond with shouts of support, some dressed in Puritan clothing, others not. A couple of helicopters circle high above, their roaring blades adding to the surrounding chaos.

And while the energy continues to grow in my chest, I make sure to keep in step with the churning crowd and keep breathing.

A group of guards comes into view ten feet ahead. I angle my face away and let the throng shuffle me past them. Then twenty yards further forward, the current surges to the side, heading toward the access road.

I lift my head for an instant and spy the hundred-and-fifty-yard tarmac corridor, metal barriers running along both sides. It links a feeder road beyond the Docklands area with the only entrance to the summit building not locked up tight.

Natasha leans in. "Paul Hawcross," she says. "He must be arriving at any moment."

I nod, the people around us pressing in the direction of the tarmac corridor with muscles tense, feverish movements, and desire flaring in their eyes. I try to imagine Gabriel appearing on stage, convincing them.

Another waft of cordite hits my nostrils, and then it's gone again. My gut continues to twist.

We are still being driven toward the media enclosure, only thirty yards away now, the access road just in front. And my gaze falls on several guards patrolling it, some of them glancing in our direction. I plant my feet to slow our movements.

Natasha tries to peer beyond them.

"Can you see her?" I ask. We're looking for the female reporter we stole from last time.

"I don't think so," Natasha shouts above the yelling crowd. "But seven or so crews are still recording. And if one is her, she could easily recognise us from up there."

I nod, trying to follow Natasha's gaze while my fingers rummage absent-mindedly into my pockets. Firecrackers, mini box-cutter, lighter, burner phone, cable ties.

The throng surges faster and shoves us harder toward the access road and the guards, the din growing ever louder. And I have to anchor myself as people flow on both sides of me, my eyes fixed on the platform. At least three of the reporters are women, one of them with blonde hair. I chew my cheek.

The shouting continues to intensify at our backs, and a part of my brain processes the individual words.

"Bigot! Racist! Zealot!"

I turn. And behind me, the crowd's much thinner than it was, people scrabbling to get away from something.

I blink.

Against the backdrop of the feeder roads, a new horde of

people is striding directly toward us, only fifty feet away. They must be thousands strong, of all nationalities, the majority Middle Eastern. And they're all shouting in unison – a protest group – their arms raised and fingers jabbing at the summit building behind me.

The intrusion is perfect for the cameras, and Paul Hawcross's supporters at my back yell even louder.

My mouth gapes. This has been planned. The protesters continue their approach, thirty feet away from us now.

Grabbing Natasha's hand, I spin toward the summit and plough directly into the crowd. But we find our way blocked by a thickening line of Paul Hawcross's supporters, all bellowing and pressing in our direction, establishing some kind of shield to the building behind.

I try to yank Natasha laterally toward the access road instead, but we're too late. Several supporters plant themselves before us, forming a defensive arc around the approaching protest group. One of Paul Hawcross's supporters shoves me backward, and the pain screams in my rib. I grit my teeth and swivel.

The leaders of the protest have halted just behind us – two robed men with a thousand of their fellow protesters at their backs, all staring in our direction.

We're right in the fucking middle.

My heart beats faster as I grip Natasha's hand. "Don't let go."

And with that, I start the count and still my mind. Amid the building chaos, the shimmering world spreads out easily around me, the movements of the frothing crowd resolving into a choreographed dance. Each shift arises in my awareness an instant before it happens.

Facing the wall of Paul Hawcross's supporters, I feint one way. A burly guy tries to block me off, and I dart into the minute gap he leaves behind, tugging Natasha with me. The people behind him react, dashing to get in my way. And again, their movements create spaces I hasten toward before they even form.

Yet with the crowd so tightly packed, even beyond the veil, our progress is incredibly slow. And with every movement, more shouts ring out from our sides – shouts of alarm, not challenge, and from supporters, not protesters.

I find my head turning, and my eyes go wide. The protest leaders are right at our backs, using Natasha and me as icebreakers to slice through the crowd, their comrades spilling in behind.

I blank my mind entirely and peel the veil further back. As time slows, I channel more energy into my legs and arms. I yank Natasha faster onward, scamper into gaps, and shove between supporters where necessary, though the pain in my rib yells at me with every contact.

Still I can sense the protest group right behind us while several supporters press in at our sides, teeth clenched and fists raised. I can't help scanning the surrounding throng, my eyes searching for patrolling guards, and I catch a glimpse of the two protest leaders scrambling closer in our wake.

With jaw clenched, I stumble to a stop. One of the leaders knocks into the back of my shoulder, and I'm already spinning, my thoughts firing. The veil slips back before my senses.

"Go back!" I shout and jab a finger between the heads of the protest leaders.

The two robed guys simply stand and stare, their eyes narrowed and chests heaving, while Paul Hawcross's supporters yell at them too, spittle flying. The energy continues to build inside me.

Again, I force my mind to still and peel back the veil. And this time, I channel as much power as I can up my throat, preparing the priest's command voice.

"Go back!" I yell right at the leaders.

The words hit them dead on, and both robed guys stumble away from me, features slack.

And their movement's like a dam breaking. Paul Hawcross's supporters dive into the gap they left behind and begin pressing them further backward. I can only watch as the protesters are shoved away from us, from the summit building, the cheers ringing louder from the prime minister's supporters.

Someone leans over and slaps me on the shoulder, and more people congratulate me, left and right. The darkness rises at my core as I swivel away, the veil still pulled back. I glimpse a black outline, a shadowed figure amid the throng, thirty feet distant, watching on. And a hint of sulphur bites at my nose.

My breath stops. My heart seizes. And I spin back. No one's there. Only the heaving throng, the baying supporters, and the scent of sulphur lingering in my nose.

A shiver runs through me while more people pat me on my arms, my back.

"Let's get out of here," I say, turning to Natasha.

I lead her through the crowd toward the media enclosure, the shouted congratulations ringing on in my ears. People step out of our way and clasp me on the shoulder as we pass. And while my body yearns to shrink, the void deepening inside, I can't help keeping my head raised, my eyes scanning for the shadowed figure.

There's no sign.

41

I PRESS ON FASTER, the access road only fifteen feet away now with a dozen people between us and the metal barriers. The road runs across us in a straight line, right up to the summit building's entrance. And adjoining the road, directly opposite us, is the media car park. It's square with space for twenty vehicles along with the raised platform on its far side.

Plus, I can make out the security checkpoint where the end of the car park meets the access road. Two guards stand there, allowing a reporter and camera operator past. The crew hurries down the remainder of the access road toward the building's entrance.

My hand dives into my pocket, my fingers groping for the firecrackers. I grab two out, plus the box-cutter and lighter.

"Three crews are still recording on the platform," Natasha says. "More of them in the car park. The woman may still be there."

"We can't wait," I say, using the box-cutter to slice the firecracker fuses shorter. "And there's no time to plant these properly."

Natasha frowns and says, "What are you going to—"

"Follow me," I say.

I shove through the remaining people till I'm only a few

feet from the metal barrier. Then I light two of the firecrackers. I count to eight and hurl one over the head of the nearest guard along the access road and the other in the opposite direction beyond the guards on the checkpoint.

Natasha joins me a moment before the explosions ring out. Loud, but not too loud over the din of the crowd.

Everyone nearby swivels away, gazing in opposite directions, the guards in the access road included.

I plough forward and leap over the barrier, Natasha scaling it just behind me. We sprint across the access road toward the media car park and manage to get to within a few feet of the first van.

A loud voice barks from the side, "Hey, stop!" as more yells ring out from behind.

I can't help turning. And sure enough, several people are trying to follow us over the fence, a mini-stampede after the firecrackers.

The channel guards zero in on these infiltrators, but Natasha and I are already well past. We scramble beyond the bonnet of the first van and dive down the gap between it and the second.

The yelling from the guards gradually ceases, replaced by the resumed shouts from the crowd, and the thrum of anticipation grows in the air. Paul Hawcross's appearance is only minutes away. I try to calm my breathing and scan the enclosure.

The platform's now empty of media crews while half a dozen hurry to and from their vehicles, equipment in hand. And there's no sign of the female reporter.

Natasha grips my arm, her eyes fixed on the security checkpoint. The two guards remain there, positioned between the enclosure and the rest of the access road. I watch another couple of reporters and camera operators hurry past them toward the building entrance.

"They have security wristbands," she hisses.

"What?" I ask.

"The media crews," she says, her fingers tightening around my forearm. "Each one has been given an electronic fob. The guards are scanning them at the checkpoint." She points. "We'll each need one to get through."

My heart stops as I scour the remaining media crews. Sure enough, coloured wristbands decorate their wrists. Plus, a guard at the checkpoint grips an electronic reader in his hand. The void blooms wider at my core.

"Can you steal two?" Natasha asks.

I shake my head. "No way," I say, my gut twisting further, my palms sweaty. "We'll just have to take the place of one of the crews."

"*What?*" Natasha says.

"And we'll have to trap them inside one of their vans, somehow," I say. "Or they'll alert the guards, and we'll be screwed."

Natasha turns back to the enclosure, her face pale, and I search the remaining media crews hurrying across the car park. Each camera operator and reporter also has a security pass around their neck.

"Most of them are men," Natasha whispers.

It's true. Four – no, five – male reporters are dashing to their vehicles, the car park emptying. The only female reporter I can see is scampering toward one of the larger vans in the far corner – a major network.

She's shorter than Natasha with a heavier build and darker hair. My heart beats faster.

"Could you pass for her?" I ask, pointing.

Natasha follows my gaze. "Maybe," she says, the doubt clear in her voice.

The woman jerks open the rear door and jumps inside, followed by a cameraman. He slams the door behind them.

"Well, you might need to," I reply.

I thrust my way out from between the vehicles and begin striding toward the woman's van, without a security pass or wristband, and in plain bloody view of everyone. I force myself to breathe, to maintain a steady pace, while doubting voices screech and wail.

A male reporter glances at me as he passes. He stops walking, his eyes tracking my movements as if he recognises me. I keep going, making sure to keep my gaze straight.

Thirty feet from the van, visions assail me of the two crew members inside, probably ready to jump out at any moment. I speed up a little, leaving Natasha in my wake.

Twenty feet. Still no one accosts us.

"Be careful," I say over my shoulder. "Keep out of sight." Then I just dart right up to the van door, yank it open, and plunge inside, slamming the door closed behind me. Then I spin.

This van's much larger than the one we stole from. The extended walls are covered by the same equipment – cameras, microphones, digital displays. The reporter's standing on one side, microphone already in her hand and fob on her wrist, while the cameraman's on the other. His camera rests down by his leg, a spare battery in his free hand. They both gaze at me, faces blank.

I don't move, either. A third set of eyes stares at me from the back – a man, heavily built, with dark trousers, a white shirt, and a belt packed with a baton and some kind of gun.

Every one of my muscles tightens. He's their personal security, probably hired because of our antics at the rally. The guy doesn't open his mouth to speak, doesn't challenge me. My heartbeat drums as he simply lowers his centre of gravity and raises his arms, fingers out like claws.

I swivel, and the guard rushes at me. One stride and then another – the guy is light on his feet. He lunges, and I duck as he reaches for my shoulder. I let my knees collapse and tilt my chin backward a fraction. The guy's arm sweeps an inch over my head, leaving me with the mixed scent of soap and sweat. His shoulder bounces off the inside of the doors and the van rocks on its wheels.

My gaze finds the female reporter while her cameraman

cowers on the opposite side. She's already grabbing at something from the middle of the side wall.

A phone.

She yanks it from its cradle and starts jabbing at the buttons, her face intent. I push off the back door and leap toward her, shooting my arm out, my fingers reaching. I manage to grab the spiralling cable to rip it from its socket while pitching over forward.

I go down on my knees and then glance up. The reporter's standing over me, the phone still in her hand with cable dangling from the end.

A hand shoves hard against my shoulder and slams me back against the wall. My rib pounds, and I grit my teeth against the pain.

The guard looms above me and brings his elbow careening toward my face. I jerk my head to the side and out of the way of the strike. The movement takes my nose to within an inch of the reporter's chest, and she whips the phone toward my temple just as the guard lines up a punch with his other hand.

My mind stills, the veil peels back, and the shimmering world extends around me, my heartbeat louder in my ears. I can sense the motion of the reporter's arm and the coming arc of the guard's fist.

My hand darts upward, fingers spread, and I grab the reporter by the wrist that's holding the phone an instant before it crashes into my head.

In slowed time, the guard's fist barrels toward me. I yank the reporter sideways – a shield between me and the guard – while I grasp her by the collar with my other hand and force her head upward. She shrieks with the sudden lurch, the sound elongating behind the veil as the guard's fist careens toward her.

The guard's eyes go wide, and he pulls the punch a fraction. Yet when his fist connects with the side of her jaw, the impact still snaps her head right back. The woman's knees give out, and I catch her under the arms before lowering her gently to the floor.

The guard's eyes narrow. His face reddens, and his breathing accelerates. And behind the veil, I can feel the guy's rage, the energy building in my chest.

He tenses his shoulders and grabs out the baton from his belt, his knuckles white around the handle. The cameraman scrambles right into the far corner by the doors, his camera on his knees.

My eyes shoot back to the guard, and he flies at me, baton raised. He swings it at my shoulder and forces me to scramble out of the way, straight into a crouch in the opposite corner. Then he raises his foot, grips the headrest of the driver's seat, and kicks out hard at my head.

I press my heels against the back of the passenger seats and spring forward, just missing his leg.

I go into a roll, ending up a couple of feet from the rear doors. Then I whirl back around, my rib thumping.

The guard's facing me once more, his nostrils flared and arms tense. He swaps the baton from one hand to the other and grabs something else from his belt – a taser gun, even bloody larger than the one from Haniel's club. He raises the barrel and points it at me.

I channel the power into my legs and feet, and I lunge at the guy, my hands out. I catch him in the stomach with my shoulder, and while pain shrieks in my rib, I keep pushing, driving the guy back. But I manage only a couple of feet. The guy's shoving hard in the opposite direction, and he's fucking strong.

Worries spark in my mind, the veil slipping back before my senses. I clench my jaw and focus harder on the fire in my chest, the shimmering world expanding again. The guy shifts his weight, and I can feel his hands rising above my head, his fingers clenched around the handles of the gun and baton. The back of my neck's fully exposed underneath.

I inch my knees beneath me and channel the energy

throughout my entire body – from my shoulders down to my heels, concentrating intently.

The guy whips his hands downward, and a roar issues from my mouth as I explode upward at the same time. I shove hard from my toes and drive my shoulder directly into the guy's chin from below.

The guy's jaw snaps shut, and he drops the baton. Thrusting harder upward, I smash the crown of his head into the roof of the van. My shoulder sears with pain as his chin digs into it. The taser gun clatters to the ground as well, and his sudden weight presses down on me as he blacks out.

I stumble for an instant and then step aside as his body crumples to the floor.

My gaze flicks to the cameraman. He's still crouching in the far corner of the van fifteen feet away, gazing at me with eyes like dinner plates, his mouth gaping. He's even got his camera trained in my direction, his finger on the controls.

And now his other hand reaches for the inside door handle. My thoughts start up, the veil sliding before my senses again, and my mind estimating distances and times. The guy continues to stretch his arm toward the door, too bloody far away for me to reach him in one leap. I picture myself grabbing up and using the taser gun by my foot – likely instant coma at least.

I bite my lip.

The guy shoves down on the door handle, and I ignore the gun, taking two quick steps and then throwing myself at him. He drops the camera and thrusts the door open, barely managing to get his head out at the same moment I reach for his legs.

I miss one but catch hold of the other, my fingers wrapping themselves around his calf. Then my chest hits the van floor, and the pain in my rib screams again.

The guy kicks out at me viciously. My vision blurry, I throw my upper body out of the way while keeping hold of the guy's leg and rolling around on my fucking belly. He lifts his foot again and is aiming a kick at my grasping hand when a voice calls out.

"What are you doing?" Natasha asks.

The guy spins and stares through the gap in the door. I can barely see her calm face gazing back at him.

He stands there, his eyes huge. I scramble forward, my breath held against the biting pain, and grab a boom microphone holder on the inside of the open door. Natasha watches on, and I yank the holder toward me while she pushes hard on the door, crashing it into the guy's forehead.

The door slams closed, and the cameraman topples over me onto the floor. He lies there unmoving.

Then the door opens again. And Natasha stares through it, her eyebrow raised at my sprawled figure.

"Well, you look a sight," she says. "Are you done yet?"

42

I CAN ONLY NOD back at Natasha through the open van door, my head woozy with pain. She jumps up beside me and shuts the door.

"Why did you take so long?" she asks.

"They had a guard," I say, pointing stupidly at the third unconscious body.

"Well, hurry," she says and squats by the reporter, reaching for her security wristband. "Our man will be arriving imminently, and the crowd knows it. They are going crazy out there."

My heart's beating fast again, and I blink through the pain, focusing on the side walls instead while scanning for places to tie up the crew. Yet all I can see is communications equipment – a hundred ways for them to contact the outside world.

Natasha's pulled the fob and security pass off the reporter and goes to work on the cameraman.

"Jake, come on—" she says.

I push past her and dash for the doors, grabbing at the cable ties in my pocket.

"Tie them up as best you can," I say and throw the ties at her feet.

She straightens. "Where are you going?"

"There's something we need to do," I say, yanking a small toolbox from the corner of the van. Then I shove the rear doors open and jump straight out onto the car park.

Pain shoots up my rib, and the calls of the crowd ring loudly in my ears, like animals baying. Plus, there's the sound of revving engines, somewhere in the distance.

I shut it all out and dart around the corner of the van – driver door, bonnet open, van battery. I wrench at the wire connectors with a pair of pliers, fail … and fail again. It takes me four attempts to disconnect the bloody things. Then I slam the bonnet shut and scramble back around the van and into the rear.

Sure enough, all the equipment's dead. And all three people remain unconscious. Natasha's cable-tied the reporter to a few hooks and looped handles. And she's doing the same to the cameraman. Three mobile phones lie piled by the door, the guard still sprawled at her feet.

"He's too heavy for me," she says.

I nod and drag the guy into the far corner of the van where I tie him up with cable ties and the phone cord. I make sure not to bind his neck too tightly.

"You will need these," Natasha says and thrusts the security tag and the fob at me.

One goes around my neck and the other on my wrist. I grab the three mobiles, jump out of the van, and chuck the phones underneath it. Then I heave the camera onto my shoulder and begin hurrying between the other vehicles toward the checkpoint with Natasha just behind.

The sound of the crowd vibrates my skull, and I peer up the visible slice of access road. Still empty. No sign of Paul Hawcross. However, my gut continues to twist, the noise of rotor blades growing deafening in my ears from the three bloody helicopters circling the summit building. My gaze climbs to its top, blueprints flashing through my mind. The fire door on the roof is invisible from everywhere except the river and the fucking air.

Natasha runs at my side as a helicopter swoops low over us. "They will make it without using their powers," she says.

"If they come at all," I mutter back.

"The angels will come," she says between snatched breaths, "but we need to get that damn door open first."

I barrel right up to the security checkpoint and halt in front of one of the guards, my chest heaving. I hear more screams of excitement behind, and I spin.

And the sight makes me wobble in place. A column of three black armoured cars is approaching, just thirty yards away, with tinted windows and huge wheels. Each one is like a tank, crawling unerringly toward us as the crowd froths on either side of the access road. The front vehicle revs, the smell of diesel stronger in the air, and for an instant, I notice a familiar scent underneath.

Sulphur.

A shiver rolls from my calves up my back. I try to still my thoughts, but staring at the cars, memories surge, my vision hazing over …

I see scenes of hell, the scarred landscape, the erupting lava, the raging clouds. Plus, the black creatures – the pneumas – scuttling all around us.

I grit my teeth and force my gaze away to focus on the guards at the checkpoint instead.

"You're late!" one yells.

I blink back at him and open my mouth, yet my vision fogs once more, more images forming before my eyes …

The devil. Suit so dark. Bone-white skin. Smoke seeping from cuffs and hems. His mismatched eyes are fixed on mine, his slender fingers motioning me toward him.

The cars rev louder, and the guard shouts again, words indistinct. I have to tense my legs to stop them from trembling. Natasha yells back at the guard, and thrusts her own fob forward to be scanned. Then she grabs my wrist and hoists it toward the electronic scanner.

My gaze flits to the summit building, fifty yards away, just the remaining length of the access road in between. Metal barriers line both sides, the throng seething and frothing behind them like wave tips. And to one side of the building, a great many thousands of supporters swarm together on raised seating in the shape of a gargantuan clam shell.

The guard yells at me directly and jabs his finger down the access road, at a cavernous mouth-like entrance to the building, big enough to swallow the cars. And standing to the side of it, along with several security guards, are three guys in suits. Two of them are immaculately turned out, the last with tousled hair, an open shirt, and a rumpled jacket.

The air turns to concrete in my lungs. Natasha hurries forward between the guards, and I grab her hand.

She spins and hisses, "What is it?"

My mouth opens, but nothing comes out. I swallow.

"It's Ben," I croak.

She goes white, but doesn't look, simply holding my gaze.

The engines growl behind us, the vehicles only twenty yards away now and steadily approaching. My heartbeat's so loud I'm sure the entire crowd can hear it.

"Come on!" the guard yells and shoves at my shoulder. "Get going down the road or get out of the way!"

Still, I remain rooted, my eyes glued by the dark entrance with Ben right there, while the veil's so thin before my senses. His demonic form appears – torn clothes, smoke issuing from the rips, glowing embers inside. Again, the void grows at my core, darkness taking over my insides. The cars rev ever louder.

I shake myself, tense my legs, and make sure not to turn away from the dark. Instead, I imagine Father Thomas at my side and feel his hand on my shoulder. I summon the energy in my core and then squeeze Natasha's wrist.

"Let's go," I say.

I lumber between the guards and toward the summit building. Even fifty yards away, I sense my gaze drawn to Ben, the veil peeling back from my senses, his body growing, his demonic form emerging further before my eyes – the slashed face, the gleaming eyes …

I rip my eyes away and swivel the camera a fraction, using it to hide me from the front while the angle of my head hides my face from the rear. Then I usher Natasha behind me and shamble slowly toward the building, my lens aimed at the crowd.

They holler and rage, spit flying and eyes aflame. Hands are either reaching for the cars or beating the air at a section of crowd near the entrance, and that's when I spot them.

The protesters. Fifty or more placed right by the building, many of them gripping placards over their section of metal barriers, each one screaming at Paul Hawcross's cavalcade. His supporters yell back even louder – a perfect spectacle.

And sure enough, just inside the mouth of the entrance, a couple of cameramen push up against each other for the best footage. A line of security guards stand poised before them, to either side of Ben and the demons.

We're edging closer, only ten yards away from them now – and also from the cars at our backs, their distance shrinking with every second. The heat prickles up my spine, the scent of sulphur undeniable, and my heart thumps painfully against my ribs.

Still I keep my steps steady, my camera pointed at the crowd, and my face averted from the cavalcade and the demons. I try to picture us slinking past them and the guards.

"Hey, you!" a guard yells, barely audible above the baying throng and the helicopters' rotors.

I ignore him and continue shuffling toward the entrance, parallel with the protesters now. Natasha grips my arm and presses in close.

"Camera crew!" the guard yells louder.

I fix him in the corner of my vision. The guy's motioning

us over, his arm churning wildly at the air, and Ben's standing right at his side.

My spine turns to ice.

"Over here, *now*!" the guard shouts.

Nevertheless, I don't turn. Instead, I take a trembling breath, still my thoughts, and risk peeling back the veil. The shimmering world starts to unfurl and sensations bombard me: yells from the protesters, screams from Paul Hawcross's supporters, shouts from the guard. My head rings, and I don't tune any of it out. I let everything play through my mind …

The helicopters above. A baying crowd. Protesters. Cameramen. Security guards. Access road lined with barriers. The demons. The vehicles behind us, continuing to creep closer. All of it.

The kernel of an idea forms at the back of my mind.

I start to spin. Natasha goes to stop me, but I whirl all the way around and risk facing the approaching cars, fixing my camera on them. They're only five yards away now, the entrance a bit further behind me, and I start padding backward.

"Start your report," I hiss to Natasha, the veil slipping back before my senses.

"What—" she starts.

"Your *report*," I say, louder, training my camera on the nearest vehicle.

Natasha goes silent, simply keeping pace with my retreat. Then she brings the microphone to her lips.

"You join us here," she begins, "at the start of …"

And I tune out her ongoing monologue, all my attention on the sounds to my sides – the protesters yelling, the supporters shouting back, and behind me, the same guard's voice.

"You can't go out there …" he says.

I swivel my head a fraction. The guard's gesticulating at one of the other camera operators, a few feet inside the entrance.

"He's got the shot," the cameraman shouts back, jabbing his finger at me. "Why can't I?"

I lean in toward Natasha. "Speak louder," I say.

She does, and a few moments later, I hear a scramble of footsteps. The cameraman and his reporter dash out of the entrance and start filming the convoy at our side.

Keeping my camera trained on the approaching cars, I edge to the side of the access road right up to the metal barriers with the protesters beyond them, the closest members yelling klaxon-like in my ears. And despite the heat, another shiver rolls through me. The cars are less than ten feet away now, the smell of sulphur so strong in my nose.

I take a quick breath and slip a foot beneath two of the metal barriers, making sure to place it right under the join. Keeping my body steady, my camera still fixed ahead, I push the barrier upward with the top of my shoe, trying to unhook them.

The thing doesn't move.

The vehicles continue their approach. The blackened windows are only five feet from me now, and the crowd screams louder, the protesters leaning further over the railing to my sides. My heart hammers in my chest.

I push harder at the join, trying to force one barrier upward and my rib aching more with the effort. Again, nothing happens, with dozens of protesters hanging over the railing. Too much damn weight.

Sweat breaks out across my forehead. My hands shake, and the first car draws almost parallel with our position.

Again, I work to steady my breathing. Then I go behind the veil again, summon the energy at my core and, ignoring the flaring pain around my rib, shove myself against the railing. I thrust backward with everything I have. The barrier leans away from me, the protesters sent scrambling, the weight gone.

My foot finds the barrier join, and I jerk it upward. I hear a click, and the hooks pop free of the loops.

The protesters surge forward again and throw themselves into the freed barrier, which shoves it wide open. I dart out of the way while a dozen protesters stumble onto the access road. More pour in from behind, and soon they're surrounding the cars, banging on bonnets, yelling at the windows.

The screams from the supporters become even more crazed. A number of them climb their own barriers and jump into the access road. The second media crew films it all.

I guide Natasha back toward the building. Several guards stream out of the entrance to our side along with another media crew, their camera aimed at the unfolding chaos. I hold my breath. Ben moves with them, his hands out, and one of the two suited demons goes with him. Both have their backs to us now.

My back hits the summit building wall, right in the corner of the access road, and I remain there, rigid, my eyes fixed on the growing fray before us. The third demon still hasn't fucking moved. He's still in front of the entrance, only a pace to our side. My pulse fires, and my legs shake.

The security guards dive into the midst of the throng and start hauling protesters and supporters apart, yanking the two media crews back through the entrance.

Fingers close around my arm, and my entire body tenses. But I force myself not to react, and just glance to the side.

It's another guard with his hands on Natasha and me, tugging us toward the entrance along with the others. And beyond him ... the third demon, gazing out at the tumult, only a few feet away.

Claws of dread squeeze my chest. Panicked thoughts and visions start to arise, and I let them all come. A memory hits me of Haniel's ancient city, and I blank my mind entirely. I focus again on the sensation of nothingness, concentrating on sending the energy in my body out through my feet into the ground, through my hands into the air.

Colours dim and images blur – the forms of the guards,

the demon – and I force myself to let them all go, to ignore my screaming mind. The black outline of the entrance looms ahead, and I simply lurch toward it, the faintest string of attention on my legs, on keeping them moving. My mind becomes an empty vessel. My body insubstantial. No mass. No form.

Shapes flash before my eyes – outlines of light and dark. I don't cling to any of them but just let every sight, every sensation arise and disappear against the background of my awareness. I lose all sense of time as I feel myself lumbering on forever.

Fingers grab my arm and squeeze.

"Jake," Natasha says. "Are you okay?"

43

"Speak to me," Natasha says.

I turn on the spot, my brain slowly unscrambling.

Something bumps against my leg, and I stare down at the camera in my hand, somehow now off my shoulder. The veil slips back before my senses, and more sights and sounds infiltrate my mind.

We're standing in a shadowy underground car park, with space for about thirty cars. And though every bay stands empty, it's a hive of activity. A stream of guards scramble past us toward a ramp up to the entrance, and I have to back right up to a concrete wall. The sound of shouting and engines revving is still clearly audible from outside.

"Are we through?" I ask.

Natasha nods. "We're through, and you walked right past that demon. He didn't even *look*."

I hear a tone of astonishment in her voice and see that strange look in her eyes again – curiosity or excitement. But my stomach turns over, and my gaze finds the car park entrance, the protesters out there, and the void grows once more. They're swarming the cars, fists banging on the chassis and windows, and the media crews broadcast it all for the world – a prime minister under siege, the target of foreign intruders.

Nausea bites at my throat, and I sense the growl of monsters down in the darkness. I close my eyes and breathe deeply while Natasha squeezes my forearm again.

"We *did* it, Jake," she says, her tone animated. "We made it inside."

I nod, my insides constricting more. "Did we, or did they let us?"

Natasha shakes my arm, and the look of excitement in her eyes burns on. "We are here, exactly where we wanted to be, but the hardest bit's still to come. And we *have* to move." She grips tighter and starts pulling my forearm. "They will have the entrance clear in minutes."

People continue to hurry past us in both directions, and my eyes track a group in civilian clothes heading toward us and away from the entrance. I shake myself and hasten behind the stragglers. Natasha and I follow them up another ramp and through a set of double doors at its top.

None of them glance back at us, and we end up in a wide corridor that curves in both directions, running around the massive auditorium in the middle of the building. The passageway is full of more bustling people – dignitaries with their attendants, security guards, and more of the civilian men and women in tailored suits with earpieces, security tags, and electronic tablets in their hands. They look just like the ones I saw in Paul Hawcross's headquarters.

Tension knits my shoulders, and I avert my gaze, though I can't help keeping the nearest group in the corner of my eye, scanning for any sign of recognition. But they continue down the passageway without looking.

I turn the other way and hurry after a set of dignitaries. Then I duck into a small recess out of the main corridor, Natasha at my side.

"You remember—" I start.

"Yes, yes," she says. "Along to the end." She nods back

down the passageway. "Up two flights of stairs, opposite gate G. Then take the smaller of the corridors toward the rear of the building." She points upward. "Climb one more flight of stairs and the roof fire door is at the end of the hall."

I can only nod.

"And you?" she says, tilting her head, a smile parked at the edge of her mouth.

"Basement," I say. "Security room. Turn off the alarm system."

"Great," she says.

But she doesn't move, and I don't either. The twisting in my gut from outside hasn't eased a bit.

Gazing into her eyes, I find myself trying to capture an image of her face, to sear this moment into my memory. My heart beats faster, and my hands go sweaty. She smiles again before she leans in and kisses me on the lips.

My eyes go wide.

"It's okay. I'm with you," she says and then grips my hand. "I will be fine."

I go to open my mouth, but a burst of noise from behind makes me turn my head. The people in the corridor are hurrying faster, either away from or toward the double doors, an increased frenzy to their movements. And the energy starts to build at my core.

Natasha squeezes my fingers. "You be careful," she says, that familiar crease across her forehead.

I squeeze her hand back. "I will," I manage to say. "Give me ten minutes. Any longer and we'll miss the angels."

Natasha nods and checks her watch. "Message me," she says and taps the burner phone in her pocket.

With that, she's gone, hurrying back along the corridor past the double doors.

For a moment, I just stand there and watch her go. Then I take a deep breath and hoist the camera back onto my shoulder. I turn, and with an ache in my chest, I hasten on down the side of the passageway.

My feet take me past more of Paul Hawcross's people. I keep my head straight, and while no one stops and stares, a few glance in my direction but then allow their gazes to linger. Sweat climbs my back, and I quicken my stride.

A door approaches. Stairwell. I check both directions and slip through.

The wide shaft is empty, just brightly lit concrete walls and rubber steps running up and down. I listen hard. Silence. Then I hurry downward, the camera still on my shoulder without a media crew anywhere near – the worst disguise ever.

I get only six steps from the next landing down when the door below is thrust open. Three people stride through – a woman and two men, all young and all in their sharp suits with earpieces.

I whip out my burner phone as they head for the steps upward. And their eyes find me as I press the phone to my ear.

"Yeah, I'm almost there," I say, trying an exasperated tone and clumping down the steps toward them. "Will be just a couple of minutes."

I pass them by on the stairs, my shoulders tensing. Again, no one stops me, and my feet propel me on in the direction of the basement and the security room. It's probably full of guards and all out of bloody bounds to anyone who doesn't work there.

I stop in place, my fingers gripping the handrail. Then I glance back up the steps at the three suits still climbing. They've reached the door to the level above.

"Wait!" I shout.

The footsteps pause. One of the guys gazes down the stairwell, his security pass hanging from his lapel pocket.

"Is this the right way?" I ask, leaping back up toward them, the camera bouncing on my shoulder.

I reach the top of the first set of steps and start on the next. The three of them stand in a line on the landing, and I keep my gaze pinned to the guy who's furthest away, nearest the door.

"To the pit?" I say, almost at their level now.

None of them move. They only stare as I stride past the first guy, angling my torso toward the woman beside him. I stumble into her, my fingers grasping for her security pass, and miss. She darts backward and out of reach.

Which leaves me staggering toward the furthest guy. I manage to right myself a few feet away, the other two at my side.

"The pit?" he says with a Spanish accent.

I pause a moment, my mind groping.

Then I step forward till I'm only a foot from him, my camera extending over his shoulder. "Yeah, the pit," I say. "For the cameras, the reporters."

The Spaniard opens his mouth and nods. "Oh, yes," he says, retreating slightly. "It is up one level and then round the other side." He glances upward.

"Upstairs?" I say.

I follow his gaze, swinging my camera toward his ear and leaning forward till we're almost chest to chest. My fingers grip the security pass clipped to his lapel.

He ducks to avoid the swinging camera, angling his head away. And I pull back, stripping the security pass from his jacket.

I palm the pass, making sure to keep his colleagues behind me. "Sorry," I say, forming a sheepish grin.

"Yes, upstairs," he says, his voice tight.

"Thanks," I say.

Two of them turn away while the Spaniard fixes me with a stare, his eyes narrowed. I focus hard on keeping still, on maintaining my smile.

Eventually, the guy swivels away. "You better hurry and plug in," he says, waving a finger. "No separate transmissions allowed."

I watch him follow his colleagues through the door. I

pocket the pass before blundering down the stairs again, the camera held out to one side now.

My feet take me down one storey and then two more till I reach the deepest level. Spying no one the entire way.

The door opens without a sound, and I peer out. Curving walls head in both directions with a couple of closed single doors on one side, a set of double doors on the other, portholes in all of them. The passageway's empty. Not a soul. And not a scrap of cover, either.

Heart beating, I hurry to the right, placing my feet as lightly as I can, and still my footsteps resound with the faintest squeak on the rubber floors. I keep going and get within twenty yards of the security room when the noise of clomping footsteps comes from behind – heavy-duty boots.

My adrenaline fires. I dash toward the inside of the corridor and then scamper along it to the next set of double doors. Male voices sound up the passageway, getting closer.

I force myself to check the porthole, but I can see only darkness. I push the doors open and dart through into an enormous cave-like room. Then I edge the doors closed again and stare around.

The space is a hundred yards long, at least as wide at the far end and almost half as high, faintly lit from above. I find myself gazing upward at what must be the underside of the stage and of the seating area opposite it. Each hangs over space, propped up by massive telescopic legs that can be moved up and down to lower or raise the stage. It resembles the underside of an enormous insect.

The space is empty. And with half of my attention trained on the corridor outside – listening for footsteps – I can't help gazing around at the engineering mastery.

While a lowered stage means a steeply banked seating area, here Paul Hawcross has raised the stage and the indoor seating as well, flattening them to line them up with the massive clam-shell stepped area outside. This allows his followers to view him through the glass wall.

In between the stage and seating, he's kept a narrow gap for security – maybe twenty feet across – that plunges right down to the basement floor. Through it, I can see a massive crucifix perched right at the edge of the stage, along with a slice of the retractable glass roof beyond. The sound of chatter echoes down through the opening.

Listening to the distant babble, my chest starts to squeeze, and visions bombard me. My sight hazes, and I'm suddenly transported ten years back …

To my childhood home. The faint sound of the gang talking, laughing, while I'm locked in the chest, in the dark, my body trembling. The memory so fucking real.

Heat rises at my core, my arms tense, and my breathing accelerates. And there it is … The faintest scent of sulphur in the cool filtered air.

I whirl around, my eyes probing the darkened space. The shadows are deepening in the corners, and the outlines of black limbs and scuttling shapes appear and disappear in the blackness, getting closer.

I spin back to face the double doors, shove the nearer one open, and thrust my way through with my breath held.

The corridor's empty. I scan the passageway in both directions, but there's no sign of the guards, and I hear no sound either. The visions diminish in my head.

I take a breath and then hurry down the corridor, the camera gripped in one hand, with time ticking down. I pass one door. And another. My eyes focus on the third – the security room. Again, I check the porthole.

And find myself staring straight at the chest of a guard, his white shirt, name badge, and security tag only a few inches beyond the door. And he's turning toward it.

I stagger backward, every muscle tense. The guy pushes down on the door handle. And I throw myself further down the curved passageway. I pass an equipment room on the outside and sprint for the next inside door, thirty feet away.

The security guard steps into the corridor at the same

moment as my feet skid to a halt in front of the doorway. I flatten myself within it and push my back against the port-hole window, the camera held down behind my legs, just as the two other guards join the first in the passageway.

"They'll probably do another sweep," the guard says, speaking through the door to whoever's still in the security room.

The guy goes on talking, but my focus slips, my attention drawn instead by a prickling sensation climbing my spine, a scratchy heat. The wooden door feels strangely warm against the back of my head and hands.

My gut twists further, and despite the heat, a chill sidles around my insides. My neck rotates, and while every voice screams at me not to, I peer through the circular window.

The room has a wall covered in screens and mixing desks – some kind of production suite – with images of the raised stage visible through various monitors. The live footage from multiple media crews shows the huge crucifix right in the centre of each one.

Before the screens sit two chairs, the far one empty. And staring at the nearer one, I feel as if hands grip my chest, my throat. My heart stops, and I can't move. Can't breathe. Can't look away.

Lucia – the female demon from Paul Hawcross's head-quarters and from the rally: flaming red hair, a grey pencil skirt, and a jacket. She's sitting side-on at the controls of the production suite, back ramrod straight, staring at the monitors.

My hands shake. I feel her power through the door, her draw, like she's got hooks around my ribs, pulling me toward her. And I find my body pressing against the wood, my fingers reaching for the handle, getting ever closer …

I quieten my mind, tense every muscle, and rip my gaze away. Scrambling out of the doorway with my legs almost tripping over each other, I stumble into the middle of the corridor.

“We’ll see you in fifteen,” the guard yells out. He and his colleagues are all standing in the centre of the passageway now. Easily visible. Only ten yards away.

I go still, my body rigid and heart pounding. The three of them turn and walk the other way, back in the direction they came.

Yet there’s no relief. Images from the porthole window bombard my mind, and the suited Spaniard’s words come back to me … *no separate transmissions allowed*. Lucia is in charge of all video output. So, even if Gabriel does come, does reveal himself, Lucia could end the broadcast in a moment and ruin everything.

As if they knew the plan.

My heartbeat quickens. The chill deepens at my core, the monsters still growling down in the darkness, and I breathe – once, twice – trying to find some calm.

Yet it doesn’t come, my insides tightening further, time still fucking ticking down. Three minutes before Natasha opens the alarmed fire door and brings every guard and demon in the building down upon her.

I clench my jaw, steel myself, and lurch back up the corridor.

44

I LUMBER to a stop by the security room door, my legs shaking, and force myself to peer through the porthole.

Two security guards, both sitting with their backs to me at a desk that's absolutely massive, covered with copious panels and countless tiny lights and buttons. A fucking labyrinth of an alarm system with a patrol visiting here every fifteen minutes, meaning there's no way I can take these guys out.

I suck in a breath and reach for my stolen security pass. I clip it onto my shirt and then turn the door handle and push. I get halfway into the room when something bumps against my legs. The bloody camera.

I quickly dump it outside the door and bumble on into the room.

Both guards swivel their chairs to face me. One of them jumps up. He's larger than his colleague, with a square frame and sleeves rolled up over muscled forearms, each one blue with tattoos.

"Who the hell are you?" he asks, staring daggers.

I find my eyes drifting to the room's CCTV screens. Several hang above the desk, showing multiple angles of the auditorium interior. And the side wall is covered by many more – maybe fifty in total, each displaying revolving images of the building's numerous corridors and rooms. Some are full of people, but most are empty. And *there* – the picture of a wide passageway, a single person moving across the far end, visible for an instant. Slim build, female, the outline of long hair down her back.

Tattooed Guy starts to follow my gaze, and I dart further into the room. I take a few hurried steps and position myself right in front of that section of monitors.

"Routine check," I say, unclipping my security pass. I hold it up.

Both of the guards frown back at me. The guy who's still seated is older, with a thin build, pinched features, and a permanent scowl.

I anchor my feet and try to settle myself. "We need to understand how you're monitoring risks," I say.

The guards glance at each other, their frowns deepening.

"We already discussed—" Tattooed Guy says.

My chest tightens, and I shake my head, forcing the energy up my throat. "Not good enough," I snap and take another step forward, shaking the security pass in my hand. "D'you know how many threats Paul Hawcross faces every day?" I jab my finger at both of them.

Old Guy glances at the security pass, and I quickly pocket it.

Tattooed Guy opens his mouth. "They told us—"

"Terrorists, assassins ... More than you can imagine," I say. Then I raise my hands, palms facing them, and soften my tone. "I just need to make sure everything's in hand. That's all."

I make a sweeping gesture across the guards' desk with my arm, peering more closely at the various panels of lights and buttons, each one bloody identical-looking.

The guards just stare at me.

"How would you know if the building's being infiltrated?" I say, bringing my gaze back to Tattooed Guy standing before me.

He returns my stare, his lips tightly pressed together. I don't look away.

"Every door and window is alarmed," Old Guy says, sitting forward in his seat.

"And you'd know here first. Right?" I say. My eyes find a particular panel on the desk, one to the far side of Old Guy. It's got thirty or so tiny lights, each one with a button and tiny label underneath. I point to it. "Every light's a different door?"

The older guy narrows his eyes.

I pad up to the panel and lean down over it, my pulse speeding up. Natasha's CCTV monitor is now unobstructed to my side.

"Let's see," I say, raising my voice a little. "Buttons to click them off, maybe one row for each floor?"

I mime pressing a few buttons, and Old Guy rolls his swivel chair toward me, nudging me away from the panel.

"No, this one," he says through a clenched jaw and then motions to a much larger panel on the opposite side of the desk from the CCTV cameras. It's covered in many more lights and buttons, probably well over two hundred. "Every individual circuit is registered here. If a door's alarm is triggered, its LED lights up, the building goes on high alert automatically, and if it's not stood down in three minutes, the external alarm is activated."

"Hundreds of different circuits," I say with a nod, trying to look impressed, though my stomach's plunging. I point toward the row of three larger red buttons at the top of the panel. "Unless you activate it sooner?"

Old Guy frowns. "Right ..." he says.

I swallow. "But what's to stop someone disabling a certain door?" I ask, bending down further to read the tiny labels.

They're all unintelligible, each one a mixture of different bloody letters and numbers. Like a foreign language.

Tattooed Guy shakes his head. "Can't be done," he says

and steps up to Old Guy's shoulder, folding his arms across his chest.

I straighten. "What, even from here?" I ask, my heart racing and my mind conjuring images of Natasha reaching the end of the roof corridor, only seconds away.

"No," Old Guy says with a smile. "Each door is linked. Any attempt to disable a door would trigger the entire system. It's foolproof. Tested every two days to make sure."

My stomach sinks through the floor. I clear my throat. "Good to know," I manage to croak out. "Excellent."

And I find my gaze drawn to the bank of CCTV monitors on the side wall again, over the guards' shoulders.

And sure enough, there she is. Natasha. Poised before the fire door, an emergency exit bar across it. She glances down at her wrist. Pauses a second. Then reaches out—

I thrust my arm out toward the top of the panel. Tattooed Guy reacts in an instant and leaps forward to stop me, but I'm too fast.

Natasha presses down on the bar. A single LED illuminates on the panel at the same time as I slam my hand down across all three of the red buttons.

45

EVERY LED on every panel illuminates immediately, and a whining alarm fills the room. Tattooed Guy shoves me hard away from the desk.

"What the hell are you *doing?*" he demands, real venom in his tone.

I begin edging toward the side of the room. Tattooed Guy presses two of the red buttons again and then wheels back to enter some kind of code into his keyboard. But the alarm doesn't shut off. It continues to blare, a single LED still illuminated on one of the panels.

Natasha's fire door.

Both guards gaze down at the lit LED, brows furrowed.

I throw my arms in the air. "You see!" I say, putting a vindicated tone into my voice. "Something *is* wrong."

I point to the single lit LED while continuing to edge toward the CCTV monitors on the side wall. I position myself directly in front of the one showing the fire door, a part of my brain picturing the angels pouring through it, though I force myself not to turn around.

The alarm whines on, both guards still frozen in place.

"How long did you say we had?" I say. "Three minutes?"

The older guard nods absent-mindedly while Tattooed

Guy taps his finger against the bottom of the desk. But still neither one does anything.

"And when the time's up, where would the main alarm go off?" I say. "Would it ring all through the building?"

The older guard's brow shines with sweat now. He tries to nudge Tattooed Guy out of the way to get to the panel. The younger guy doesn't move.

"You think the prime minister will be impressed?" I ask, the tinny alarm sound echoing around the room. "If this is the way we kick off his summit?"

Jaw clenched, Old Guy shoves his colleague's hands away from the keyboard, punches in another code onto the main monitor screen, and then jabs a couple of yellow buttons to his other side. The alarm extinguishes immediately, the single LED with it.

I take a slow breath. Both guards turn to face me, Tattooed Guy still on his feet. I swallow and then fake a smile.

"Well done," I say, my voice a little shaky, as I back away toward the door.

Still the guards stare at me, their gazes hardening.

"I'm satisfied," I say. "Everything seems to be in order."

Tattooed Guy steps toward me, forearms bulging. I point at the CCTV screens above their main monitors, the internal seats in the auditorium completely full now.

"Hadn't you better ..." I say, my other hand searching for the door handle behind my back.

Both guards swivel, and I quickly shove the door open and slip through, closing it silently behind me. Then I dart to the side, place my back to the wall with the camera at my feet, and breathe.

The corridor's still empty, and my eyes find the security room door, images coming of it bursting open.

Nothing happens. No sound of raised voices.

Gradually, my breathing calms. I grab the burner phone from my pocket. One message received ...

Fire door open. Back below now. See you at rendezvous?

I read and reread it, waiting for more of the tension to ease. It doesn't. My eyes keep flicking back down the corridor, toward the production room and Lucia in control of all fucking audiovisual output.

My fingers clench, my gut as constricted as ever, and I shut my eyes, forcing myself through the options.

I can't enlist the angels. I'd never find them, and what would make them battle Lucia? I can't reveal the bigger plan.

My pulse beating faster, I open the phone's inbox again. And with heart aching, I begin typing out a message.

Just got one more thing to do. Will see you soon.

I hesitate and then delete the last four words with trembling fingers and add two more, tears pricking the corner of my eyes.

Go well.

I pocket the phone, breathe deeply, and shake myself. The phone buzzes in my pocket. I ignore it and grab the camera instead, hoisting it onto my shoulder. Then I begin to pad back down the corridor. Every step's an effort, my doubts screaming at me. And all too soon, I'm standing before the production room door.

My fingers reach for the handle, and before I have the chance to retreat, I shove it down and push the door open.

My body jolts, my stomach lurches to my throat, and my eyes go wide. Lucia's already gazing up at me from her mixing desk, her head turned and spine straight. With burning red hair and brighter lips, her eyes are trained on mine as if she's been tracking my approach through the wall the entire time.

I can only stare back, my mind a mess. The veil's so thin, and I sense it beginning to peel away, her demonic form appearing before my eyes. The grey suit becomes metal plates embedded in her chest and legs, red eyes peering back at me. I barely keep my thoughts running, the shimmering world at bay.

"What do you want?" she asks, her voice entirely emotionless.

My lips part. But nothing comes out, my thoughts still shrieking. I manage to force my eyes away, to take a couple of faltering steps into the room. I fix my gaze on the monitors before her.

"A media crew is missing," I find myself saying, the camera wobbling on my shoulder while my doubts yell louder.

So fucking what?

Still, I keep my eyes on the two CCTV camera monitors showing the seats opposite the stage – the media area crammed with television crews. Many of the reporters are recording pieces to camera, their overlapping voices playing through speakers on the desk.

I point to a tiny gap near the rear of the crews. "There," I say and keep my arm raised, my hand shaking.

Eventually, she turns back to the screens and follows my gaze.

"It means nothing," she says. "Enough are present already." And she goes still, gazing on at the screens as if I don't exist.

I tiptoe behind her, the sweat building up my back, and my eyes scour the room for weapons ... Fire extinguisher strapped to the wall in the corner. Spare office chair to her side. Camera on my shoulder. All either too heavy, too bulky, or too bloody far away.

The room's big, but there's nothing more. Only keyboards, mice, coffee cups, and a host of computer equipment, most of it built into the console. Plus the screens she's staring at – two attached to the soundproof walls, and the smaller ones on flexible mounts to the side. Absolutely fuck all else.

My gut continues to tighten while my pulse accelerates. Sweat's forming across my brow, trickling down my face in the growing heat.

I reach the far end of the desk, side-on from Lucia and

only a couple of feet away. The smell's more intense: cinnamon plus a charred scent underneath, sickly sweet.

She continues to stare at the screens directly before her, at images of the raised stage. Curved tables cover it, with well over a dozen people sitting behind them – world leaders. Only the lectern remains empty in front with Paul Hawcross's arrival imminent.

I take a breath and try to relax, but my heart's still a jack-hammer in my chest, the sense of darkness, of the abyss so deep inside me.

I lean down, place my camera on the floor, and edge my hand toward the nearest keyboard on the desk, keeping my eyes on the screens the entire time.

She doesn't react but simply continues to stare forward. And as my fingers draw nearer the keyboard, it's as if the room becomes hotter, the light dims more, and the shadows creep inward from the corners. Plus the smell worsens and the sense of stillness increases, the sound from the speakers growing quieter in my ears.

I swallow and force myself to breathe, the air scorching my lungs while my lips mouth silent prayers.

Then I tense my stomach, grab the keyboard in one hand, and hurl it at her.

46

The keyboard flies toward Lucia, covering the few feet between us in an instant. And, from complete stillness, the female demon moves like a coiled spring.

Her hand darts up and diverts the flying wedge of plastic, sending it crashing into the wall behind. Then the same arm shoots toward me, her hand grabbing for my throat. She doesn't even turn her head from the television screens.

It takes me every ounce of will not to dodge out of the way. Instead, I still my thoughts, channel the energy down my arm, and grasp the nearer monitor on its extendible arm. I yank it in front of me, right into the way of her speeding hand.

Her fingers smash straight through it, and the display shatters with a muted crash, sending plastic shards flying. I barely manage to keep my eyes open to see her fingers burst out the other side, tighten into claws, and strain for my extended neck.

I lean back just in time, her hand stopping inches from my throat. Then I force the veil back further and feel the power building in my shoulder. I jerk the monitor down, ignoring the pain in my rib. The screen tears free from its extendible arm and drags Lucia's trapped arm downward, her head toward me.

She starts to turn.

In slowed time, I tense my chest, my shoulders, my arms, and thrust the screen away from me as hard as I can. Right at her forehead.

The monitor smashes into her with a dull clunk. And while it would have taken a normal person's head off, hers hardly moves at all.

The doubting thoughts screech, and a chill grips my insides while monsters laugh on in the black. Again, I drive the sensations away, plant my feet, and tug the broken screen to the side. I shove hard at her elbow joint, trying to bend her arm backward to break it.

But I can't move the thing more than a few inches. And as I push, she continues to turn her head. Painfully slowly.

Behind the veil, her demonic form resolves itself, and I find myself staring at the spikes embedded along the top of her shoulders and backs of her arms. The metal plates cover not only her chest and stomach but her thighs and calves as well, sections of smooth flesh in between. The upper half of one side of her face is coated in steel, while twin red eyes burn, each one filled with swirling flames, inhumanly large.

The longer I stare at them, the more I feel them pulling at me, like I'm standing at the edge of a well about to tip forward, to tumble in. And the sense of stillness increases further, as if the rest of the world's been banished, while the shadows continue to deepen around me.

She grabs the broken monitor with her other hand, rips her trapped arm out of the shattered casing, and flings the screen at me.

I launch myself to the side, barely getting out of the way, but my foot slips on bits of plastic as the broken monitor smashes into the wall at my back. And I go down on one knee.

Lucia slowly gets to her feet, the image flitting between

the auburn-haired beauty and her metal-plated form. The door's behind her and the corridor beyond. My mind conjures images of Natasha wandering the building alone, unprotected, and surrounded by demons.

The ache fills my chest, so easy to turn into fire, and I focus on the flames, building the energy at my core. The veil peels back automatically, and my feet grip the floor beneath me. I rock forward, tense my legs, and explode up toward her to throw myself at her midriff.

She meets my charge, and I catch her in the stomach with my shoulder. I shove, feet straining at the ground, my voice roaring with the effort.

She slides back a little, her hands clamped on my back and sharp nails digging into my skin. Then she grabs me and lifts me effortlessly into the air, tossing me to the side. I don't let go. My fingers grasp her by the shoulders as she spins me around, my body fucking parallel with the ground.

My feet hit the wall, and I bend my knees and thrust back hard against it, using the churning energy inside. Her balance shifts, and she slips backward. My hands grip her tighter, and I continue to leverage my weight down upon her, just managing to drive her into the floor beneath me.

Her back hits the ground, and I am able to keep on top. I end up kneeling astride her. She's so close now, the sickly smell so strong in my nose and the steel plates blazing hot beneath me, the heat almost unbearable.

The fire rages within me as well, the energy surging hotter through my veins. With my teeth clenched, I grab her head and slam the back of it into the floor, ignoring the burning sensation in my hands.

She doesn't react at all. Just lets me do it.

And with the flames continuing to blaze inside, I grasp her neck, swivel her head halfway around, and smash the uncovered side of her face into the ground again. And again. And again. Harder each time. Till my arms shake with the effort.

Still she doesn't fight back.

My thoughts start up, the veil slipping into place before my senses again, and her demonic form recedes, the suited lady appearing before my eyes once more. I lean over and glimpse her human eyes. They're unmoving, still empty of emotion.

In the next instant, I feel her hands underneath my chest, and without the added reaction time of the shimmering world, I sense the movement coming, but I'm no way fast enough. She thrusts me off her, sending me flying upward, and I spin through the air, my arms and legs flailing and my hands grasping. The ceiling smashes into my back, and the impact drives the breath out of me, causing the pain in my rib to flare wildly.

My body falls again, my lungs hungrily sucking in air, the breath bringing only more pain. I still my thoughts once more and try to peel back the veil, to slow my fall. I start to rotate my legs underneath me.

The ground comes so fast, and I land hard on one foot and one knee, off balance and stumbling backward. My feet trip over bits of the shattered monitor casing, and toppling over, my back hits the wall behind. I collapse down it, my legs stretched out. The pounding in my rib's like an extra heartbeat.

She stands before me, her empty eyes fixed on mine. Then she blinks and brushes her lips with her fingertips. They come away red.

She frowns at the blood, and her tongue appears through perfect teeth. She licks her fingers, and her eyes find mine again. I work to steady my breathing.

She reaches one hand behind her back and draws something out – a bone handle connected to a long metal wire, curled into loops and razor-thin while the end thickens into a barbed hook. Her lips form a faint smile.

My eyes search the space to my side, my camera only a foot away.

Her hand shoots downward, and without the shimmering world, the movement is near instantaneous. A flash erupts to the side of my head, combined with an enormous cracking sound.

The camera. Now split entirely in two, the lens section separated from the main body. Tendrils of smoke rise from the gashed metal while an acrid scent fills my nose.

My eyes find Lucia again. She's slowly winding the wire back up between her hands, her smile that bit wider.

With my heart beating furiously, I glance the other way, scanning the floor for some kind of protection ... the swivel chair, the fragments of the monitor casing, the fire extinguisher beside the desk.

The flash comes again, only inches from my nose, the light blinding. The crack of the whip rings even louder in my ears, and my body jerks away from the impact, prompting a stabbing pain in my side. I take a quick intake of breath and my fingers go automatically to my injured rib.

Lucia gazes at my chest and tilts her head. I yank my hand back down by my side. Too late. Lucia's whip hand shifts again, as fast as before, and I catch just a glimpse of metal arcing through the air. The next thing I know, her barbed hook spears the skin over my wounded rib, striking the bone underneath.

My mouth opens wide, but no sound comes out, the pain in my chest augmenting to a loud screaming. My gaze finds the circle of blood over my throbbing rib, and Lucia's smile widens again, her hands coiling up her whip and her eyes still fixed on my torso.

My rib pounds, and my fingers start to reach for it, but I tense my arm. I keep it rooted to my side, images coming of her taking my entire hand off at the wrist.

Her smile doesn't waver. The bone handle simply blurs downward once more, and the hook tears deeper into my skin over my rib. I feel another explosion of pain, like my torso's on fire. My body bucks and writhes on the floor, which augments the agony even further. My vision blurs, and I need to grit my teeth to avoid passing out.

I force myself to calm. To still. And I lie there, my head propped up against the wall, with every part of me sweating. More blood seeps from my chest and stains my shirt as a wave of exhaustion settles over me. I feel a massive urge to close my eyes, to slow my breathing, to do nothing. Any movement just brings more agony.

Yet I begin the count and empty my mind. Despite the augmented sensations of the shimmering world, I push the veil back. My jaw clenches against the amplified pain, and I force my attention onto my memories of the room …

Bits and pieces strewn everywhere. Chairs, monitors, keyboards, fire extinguisher. And while I feel my attention drawn to the side, I don't move a muscle. I don't even try to peer that way with my peripheral vision.

Instead, I fix my gaze on Lucia's demonic form. Behind the veil, she grows before me, the metal plates forming again, the spikes appearing from her shoulders and arms. And the heat rises like the fire's inside my body, inside my bones, burning my injured rib from within. The gloom continues to press in on me, shadows creeping across the floor and pushing in from the corners of my vision.

Still I don't move. I simply continue to force back the veil, to augment the sense of connection with every object around me as the pain screams ever louder in my chest.

Lucia raises her hand with the whip and brings it crashing down again. In slowed time, with the instant of foresight, I'm already moving. I clench every muscle in my stomach and throw myself to the side, gritting my teeth against the resulting agony just as the whip slams into the ground a few inches from my back.

My hands shoot outward. I don't look as I simply reach out for where I sense the fire extinguisher is, strapped to the wall. My fingers rip the metal cylinder from its housing, and I roll back, thrusting it out before my chest as Lucia brings the whip handle crashing down again.

The coils fly, and I feel them wrap around the cylinder between my hands, biting into the thick metal without chewing through. I keep my head back to avoid the stinging hook.

Then I grip the extinguisher tighter to channel whatever energy remains into my shoulders, and launch it at her. She ducks and yanks her bone handle to the side, whipping the extinguisher out of the way of her body.

I'm already scrambling to my feet, pushing against the biting pain as my fingers reach for the split camera at my side. I grip the lens and bring it back behind me, my arms tensing while my doubts roar. Then I sling the camera lens at her as well.

She takes a step back, brings the whip around, and simply lashes it out of the air. I lift my foot, channel energy down my leg, and kick out at one of the swivel chairs. I send it careening toward her, but she arcs the whip back in front of her. It loops around the spindle of the chair and casts it out of the way, too.

Still, I keep going, lowering my arm as I bound toward her. My hand sweeps everything off the desk – keyboard, computer mice – in a shower of plastic, all aimed at her uncovered midriff, right between the metal plates.

She doesn't even move this time, simply letting everything bounce off her and fall to the ground. My doubts bellow ever louder, and the blazing pain in my rib continues to pull at my attention.

I focus on the desk to my side, grab a coffee cup from the back, and fling it toward her head. She takes another step backward to avoid it and doesn't even use the whip this time. She ends up by the corridor wall, a foot in front of the door, blocking off my escape.

Then she raises her whip, the coils falling behind her shoulder, and that smile returns to her lips.

I just stand there, my thoughts starting and pulse hammering as the darkness claims me inside and out. While the shadows continue to deepen across the surrounding walls, her eyes burn ever brighter in the growing dark.

She brings her arm forward as the door bursts open, smashing into her shoulder from behind.

47

ELETH, dressed in full armour – breastplate, helmet, and wrist bracers – is glowing brilliantly, and her arms fly. She thrusts her way through the production room doorway, sword flashing through the air. Lucia stumbles away from her, knocked off balance by the door. She spins, bone handle lifted, and brings the whip around to block Eleth's attacks.

The emissary keeps coming, delivering strike after strike with her sword in a mixture of sweeps and thrusts. Each one drives Lucia rearward, her whip flashing left and right in defence. I back into the corner of the room, out of reach of the blade and coils, my rib still yelling with pain.

Eleth lunges, her sword outstretched, and forces Lucia to dodge and deflect the blade with a slash of her whip. The demon steps immediately forward and presses in at Eleth from the side. Lucia delivers three quick strikes with the whip, each one almost too fast for me to see. Eleth parries desperately and backs right up against the control desk.

I just stare on. The attacks are so rapid, I'm barely able to follow them.

Eleth dives out of the way of another strike and opens her mouth to yell, "Now!"

With another flash of light, Nakir hurtles through the

door, side-on from Lucia. He falls on her with sword swinging while Eleth pushes back from the desk and attacks her from the opposite side.

All I can make out now is a blur of movement as silver arcs flash through the air. All three of them strike out while somehow avoiding the walls and ceiling of the confined space. The two emissaries attack Lucia from different angles, and the demon keeps her whip spinning, the coils arcing at impossible angles, somehow deflecting both swords with single strikes.

Nakir presses a step closer, his sword flashing to either side of him, wrist spinning in a single-handed grip. He darts inside Lucia's slashing coils, his blade reaching for her uncovered neck. The demon blocks it before delivering a lower strike and then a higher one. She forces Nakir to alter his defence and pushes him backward again.

She maintains her position in the middle of the fight, trading attacks with each of them, and each whip crack sends vibrations through my bones. Soon, the emissaries' muscles are quivering, their skin slick with sweat, and their movements gradually slowing. Yet Lucia fights on undimmed, clearly using whatever powers she has, which may be how the emissaries found us.

Eleth deflects one of Lucia's strikes before trying to backhand the demon with a golden bracer. Lucia steps to the side, watches Eleth's hand pass harmlessly past her face, and then leans in and smashes Eleth in the forehead with the end of the handle.

With an audible crack of bone against bone, Eleth's head snaps back, her eyes wide and lips parted. Lucia keeps moving. She lashes the whip at a swivel chair, wraps the coils around its metal stem, and hurls it directly at Nakir, all in an instant. The chair careens toward the emissary, too big to deflect with his sword. Nakir has to dodge backward out of the way and ends up losing a few feet and as many seconds.

Lucia's already facing a stunned Eleth.

I reach out an arm, a shout stuck in my throat, while Eleth raises her sword. But Lucia kicks it out of her hand, smashes her in the head with the handle again, and then looms above her. She brings the coils of her whip across her body to the side, ready to decapitate the emissary.

I dart forward, starting the count in my mind and peeling back the veil. The resulting agony in my rib makes my vision wobble, but I ignore it and launch myself at Lucia, channelling all my available energy into my chest and my shoulders. I cross the six feet in a moment and spin side-on to barge her out of the way from behind.

All the while, the demon doesn't attack but simply holds her whip primed across Eleth's body

I aim my shoulder at the space between two of Lucia's metal plates, but she spins to dodge my thrust. Then she swings her free arm and smashes me on the side of the head.

My vision blurs, and I'm left toppling into space. My body hits the ground, and I go into some kind of roll, my rib screaming. I end up on my back, gazing up at Lucia.

She's turned on me, her whip handle held out at waist height.

Eleth is still weaponless off to one side, and Nakir tries a sword thrust from the other direction, which Lucia easily pushes aside with her metal coils. Her eyes never leave mine.

She raises the bone handle above her shoulder, her metal spikes glinting in the reflected light. She starts to bring the whip down toward me as I scramble backward on hands and feet.

"No!" Eleth yells and throws herself between us, lifting her arm to deflect the blow.

The whip connects with her arm just above her metal bracers, the coils biting deep into her muscled flesh.

Eleth screams, and Nakir yells out, scrabbling to get to her. Lucia doesn't hesitate an instant. As I'm clambering to my knees, the demon yanks back on the whip handle, rips the coils from Eleth's arm, and strikes again. She sends the hook crashing into the emissary's throat from one side.

The emissary's scream is cut short. Her eyes widen. Her mouth opens and closes, desperately trying to suck in air while blood spills from the ragged hole in her neck. Her eyes turn glassy, her body goes limp, and her glow diminishes, the shadows pressing in ever closer around us as she collapses to the ground.

With hands clenched around his sword, Nakir lets out a louder yell. My skull shakes with it, the energy vibrating my bones. My core's swamped in darkness, the veil back in place while the monsters rumble ever louder in the deep.

The emissary throws himself at Lucia, his sword flying faster than I've ever seen. The demon repels him with more strikes from her whip, each one pushing his blade aside, the repeated clash of metal ringing loud in my ears.

I scramble to my feet and back away to one side of the room. Nakir keeps fighting, keeps slashing and lunging. Lucia's coils rip his cheek, a thin red line curving downward from his temple to the line of his jaw. Still he keeps coming, his attacks yet wilder. He thrusts himself between Eleth's body and Lucia, blood trickling down the side of his face.

They move so fast now, my thoughts still automatically, the veil peeling back once more. Even in slowed time, I have to concentrate hard to make out each attack.

Lucia's so quick, so strong. She turns each of Nakir's attacks away. She uses the coils of her whip to seize objects – fire extinguisher, shattered monitor, keyboard – before sending them careening at Nakir.

The emissary is forced to defend himself against the flying objects, not Lucia. The demon lands another strike with her whip on his arm and then his shoulder. Her coils open new lines of flesh between the sections of Nakir's battered armour. His face contorts. His jaw tenses, and still he fights on, swinging the sword in crazy arcs and lunging for a killing stroke.

Lucia keeps landing hit after hit, the metal hook flashing, always targeting his extremities – arms, hands, thighs, shoulders – never a mortal injury. She continues to reduce his skin to bloody rags, yet he remains fighting at Eleth's side, refusing to be pushed backward.

I stand watching from the edge of the room, my eyes glued, rib throbbing, and feet welded to the floor. The void's still so wide inside me, the image of Eleth's motionless body etched in my mind. I sense Lucia sidling into my head, scouring my thoughts, waiting for my move. Yet my brain's yelling at me to act; Nakir has only moments to live.

The emissary swipes again. Lucia knocks the blade lazily out of the way with her whip and then lands another strike on his other cheek, opening an even deeper gash.

My heart's like a rabid animal in my chest as I start the count and quieten my thoughts completely. I peel the veil back further, the shimmering world opening out around me. And while the sensation of connection builds with every object – monitors, bits of camera, fire extinguisher, desk, walls, ground – I don't allow my attention to rest on any of them. Instead, I breathe deep and let my body take over.

I find my hand reaching down and to the side. Without looking, I feel my fingers curl around the handle of my severed camera. I grip it tightly, raise it up, and lurch on toward Lucia from the side, toward the arm where she's holding the whip.

The demon strikes out at Nakir again. In slowed time, I glimpse the coils flash through the air before smashing into his wrist bracer. Vibrations roll up his arm, the impact almost making him drop his sword.

I lift the broken camera beside my shoulder, only three feet from Lucia now. And feeling the demon still probing my thoughts, I fix my eyes on the side of her neck, the adrenaline like molten fire in my veins, my pulse a torrent behind my ears.

Nakir grips his sword with both hands and brings it back

for another wild swing at her chest. While I keep my focus on Lucia's neck, my hand sweeps the camera body up from behind my head.

Lucia calmly turns her torso toward me, her whip raised. She brings the coils back to send them flying at Nakir, to block his strike and send him reeling, while her other hand sweeps across her body toward my lifted arm, her fingers like steel blades.

I keep my eyes trained on the side of her neck and dive deeper into the shimmering world, concentrating hard on the resulting currents in my body. I don't bring the camera crashing down on her. Instead, as she slashes the handle at Nakir, I thrust my hand upward into the space behind her swinging arm. With feet rooted, I anchor it there with everything I have.

The lashing coils collide with the camera's body in mid-air, curling around it, biting into the metal, and drawing nearer to my fingers. And while I'm desperate to let go, I grip the camera handle ever harder.

In slowed time, the metal wire wraps itself around the camera case numerous times, the hook embedding itself in its side as burning sparks shower the back of my hand. Lucia's head turns toward the case, her eyes widening. She jerks her arm and tries to disengage the whip.

And I hold on yet tighter, the back of my hand on fire and my shoulder almost ripped from its socket.

Nakir never stopped his wild swing. He brings his sword up in a broad arc from thigh height to above her head, the tip of the blade slicing deep into Lucia's bare neck.

Blood sprays, splattering Nakir's front, and she totters. As I stare at her, my thoughts start up, the veil slips back before my senses, and Lucia's demonic form fades away. She becomes a woman in a business suit, the colour draining from her cheeks and her lips, her muscles slackening. The smell and heat disappear also, the darkness banished back to the corners of the room, and her body topples face-first onto the ground.

Nakir teeters for a moment and then lets his sword fall as he drops to his knees at Eleth's side. He reaches out so gently, lifts her by the shoulders, and rolls her over slowly. He pulls her carefully onto his lap, and the tears come, his lips mumbling a strange language as he rocks her back and forth.

I can't take my gaze from her limp body, her vacant eyes. My mouth opens, though no sound comes out, the pain in my chest a colossal weight with the abyss as immense as ever.

"I'm so sorry," I say, my voice shaking.

Nakir doesn't look at me. Doesn't speak to me. Instead, he turns away, his back and shoulders tense. He grits his teeth and simply squeezes Eleth more tightly.

I breathe, trying to stand still, but faintness grips me. I stumble into the desk at my side and then glance down and spy my stained shirt and the large crimson patch around my rib. More of the adrenaline fades from my system, and the pain reasserts itself.

Nakir continues to hold Eleth to him, softly whispering in her ear. And while my eyes find the door, I don't move toward it. Instead, I step to Nakir's side and put a hand on his shoulder, my fingers still stinging from the burning sparks.

Again, Nakir tenses, his fists clenched. I keep my fingers there and then squeeze, the weight huge inside me as we breathe together.

"I'm so, so sorry," I whisper.

He doesn't react. Doesn't rip my arm off. Just remains kneeling there, the tears falling faster. I straighten, a clock ticking loudly in my mind, and my feet take me lurching toward the door.

48

I STAND in the spare equipment room, fumbling the buttons of a stolen shirt. My mind keeps flitting to the production suite only a few doors away, the void still gaping inside. Nakir holding Eleth in his arms, the tears streaking his cheeks. All my fault again. And every time I see Eleth, the vision morphs into one of Natasha lying there, the ache almost paralysing in my chest.

My fingers shake more, and I focus again on the buttons. I finally do them up, the burnt skin on my hand stinging more intensely now. Then I grab a jacket off a hanger and haul it on over the strips of spare shirts I've used to bind my rib. Yet my side still feels wet with blood.

I stagger out of the equipment room and on down the basement corridor. Still empty. Outside the double doors to the technical area, my feet stumble to a halt. A muffled sound emanates from behind them, a faint vibration climbing my legs while my gut twists again.

I force myself to open the double doors, and sure enough, Paul Hawcross's distant voice hits my ears. The individual words are unclear, though my chest resounds with the power, the confidence. No apparent worry about any angels in the building … or Gabriel. And as I stare across the cavernous space, the shadows slink toward me again, their shapes twisting into the outlines of scuttling legs.

My pulse quickens, and I slam the door before pushing myself faster down the corridor. Then I barge straight through the stairwell door.

I jump the steps, the pain flaring in my rib while the stickiness grows under my mock bandages, my head increasingly woozy. Still, I keep climbing and don't let up the pace.

First level. Second level. I fix my gaze on every door, ready for guards to burst through them. No one does.

Third level – ground floor. No sound beyond the doors, everyone undoubtedly in the auditorium. I almost peep through to check the corridor but force myself on upward.

Fifth-level landing. My chest's heaving, the throbbing worse in my side, my back wet with blood or sweat. I nudge open the door to peer out.

Another empty corridor. Paul Hawcross's voice echoes against the curving walls, the dull roars from outside the building audible. And no sign of Natasha.

My heart beats faster, and I take off down this new passageway, around the top of the auditorium, while more images bombard me of Eleth's inert body, and then Natasha's, her vacant eyes, a gaping hole in her neck.

My head swims and my lungs seize. I grip the wall for support and then stumble on those final twenty feet. The balcony room doors come into view around the corner, though I can barely look, my breath held, my back rigid.

Through narrowed eyes, I glimpse her. Outside one of the balcony doors and facing away.

"Nat," I say, my voice so hoarse.

She spins, her face lighting up, and takes several running steps in my direction. She throws her hands around my neck.

My arms fold around her back, and I burrow my face in her hair, ignoring the throbbing pain in my side.

She pushes away from me. "What is it?" she asks, pulling my jacket aside.

She draws in a quick breath, and her fingers go to her mouth. I follow her gaze. The growing patch of red is all too easy to see on my right-hand side at the base of my ribcage. And staring at it, a weakness creeps up my legs, a new drowsiness coming over me.

"Well, you don't look too good," she says, forcing levity into her tone, and her eyes meet mine. "What happened?"

"I'll tell you later," I reply. For an instant the void is gone, replaced by a brimming joy in my heart. I grip her hand and squeeze it.

Yet my insides don't untwist, that telltale constriction in my gut all too obvious.

My gaze finds the balcony door behind her while Natasha's staring again at my chest, that strange look back in her eyes, the same mixture of curiosity and excitement.

"Is it locked?" I ask.

She glances up at my face, her lips parted, and then shakes her head.

The door has the same porthole window as the others, several empty seats visible beyond. I press down on the handle and push.

The balcony's ten feet by six with half a dozen velvet chairs and a sculpted barrier around the edge made entirely of glass. But again, Paul Hawcross's voice seizes my attention. Not only is his vitriol now louder, but I feel my whole body vibrating with its power; a level of command voice far surpassing even the priest's.

I need to consciously shift my focus and take in the curved space around me.

The auditorium is massive, well over two hundred feet wide and considerably longer. Our balcony faces across the interior, a hundred feet above the edge of the stage. The huge domed roof stretches overhead, one half of it made of glass, which slopes down over the rows of internal seating. And though the blueprints showed it can be covered, right now natural light streams through, the blue sky clearly visible up above.

Natasha pads through the door at my side, and I shut it silently behind me. Then I lower myself down onto my stomach, gritting my teeth against the pain, and crawl forward toward the glass barrier. I stop when I'm just a few inches from the edge.

I can see everything. The stage stretches out below me. The rear half is raised six feet with three concentric rows of semicircular tables, each one covered by purple silk. And well over fifty people sit behind them in ornate chairs, all decorated in varying fineries. The world leaders, probably the heads of the largest Christian countries on earth, and they're all here.

The sight takes my breath away.

And in the centre of the tables, in the middle of the raised part of the stage, stands Paul Hawcross. It's hard to look anywhere else. He's dressed in his customary simple dark trousers and white shirt, with hands gesticulating as if he's conducting an orchestra of millions.

Natasha lies down next to me, wriggles forward, and presses into my side. For that moment, I'm back in our home, beside her on the mattress, hearing the prime minister's voice coming through the holes in the wall. And then, just as suddenly, I'm here, listening to it live and booming louder than ever, like a gong inside my brain.

"In the West, we have been lied to, over and over!" Paul Hawcross says, spitting the words. "Our power stripped away by those who vowed to help us. Political leaders, corporations, financiers."

The prime minister speaks without a visible microphone, wandering out from behind the lectern. Nevertheless, his amplified voice resounds around us, giving him a supernatural air. The microphones are clearly hidden somewhere in the stage. Bloody clever.

"Their sins have been pride, gluttony, but worst of all, ignorance!" he says. "Because it let true evil into our lands."

He holds one hand out toward the audience, palm up. Across the lower half of the stage and the twenty-foot gap sit the media – fifty or so television crews from all over the world. They all sit crammed together, with every camera trained on the prime minister and the heads of state behind him.

Above the media, they've packed more VIPs and religious leaders along the remaining tiers of internal seating. Its rows slope gently up to the bottom of the glass wall and the clam-shell area beyond.

My mouth gapes. A sea of people swamp it, an ocean. Hundreds of thousands of supporters look on, all of them hearing Paul Hawcross's voice through banks of speakers and watching him on massive screens. All of them bay and leap up and down in response. The pulsating crowd stretches as far as I can see.

"Crop failures, droughts, famines," Paul Hawcross yells, counting off the disasters on his fingers. "These aren't about science. They're about *faith*." He clenches a fist. "We are being punished for our lack of purity, our absence of godliness."

And with each accusation, the shouts from the crowd outside get louder. I bite my cheek, my eyes scanning the space for any sign of angels, for any sign of Gabriel. My heart pounds yet harder in my chest, my gut continuing to twist.

"But I come with good news!" Paul Hawcross says, lifting his arm once more. "For I am the hand of God, and you are my holy army! Here to combat the devil, in all his guises. The powers I have are God-given." He lifts his chin and raises a finger to the sky as if he's pointing at us. "Here to inspire the pure, to expose the hollow, to root out deceivers!"

My adrenaline fires again, my side throbs with pain, and a realisation starts to take root in my mind, the void growing at my core again.

"Gabriel ..." I find myself whispering.

Natasha turns, and I keep my eyes fixed on the stage.

"He's not coming, and he never was," I go on. "This is his revenge on us." The darkness is filling my insides, choking my lungs, and images come of the angels we brought around us, here to witness Satan's triumph first-hand. "This isn't our plan. It's the devil's." My voice falters. "We've helped crush the tiny resistance there might've been."

The sound of hissed breath causes me to turn.

Natasha has scooted toward the balcony door and is sitting with her back against it, her knees bent and her face completely white, that same strange look in her eyes. It's even more intense now – a great fierceness in her expression, with lines of tension around her mouth and cheeks.

My pulse quickens yet further. I push myself up and away from the barrier. "What is it?"

Natasha's mouth opens, but nothing comes out. She touches her fingers to her lips instead, her hand trembling.

"No, no, no, no, no ..." she says.

I reach out my hand toward her, but she pulls away. She shifts a knee and shuffles to the side.

"Nat, what's going—" I start.

She shakes her head and shuts her eyes. When she opens them, tears dot their corners. Then she takes a slow breath, a hint of redness returning to her cheeks. And when she speaks, her voice quivers.

"I'm here for you *now*," she says, her gaze finding mine.

I blink. "Of course."

She shakes her head more forcefully this time. "*No*," she says, her breathing speeding up. She tries to settle herself. "Those words Father Thomas spoke to you. That I would be there for you before the end."

My stomach plummets, as if I'm falling down an endless well. An enormous desire grabs me to charge back out of the balcony door.

"*This* is the end," she whispers, reaching out and gripping my hand.

She pulls me close, and I hardly feel the sting of pain in my side. She cradles my cheek with her other hand and then leans in, closes her eyes, and kisses me. I stop breathing. My eyes are still open, staring past her shoulder.

Her lips linger on mine. Then she pulls back, tears tracing their way down her cheeks. My fingers entwine with hers.

"What is it?" I ask again, more slowly this time, the prime minister's voice growing increasingly distant in my ears.

"I ... I know what the story is," she says.

I can only stare back.

"The bigger story, Jake, the myth we have been looking for, the narrative Father Thomas tried to help us find," she says.

"Revelation—" I start.

"It's not Revelation. It's not," she says. "It's the most powerful story ever told." Her voice trembles. "The one that touches more people on this planet than any other."

She glances toward the sky. "I can't believe I did not see it before," she says, her features tightening with a look of pain. "But who could have imagined it?"

"Imagined *what?*" I press.

Yet crouching there, I feel the darkness expanding out around me, the monsters howling and screaming in the deep, my gut twisting more than ever.

"The immaculate conception," she says. "You never knew your father. Did you? Your mother never spoke of anyone. And now you are pursuing the same vision as Father Thomas – to democratise your abilities, to empower us all."

Natasha sits forward on her knees. "The kingdom of God is at hand," she says, and even though it's quiet, her voice resonates as if she's standing in a pulpit. "You are handing out its keys, helping us know its mysteries. That's what the Bible says."

My mouth opens, and I shake my head automatically.

"I have watched you," she says, the words coming more

quickly now. "An unbeliever. Standing up and preaching to angels. Convincing divine beings to follow your cause."

Her eyes blaze, all past deadness gone, and I sense a part of my brain shutting down, numbing out.

"You're right," she says, working to keep her voice steady. "We are not waiting for Gabriel." Then she jabs a finger at me. "It's *you*. This entire time, we've been trying to persuade others. The angels. Gabriel. But this is *your* role, *your* time." She jabs the finger at me again. "You are here to inspire the world, just as Jesus did two thousand years ago."

Then she tilts her hand downward till her trembling finger points at my chest. I follow her gaze. She's gesturing toward the bloodied stripe across my side, and the memory comes of an image in Father Thomas's church. Jesus crucified. The slice across his lower chest, the injury from the Roman spear, in exactly the same place.

Gooseflesh forms across my neck.

"Nat, that's crazy," I breathe.

She straightens up and lifts her chin. "It may be," she says, nodding once. "It may be total fantasy. We cannot know. That's the point. Yet we have to go on anyway." She points at me again with her lifted finger. "Those were *your* words, outside Gabriel's building."

My mouth opens, more arguments revolving around my head, but nothing comes out. My mind is entirely scrambled.

Natasha grips my hand again, her eyes red now, tears falling from her chin.

"I'm so sorry," she breathes.

And the image returns of Jesus in the painting. Crucified.

Natasha's hand squeezes tighter and doesn't let me go as the darkness fills my entire body. It's so immense I can barely breathe with it, barely think.

I push up off the floor and force myself to stand. If I remain stationary, I'm not sure I'll ever move again.

My feet stumble on toward the edge of the balcony. With each step I take, Paul Hawcross's voice grows louder in my ears, the clamouring yells from outside ever more powerful. My eyes find the wall beyond. It slopes downward toward the ground, almost vertical, the incline growing that bit gentler the nearer it gets to the stage.

The stage, the twenty-foot gap. Then fifty television cameras and two hundred thousand people beyond. Millions or even billions more watching around the world.

My legs shake, my breaths coming raggedly now. I grasp the wall to brace myself, and doubts scream. Even so, I swing my leg over the barrier, my gaze fixed on the ten-foot crucifix at the centre of the lower part of the stage. And I hear Father Thomas's voice in my mind ... *Trust this.*

I get one foot onto the thin lip on the far side of the railing. There's an audible hush from below, and I'm vaguely aware of a pause in Paul Hawcross's speech.

I start the count and try to still my thoughts. Then I swing over the other leg and bring both feet side by side till I'm standing with both heels on the outer edge of the balcony, the hundred-foot drop below me. My stomach climbs my throat.

And in that instant, I'm no longer standing two-thirds of the way up an auditorium wall. I'm perched on the umpteenth floor of Gabriel's headquarters, the shattered window before me, nothing but the night sky beyond, with Father Thomas at my side.

"Go well," Natasha says from behind, the hush continuing to build below. "I'm with you."

The ache sears my heart, and while every part of me wants to turn around, to find her eyes again, I take one foot off the balcony lip, place it flat on the sloping wall to my side, and let go of the railing.

49

I BEGIN TO SLIP, the wall slick under my feet and hip, and the auditorium stage barrels up to meet me. I start the count, try to keep my mind quiet, and focus on peeling back the veil. But it's so damn tough. My doubts rage louder, my body picking up speed, and the near-vertical wall is slipping by faster above me.

I throw my body against the tiles. Increase the friction of my slide. And bite down on my thoughts to force back the veil. I concentrate hard on the sensation of the wind against my skin, on the air billowing all around me. I picture it as water and imagine myself diving, not falling, being forced back up toward the surface.

Time slows, and the air thickens around me. My fall slows, too, the slope lessening, while each tile join drags at my calves and jars my bones. I skid down the final few feet and slam down into the stage, heels first. The shock ricochets up my bones, and pain spikes my rib, my knees bending to take the impact.

I go into a forward roll, spring back to my feet, and stumble a few paces across the lower part of the stage. The raised part with the podium is on one side, the twenty-foot gap before the media pit on the other, and the crucifix is directly in front of me, fifty feet away.

The hush deepens, and hundreds of sets of eyes fix on me from inside the auditorium. Hundreds of thousands from outside. Plus, many of the cameras are now trained in my direction.

Sweat breaks out at the base of my spine, and the veil slips back before my senses, the shimmering world dissolving.

"It seems the devil appears in all kinds of guises," Paul Hawcross says. He's staring down at me from the podium, both hands gripping the lectern. "To throw us off. To prevent us from pursuing our divine goal."

A few cries of anger come from the crowd, and I spin, darting my gaze between the doors to either side of the stage. They remain closed, no guards or demons bursting through.

A lightness forms in my chest and then vanishes the next instant. Paul Hawcross is staring at me with eyes narrowed and lip curled. Not a hint of surprise or concern in his expression.

"This is exactly what we must guard against!" he booms, motioning in my direction. "A prime example!"

More of the crowd stirs behind me. More shouts ring out, and I just stand there, my gaze flicking between Paul Hawcross and the audience. A few people are on their feet now, jabbing their fingers at me.

The prime minster keeps going, his voice continuing to rise. "It is a reminder that the devil skulks in our midst." He leans over the lectern toward the audience, most of the cameras focusing on him once more. "He may try and thwart us in every moment, but he will not daunt us! Will not deter us!"

The cries grow louder from within, and beyond the glass wall, the sound reverberates in my bones.

My lungs squeeze, and in that instant, it's as if I'm back in the school hall with the preacher, all those eyes on me, my legs gripped by the huge compulsion to flee.

"Blessed is he who hears these words of prophecy!" Paul Hawcross goes on, his voice ringing out and his hand sweeping over the audience. "For the time is at hand!"

More cheers ring out in approval, and I steel myself, clench my fingers together, and open my mouth, my mind desperately scrambling for something to say.

"Our world has languished in moral darkness for *far* too long," he continues, starting low again and building toward a crescendo. "And now heathens are flooding to our shores, bathing our towns and cities in blood. And despite the many warnings, the many divine signs, so many do not repent of their sins!"

A man in the audience jumps to his feet and stabs his finger directly at me.

"Sinner!" he yells. "Sinner!"

The prime minister merely smiles. The pulse thumps behind my ears, the darkness squeezing tighter around my lungs. Then another memory comes. Crouching before my mother that final time, her hand pressed to my chest. The pain and love exploding inside me.

I face the void within, feeling the darkness as fully as I can. Then I open my mouth again and force the words out. "These sins!" I yell, the words amplified by the microphones built into the stage. "They're committed *against* you, not *by* you!"

I hear a combined intake of breath from the crowd. Some of the TV cameras shift toward me once more, and Paul Hawcross's eyes dart toward the wings of the raised stage. He gives a near-imperceptible shake of his head and then swivels to face me again, the smile back on his lips.

I push myself on. "You're *all* victims," I say. "Of a war not between religions or nations but one for your heart. And it's been going on since the start of our civilisation!"

Paul Hawcross straightens himself behind the lectern, his features cool and composed as more shouts rain down on me from the crowd.

I point up at the prime minister, my hand shaking. "Do you not recognise the words of Revelation?" Then I shift my gaze to the leaders at his back. "The false prophet will go forth to the kings of the earth and gather them together for war," I bark, trying to put energy into the words of scripture Natasha taught me. "Don't you recognise this man's design?" I motion toward Paul Hawcross again. "He's leading you to war, no? Isn't that why you're here?"

The shocked silence grows. Many of the leaders stare back at me with lips pursed and postures tense, their expressions ranging from surprise to outrage.

Paul Hawcross snorts audibly and raises his arms again, facing the audience and the masses beyond. "How can it be *false?*" he shouts, the words like hammers to my sternum. "It is a holy crusade. With the depravity, the corruption, the evil that straddles our land, it is needed now more than ever." He tightens one hand into a fist. "For years, devils have been plotting against us. And now these heathen armies rise – armies of the North African, Arabian, and Southern Asian peninsulas."

I open my mouth, but the prime minister cuts me off.

"They send their soldiers to *every* country, into *every* community!" he continues, the power of his voice still vibrating my chest. "The terrorists kill our families, our children. We must be vigilant!"

A woman in the audience points directly at me. "He's got a bomb!" she yells, her tone shrill.

Several people shout out in alarm, and as the energy builds inside me, I force it up my throat.

"I have no bomb, no weapon!" I yell and pull apart my jacket lapels with shaking hands, revealing my white shirt and the growing bloodstain.

More whispers break out across the audience. Half a dozen people are standing now, clear alarm in their expressions. Monsters howl deep inside me, Michael's words resounding once more in my brain … *You're nothing but the devil's puppet.*

My jaw tightens, and I use the building energy to still my thoughts and peel back the veil. As the shimmering world expands around me, again I just open my mouth and let the words out.

"The true danger is there!" I yell and jab a finger at Paul Hawcross, my own command voice vibrating the air. "He leads you into a religious war. And for what? For nothing but fear and death, superstition and worship. Billions begging for deliverance and salvation. Unprecedented belief in gods, in the devil. Their names spoken in prayers every minute of every hour of every day."

"God *should* be in our hearts, in our prayers!" he bellows even louder, his fingers gripping the lectern tighter, his face reddening.

"But you do *not* serve God," I shout back, his anger building the fire in my chest. I spin back to the audience. "For our prime minister is a pawn!"

Half of the audience are standing now, more cries of fury erupting from among them, several people gesticulating wildly at me. And the hordes outside roar and rail, their din vibrating the glass wall.

The prime minister goes to speak, but this time I cut him off, raising my voice above his.

"Paul Hawcross is the false prophet of the book of Revelation!" I shout out. "He's been forged in the role of the Antichrist by his master, a being who's walked this earth since the ancient times!"

Most of the audience is shouting now, while a few watch on with stunned expressions.

Paul Hawcross glances toward the wings again. He nods this time, and three guards appear out of nowhere, hurrying toward him across the raised stage.

I force myself to face the crowd again. "Forged by

someone who's in this very building," I continue, channelling whatever energy remains in my chest.

Footsteps clomp across the raised stage at my back. More of the audience hush, and my heart starts to race. Yet I don't turn around. Don't look. Instead, I concentrate on the crowds before me, on the cameras trained on my face. With the veil still peeled back, I try to imagine reaching out to the billions watching beyond, to feel a sense of connection.

"The devil is a *real* being, with powers generated from our beliefs," I say, staring back down the lenses. "He and the angels have been milking this for thousands of years, but they were real people once, like you and me. Before they stole our divine spark, stole our birthright … our faith."

"This is blasphemy!" someone yells.

The guards' footsteps turn into larger thwacks as two of them jump down to the lower part of the stage, only forty feet behind me.

My hands reach toward the audience. "It sounds insane. I know!" I say, speaking more quickly. "I'd never have believed it myself. I was an atheist, a cynic. Yet I've had my eyes opened to what I'm capable of, what we're *all* capable of. All cultures, all religions – *everyone*."

The footsteps draw nearer, dividing up and approaching from both sides. The nearest guard is only ten feet behind me, and the hush deepens in the crowd.

While every ounce of my training urges me to spin around, to face the coming threat, I step right up to the gap, the massive drop below me, and gaze out across the audience.

"All you have to do is *believe*," I say, my fist clenched. "And we can take back our power. Reclaim our potential."

Beyond the veil, I can sense the nearer guard lunge at me, his hand stretching, a dark blur in the corner of my vision.

"And I will show you how!" I yell and whirl around.

50

THE GUARD GRASPS at my arm from the side. I yank it away at the last instant, pain stabbing at my rib, and my head goes woozy.

The guard stumbles toward the lip of the stage, having missed, and I push the veil back further. Pain flares even more, and I clench my jaw against it. I feel into everything around me – the guard trying to right himself, the stage edge only a couple of feet from our toes, the cameras trained on me across the gap, plus the second guard approaching from behind, fifteen feet away now.

The first guard brings his arm careening upward toward my face.

I shoot my other hand across my body and grab his wrist out of the air. Then, channelling the energy down my arms and legs, I haul him further across me and dart forward half a step, slamming my shoulder into his chest.

The guard's medium in build with a fully stocked security belt and a neck so thick it's almost non-existent. With the energy coursing through my body, he bounces straight off me and stumbles backward toward the edge of the stage, his eyes wide.

I open my mouth again, and the words just come. "We've given our power away for far too long," I yell.

No-neck teeters further backward, the fifty-foot drop just behind him, his arms flailing. With one hand, I grab the guy's tie and hold it fast while my other fingers yank the cable-tie handcuff from his belt. I slip my free hand through one of its plastic loops.

The second guard continues his silent approach from behind, but I don't turn. I simply reach out with my senses, feeling the soft placement of each of his feet – heel to toe – only five feet away.

I keep my eyes trained on the audience, on the cameras. "Reclaim your divine spark!" I shout, the energy continuing to build at my core, my chest vibrating with my command voice. "Take back your faith!"

There's near silence in the room. Well over two-thirds of the audience are on their feet now, their eyes darting between me and the second guard at my back. I can sense his arm sweeping around my shoulder – lightning-fast – aiming for a chokehold.

I plant my feet, pull on No-neck's tie to help him balance, and thrust my free hand with the loop up and across my body to the side of my head. I place it right in between the second guard's arm and my neck, just quickly enough to stop him strangling me.

The guy grinds his teeth and squeezes tighter, pulling my blocking arm against my throat. And now with his balance restored, No-neck raises his arms and prepares to grab me.

The guards' rage fans the flames at my core. I twist my blocking arm and grasp the second guard's wrist by my neck. Then with my free hand, I grip the tip of the cable tie that's around my forearm, wrench my arms in opposite directions, and swivel my hip. This tosses the guy over my shoulder and yanks the plastic loop from my arm onto his, tightening it around his wrist.

The guy's better built than his colleague, with a huge chest and muscled arms, but only spindly legs. He gives a cry of shock as he stumbles toward the edge, bundling into No-neck, just as the first guard tries to rush me.

I keep my gaze on the audience the entire time, feeling the shimmering world all around me.

"We can all do so much!" I say, the words still just coming, my weight pivoting. I let go of Muscle Man's wrist and clamp my fingers onto the empty cuff loop while lifting one knee into the air. "What matters is what we *believe*."

No-neck dives around his colleague's stumbling body, and this time his hand darts to his belt, clasping his large taser gun. He lifts it toward me at exactly the same moment I kick out with my raised leg.

The energy courses down my calf, and I smash my foot into his lifted hand, sending the gun flying.

The second guard – Muscle Man – swings his uncuffed fist at my jaw from the side while No-neck grabs a billy club from his belt dead ahead of me and yanks it up toward his shoulder to strike.

Behind the veil, I sense both attacks coming, and in slowed time, I don't alter my movement, don't jerk one way or the other. I simply pitch my weight forward to bring my lifted leg down between No-neck's feet while spinning my body around. My jaw clenches as I slam my back into his chest, my rib blazing with pain.

Muscle Man's punch flies by my ear, missing my temple by an inch. And with No-neck behind me now, I clamp his arm under mine, his hand with the billy club stretched out before me.

No-neck tries to wrestle his arm free. I squeeze it tighter between my left biceps and side, my jaw clenched against the growing pain. With my right hand still gripping the empty cuff loop, I yank Muscle Man's bound wrist down hard into his colleague's hand with the club and then again, till eventually No-neck drops the weapon.

Muscle Man stumbles in front of me while I thrust my

right hand through the open loop and haul the cuff to the side as I swivel, pulling him further off balance. With No-neck's hand now empty before me, I grab his wrist with my right hand, clasp the tip of the cable tie with my left, and yank my hands in both directions again. The cuff tightens easily around No-neck's wrist, just as it did his colleague's, leaving them both cuffed together and stumbling a few feet from the stage's edge.

I hear gasps of shock from the crowd and glance up. Beyond the veil, there's another noise in my ears: stomping footsteps across the lower part of the stage.

My gut twists again, and I turn toward the sound. Paul Hawcross remains standing rigidly at his lectern. Below him, only twenty feet away, a third guard is advancing across the lower stage, the taser gun in his hand already pointed at me.

He fires. I hear a crackling sound, and time slows even further, every thought banished from my mind. My knees bend, and I throw myself to the side, behind Muscle Man, just as the wires shoot past my shoulder. I end up only a few inches from the edge of the stage.

The third guard's face glows puce, veins prominent in his neck and every muscle tense. He drops the gun and breaks out into a run, grabbing his stun baton from his belt. He fingers a button and giant crackles of blue electricity shoot down the two-foot-long blade – enough to bring down a fucking elephant.

And the guy barrels toward Muscle Man, the baton raised, forcing him back into me. I can feel the yawning drop just behind my heels, the updraught fluttering my jacket, and my stomach turns over.

Muscle Man instinctively tries to scramble away but rebounds back to No-neck, pinned by the cuff. The baton's only a foot or so from his chest.

"No!" Muscle Man yells, his arms up.

Angry Man keeps on coming, his teeth gritted.

And while thoughts scream at me to leap far to the side, I

anchor my feet and grab the plastic join between the two cuffs. I channel the energy into my arm and yank Muscle Man out of the way of the stabbing blade.

Angry Man doesn't let up. He tracks our movement and continues to thrust with the baton. He jabs at me between his colleagues' limbs, the weapon passing only inches from their skin.

The guy's fury drives my own, and I grip the cuffs tighter, pulling both trapped guards away from the edge while still keeping them as a shield between me and Angry Man's attacks. Both of them track him as well, their free arms raised and palms out.

"Stop, man, stop!" No-neck yells.

Angry Man keeps on thrusting at his colleagues to get to me. I keep yanking them out of the way. My side's sticky with blood, and exhaustion grips my limbs. My head pounds, and my eyes remain glued to the flickering blade, the crazy levels of electricity. My thoughts start up, images coming of me dead, or him, or them, or all of us.

Angry Man lunges. I jerk the guards to the left, and the baton crackles a hair's breadth from No-neck's arm, the caustic smell biting at my nose.

Angry Man sets himself to go again, and I take a breath, starting the count and stilling my mind. I dive further behind the veil. Pain screams in my chest, but I blink through it. I focus intensely on Angry Man's movements, on his shifting weight, on the tensing of the muscles in his neck, his arms.

And instead of keeping my distance, I press closer to Muscle Man. I hover just behind his shoulder, my fingers still wrapped tightly around the centre of the plastic cuffs.

Angry Man's mouth curls up fractionally in a smile. With teeth bared, he lunges further than he's done before, thrusting the baton right between the guards, directly at my chest.

Pushing away the compulsion to scramble backward, I grip the floor with my toes and throw my weight toward No-neck, rotating my shoulder as the baton passes me. It's so close the heat stings my injured side.

Muscle Man lunges away from the strike as well, moving in the opposite direction, and his heavier weight drags No-neck with him.

I shoot a leg out in front of me, right in the way of No-neck's scrabbling feet. His ankles collide, and he stumbles forward toward Muscle Man, the third guard still reaching between them.

Angry Man swivels to the side and shoots out his free hand to protect himself from No-neck's toppling body, the stun baton still extended over the cuffed hands of his colleagues.

No-neck tumbles into him. With one set of fingers, he shoves at Angry Man's chest while the other grasps at Muscle Man's cuffed hand, trying to regain his balance.

And at the same time, I jab my forearm under the middle of the plastic cuffs and thrust upward hard, shoving Muscle Man's arm straight into the blade of the stun baton.

I leap backward, breaking contact, but still the blue electricity jolts up my spine. The full shock leaps from baton to Muscle Man's arm, and then from him into No-neck, all the way through his warding hand into Angry Man.

For a long moment, the electricity's powerful enough to turn three large men into a vibrating mass, their limbs convulsing.

Then the baton jerks away, and they all collapse in a heap.

51

ABSOLUTE SILENCE REIGNS.

I kick the stun baton away and examine the three guards, checking their chests. Each one is still breathing, and beyond them, Paul Hawcross remains at his podium, his head turning left and right. His eyes dart to the doors at either edge of the stage, but no one comes through. Many of the leaders behind him are on their feet, their curious eyes fixed on me.

Swivelling to face the crowd, my legs tremble, and I almost topple over, barely righting myself.

Nearly everyone in the audience is standing as well, all staring at me, the TV crews following my every movement. Still, no one comes to interrupt.

Yet my gut's twisting again, fresh worries niggling. The veil slips back into place, and my vision hazes for an instant, my rib burning.

Mutters break out in the audience, and small groups whisper to each other. I clench my fingers and push myself on.

"You're *all* capable of this, and so much more," I say, but my amplified voice is so hoarse in my ears.

The muttering continues, and my heart's beating ever faster, the wetness growing around my side. I tighten my shoulders, concentrating hard on the energy at my core, and press back the veil again.

"Faith is the very fabric of reality," I yell, louder now. And then Father Thomas's words come to me from the very first time we met. "If we only believe in the mundane, that's all we'll experience!"

Some of the muttering grows quiet and eyes turn back to me, though my insides constrict tighter.

"The angels and demons understand this better than anyone," I press on, speaking faster. "A very long time ago, they were mortal, like you and me. And they've been extorting your devotion ever since, using it to build their powers, to prolong their lives." I sweep a raised hand across the crowd. "The miracles you pray for are *yours* to perform."

The silence deepens.

"We all ..." I say, and then my brain falters and my lungs squeeze. The devil's mismatched eyes blaze in my mind – azure blue and emerald green. The vision pushes everything else out.

I swallow, set myself, and open my mouth again. But nothing comes out with my throat clenched so tightly. The devil's image is growing before me, motioning me toward him, a smile on his lips.

My gut twists even more, my blood going cold. I tip my head back. Tense my chest to hurl out the words.

The devil, he's real! The devil is here!

Yet all I can manage is a croak, my throat so constricted that it's becoming difficult to breathe.

There's a collective buzz of anticipation from the crowd as a number of people glance to one side. Although I stiffen my neck and shoulders, my head still turns.

A man is ambling toward me from the side of the lower stage – fine features, dark hair, grey jacket, trousers, and tie. And with the veil so thin before my senses, another image hovers there, superimposed.

My exact memory from hell.

Suit of absolute black. Bare feet and hands, his skin bleached white. Smoke rising from beneath ragged cuffs and hems. Slick red hair, with the horned mask that covers one side of his face. And an outline of darkness surrounds him.

A new jabbering starts up in my ears, the smell of burnt sulphur in my nose.

Again, I try to force the words out, but my mouth just opens and closes like a fish. My internal alarm's bleating at a level I've never experienced – my gut twisted entirely over – while the abyss plummets inside me, the monsters roaring in the deep.

I find myself inching backward along the edge of the stage toward the ten-foot crucifix at my back.

Satan in his human guise bows to the audience, his tie hanging down. "Sincere apologies for the intrusion," he says.

An emotionless smile crosses his features, and his eyes sweep across the crowd inside to the leaders behind the podium. More of them shift their gaze to him, and a number sit back down in their seats. And all the while, his devil form never turns away from me, and his gleaming eyes hold mine.

"You come before me, why?" he says, the words implanted directly into my brain, the tone flat with just a hint of curiosity. *"With what hope?"*

Even with the veil partially peeled back, my brain's a riot of thought while the devil continues to address the audience.

"We will deal with this terrorist," he says.

I stare straight back at him, trying to devise some kind of idea. But the crowd won't act, the angels won't either, and there's no fucking way I can fight him.

Satan narrows his eyes, and I can sense his mind infiltrating mine, like smoke penetrating my ears, my temples throbbing with heat and pain. I begin the count, trying to still my thoughts, to shove him out. But his words simply repeat more powerfully in my brain … *With what hope? With what hope?*

I stumble backward, my doubts jabbering ever louder.

"We'll be closing the auditorium roof," the devil says out loud, and his eyes flick lazily upward. "A purely precautionary measure."

A metallic clank sounds, and the massive grey cover starts to creep across the glass dome above, crawling slowly from the back of the stage to the front and blocking out more of the sky above the audience. Eventually, it'll continue downward over the entire glass wall, shutting us off entirely from the world outside.

"Just in case he came with others," the devil goes on.

I feel my gaze drawn to the growing area of shadow toward the rear of the stage. Something's moving in the darkness – the faintest outline of four-limbed creatures. Legions of them all edge forward as the gloom expands across the raised stage, several feet behind the leaders' tables.

The devil continues his approach, and my feet shuffle faster back along the edge of the stage, almost halfway across it now. Again, I try to force my mind to think, but pain flares behind my temples, his presence tunnelling deeper inside my head while the heat rises so much it feels like my brain's cooking. I have to tense my arms to avoid gripping my ears.

Satan's horned face continues to stare at me as I retreat, while his human form speaks to the audience, the words ringing across the auditorium.

"Apologies again, ladies and gentlemen," he says. "As the head of security for this establishment, I wanted to come and attend to this matter personally."

More of the crowd settle back into their seats, their hands folded calmly on their laps.

"This is exactly why we were so pleased to have the prime minister address us today," the devil's human form calls out, and he raises a hand toward me. "This is exactly the kind of menace he will protect us from."

The devil continues his advance, thirty feet away, pressing me rearward till the back of my head collides with the crossbar of the crucifix.

I start to dart around it when Satan tilts his head, and my body lurches to a halt, his presence like squeezing fingers around my mind. I pull at my feet but find them stuck to the floor, unable to bloody move. My calves begin to quiver violently.

"A drug user," the devil says out loud. "An addict. High on some prohibited substance and now on a comedown."

Again, I try to still my mind, to scramble away. Yet my thoughts are rabbiting wildly now, my legs shaking more, the sense of darkness huge.

"She's here. Isn't she?" The devil's words ring in my head, his eyes fixed on mine. *"The lovely Eve?"*

And no matter how hard I try to quiet my mind, images come of Natasha, of us lying together on the balcony floor, just above the stage.

Satan's smile widens a fraction. *"Interesting that you fought so hard to protect her,"* he goes on. *"And now you bring her to me."*

My entire body trembles, and the void's now a gigantic abyss at the heart of me. The compulsion to simply cast myself off the edge of the stage is enormous, the doubting voices shrieking.

The devil pads slowly onward, only ten feet from me now. I grit my teeth and, with him still encamped in my brain, with my mind still jabbering, I focus on one solitary thought … *I'm here for a reason. There has to be something.*

I shut my eyes and concentrate hard on the sensation of the crucifix against the back of my head, of my feet on the ground, of the throbbing pain in my rib. I start the count and focus intensely on the escalating numbers. Gradually, I'm able to still my mind and peel back the veil.

There has *to be something.*

With the shimmering world opening up around me, I sense the devil probing yet deeper into my mind. And for the first time, I abandon my fierce concentration and stop trying to shut him out. Instead, I let my attention run free, flitting between memories of everything I've seen since Satan appeared … everything I've done …

And after what feels like an age … nothing comes.

My eyes open, and I jump, my rib pounding.

The devil's standing right before me now, only two feet away. His mismatched eyes stare flatly down at mine, and the heat becomes a furnace in my head.

"We'll have this insurgent out of here before you know it," Satan says out loud, his human form facing the audience.

They're all staring at me – the crowd inside and out, along with the leaders behind the podium. The cover continues to edge closed high above, now halfway across the glass dome, the shadow slinking across the raised stage, allowing the black creatures to creep ever nearer.

I blank my mind again, keep the veil peeled back, and focus harder on everything I've observed – structures, objects, people. I let my attention linger on each memory while the devil holds my gaze.

"Whatever you devise, I can see," he says in my head. *"Whatever you attempt, I can use against you. You* know *this by now."*

My heartbeat races, the void colossal. It crushes my heart, strangles my lungs, and swamps every nerve. I have to work ever harder to breathe, sucking in tiny mouthfuls of air.

"So, I ask you again," the devil continues inside my head. *"You come before me. Why? To do what?"*

My eyes close, and I don't try to start my thoughts. I just feel into the darkness, letting it fill every cell of me, and in the shimmering world, I reach out to the devil through my mind.

"Nothing," I say, projecting the word directly into his head.

He frowns, the faintest crease forming across the visible side of his forehead. Then he raises an eyebrow.

I feel a growing lightness amid the dark, a growing certainty in my heart.

"Nothing," I say again. *"There's nothing I can do. I know that."*

The pain's like needles in my brain as Satan digs ever

deeper, scouring my mind for hidden thoughts and ideas. I let him fully in. He prods and pokes for the memories he knows are there and amplifies their intensity to incredible levels …

The devil killing Father Thomas in hell, driving his body repeatedly into the rocky ground. The pneuma grabbing up my mother in her nightdress, smashing her head into the kitchen counter.

And through it all, the sense of lightness remains, the feeling of fierce pain and love coalescing, my heart swelling with it. The wave of emotion sweeps the veil far back, and I find that I can reach into the devil's mind.

Hardly anything is there – only a barren landscape with vast and swooping flocks of thought, no memories or feelings whatsoever.

I let out a breath and shift my position against the crucifix behind me.

"It must be so sad," I say, projecting the words into his head. *"So lonely."*

Satan bares his teeth, and his cheeks redden. He steps right to my side, the heat against my skin almost overwhelming.

"I … will … destroy … you," he hisses, drawing out each word inside my mind.

"Go ahead," I convey back. *"It doesn't matter. I know I'm meant to be here. How could things be any other way? If you kill me, it'll simply be an example of the evil humanity has to free itself from."*

I find myself able to speak out loud simultaneously, just as the devil did.

"Be clear, this is no normal man," I yell to the crowd, the amplified words ringing out around me. "He is the force behind our prime minister, and you know him as the devil. He's come here to start a war, to enslave you in fear of him. However, you can take back your power right now!"

Many of the audience shift their gazes back to me, several standing up again to get a better view. A man in a brown robe squeezes along his aisle to see past the people before him while the roof continues its slow close above us.

The devil slaps a bone-white hand on my shoulder, his teeth still bared. *"But your death does not need to be easy,"* he says inside my mind.

He stares into my eyes, his fingers tightening and his hand growing increasingly hot. In the next instant, pain explodes within my chest, my legs, my arms, like shrapnel ripping through every part of my body.

I tense my muscles and scream to ease it, but the agony doesn't subside. It mounts further ... and further, like the bits of metal are being yanked and twisted around in my flesh. The more the pain comes, the slower time moves, till my breathing stops, my lungs solidify, and my body goes rigid.

I try to force my thoughts into action, to fabricate any distraction to cling to, yet still the agony remains, constantly building, continuously growing. The passage of time loses all meaning. My vision darkens, and my external senses shut down till my entire existence is pain – nothing before or after, only pain. As if every nerve end's shrieking.

Finally, light appears through my closed eyelids. My breath comes again, and the pain gradually recedes, leaving a crushing hollowness at my core.

It feels like a lifetime's passed. Yet as I tremble there, staring out, the man in the brown robe has barely reached the end of his row. The cover's in the same place above me, just over two-thirds of the way across the roof.

Satan maintains his grip on my shoulder. *"You see?"* he says, the words again revolving around my head. *"It's futile. I can continue this until you submit. Until you get on your knees and beg."*

My body shudders violently, and my thoughts scramble. It takes all my remaining energy to remain upright and not crumple to the ground.

The devil raises an eyebrow. *"Would you like me to take the pain away?"* he says. *"To remove you from all of this?"* He nods. *"I could. In an instant."*

The smile returns to his lips, his fingers like burning needles against my skin. And still I can't fucking move.

Cold panic grips at my limbs, but I shove it away, quiet my thoughts, and push back the veil again. I manage to inch my head around toward the crowd.

My mouth opens, and I channel the energy up my throat to hurl the words out. "You're all free—" I start.

Satan tightens his grip, and the burning pain erupts inside me once more. It rises faster and even higher than before as time slows.

The urge grips me to banish the veil, to diminish the sensations, to hide behind my thoughts. But instead, I concentrate harder on the shimmering world, on the feeling of the pain ripping through my body. And, remembering Harmony, I focus on dissipating it out into everything around me – through my feet into the stage, through my fingers and mouth into the air.

Gradually, I cease to be just this body and this mind. And I become everything: the crowd beyond the gap, the crucifix at my back, and the stage beneath my feet – even the air that surrounds me.

Doubts fire. Visions come of these sensations being forever more. Yet I banish them all and become nothingness, beyond time and identity. And in that state, the pain spreads out as well, suffuses everything, and becomes incrementally easier to hold.

Eventually, time speeds up once more and sensation rushes in – light before my eyes and sounds in my ears. I come back to myself so hard that the flood of pain almost makes me retch. Satan is speaking to the crowd again, his words like spikes in my brain.

"Apologies once more, ladies and gentlemen, for this continued disruption," he says. "It will just take a few more moments."

He speaks simultaneously in my head.

"We can repeat this as many times as you want, worse every time," he says. *"You will repent eventually. It is inevitable."*

And I reply immediately, the connection all too easy to make with the veil pulled so far back, the feeling of love and darkness still brimming in my heart.

"I won't give up," I say. *"Do what you want. I'm here to serve humanity's liberation. Whether that happens now or in two thousand years, it doesn't matter."*

And at the same moment, I concentrate on the energy in my chest and thrust it up my throat. "Divinity isn't outside you!" I shout to the crowd.

The devil's fingers press into my shoulder. The pain mounts faster than ever. I scrunch my eyes shut and, amid slowing time, my scream rings in my ears – the horrible sound stretching out.

Then a flash of light detonates to the side, easily visible through my closed eyelids. And I hear a huge gasp of shock from the audience.

52

Satan yanks his hand from my shoulder and his presence from my mind. Time speeds up once more, the agony vanishes, and the veil's back in place before my senses.

My eyes shoot open and then squint against the brightness.

The devil's staring off to the side toward the raised stage. The entire audience is doing the same, many of them with arms covering their faces, shielding their eyes from a fierce light that reflects off every surface like a million burning suns.

I follow their gaze, my pulse firing. Gradually the flare diminishes, while the gasps and exclamations only grow louder from the audience.

A colossus stands poised at the back of the raised stage, encased by a radiant halo. He's at least two feet taller than a normal man, with an impossibly muscled build along with brilliant armour – a shining breastplate with sculpted leg and arm guards. And behind his shoulders, a golden cloak extends to both sides of his massive chest before rippling down to the ground.

Gabriel.

Paul Hawcross and the leaders clamber to either side of the tables as he launches himself onto the centre of the rearmost one and then marches forward. He traverses the huge tables in single strides, right to the edge of the raised stage.

His eyes flick down to meet mine for an instant, and then he gazes out across the crowd again.

No one's sitting any longer. Everyone is either on their feet with mouths gaping or down on their knees, hands pressed together. And every camera is trained on the archangel.

As the glow continues to ebb, Gabriel's human form appears, superimposed on his angelic one, this time dressed in a white suit that's so bright it glows.

"I am Gabriel, archangel!" he calls out, the sound filling the hall. His voice echoes from every direction in multiple keys, like the layers of ringing bells. "I am the guardian angel over serpents and paradise. The first of the pantheon. Lord over the many!"

The air hums, and new gasps of surprise come from the audience. More people bow down before him.

"I have been a light to your fathers and mothers, and their ancestors, as history has stretched back to its very beginnings," Gabriel goes on. "And I have walked this earth for *thousands* of years!"

The devil retreats several steps toward the side of the stage, and I slump against the ten-foot crucifix, barely able to move. The pain's a spear in my side, my legs about to collapse.

The cover continues to close above us, now three-quarters of the way across the roof.

"I have been the sower of miracles, the great balancer," Gabriel calls from the front of the raised stage. "And I come before you now to perform my most important of acts. The great revelation. My final testament!"

His chest swells and his aura blazes again. However, peering closer, I can pick out the scars on both cheeks, barely visible behind his intense glow. His armour covers strips of material wound tightly around his torso, legs, and shoulders, keeping his injured body together. Plus, his stance; it's hardly noticeable, but he's standing with more weight on one leg than the other.

Satan is staring up at Gabriel also, scrutinising his form and posture with narrowed eyes.

"It is true," Gabriel says, his voice ringing out. "I was human once. We all were – all the angels and demons that live around you, invisible to your eyes. And the powers we have are not ours by right. It is as you've heard it." He clears his throat and lifts his chin. "Your divinity is not outside you."

Then Gabriel raises his arms and rises into the air. He floats clear of the raised part of the stage.

Cries of shock ring out from the audience. Some people scramble to get away, while others press closer to the stage. I blink. The veil starts to pull back, and the image of Gabriel's cloak morphs into huge rippling wings that arc up on either side of him. The light's almost blinding, and the heat scorches my forehead and neck.

With two wing beats, Gabriel descends gently to the back of the lower part of the stage, touching down on the opposite side of me from the devil.

I glance at each of them, both only thirty feet away, my position right in the fucking middle.

Beyond the veil, the devil's horned face smiles, and Gabriel points a massive hand at him.

"This is indeed no ordinary man," he says. "He is as old as I am, and you know him by many names: Satan, Baphomet, Lucifer, Fallen One, Beelzebub, Moloch." His voice grows louder with each word. "All contrived to create what sustains him – belief in his evil. The more you fear him, the more his power grows."

Gabriel takes a step toward the front of the lower stage, the hilt of his massive sword clearly visible over his shoulder while he keeps his gaze fixed on Satan.

"He aims not to inspire but to enslave you," Gabriel goes on, his voice vibrating my chest. "He would reign over a world of war and darkness while you, my children ..." – he draws himself up taller – "you belong to the light, the sacred. *That* is your potential. And *that* is why I have come."

Sweat glistens on Gabriel's brow. And while he moves with the faintest limp, his gaze is as fierce as ever, his aura blazing.

The devil continues to stare back at him from across the stage.

"You have lost," Gabriel says.

Satan replies, *"On the contrary."*

And I can hear both voices in my head.

"I will keep bringing this message to the wider world," Gabriel says. *"For perpetuity. For humanity's liberation."*

His gaze flicks to me as he uses my own words. I blink. The devil unclasps his hands and reaches one behind his back.

"Who knows if you'll ever see the wider world," he says.

And the devil brings his hand back in front of him, something gripped in his fingers. I stumble backward, and my hip knocks against the side of the crucifix. More shocked cries echo out from the crowd.

Satan holds a white rod composed of three vines, and though it starts out a couple of feet long, the weapon quickly grows, the vines extending upward and snaking around each other till they form the familiar three-pointed head of the eight-foot trident, identical to the one Gabriel broke in hell.

"And who knows if this is even visible from outside," the devil muses, making a show of gazing through the shrinking glass wall. The cover has reached the top of it and is now inching down its face. *"Particularly as the feeds to the cameras and screens can so easily become interrupted."*

The memory forms immediately in my mind … Lucia. Lying dead in the production room. My heart speeds up, my hands quiver, and I bite down hard on the thought. I concentrate desperately on pushing the vision out of my brain. I can't help glancing at the devil.

His gaze is still on Gabriel, fifty feet of stage between

them. The archangel's glow has diminished a fraction, but his expression remains fixed. He raises a hand behind his shoulder and draws out his huge, dark sword.

The crowd falls silent again, the air thrumming with a growing charge. Every single hair on my neck and arms stands up.

"And when you're dead," the devil continues in our minds, *"the story told of this will be just another miracle conjured by our good prime minister, yet more evidence for his holy quest. You will only add to my victory."*

Then he glances up toward the podium, and with the roof continuing to close, the band of shadow extends across over most of the raised stage now, the gloom so dark the global leaders have long since fled. And inside the blackness, I can barely make out the four-limbed creatures, creeping forward with the shadow's edge, as the jabbering sound rises in my ears.

The smile grows at the corner of Satan's mouth, the trident held tightly at his side. And again, Gabriel's glow ebbs a little.

"And there is no doubt," the devil says, his head tilted, *"you* will *die."*

Gabriel leaps toward him, crossing the space between them in a heartbeat. He looms a whole foot above the devil, and his sword cleaves the air so fast there's a pop in my ears. Satan swings his trident upward. I can't help flinching. The devil smashes the end of his weapon into the blade and leaves my skull vibrating.

The archangel attacks again, the strikes and counterstrikes far too quick to see, and I can sense my thoughts stilling, the veil peeling further back. Which leaves the pain screeching in my side, the weakness still growing in my limbs while the attacks resolve before my eyes.

Gabriel slashes and stabs with immense power, following each strike with another one, never letting up. The devil twirls his trident in a blur around him, always bringing it to block Gabriel's blows an instant before they arrive. Each move is simultaneously attack and defence. He deflects one of Gabriel's strikes with the foot of the trident before swinging its tip in a slashing arc toward the archangel's head.

I rip my gaze away from the fight and start scanning the stage for some kind of weapon. The three guards remain sprawled out on the floor, twenty feet to one side. And there lies the stun baton, a couple of yards further on.

I spring toward it when a voice barks in my head. *"This … is … not … your … fight,"* Gabriel says.

My gaze snaps back to the archangel, his phrase swirling around my mind along with a vague memory.

The devil presses Gabriel back toward the upper stage, toward the black creatures beyond. The archangel emits a roar like thunder, his glow blazes, and he lunges at Satan. He swings his blade faster, harder. Barely visible even behind the veil.

The devil is pushed back for a moment, but he counters again, the trident continuing its whirling motion. He blocks one of Gabriel's strikes, and the black sword cleaves a five-foot gash out of the raised stage. Then Satan begins interspersing strikes with evasions, one instant crashing his weapon into one of Gabriel's enormous blows before darting out of the way of the next. Gabriel ends up lurching from one side to the other, unable to right himself.

Satan stabs at Gabriel's chest with his trident, forcing him all the way back to the raised stage. The cover's almost at the bottom of the glass wall now, the blanket of shadow covering the entire upper platform. Black limbs dart out of the darkness, talons grabbing for Gabriel's shoulders. They yank him further off balance, making it near impossible for him to fight.

A chill climbs my spine, and my body spins, my eyes scanning for the stun baton once more, for the guards' taser guns. Then I stop.

Gabriel's words blaze again in my mind. And the memory hits me … The janitor, in Paul Hawcross's headquarters, moments before he died. He uttered the very same words. *This is not your fight.*

I clench my jaw and swivel around to face the crowd once more. The vast majority are on their feet now, some with their hands clasped in prayer and others swaying back and forth in exaltation. But all gaze upon the supernatural beings in the divine rapture of worship, as if Gabriel's words, my words, meant absolutely nothing.

The growing weakness pulls at my limbs like weights, the patch of wetness seeping across my entire back. Still, I open my mouth and fling the words out.

"Please, please!" I yell, my voice coming out all raspy, barely audible among the clashing weapons.

No one in the crowd looks at me.

I plant my feet. "This is about you, not them!" I shout louder, jabbing a shaking finger toward the audience. "You!"

Still everyone remains gripped by the fight over my shoulder, the cameras included.

The fire sparks in my chest while the pneumas' jabbering grows louder in my ears. And suddenly, the memory seizes me of the creatures swamping Gabriel in hell, raining stones down upon his shattered body, the devil triumphing.

I find my fingers gripping something tighter to my side: the crucifix. The top of the crossbar is several inches above my head.

Without thinking, I grab it with two hands and start to pull myself up. The pain is enormous, spreading up the side of and across my whole chest, while the exhaustion eats away at the strength in my shoulders and arms. Still, I don't let go. I simply push aside the doubt and pain and dive deeper behind the veil. I summon the sparking energy from somewhere, from anywhere, and I fight to haul myself upward, straining every muscle and shouting with the effort.

Finally, I manage to drag my stomach onto the bar's flat surface, panting hard, and climb shakily to stand.

The gap looms before me, sixty feet down now to the basement floor. My head swims, and my body tips forward, the weakness pulling at my legs. I barely grab the top of the crucifix to right myself.

Gabriel shouts with pain and rage behind me, the pneumas' jabbering ever louder in my skull, and the sound of trident smashing sword echoes around the auditorium.

I tense my neck and force my gaze straight. My eyes find the media crews at the front of the crowd, a few of the cameras hanging right over the gap. A couple have shifted their lenses toward me, but most remain trained on the battle behind.

I take a breath and, with hands shaking, summon whatever power remains in my core.

"Listen, please!" I yell, projecting my command voice as far as I can. "This is your potential, your birthright! Don't give it away! Don't waste it!"

Still most of the crowd and cameras keep their gaze on the fight. Almost everyone has their hands clasped together now, many of them babbling their prayers out loud. Then numerous expressions contort in anguish.

My muscles stiffen, and I swivel.

The devil is slashing wildly at Gabriel, pinning him against the raised stage while the pneumas claw and tear at his body from above. Gabriel slashes left and right, barely able to fend off Satan's blurred attacks. And his muscled form is now drenched in sweat, the scars more obvious through his diminished glow.

Then he does the strangest thing.

He takes his eyes from the devil and glances up at me, a gleam of excitement in his gaze.

"This is my part," he says inside my head.

My mouth falls open.

Gabriel drops his guard, lets his blade slip a fraction. The devil darts forward, grips the trident with both hands, and stabs the archangel right in the stomach, all three points digging in deeply.

A mixture of gasps and strangled cries erupts from the audience. While Gabriel's features don't alter at all. His eyes blaze as he stares up at me, his aura continuing to diminish.

"Now, you do yours," he continues, again the words spoken for me alone.

Then he moves like lightning. With his free hand, he grabs the devil's wrist and yanks the trident toward himself, spearing himself even deeper with the three spikes.

Satan tries to pull his hand away. To wriggle free. But Gabriel holds on tightly. And with gritted teeth, he thrusts his other hand upward, sword arm shaking, and drives the blade up into the devil's side. He slices deeply between his ribs.

The devil gives a cry of shock, a quick intake of breath. My fingers clench the top of the crucifix as blood gushes down Satan's side. And Gabriel's words echo in my head … *Now do yours.*

The devil topples, pulling Gabriel with him. And again, I find myself turning and facing the audience from ten feet above the stage.

Every single person's standing now, some craning their necks to see and others chattering with the neighbours. More conversations start up every second.

My eyes find the gap just in front of me, and the sixty-foot drop to the hard basement floor. My stomach climbs my throat.

I take a deep breath and focus on peeling the veil back even further, on expanding the shimmering world. And in that moment, all sound dies, leaving my heart as a metronome in the silence. And my vision hazes, the media crews and audience becoming a moving blur before me. My chest continues to heave, but slower and slower again as time ebbs to a crawl.

My eyes scan to the side. A presence stands there, a familiar aged smell in my nostrils and a sense of warmth in my heart.

Father Thomas.

His image hovers on the opposite side of the crossbar, dressed in his habit and dog collar, his eyes shining and his stick held in front of him. He faces the audience as I do, gazing out across them.

His lips form a wide smile, and I remember the very last words he said to me ... *I'm always there.*

And again, I'm not balancing on the top of a crucifix. I'm at his side in Gabriel's office building, about to plunge out of a fortieth-storey window.

But my legs wobble, more doubts coming. The priest's descriptions of the leap of faith, how it took decades to master, the ultimate accomplishment of his order.

Then it's as if I can hear his voice in my head ...

Belief is everything.

The image of the priest dissipates, and still behind the veil, sensation bombards me again. I feel the threads of connection to everything in my vicinity – the crossbar under my feet, the stage beneath that, and the thousands of people across the auditorium, the sound of their chattering discussions rising in my ears.

I raise my arms at my side to form a human cross and shuffle forward, right to the edge of the crucifix top.

A new hush descends, and I sense a thousand eyes on me now. Every camera lens swivels in my direction, and with the shimmering world all around me, I focus only on this moment. All thoughts vanish, and in the resulting space, I feel a growing certainty, a sense of completeness – nothing other than the knowing of a tapestry being continually spun, all of us interweaving threads. Nothing else to happen but *this*.

Thy will be done.

How could it ever have been different?

The weariness grabs at me again, pulling me forward, and I let it, feeling my weight shifting and my body tipping. And with arms spread, I begin to fall, my gaze inching downward from the audience on their feet, to the media pit and all the camera lenses, and then the blackness of the basement below.

I plummet. The gap rushes up to meet me and the wind billows against my skin. Behind the veil, I will it to thicken around my limbs, to caress my body, to slow my descent. There's no exertion, just the effortless connection I feel to everything around me. The total confidence that this is exactly where I'm supposed to be, the monsters entirely silent in the depths. And the faith that all that's happened has built to this moment.

And so, with arms stretched outward, I pull the air tighter around me, and I fall …

53

I WAKE up with a start and blink. Darkness surrounds me, except for a faint glow off to the side somewhere. I'm lying on a soft surface, a blanket over my legs, the air cool against my skin, fresh to my nose. I hear the faintest hum in my ears, some kind of air conditioning unit.

I push myself up on my elbows, and pain throbs across my side.

"Hush … hush," a voice says from close by.

Padded footsteps are followed by fingers touching my chest, gently pressing me back down.

I tense my stomach and resist, thoughts sparking and dying, my brain entirely scrambled.

"Jake, it's okay," the voice says again, tone warm.

Natasha. My vision comes into focus, and I can barely make out her features in the darkness – her large eyes, the curve of her mouth, a braid of long hair falling over her shoulder.

A bone-heavy fatigue pulls at my entire body, every muscle aching. Natasha keeps pressing down on my chest, and I let myself relax back down onto a pillow, a couch below me. My bloodied clothes are gone, replaced by some kind of cotton robe and trousers.

"Where are we?" I ask, barely managing a croak.

"Safe," she whispers. "Don't worry. I'll explain."

My vision continues to clear, and I glance around.

We're in a wide room, my couch in one corner. Windows line both neighbouring walls, each one covered by blinds, and a door stands in the centre of one of the opposite walls, golden-framed paintings covering a good deal of the rest. Several plush sofas have been positioned around the room, plus a sprawling desk in the far corner, all corporate-looking and expensive.

To the side of the door, the faint glow resolves into a flat screen mounted halfway up the wall. The sound's muted, the television the only source of illumination in the room with the brightness turned down.

I lift my head. The channel's tuned to a news programme – a female anchor speaking to the camera, a picture of the summit building over her shoulder. The image cuts to video footage of the auditorium interior, the stage, the crucifix at the edge. And a figure leaping from the top, then plummeting into the gap, the camera following them right down into the darkness.

My heart beats faster, and I strain to rise.

"Jake, no," Natasha says, both hands on my chest. "You must rest. You've lost a lot of blood."

I scrunch my eyes shut against the pain and keep pushing, forcing myself up into a sitting position. My head spins, and a new pounding starts up behind my temples.

"I'm okay," I say, and my gaze finds the television screen again.

The shot's now a blurred close-up of my body, arms spread like a human crucifix, the slash of red visible across my side. And then the leap into the gap.

Natasha crouches by me.

"What happened?" I whisper.

"You survived, Jake," she says, the faintest tremble in her voice. "With barely a scratch." She clears her throat. "As soon as you jumped, I sprinted down through the building to find you. The basement was chaos, people running everywhere. You were sitting up, technicians all around, most in absolute shock. She was there—"

I grip Natasha's arm. "She?"

Then I notice that the sliding door's already halfway open. A figure standing in the gap.

My body tenses, my rib throbbing, and then my brain clicks.

"You're awake," Harmony says and hits a switch.

Floor-level bulbs illuminate to either side of the door, and I have to squint a little with the new light. It's dim, though, and darkness remains over much of the room, my couch pressed into the brighter corner, right by the window.

Harmony's wearing the black trouser suit I remember with its high collar, one hand on the door frame above her head, the other on her hip.

"Surprised?" I say.

A genuine smile touches her lips. "A great many people would be," she says.

The news programme continues to play on the television to Harmony's side, now showing interviews with people outside the summit building. A huge crowd has gathered behind the reporter, all huddled around a sprawling mound of home-made altars with candles, signs, and flowers.

And again, I try to bring back the memory of landing. But it's all just a blank in my mind.

Natasha sits down at my side on the couch and follows my gaze toward the television. She's wearing a set of clothes I don't recognise – low-cut skinny jeans and a top that hangs off her shoulder.

"The frenzy in the basement was extraordinary," she says. "Hordes of people trying to get to you, to touch you, to see you, the media also."

She shifts her gaze to our visitor.

"Harmony got you out of there," Natasha goes on. "She

had five cars waiting in the garage area." Natasha faces me and holds up the fingers on her right hand. "Five."

All the while, Harmony doesn't move. She simply stares back at us, arms now folded.

"We got you into one of them and then all five took off," Natasha says. "They started in convoy and then split up, each one heading off in a different direction, which meant no one could follow us. Our car came to this building."

Some memories of the journey return, and I press my hand to my side, feeling a springy texture under my fingers.

"See, you no longer look *too* bad," Natasha says with a grin.

I peel back my robe to find a bandage over my rib.

"They had a doctor here," Natasha continues. "She stitched your wound and gave you a transfusion, all the equipment already in place."

"Already in place?" I ask, looking up.

Natasha nods.

"Impressive," I say and then sniff the air and glance at the patch of shadow in the opposite corner of the room.

"And how long have I been out?" I ask.

"Nearly thirty-six hours," Natasha replies.

"And you've been here the entire time?" I ask, and my eyes flick to Harmony.

She's still staring at me. In fact, she's not looked anywhere else since entering the room.

"Almost," Natasha says, the slightest tightness in her tone. "I have stepped out a few times."

"But aside from that, you've eaten here, slept here, got changed here?" I press.

"Yes," she says with a frown. "They have wardrobes full of clothes."

I sniff the air again, taking in deeper breaths. And there it is, the faintest smell of cordite, almost undetectable with the fresh scent in the room.

I spin on the couch. Fix my gaze on the deepest pool of darkness in the far corner.

"Going to announce yourself?" I ask.

There's no reply. And peering into the gloom around the sofas, shapes swim before my eyes. I don't avert my gaze.

"All in good time," a voice says out of the black with that familiar playful and aristocratic tone.

Natasha starts and swivels her head. Haniel appears out of the shadows, lying propped up on a sofa, his aura glowing. He's wearing a white suit, a half smile on his lips.

"Why are you here?" I ask.

He shrugs and says, "Relaxed environment, good company." A nod toward Natasha.

She flushes at my side, and my chest tightens. I try to rise to my feet, though the fatigue pulls harder at my limbs. I wobble, grip the couch, and push myself to standing.

"But you organised all this?" I ask. "Why?"

"Do you have any concept of how many people are searching for you right now?" Haniel says, gazing up at me from his reclined position. "You are a global phenomenon, Jacob. Plenty of religious groups have named it blasphemy, while others are calling it the second coming."

I simply stare back at him.

"Naturally, the rationalists are attempting to disprove it," Haniel says and begins inspecting the nails on one of his hands. "And some of their theories are quite fascinating, involving wires and clever lighting techniques. The use of a double." He drops his hand and smiles wanly up at Harmony. "Charming. Isn't it, dear?"

"Multiple cameras filmed the entire fall from different angles," Harmony says. "The global news channels play the footage almost constantly, analysing it, discussing the implications, reviewing your message."

My mind continues to clear, flashes of memory returning to me.

"And the devil and Gabriel?" I ask. "What about their bodies?"

"There was no sign of them," Harmony says.

"What?" I exclaim, leaning forward, pain flaring in my rib.

"In all the chaos, the angels removed Gabriel's, while I believe the demons have removed the devil's," Haniel says, his voice still as light as ever.

"But that couldn't stop the forensic scientists," Harmony says.

I whirl back to find that hint of a genuine smile on her features again.

"Government ones and several private companies also, we made sure of that," she says. "They've collected the blood and will conduct DNA analysis to determine their ages. The data should be pretty incontrovertible – two beings, both thousands of years old."

Angelic rule undermined even more. I swivel to face Haniel again. He's staring at me, sporting a wry smile.

"Did you know?" I ask. "About our plan?"

He shrugs once more. "I had an inkling," he says. He holds my gaze and winks.

My mouth opens, and Haniel gets smoothly to his feet. Though the aura still surrounds him, it's dimmer than in our previous meetings, the glow somewhat paler. He brushes down his jacket and trousers.

"There is one more thing," he says, facing us. He clasps his hands behind him. "Proposals have already been made. It was inevitable."

Natasha frowns. "Proposals?"

Haniel nods. "A group of angels, seeing the potential of a new saviour, a new age, the devil vanquished," he says, turning to me. "An opportunity to create a new pantheon, a new example for humanity at the dawn of a new era. They are offering protection and an opportunity to write your own gospels. New ones."

The angel holds my gaze, and I search his expression and

tone for any sign of excitement, of showmanship. But it remains neutral, and I see only heaviness in his eyes, plus a smile on his lips.

"I think you already know the answer," I say.

Haniel heaves a sigh, and Natasha squeezes my arm.

"I do," the angel says. "But I thought it only right to pass on the message." He turns to Harmony. "I am honourable. Am I not, dearest?"

Harmony raises an eyebrow. "Sometimes," she says.

Haniel grins, some of the glow returning to his face. "Well," he says and swivels for the door. "It's never too late to begin." Then he motions toward Harmony. "Come. Let us leave this couple in peace. I am sure they have a great deal to catch up on."

Haniel turns and winks at Natasha this time, who blushes crimson. And I watch Harmony and the angel pad out the door.

54

THE DOOR SLIDES CLOSED, and I keep my eyes on it. No one else enters as the silence stretches. No sound emanates from floors above or below.

My head turns, and I notice the faintest twisting in my gut, my gaze drawn to the vertical windows beyond the couch.

"Where did they bring us?" I ask.

"The city centre," Natasha says. "A twenty-minute ride from the summit building."

I pad over to the window, peel back the blind, and gaze out upon a nightscape full of skyscrapers. Lights dot each of the many storeys while their steel and glass surfaces taper out in familiar curves.

The financial district. Our apartment on the thirtieth floor or so of some lofty building.

I gaze downward, and with the five-hundred-foot drop to the ground, memories swirl of the gap beyond the crucifix. The feeling of weakness tugs at my limbs, and my vision swims again. My fingers squeeze the glass.

But I don't pull away, my pulse thumping behind my ear, my eyes gripped by the sight directly below me.

The new train station, with several cranes dotted around

the building site. They're still reconstructing the place after the train crash, where the whole thing started.

Natasha moves to my shoulder.

"Somehow, he predicted it all," I say.

"Who?" she says.

"Gabriel," I say. "The very first time I saw him. Down there." I nod toward the station below. "He said it'd be better to die now than to face what was coming."

She follows my gaze and pauses a while. "Maybe, deep down, he recognised his time was up," she says. "So, he ended up making the ultimate sacrifice." Her voice softens. "Inspired by you."

I continue to stare down at the building site, completely empty now, the surrounding area as well. Everyone is probably at home, watching the bloody news.

"And what about Father Thomas? Do you think he knew?" Natasha asks after a while.

She's smiling, such warmth and sadness in her eyes. And again, I feel the priest's presence next to me on the crucifix.

I shrug. "How could he? How could anyone have truly known?"

I gaze back out of the window and the constriction in my stomach doesn't let up. It's joined by a prickling sensation in the middle of my back. I take a breath and let my gaze wander; it's drawn toward the nearest skyscraper, only a hundred feet away.

My eyes squint. There's a single storey with every light illuminated, directly across from ours. The windows stretch from floor to ceiling, and in the centre of the floor stands a figure, his hands on a railing before him.

I gasp, my heartbeat hammering again. His face is lit from the front also, all too easy to recognise.

"What is it?" Natasha says, her voice tight, her eyes on me.

My mouth opens but nothing comes out, my gaze still fixed on the figure. He's dressed in his customary rumpled suit. He lifts a hand off the rail and points upward, jabbing a finger at the sky. Then he turns and ambles toward the back of the floor.

I let the blind fall back against the window and edge away. Natasha continues to stare.

"What—" she starts.

"It was Ben," I say, my voice shaky.

Natasha blinks.

"He wants to meet," I continue. "On the roof."

"*Meet?*" she says, her voice high and her eyes wide.

I swallow and then nod.

Her face drains of colour. "You are not seriously thinking ..." she says.

"I am," I say, memories returning of those few moments in our conversation, in his conference room.

"But the demons got the devil's body," she says. "Ben could be—"

"It's okay, Nat," I say, squeezing her arm. "Trust me."

She bites her lip, and I nudge her toward the door.

"Can we get out?" I ask.

She frowns as she paces to the door and then slides it open. "Of course," she says. "This is not a prison."

The corridor outside is as plush as the room, and then there's a lobby area. With the help of a key card, Natasha operates a lift, which takes us to within two floors of the roof. We climb maintenance stairwells with their rubber floors and drab lighting. The fatigue grows in my limbs, and I need to take regular breaks, catching my breath. Eventually, we reach a set of steps that end in a fire door at the top.

Natasha grips my arm at the base. "Jake, are you sure?" she asks.

I find a smile pulling at my mouth. "Trust me," I say again.

She takes a breath and follows me up the stairs. I press the handle at the top and push open the door.

The roof's square, over a hundred feet wide with a series

of satellite dishes and air conditioning vents installed over its flat surface.

A figure stands by the far edge, facing away from us, hands in the pockets of his trousers. The suit is even more crumpled than before. The wind pulls at his tousled hair, and beyond him, patches of stars are barely visible between banks of dark clouds.

I don't approach, and he doesn't turn. Fifty feet remain between us. My fingers tense at my sides, my heart thumping again while the wind bites at my skin through the cotton robe.

"Where's the body?" I demand, hurling my voice into the gusts.

For a moment, Ben says nothing. He simply continues to stand there, the wind bringing the faintest scent of sulphur.

"Safe," he says eventually.

He turns to me, his hands still in his pockets and his face framed in shadow.

"Is he dead?" I ask.

"Wasn't me who pulled him out," he says. "Or Lucia, for that matter."

His voice is as flat as it was in the conference room, in those moments between his bouts of frenzy. Only now it's combined with a faint bite.

"Is he *dead?"* I ask again, louder this time.

Ben shrugs. "Probably. That was quite a wound." Then he tilts his head up toward the stars. "Have you had the offer yet?"

I take a breath and then eventually say, "Yes."

He nods. "Figures," he says. "You're naive if you think the angels will renounce their rule." His voice deepens, and I sense the veil thinning before my eyes, his demonic form – Mammon – pressing in, the outline of smoking gashes appearing across one side of his clothes, his face.

I don't turn my eyes away.

"They'll fight tooth and nail to reclaim their power," he growls. "You know that."

Natasha straightens at my side. "They can't," she says.

Ben steps forward, his boyish features visible in the reflected light from the neighbouring buildings. No sign of Mammon. His mouth splits in a wide smile.

"Their backlash is certain," he says. "And if they can't court you, they *will* kill you. The demons as well. They have just as much to lose."

My throat tightens, and I shiver in the swirling gusts. Still, I take a couple of steps toward him.

"But you won't. Will you?" I say.

Ben snorts and then shrugs again.

"I know you won't," I say. "Because at your core, you never agreed with the devil's view of the world. Did you?" My heart beats even louder in my chest, my throat so dry. "You *want* to believe. I know you do."

This time Ben goes entirely still, and his face disappears into shadow once more. I can sense Mammon behind the darkness again, his scarred face and single red eye.

"We all need to make a choice," I say. "You told me that on the top floor of your building." I reach out a hand. "Join us. We won't side with angel or demon. We're here to create something new."

Mammon laughs, the sound vibrating my sternum. Then he shakes his head.

"The same naivete as when we first met," he says.

"Yes," Natasha says, her voice ringing in the night air, "yet here we are."

Mammon turns slowly back toward the edge of the roof.

"Yes," he says. "Here we are."

And he gazes out into the night, his back to us.

"Just remember," he says eventually, his voice barely audible. "Be it angels or demons, they *will* come for you."

He whips his hands from his pockets, grabs the lip of the building, and leaps over it, disappearing from sight.

I jump forward, the stitches pulling over my rib, and dash for the roof's edge to peer over.

The floor below extends out another twenty feet on all sides, fifteen feet down or so. Then the floor below does the same.

And there's no sign of anyone.

I'm scanning the shadows when Natasha hooks her arm around my middle and tugs me backward.

"Let's get out of here," she says.

I nod, the wind blowing wilder around me. We turn and hurry back across the roof, down the stairs, and into the lift. By the time we reach the apartment door, I'm moving slower, the adrenaline having bled from my system and the fatigue pulling at my limbs.

Natasha opens the door with the key card and helps me back into the plush room. I scour the corners for dark outlines or blurs of movement. Nothing. Then I shuffle to the couch and lower myself down, my rib throbbing now.

Natasha nudges me over and lies down at my side. She places her head on my chest, a new warmth kindling there. I smile.

And though another wave of tiredness washes through me, I don't close my eyes. Instead, I rest my hand on the back of her head and run my fingers through her hair.

"He is right," she says, her voice barely a whisper. "They will come for you."

My breathing continues, slow and easy. No new tension in my muscles or lungs.

"I know, but that's okay. It has to be. Right?" I say eventually. "Whatever happens, we'll meet it when it comes." I hug her tightly, and she squeezes me back. "But right now, I choose this."

JAKE AND NATASHA WILL RETURN. Thank you for reaching the conclusion of the trilogy. The tyranny has been broken but what lies ahead? How will humanity respond to its newfound potential powers? What fresh threat will emerge to exploit the inevitable turmoil that will follow?

IF YOU'VE NOT ALREADY DONE SO, join my reader list to stay updated on the next instalment in The Faith Series and receive exclusive bonus material. Simply visit:

https://www.thefaithtrilogy.com/death

We look forward to seeing you there!

SPREADING THE FAITH?

Thanks again so much for accompanying Natasha and Jake right to the culmination of their adventure. If you've enjoyed the trilogy and have a moment to spare, I would greatly appreciate a short review on Amazon. Even just a sentence is wonderful, and reviews make a big difference in helping new readers find the series. Thank you!

FACTION - YOUR FREE EBOOK IS WAITING

Destroying Gabriel's disease was just the beginning. Now Natasha and Jake are on the run, hiding from an irate archangel, and being urged by Father Thomas to develop the abilities they'll need for the coming fight. Natasha's desperate to discover Gabriel's plan, to identify angelic activity, while Jake's working hard just to keep them safe.

Yet perhaps he's looking in the wrong place.

When the gang that enslaved him for six years re-emerge, they aren't merely seeking their best thief; it turns out a growing Mandem army want Jake for a specific job, and one that bears all the hallmarks of the angelic activity he's trying so desperately to avoid.

Jake soon realises that what's at stake isn't just his own freedom and Natasha's safety, but the freedom and safety of a growing army of the downtrodden – young grunts just like him. And as Mandem's plan unfolds, it becomes clear that there won't be a corner of London unaffected.

In this heart-pounding tale of survival and rebellion, Jake must confront his past, harness his powers, and lead a revolution against forces both human and divine. The fate of a city hangs in the balance.

If you have not already received it, get a free ebook copy of the short story between Faith and Wrath - Faction - along with more bonus material and updates on the next instalments in The Faith Series, by visiting:

https://www.thefaithtrilogy.com/death

ABOUT NICK NIELSEN

Nick loves reading clever, fast-paced, and engaging fantasy stories which say something about the real world we live in. So much so that he decided to write them. Professionally, he's an award-winning entrepreneur, the director of the social change agency Osca, and the founder of Envision - a Guardian Charity Award winner. He's also a winner of the Shackleton Leadership Award. In his fantasy stories he leans heavily not only on his professional background working in the area of behavioural psychology, but on his twenty-year experience learning from real magicians - practitioners of the mystical arts - from Eastern, Western, and African lineages. Nick lives in London with his wife, two overly chilled teenage children, and one neurotic bunny rabbit.

ACKNOWLEDGMENTS

First to you, the reader, for not only investing your valuable time in this book but also for continuing through the scrubland of the back matter to find out who I might be humbly thanking. And first of all ... this is you. Your care and attention are the reason we authors write - to entertain, enliven, and bring you joy. But this is only possible because of your curiosity and commitment, without which there would be fewer stories, and the world would be a considerably poorer place.

So thank you. I sincerely hope you found the investment worthwhile.

Continuing on, there are a great many people to thank. Foremost is Leslie Watts, this trilogy's amazing editor. When I first came to her five years ago with the story idea, she showed nothing but enthusiasm for the project, despite the roughness of my writing. I am so thankful for her kindness and enduring patience in helping me to improve my craft over the innumerable drafts, for her dedication to the project over the five years it took to complete, and her absolute commitment to the craft in not letting me run ahead and publish before the books were as good as we could make them.

In finishing the final versions, thank you so much to Amanda Brown for her love of the words, and to Alison Birch for her eagle eye. Thank you also to Stuart Bache for the wonderful cover designs.

And then there's my amazing tribe. Thank you Eva and Luke for your love, patience, and impatience with this project, and for understanding the stupid thing their dad does every single morning at five am. Thank you, Beth for always being there, for being my biggest supporter and most demanding critic, and for more than I can ever say. Thank you to a mother whose heart and home are always open, and to a father for whom it all became too much in the end. We miss you, we honour your choice, and we thank you for everything you gave us. Thank you, brothers and sisters - Thomas, Trine, Sach, and last but definitely not least, Steph. Thank you, fellow story craft lover, both for the ongoing support with this project and for walking alongside me on this crazy journey.

Thank you to my own Father Thomas - Colin, Saniel, and Krishna. My debt of gratitude to you, your care, and your work is also more than I can express.

Thank you to my readers over the years - to Ian, Mark, Chris, Thomas, Debs, Ray, and Dave - and to my teachers of the craft, Danielle and Rachel and the many others. Thank you also to Shawn Coyne without whom these books would have been published five years ago, and yet so much of the richness in both them and me would have been lacking.

Thank you to Ian Craig, who was there near the beginning. And thank you to Jean who encouraged me right from the start. It's almost fifteen years ago now, and I don't know if I'd have gotten here without you.

Thank you all.

www.thefaithtrilogy.com

For any enquiries regarding this book, please email: nick@thefaithtrilogy.com

British English spellings have been used.

Book Cover by Stuart Bache.

Printed in Great Britain
by Amazon

39479688R00229